I0460063

Love Locked

The writings of Wakeman Frith and others circa 1720

Compiled and edited by

William Olson Campbell

Published by Mic Radman Associates 2015

Edition 2.01

Copyright © William Olson Campbell 2015

The right of William Olson Campbell to be identified as the author of this work
has been asserted by him in accordance with the Copyright, Designs and Patents
Act, 1988.

This book is sold subject to the condition that it shall not, by way of trade or
otherwise, be lent, resold, hired out, or otherwise circulated without the publisher's
prior consent in any form of binding or cover other than that in which it is
published and without a similar condition including this condition being imposed
on the subsequent purchaser.

First published by Mic Radman Associates 2015

All characters in this publication are fictitious and any resemblance to real
persons, living or dead is purely coincidental.

ISBN 978-0-9572658-3-7

Typeset in Liberation 11, Gabrielle, Goudy Old Style

Contents

Background i

Acknowledgments v

Monday 19th Maidenhead to Reading 1

Tuesday 20th High Bridge to Foundry Brook 41

Wednesday 21st Southcote Cut to Sheffield Lock 69

Thursday 22nd Sheffield Lock 109

Friday 23rd Sheffield Lock 131

Saturday 24th Sheffield Lock to Newbury 165

Sunday 25th Newbury 187

Monday 26th Newbury to County Lock 207

Tuesday 27 th Reading 225

Wednesday 28th Brewery Gut 241

Thursday 29th Reading to River Thames 275

List of Illustrations

Wakeman Frith's map of Reading c1720 (annotated) vii

Hoskin's sketch of the Kennet Navigation (annotated) ix

Background

The Man

Wakeman Frith was born in 1681 on a smallholding near Lanercost, Cumberland. Its renown Priory had fallen into disrepair following the Dissolution of the Monasteries, and Lanercost continued to witness the regular passage of refugees persecuted for their faith, be it Catholic, Presbyterian, Anglican or Covenanter.

Frith appears to have received a solid education from the Augustinian school associated with the Priory. He could write Latin and English by his adolescence, when he began keeping occasional day notes. By his thirties this had become a more regular journal.

In 1698 his parents contracted to a four-year indenture to pay for their passage to the new colony of Pennsylvania. They migrated in hope of secular peace and religious tolerance. Frith's younger sister died miserably during the long slow crossing. On arrival in Boston, Massachusetts, Frith discovered the family would be worked and treated as slaves on the plantation. He absconded from his parents while they waited onward transportation. Records show his parents were never released from their indenture.

The seventeen year-old spent a year or so in the Boston vicinity before drifting north. Brief residence and unplanned wandering was to be a pattern for the rest of his life. The first journal entry of this period was in 1699 when Frith was in Salem. Three years later he had recoiled into the Catskill mountains where his journal notes contain details of Mohawk culture that struck a chord with him: the tribe's Earth-centred spirituality and the Five Nation Union. There is a brief mention of a young Mohawk woman named Angeni.

By his late twenties Frith was in Bristol, England, romantically courting Grace Leeson, a merchant's daughter. She steered Frith to a small company that printed pamphlets. From there he joined the Bristol Gazette. This was a happy time for Frith, marked by few entries in his journal. Parish records show the couple married in 1714. Frith's journal resumes after their first child died aged five months. In 1717 Grace died while delivering a stillborn baby.

Frith left immediately for Lanercost. He then crossed the Pennines to spend several months in the remote Cheviots. His journal here abandons dating the entries.

He reappeared in Bristol briefly and then took a personal pilgrimage along the Great South-West Lay Line, visiting Glastonbury, Stonehenge and Combe Gibbet. Wakeman Frith arrived in Reading during May and found employment with the Reading Courant.

The Writings

While working as newsman and compositor for the Reading Courant, Frith wrote a tale of the first barge to travel from Reading to Newbury and back using the new Kennet Navigation. Frith's account is fictionalised though based on well documented events that happened during the early period of the Kennet Navigation. The blend of fact and dramatisation reveals the duality in Frith of journalist and storyteller.

Frith's journal has been utilised in Love Locked to reconstruct the story of his journalistic investigations. It also gives an insight to the person, the man who wrote the Kennet Navigation story and who fell blindingly in love with engraver and painter Catherine Lampry.

After Frith's death his writings found their way to the Bristol Gazette. They remained there until around 1860 when its successor company relocated. In 1901 they are recorded as a private donation to the W H Wills Museum and Art Gallery. They next appear in 1926 on the accessions list of Leopold Bewick, a local historian living near Reading. In 1998 Leopold's granddaughter offered the writings to a community publisher based in Reading, bringing them to light after nearly three centuries.

While editing Frith's writings, a posting was found on the Internet that diaries of Mistress Olivia Turner, daughter of Mayor Robert Turner, had been found at a derelict colonial mansion in Sazin, Kashmir. Their content added an intriguing aspect to Frith's supposedly fictionalised story and journal. It warranted an expansion of this work beyond the newsman's tale and journal.

Further research lead to the memoirs of Sir George Crockmore, which have remained in the possession of his descendants. They are included here by kind permission of Mrs Sophie Crockmore-Pettit.

The source documents from the early eighteenth century have been rendered into modern English to make Love Locked accessible to the contemporary reader. This accords with Frith's intent as he declared in a later entry of his journal, for the written story to be universally understandable and not concealed because of language. For example, the editing has seen obscure terms substituted by modern equivalents and names of locations standardised to current spelling.

The letters and diary entries have been placed in Frith's story at the place appropriate to events not the time they were written or received.

The Period

A foreigner from Hanover had been placed on the English throne in 1714. George spoke little English and after banishing his son the Prince of Wales from Saint James Palace to Leicester House, he attended fewer meetings of the Privy Council. This opened a path for the Norfolk landowner Robert Walpole to gain ascendency among the ministers of state to become the first Prime Minister. His rise was not exclusively on merit. It was Walpole who coined the phrase "All men have their price".

These nascent changes in the structure of governing the country had a counterpart in the cities, towns and villages. The early eighteenth century was the threshold of a revolution. One where technology created and changed commerce, industry and livelihood. The first patent for a steam engine was taken out in 1698 by Thomas Savery with Thomas Newcomen installing the first practical one in 1712 to pump water from the workings of the Coneygre Colliery, Tipton. Improved transport was key to this expansion. Turnpikes were making coach and wagon journeys easier and safer. Rivers were dredged, straight cuts dug and locks installed for barge traffic, heralding the boom in canal digging. By the end of the 1720s the Aire, Bristol Avon, Don, Douglas, Weaver and Yorkshire Derwent had joined the Kennet in being made navigable.

For the populace these changes were accompanied by disruption, displacement and dishonourable practices to bring them about. The period marked an acceleration of social change, underlined by the rise of a middle class of merchants and industrialists. Innovation and advancement coupled with the lure of the cities, was changing the lives of everyone from King to churl. To some it was highly benefi-cial. To many it was fearful.

Acknowledgments

To Janet Preece for her unswerving faith in this project.

For their helpfulness and knowledge the author thanks the staff at Reading Central Library, Local Studies, at the West Berkshire Museum, Newbury and at the Berkshire Record Office.

Without the people at community publishers Corridor Press, with their enthusiasm for the written word and for Berkshire waterways, there would have been no inspiration for Love Locked. Particular thanks to Alison Haymonds for her consistent support of my writing.

The author is grateful to Slough Writers for ongoing assistance, particularly Michael Pearcy, Sheila Knight and Terry Adlam for their comments and suggestions.

The background on the cover is a page from a 1726 barge ledger courtesy of West Berkshire Museum in Newbury.

About the editor

William Olson Campbell (WOC) was born in 1947 in Whitley Bay, Northumberland, then a seaside holiday resort of arcades, funfair and candyfloss surrounded by stunning landscapes. He gained a degree in Mathematics and Physics from Leeds, starting his own computing company in 1980.

He achieved writing success with short stories and plays and has been a resident dramaturg at a girls' school. He has worked as a theatre critic and columnist and volunteer editor and contributor for local community publishers. WOC has performed his prize-winning poems with an improv dance group.

Living not far beyond the Slough Arm of the Grand Union Canal he gives his time to his vegetable garden, dancing, walking and a lovely woman in a seaside resort on the south coast of England.

More about WOC is at www.wocNotes.wordpress.com/About

Further reading

The web page www.wocNotes.wordpress.com/lovelocked has the two maps, short histories of the Kennet Navigation and Love Locked and a photograph gallery of the present Kennet and Avon Canal taken during research for Love Locked.

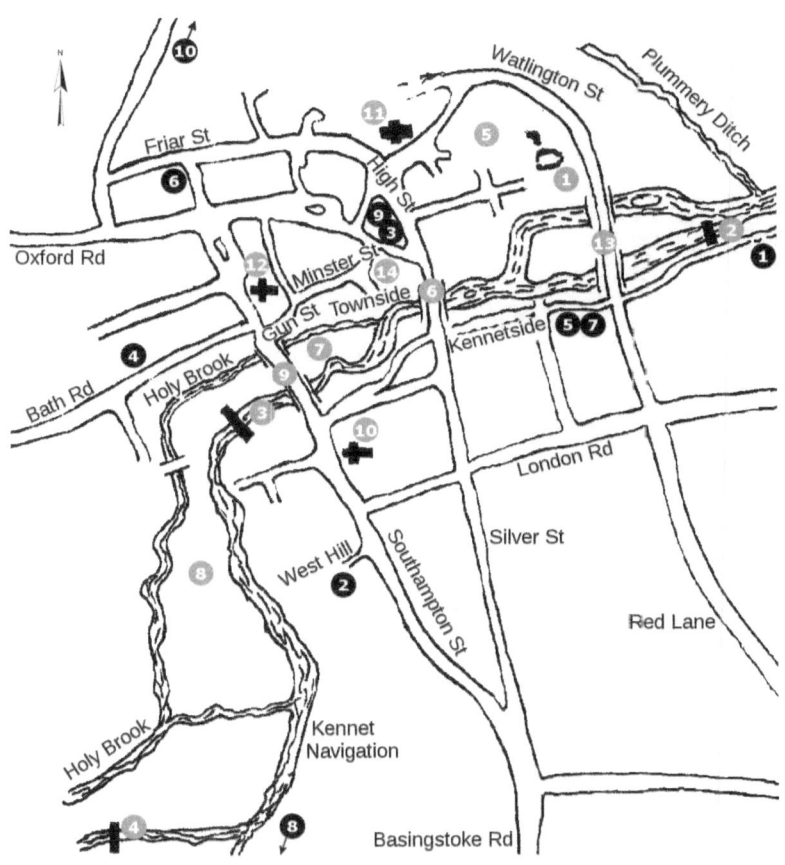

Reading places

1 Abbey (ruins)
2 Blake's Lock
3 County Lock
4 Fobney Lock
5 Forbury
6 High Bridge
7 Oracle (derelict)
8 Oyster beds
9 Seven Bridges
10 St Giles
11 St Lawrence
12 St Mary
13 Watlington Wood
14 Yield Hall

Frith's places

1 Anglers Tavern
2 Catherine's house
3 Courant office
4 Gaol
5 Kennet Koffee House
6 Mayor Turner's house
7 Middleton's Stores
8 Rose Kiln
9 Saracen's Head
10 Yedda's herbary

Map 1: Wakeman Frith's map of Reading c1720 (annotated)

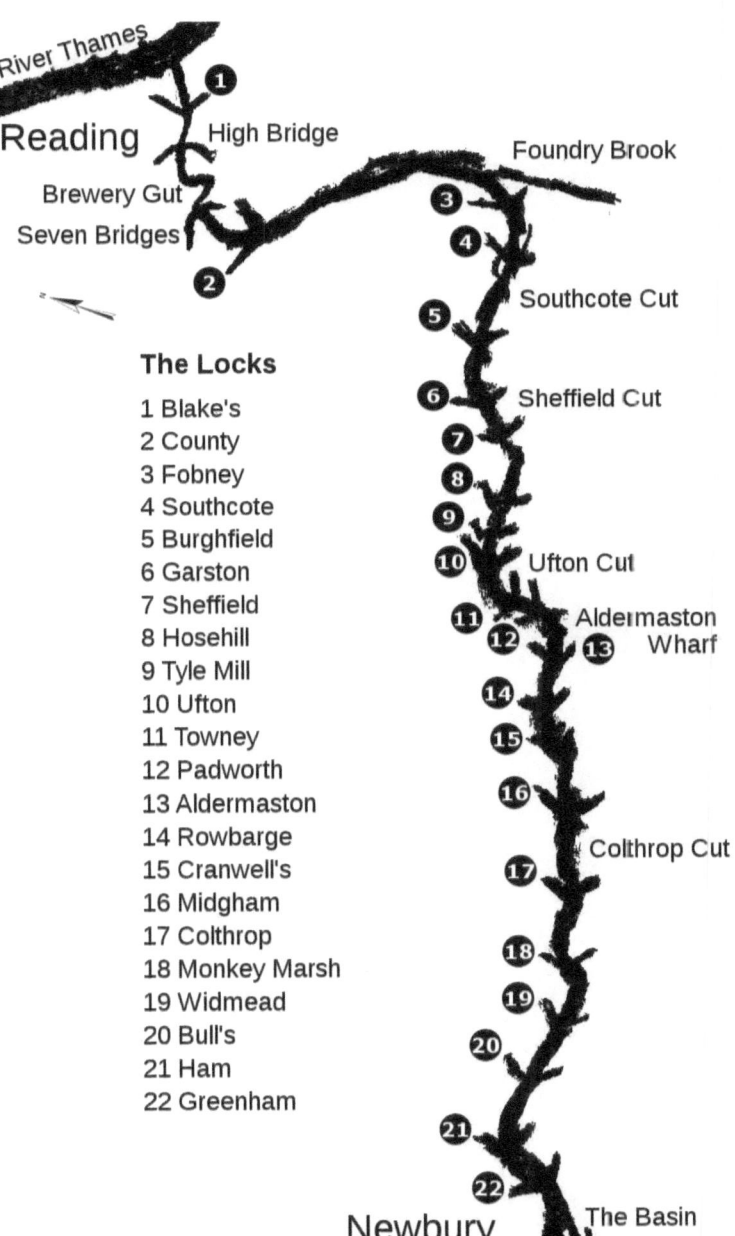

River Thames

Reading   High Bridge

Brewery Gut

Seven Bridges

Foundry Brook

③

④

Southcote Cut

⑤

The Locks

1 Blake's
2 County
3 Fobney
4 Southcote
5 Burghfield
6 Garston
7 Sheffield
8 Hosehill
9 Tyle Mill
10 Ufton
11 Towney
12 Padworth
13 Aldermaston
14 Rowbarge
15 Cranwell's
16 Midgham
17 Colthrop
18 Monkey Marsh
19 Widmead
20 Bull's
21 Ham
22 Greenham

⑥   Sheffield Cut

⑦

⑧

⑨

⑩   Ufton Cut

⑪   Aldermaston
⑫
⑬   Wharf

⑭

⑮

⑯

Colthrop Cut

⑰

⑱

⑲

⑳

㉑

㉒

Newbury   The Basin

Map 2: Hoskin's sketch of the Kennet Navigation (annotated)

The press room, Reading Courant

"French-Pox is hyphenated, Mr Frith." The editor of the Reading Courant, Mr Hyde, has stepped behind his newsman as silently as ink leaching into blotting paper. A bony finger flicks across the galley. "Poxes and coughs are hyphenated, fevers are not."

Mr Hyde moves in measured steps towards his office beyond the screw press that takes up almost the width of the room. He glides under drying folios towards his cubicle of meticulous order. Before disappearing inside he calls back, only his legs visible. "We seem to be two points short of concentration this morning, Mr Frith. Full mind to the foremost matter, if you will." He pauses in the doorway. "What people want is continuity. They do not want surprises." The door closes.

Wakeman Frith is irritated. First, that his mistake was spotted, but mainly with himself. He knows he is an excellent compositor, praised at the Bristol Gazette for his speed combined with accuracy. This morning he is aware he has been slipping into composing his future in his head to the detriment of placing the type in the galley. His future started last Thursday. The dreaming started on 8th August in Mr Hyde's office. Forty-two days ago.

Frith painstakingly replaces the spacer with a hyphen type. He is sliding the last four lines of the Bill of Mortality for London from his composing stick into the galley when his eyes are caught by 'Womrs.' He mentally slaps his wrist. Last lines are notorious for mistakes, the laxity when nearing the end of a job that shows a sloppiness. Frith alters the type so the cause of death for the two people in London will be correct on the front page of the Courant. He wonders not for the first time why people in Reading would be interested in the causes of death forty miles away in London.

Frith runs a practised hand over the galley and taps down a couple of proud type. He picks up the newspaper that arrived on the Saturday coach and compares the numbers against those he has set for the Courant. This thoroughness is what marked him in Bristol. He reads every line again. The reversed words in the galley have the same familiarity to his eyes as does his reversed face in a looking-glass. He sees only the form and not what it represents and in this detached way he recognises 'Childbed' is correctly spelt. It is only a word.

The apprentice pressman, Jake, takes the galley. The boy has been pressing the final pages since four this morning and is ready to impose this last galley into the chase to complete the issue. Frith saunters to the window with its outlook onto High Street of Reading and he watches people about their morning business, picking their way through mud, kitchen refuse and the ordure not sluiced to the kennel in the centre of the street.

A slow movement pulls his attention from beyond the window to his reflection from the surface of the glass. His keen face barely moves but he is smiling. The smile broadens as the notion of people in the street sauntering or scurrying through his translucent head tickles him. Frith's smile resides in his eyes that are often sympathetic sometimes penetrating. His medium height and slight build, and being quiet of speech and manner, at times make him as inconspicuous as his reflection in the press room window.

Staring at his smile makes Frith anticipate the thrilling excitement to be his as soon as he can get away from the press room. His stomach somersaults at the unknown possibilities. The smile slowly transforms into apprehension from a rising fear of his immersion in the joy he vowed to renounce after the childbed deaths of his beloved wife and baby. A shiver, and he forces his eyes to look through his reflection. A gravedigger is at work across the street and Frith tries to guess the cause of death of the imminent occupant of the hole. It could be almost any from the two score he has set this morning. He considers who else knows beyond the dead person's family. Yet all who can read the Reading Courant will know two people died in London of worms.

"I do not see the reason for this scramble every Monday morning." Frith is standing in his editor's office. "The list is already a week old by the time it arrives here."

Mr Hyde looks up from the papers on his desk. "The list is always one week old." The newsman has noted his editor is more often scowling over ledgers than over print copy. Mr Hyde continues, "A week's mortality figures do not change. They have numerate rigor mortis. They do not change." He raises one corner of his mouth at his wit. "It is what our readers expect and that is what we give them."

"Wouldn't they be more interested in a Bill of Mortality for Reading? Knowing why the gravedigger in St Laurence's is —"

"No they would not," says Mr Hyde calmly, nonetheless firmly. "How long have you been in this town Mr Frith?"

"As you are aware, Mr Hyde, since this May." Frith has come to recognise how his editor prefaces one of his sermons by asking a rhetorical question, and he waits with a neutral expression.

"Whereas I was born here in the year of Our Lord 1674," intones Mr Hyde. "I have lived among these good folk for over forty years. With that experience and the knowledge therefrom, I assure you they do not wish to know about local deaths. They will know all too harshly when the Grim Reaper introduces himself to their nearest. Their fascination is with death at an appropriate distance. Thus we give them numbers from afar. Faceless figures." The corner of his mouth twitches, twice.

"I defer to your greater knowledge of this locality, Mr Hyde."

"Thank you Mr Frith. Do not be put off by your suggestion not being taken up. Your ideas and innovations are always welcomed."

"I am pleased to hear that. In pursuance of which, is it not the case that the Reading Courant could be of great service to persons such as myself, new to the town, by informing —"

"Ah, your suggestion for writing profiles of notable personages. It is a radical suggestion and one that requires a good deal of thought before implementing. Whom would you consider suitable to be pricked out by your quill?"

"I have written requesting an interview with the Mayor, Mr Robert Turner. Also Sir George Crockmore whom I gather, is principal landowner as well as the Crown Judge."

Mr Hyde quietly snorts before resuming his imperturbable face.

"We shall wait with anticipation for the replies from those fine gentlemen. I did tell you, when you first mooted this incredible notion, it is unlikely for the Reading Courant."

"You did, but not why."

"What our readers already know they will not pay to read. What they do not know is through lack of interest in the subject. What they should know they will hear through the official channels and what they should not know we would not be allowed to print." Mr Hyde looks down at the ledger.

Frith ignores the implied dismissal. "I see. But I presume you are not adverse to carrying a local story should I unearth one?"

"Providing it is of interest to our readers, and is neither inflammatory nor bringing us to the attention of the Lord Chamberlain."

Frith nods, steps from his editor's office. He is looking forward to again being newsman rather than compositor. But before seeking out a story he will make his arranged visit to West Hill.

A surprising cargo

The girl's walk to get food was longer this morning. The filthy shop fifteen minutes walk from Maidenhead wharf would not let her put one more item on the slate. Two months ago she had been refused entry to the provisions store nearest to the wharf. Its bulbous proprietor behind the counter moaned it took all her effort to feed her own family and she didn't see why she had to feed another for free.

This morning the mean-eyed shopkeeper on the edge of Maidenhead had shut his ears to her pleas. In a way she was relieved for his last loaf had been flavoured with mouse droppings. Caraway seeds, he'd said. She'd wanted to tell him his kindness was smaller than one caraway seed. Instead, she meekly slid out of the shop harbouring her resentment.

The girl walked on, skirting the town centre with its coaching inns and stores priced for London travellers. She came upon a parlour-shop. Her two loaves, a quart of milk, five potatoes, a corner of tooth-break cheese and a very large fresh cabbage was chalked up against her. The broiler-faced woman sitting behind the cluttered table in the open window demanded something against the slate. The girl's shawl was far more valuable than the provisions in her pannier. It had belonged to her Mam, a reminder of those protective arms across her shoulders. The girl hunched up against the early morning air as she hurried along the three-quarters of a mile back to the wharf.

Two men stood by the stern of Barge Jeannie eyeing the girl as she approached. She was used to that having spent all her seventeen years in a world of bargemen, London dockers and taverns. She ignored them and stepped on to the barge's gunwale. A hand clamped her forearm and jerked her back. The cabbage jolted from the pannier and splashed into the Thames between the barge and the wharf.

"My cabbage!"

"That what you call it?" The man's hand lurched at her breast.

She lashed out with her clog but the man, for all his bulk, was quick. He tightened his grip against her wriggling and pulling.

"Stop yer squirming," he barked and dragged her along the wharf. The girl let herself be manhandled wondering how long his stupid game would last. "That's better." He smiled, then suddenly pitched her out over the river. He held on and hauled her back.

"It'd be trouble if Fatty went in," said the second man through an unkempt beard. "The wave'd likely drown the King's swans at Windsor."

"His Majesty King George should reward me, don't you say?" The man thrust his face into the girl's, who gagged on breath through his rotted teeth. "Be off with 'e."

"This is my Dad's barge. I'm Lynn Darville."

"Mistress Roly-Poly knows her name," scoffed the Beard.

"Maybe your dad, Lynn Darville, really is your father. Who knows with your sort," scoffed Rotten-teeth. The two men exchanged knowing looks. "But we knows for sure who owns this pile of scrap. And that gentleman wouldn't have a clod like you for a daughter."

"Not one he'd admit to," leered the Beard.

"My Dad's got papers."

"He's got leg-irons now. What's with yer surprise?" asked the Beard when the girl gasped. "It's what happens when a man don't pay his lockage and wharfage." He began reciting, "This barge's been sea-chested in loo of unpaid fees."

"It can't," cried Lynn hearing her worst fear.

"The property has been confiscated, that is to say, the ownership has been transferred to —"

"Where's Dad?"

"Maidenhead lock-up," chortled Rotten-teeth. "Or with the rats and turds," he added, giving Lynn another shove towards the river. "In there."

Lynn spun herself out of the man's grip. She had to get to her Dad no matter how far she had to run. Her clogs clacked double time against the cobbles. Distantly she heard her name, a voice that sounded familiar.

"Lynn! Where're you off to, my Beaut?" She turned to see Peter Darville standing in the narrow doorway of Messrs Hoskins. The wharfinger was trying to squeeze past him out of the hut. Peter waved a paper in his hand. "Didn't I say everything'd work out?"

Lynn gave her Dad a long hug of relief then glanced at the paper. It was a bill of lading for Barge Jeannie. She looked up at her smiling Dad, at the wharfinger striding off, at the two bailiffs. None of it made sense. Except the bailiffs. Full cargoes for their barge had been impossible to come by this last half year. Yet the wharfinger was rounding up men to load Barge Jennie.

Peter Darville was organising the cargo before his daughter could ask what was happening. Lynn emptied her pannier in the tiny cabin that doubled as a galley, then used a hitcher to probe the mud and stab the drowned cabbage.

She was surprised to see the wharf men stop loading with only fifteen cauldrons of coal in the hold. Her Dad was excessively busy making fast the tarpaulins over the hatches and ignored her questions. His only comment was to shout over his shoulder for Lynn to harness Hermond. As she heaved the collar over the big horse's head Lynn looked back puzzled by the snug-loaded barge with its empty deck.

She clambered down the three steps into the cabin Peter had built on the stern of the Thames barge. "Are we taking on cargo along the way?"

Her Dad thrust a couple of shillings into her hand. "There's a respectable lodging just over the bridge. Wharfinger 'll show you. You'll be all right there till I get back."

"Back?" asked Lynn.

"There's no need for you this trip."

"I go on every trip."

"Not this one."

"I had to give up Mam's shawl for bread this morning." cried Lynn. "We've no money for lodgings."

"Do as you're told, Lass. Jeannie's light and it's a short commission." Quickly Peter added, "Besides, wharfinger's given me a lad. This 'un, Davey."

Lynn looked at the gangling figure just into his teens and her puzzlement grew, along with her unease. She grasped for something she was sure of. "Why're we taking coal back to London?"

"Going upriver," blurted Davey, and went to unhitch the warp from the bow.

"Upriver?" challenged Lynn. "Hermond is getting old and it's me who knows when he needs a rest. Not some whippersnapper who's never seen him afore."

"I've got three extra horses."

"Dad! How are we to pay for them?"

Peter thrust the Bill of Lading at Lynn. "This'll pay for everything. And I'm telling you, you're staying put." Father and daughter stared at each other. Peter took up a softer voice. "Besides, my Beaut, it's been a long time since you had a new dress. You can buy one for when I gets back."

"Who's going to feed you?" asked Lynn, fighting her swelling anxiety by using every argument she could think of. "You know how you've been since Mam passed over."

"I won't have you talking about . . ." Peter's words choked on the grief that crippled him at any mention of his late wife Jean. He stared out of the cabin. "You're not coming."

Lynn wanted to step close to him but was unsure if she should. She had always accepted his decisions even when, since he became a widower, her instinct directed her to disagree with him. Something in his voice, something about the part-laden cargo, told her she had to be with him on this trip. She remained timid of challenging him, though the daughter stood two inches taller than the father. Lynn had seen her Dad shrink in the three years since the death of Jean Darville. This cargo had brought back some of his old liveliness and Lynn couldn't bear destroying it by arguing.

The seconds lapped by until Davey returned to the cabin. "I ain't never barged up the Thames afore. Them staunch locks is gonna be tough work even with three of us."

Peter soughed, then told Davey to fetch the other horses. "Seems I ain't been given no choice," he snarled at the river.

Barge Jeannie let slip her mooring and Peter steered away from Maidenhead wharf. Lynn busied herself on the foredeck. "No sail!" Peter snapped at his daughter. "Jennie's only part loaded and there ain't no wind."

Lynn furled the sail, coiled some ropes at the bow and watched the regular nod of Hermond's head as he clopped along the towing path. Davey led the other three behind the great Shire. Their strength would be needed at the staunch locks to haul the barge over the weir sill, pulling it against the white flume racing downriver through the gap.

Looking back from the prow, Barge Jeannie was smaller than Lynn could ever remember. The flare-up with her Dad had shrunk the space between them across the barge. Peter sat at the stern, the tiller under his right arm, but his eyes were fixed straight ahead, unseeing. Lynn noticed how weather-worn was the paintwork on the cabin that had once made Barge Jeannie the most colourful in the London docks. That had been her Mam's work. A light breeze made Lynn shiver. From habit her hand reached to her shoulder for the shawl but it wasn't there.

memoirs of Sir George Crockmore

The weather this Monday morning proving some dull indifference,

I remained abed and was rewarded in the form of Cook's new hiring bringing my breakfast. Had Cook been assigned to unearth a beauty to set my juices boiling she could have achieved no better. I ordered the girl to tarry that I might become informed of her and she the better knowing her master. She refused to sit by me but that did afford me the delight of feasting my eyes on her entirely.

She is named Penny, being fifteen years of age, the eldest daughter of Beale who is a tenant on Pingle Farm on the south border of my estates. Beale has been without trouble in paying his dues, though I recall him querulous along with others when I put the farms of my dear first wife Elizabeth on a sound financial footing after the foolish charity exercised under her governance. Beale is a man of little consequence and his wife a sour-faced weasel, yet they have produced such a gem. The girl has a delicate face with the high cheek bones and smooth skin of quality, while her eyes are those of a courtesan. Her lips are her feature, plumped satin cushions of sensual invitation. Her hair first arrested my attention when she drew back the drape. The window was a frame for her red-gold halo caressing her slender neck. Upon her entering the room I was at first in a mind to rebuke her for going about uncapped, but upon that vision was pleased to have refrained.

I had consumed the cake and drunk a good half of the ale and the kitchen maid answered my questions still standing aback from the bed. Cook had lightly poached the egg of a chicken, which I set about. Noticing my gamine companion trace her pointed tongue along those lips, I spooned the yolk unbroken into my mouth and broke it therein. Be it by design or accident, a trickle of the viscous yellow slithered from the corner of my mouth. At my signal the girl leaned across me with a napkin. She bringing her face so close to mine I considered calculated for more than wiping a spill.

Upon this thought I stayed her hand and offered the trickle of yellow towards her lips. I was rewarded with her moist tongue gliding from the corner of my mouth round my jaw. I indicated she might like to taste warmed yolk. She nodded. I took her head in both hands, pulled those luxurious lips onto mine and succumbed to her wild tongue scavenging the corners of my mouth. The tray clattered to the floor.

All did not proceed as I was by then anticipating for, though my hand had slipped under her skirt and had felt the firmness of her farm bred thighs, when I cupped my hand to explore her more intimately she pulled from me to set about smoothing hair and clothing in what appeared to be some agitation.

"You have no fear of a jealous Mistress," I said. That I was without wife she knew, but told me what I had not imagined possible – she was still a virgin. I had hitherto been convinced all such girls, taking their cue from the beasts with which they worked, opened themselves even before their flowers. This revelation ensured she was more desirous and my keenness stood unsatisfied beneath the quilt.

I bade the girl tarry until she was composed for return to the kitchen, speaking of matters inconsequential such as her room here at Southcote Hall, the correct form of addressing a lady or gentleman visitor. This latter prompted me to elaborate on the aspects of a woman that makes the one a lady the other not. First, it is the impression given, for that determines how others will greet and treat her. This is confidence, deportment and attire. The last can be purchased, the second learned and the first pretended. Beneath the dress, I asked, is not a lady the same as a kitchen maid? To this she had no answer but a blush and I volunteered a means to prove it. I despatched the girl to my poor wife's chamber wherein was a closet from which she was to pick any fine dress in which to deport herself as a lady before me.

She instantly departed, for what girl does not like to dress in rich clothes and parade in them. In far less time than any of my wives or lady I have known, the maid returned to my bed chamber wearing the burnished orange byrall that had been the love of my dear second wife. As I recall, the gown had been second in Philippa's affection only to her horses.

I enjoined the girl to walk about, swishing the dress, elevating her chin high as she flicked the fan she had appropriated. I lavished praise on her deportment, her ladylike qualities. It was none too soon before I summoned her to my bed and expended myself plentifully where no other had been. I lifted from her with the extra satisfaction of seeing the proving stain on Philippa's prize gown.

Though she lay on her Master's bed and had given him good satisfaction, I was apprehensive the girl become discomposed by the torrid minutes. I reassured her of her continued place in the household. This not having the consoling effect I had expected, I tried a different stratagem. I related the tale of faithful Penelope, the wife of Odysseus, with whom she was finally reunited after his years of travel. I explained it has been many lonely years since my last wife was taken from me and, like the first two, had left me without heir. The girl embraced me and I deemed it prudent to resist my urge to bundle with her a second time. A man is wise to forgo immediate gratification if patience will reap a greater reward.

After she was dressed again as a maid I ordered her tidy the spilled tray and ensure the gown was thoroughly cleaned adding, after a peculiar look from her, it was a necessity before she wore it again. The maid scooped it up and departed to give some excuse of her prolonged absence to Cook.

Employing shrewd thought later, I was uncertain if the omission of a cap from the maid's head was through neglect of Cook or ploy of the girl. If the latter it portends greater fun to be had from the wench, but also the need for a firm hand to remind her of her place and to whom she owes obedience.

from Mistress Olivia's diary

Mama is worse and worse. Worse one. She has spent every minute since dawn fussing after my stupid little sister. Tons more than she usually does and that's fifty hours every day. Lousy Lucy was being shown how the laundry is done. Efackins! Why would a lady need to know? The laundry maid does it and the housekeeper makes her do it properly. Lousy didn't like the heat and the steam and set upon her pathetic whimpering that sounds like a piglet tied up by its rear trotters. Now there is an idea for my dear little sister.

Worse two. The dress Mama wore to church yesterday was six years old. Six years! In front of the whole town. Lousy is four and I recall Mama wore it on every possible occasion for at least a year before she got too fat with the brat. That was our first big clash, when I advised Mama she was wearing it too often.

"At your age, Olivia, what do you know about such things?"

"I am twelve."

"This is a very special dress," said Mama dreamily. It was as if I wasn't there and that always vexes me.

"I do know! You are wearing that dress a lot because the ladies of the town are saying, 'There goes a much frequented piece'."

Slap! I shall never forget that slap. My cheek was so inflamed I refused to step from the house for a week. That was miscalculated for Mama was more than suffocating with remorse for the whole seven days. She never wore the dress again. Until yesterday.

It is a lovely dress for an old person. Cornflower blue that brightens her eyes and she knows she looks stunning in it. Alas, the whole walk to church was, "I'm dying with pleasure that I am still able to wear it." I'd die with shame – a six year-old dress!

Worse worst. It is only five days to the Forbury Fair and I do not have a new dress and Mama is showing no sign of buying me one. Seamstresses should be scrambling for the honour of making my dress. I am the daughter of Mayor Robert Turner and very pretty. But I do not want Mama choosing it. I don't want to be wearing something from the last century.

Catherine's note of Friday 16th September

Quillman, what have we unleashed? We have let slip the doves of love into a cast of falcons. My darling Mr Wakeman Frith with your logical clear mind, you could not predict this. I am soaked to my heart under a waterfall of joys. When I have to step into that other life I remain secretly drenched with the thrill of you. It is so dangerous! I wasn't looking for this. I am scared. Big, capable me!

The coach to Southwark was bumpier than ever. You should look into why the nobs aren't filling the holes in their turnpikes with the barrow loads of money they charge for travelling on them. The tolls go into their pockets while us 'bums' suffer.

This is taking ages to write. I'm a tiny bit tipsy. It's a relief to know there is no one to look over my shoulder. Brother-in-law is still out – of the house and his skull most likely. Mary says he finds his ship and gets stranded. That was quite witty for my sister. The Ship is a tavern on a street called the Strand.

Mary asked round three other alehouse widows. We quaffed lots of gin. Fay – one of Mary's friends, I didn't tell you their names did I? – asked us what we thought about having an affair outside marriage. I all but choked. She said she was giving the idea serious thought.

You know, my darling Quillman, I live in a different world to her. A different world to all of them. At first I didn't give serious thought to this thing with you. This – whatever. What we have is not like an affair – it's like coming home, like finding someone of the same species after being on one's own yet surrounded by people. This can't be wrong just because others say so. It cannot! They don't know what we have.

My lips are aching to kiss you again. Write soon, a letter for when I return to Reading. Pour your words over me so I can blossom for you.

High Bridge to Kennetside

Frith has told Mr Hyde he is visiting the ink-maker and will go on to check the morning coach from London. There are sometimes copies of Despatches with items to be edited into the Courant. This may include informing the readers which unpronounceable Hanoverian town His Majesty King George is visiting this time.

Frith enters the door next to the Courant up High Street. The Saracen's Head is dark and empty but still smoky from the clays lit and relit in its several rooms. He wanders to the back, the Petties Snug as it is known. There is neither woman nor girl in it. Frith mentally slaps his head, realising today is laundry day. He is not thinking clearly. His mind is already at his destination for this morning perambulation. Desire awaits him in West Hill yet he tantalises himself with diversion and delay.

Yield Hall Street drops to the river where Frith pauses on the crown of the single stone arch of High Bridge. He glances at the feather plume of smoke from the ale-makers that has given its name to this snaking stretch of the River Kennet. Frith emits a quiet sigh at seeing further along Brewery Gut the derelict Oracle. He had investigated the history of the place before the greater distraction in West Hill had consumed him. The Oracle had been a philanthropic workhouse, but it was destroyed by corruption and personal greed within its walls.

Further upstream is County Lock, beyond which is the widened, straightened River Kennet dug by the Kennet Navigation Company to Newbury, The Kennet Navigation. The Company's aim is to make its directors and investors wealthy. Frith wonders if this new waterway will trickle wages into the pockets of the workers and water folk of Reading. More likely the jobs and their livelihoods will flow to Newbury.

He steps down to Townside, ignores Abbey Bridge – the Watlington Wood as it is popularly called – and passes the roofless Abbey. A second example in this town, he thinks, of altruism turned into ruin by rapacity. It recalls the open nave of his childhood, Lanercost Priory in the north of Cumberland, and he abruptly turns from the violent and brutal memories.

Frith's progress along the River Kennet is impeded by Plummery Ditch. He could wander to the planks that serve as a footbridge but an awakening urge courses through him to get to West Hill, to where he wants to be. Across the river he can see his lodgings. The Anglers Tavern is the latest of many places he has laid his head since leaving Lanercost. Frith has travelled greatly in his thirty-nine years, even across the Great Ocean. He has unearthed too many questions.

Towards Kennetmouth, beyond Mayor Robert Turner's timber and coal wharf, there is another thread of smoke. This one is black. From some farmer's fire Frith supposes. He steps carefully along the weir and gingerly crosses the gates of Blake's Lock on to Kennetside. The newsman registers an animated cluster of wharf men and notes the moored barge awaiting the discharge of its deck cargo as he walks on towards the Kennetside end of the Watlington Wood. Frith passes Middleton's Provisions Store then makes a detour into the premises next door, the Kennet Koffee House.

A tightening knot has been in Frith's stomach all along Kennetside, his face has been rigid. He lets out a breath seeing Sarah at her counter and the proprietress of the Koffee House nowhere in sight. He is some frail thing inside his ungovernable body. Until he knows. For that, he must speak to Sarah.

"Good day, Mr Frith. How's you?" she says with a warm smile. Her eyes dart round the scattering of customers, checking. She sighs and speaks softly. "Oh dear, Mr Frith."

His hopes plummet, dragging down his face, wiping away all trace of his false nonchalance.

"Ain't it always the way," says Sarah with a heavier sigh. "Nothing for days." She looks sorrowfully at Frith. "Then two come along together." She beams and reaches under the counter. He knows the perfume off the envelopes.

"Your usual demitasse, Mr Frith?"

"Yes." His thoughts are already inside the envelopes, imagining the house in West Hill. "What?" asks Frith.

"Demitasse. It's what I has to call cups, says the Dragon."

"If Mrs Middleton hears you calling her that, you'll —"

"And these ain't my gentlemen no more. Oh no, they're my clientele. Dragon's got me talking nothing but foreign. I'm talking Hangover like the king."

"Hanover, Hanoverian. Anyway, those words are French."

"French! What're we using that scum's words for?"

Frith wishes he had refused a coffee but Sarah likes talking to him and he needs Sarah. "It's an affectation, Sarah."

"Is that what she's got? I knew there's something not right with Dragon. Chucked out a bunch of wharf men when they wanted to have a meeting in here. All those demitasses going begging."

"I saw some on Cutler's wharf." He puts an envelope to his nose and lets it fill his head, pushing Sarah's voice into the distance.

"They're in a lather about Thames bargemasters taking all the trade to Newbury. Not that it'll make any difference to them. That lazy load of sods do nothing from dawn to dusk. Then there's Dragon in a lather. A right bare feet on hot coals morning this has turned out to be."

"What's troubling Mrs Middleton this time?"

"She saw your letters under the counter and spewed-up the Sunday Service leftovers. 'I am not sure, Mrs Kempster,' she says to me, 'That I can condone my Kennet Koffee House being used to advance adulterous acquaintanceships.' Quite right, Dora, says me. You should take your fancy man to the Bear."

Frith almost chokes on his coffee. The idea of Mrs Middleton having a fancy man beggars belief. She would rather a dozen fancy cakes as her peccadillo.

Sarah doesn't pause. "That got Dragon preaching on about how bleeding great her marriage is, with more than a passing jab as to how I couldn't keep my husband, God rot his soul. I reckon the more a person goes on about how good something is, the more they're fooling themselves. For a start, there's very few bits of me her faithful Mr M hasn't tried to have a feel of."

Frith has heard this before. "But you never tell Mrs Middleton."

"What's the point? Dragon won't hear nothing nasty about her devoted Mr M. Timothy's a man so its just playful, isn't it? Huh, and I need my job." She turns to serve the tripe man and Frith takes his usual seat in the back corner. He will read the letters before he knocks on the door in West Hill.

The tipsy note of Friday makes him smile. The second letter causes his hands to shake.

Catherine's note on Sunday 18th September

I'm thinking of Monday. A lot. Of you, here in my house, tomorrow, oh Quillman. How will we begin, and where? I want to make as much use of the time as possible, every second. The chillier weather is coming. How more difficult for us, so we must make the best of these days.

Sorry I was so addled on Friday. I can't remember the last time. Well I can. I'll tell you when we have time for such talk.

My first try at writing was more mess than words. I hid it in my purse then forgot it was there and later gave myself such a fright seeing it again. What if someone else found it! I have burned it now – hated doing that. It was like destroying one of my sketches for a painting, but much worse, like burning to ash what you and I have. I wrote to you in wild good spirits but I remember little of what I put except this is like coming home. Something like that. Quillman, you and me are so destined for each other, it cannot be bad. It really can't.

I talk to Eliot about you, our working together and making a series of art pieces, making my drawings and your words live together. I know he doesn't listen. He's not interested in my painting. So I'm talking mainly to myself, how we exchange snippets from our pasts: yours a copy of your journal from the day of your marriage. Do you wonder why we choose the pieces we show each other?

It's early days and we don't want any fixed ideas around what we're doing. I like the fluidity of this. We can stop off and make pieces along the way. Stop off when your hands brush my face and your fingers stop along their path . . .oh.

Have you been keeping your hand busy while I've been away? I mean, holding your quill, Quillman! Oh dear, I've not put that any better. I told you I was hopeless with words. Have you talked to those farmers at Kennetmouth? There's been so many mishaps something has to be going on. Alford's kitchen garden was trampled when his cattle got loose. That man's so careful he counts every seed he plants. Oops, I'm telling you what to write. That is naughty of me – the wrong naughty!

So Monday, through the front door and hold on to each other. Ale? Later, after kissing. Might you be calling for a taste of my comfits? Am I very naughty! Will you be very polite? Will we talk about our work together? Kissing all the way?

I worry about my notes sitting in the Koffee House. If you were here right now . . . Until Monday.

An unwelcome arrival

After a particularly tough haul to get Barge Jeannie through the flash lock at Sonning, Lynn had unharnessed Hermond and ridden him bareback away from the river, away from her morose Dad. Eventually she returned to the towing path and came across the moored Barge Jeannie with Davey daydreaming on the cabin roof. He told her Peter was in the isolated house yonder. Lynn saw the name Dreadnought carved on a curve of wood over the door. Her heart sank reading on: Ales, Stout, Wines, Gin & Brandy.

Her Dad had an empty glass in front of him and six flagons of brandy in his hand. He found Lynn blocking his exit, her eyes shrunken with dismay. "You have a lot of your mother in you," he said, and walked round her to the door. "This is for later. I'll likely need it."

Lynn walked with Davey beside the horses to where a tributary joined the Thames. Lynn reined back Hermond and looked for the ferry to get the horses across.

"Keep on," snapped Peter from the tiller. "We're overnighting a short ways up."

Lynn wanted to ask how she was supposed to know that, but she preferred to maintain the uneasy calm with her Dad. They passed a burned shell of a barn and then a large wharf owned by Robert Turner Esq. The river straightened past the Anglers Tavern to a lock. It was a new style chamber lock with gates at both ends and very welcome after the staunch locks on the Thames. Lynn and Davey worked the paddles, first those of the tail gates so Jeannie could pass into the chamber, then the head gates to let in the water and raise the barge. The lock-keeper had refused to come out of his house and Lynn felt justified in not paying the lockage fee. She'd be ready for the churlish keeper of Blake's Lock on their way back to the Thames next morning.

Beyond the Thames Tavern there was a cluster of wharfs. Davey unhitched the three Hoskins horses and led them away to the stables. Lynn wondered why he hadn't taken Hermond but again held back from questioning her Dad who was busy negotiating a berth for Jeannie. Lynn counted a dozen broad Thames barges and as many empty berths yet her Dad returned saying there was no space for Barge Jeannie. Moorings were required for incoming barges even though it was late afternoon. Some berths were private, others not in use and the rudest wharfinger had bluntly stated he didn't want their rotting heap at his wharf.

Peter told Lynn to secure Hermond. Getting the big Shire aboard Jeannie had been Lynn's special task since she was twelve, after the dare she had won against some Shadwell boys. Peter raised Barge Jeannie's version of a triangular staysail that they used for close manoeuvring, and guided the barge from the wharfs. He dipped the mast under the wooden bridge and slewed right into a backwater that curved on itself into the river they had just left. Peter hove to on the outer bank where Lynn disembarked Hermond and let him eat freely on the grassy mound that rose to a ruined, flint and mortar wall.

"We need provisions," said Peter when Lynn came into the cabin. "Four days. You know what's needed."

Lynn counted the shillings he placed into her hand. "This'll be more 'n enough."

"Go over low bridge yonder and straight over next the one we come under," Peter explained. "You'll see a store called Middleton's Provisions."

Lynn climbed out of the cabin as her dad barked more instructions: "Get what we need and don't talk to no one. D'you understand? No one. Come straight back."

from Mistress Olivia's diary

The house was still in uproar from the laundry so I had Papa to myself over luncheon except for little brother Podgy Robby-Junior playing with a bowl of soapy water. I knew I would have Papa's attention if I mentioned Mama spending money. "Papa, do you like the house in the Minster Street Mama is going to buy?"

He swallowed too big a lump of turnip. I refuse to allow the loathsome stuff on my plate. They feed it to cattle in the remoter places. If there can be anywhere remoter than Reading. "A grander house would help me make a better match, Papa."

"A king's son is not too grand for you, Princess." I could see him watching over Podgy out of the corner of his eye. It is entirely rude when people address me but their attention is elsewhere. "Your mother shouldn't raise your hopes about a new house. We cannot afford it."

"Oh, Papa," I cried out. "Are we to be for the poorhouse!" He chortled but I held my what-is-to-become-of-me look.

"I have said we are able to get by, Princess."

Papa likes to play down what he has but like most men loves to brag how his cleverness or boldness acquired it. "I do own some buildings and land but I do not have ready cash to hand. All my spare funds are invested to grow into much more in the future. I won't trouble your pretty head with what that is, but rest assured it will be enough to buy a big new house for Mama."

I sensed he would like to talk about this clever investing but after several minutes the talk had not moved to an opening for me to mention my lack of a new dress for Forbury Fair. I had placed myself next to Papa's distraction on the floor and was showing Podgy how to blow soap-bubbles, as is expected of an older sister.

"These stock things are silly bits of paper," I said, acting Papa's little princess. "I would rather have jewellery or the finest house in Reading than a bit of paper that could blow away with one puff of wind."

Papa laughed and at that moment I blew the biggest bubble ever. Just as it floated from the hoop Podgy jabbed his hideously fat finger and burst it. "Or a warehouse on Kennetside," I added. I knew Papa had his heart set on another warehouse, one in the town.

I did not expect what happened next. Papa stared for several seconds where the bubble had been. "You are right my clever Princess. A warehouse is better than a paper house. I shall take the first coach to London the morrow and rearrange my affairs."

His cheeriness prompted me to ask Papa to give Mama some money for my dress. "It will only be very plain and simple because there is no time left to have one made."

"No, Princess."

My shoulders dropped accompanied by such a sigh. This was my you-don't-care-about-me sigh, which I have not quite perfected like Mama.

"You shall accompany me to London. After I have done my business at Jonathan's Coffee-House we shall purchase at the Exchange a fitting dress for my Princess."

My first visit to London! A London dress! I was so happy after Papa left, I looked into Podgy's adoring, cornflower eyes and poured the soapy water into them. His screaming had not abated one jot even as I reached my room to ransack the paltry content of my garderobe for what to wear to London.

A bitter taste

Middleton's Provisions Store was the largest Lynn had come across outside London. To the left of the door was the foodstuff with sacks of flour, wheat, meal, and root crops on the floor next to wooden boxes of vegetables. The counter was stacked with breads, cheeses, butter, dried meats and jars of pickled everything. On the right was the chandlery with ropes from brail to warp, bitts and blocks, dogs for lifting stone, sack or barrel, and piles of canvas. An archway was flanked by two columns of intricately knotted rope fenders. The air was rich with oils of flax and linseed and the dust from the grains. Underneath was the heavy odour of pipe tobacco drifting into the shop through the archway along with the rumpus of animated male voices from the Kennet Koffee House.

The owner of Store and Koffee House was sharing jokes with a customer while he measured and wrapped. Lynn saw him around forty, solid, his large gestures filling the shop. The man did not hurry and Lynn speculated if she dare add two slices of salt meat to the shopping list in her head.

"Can I help you?"

It was a quiet, lyrical voice and it's young owner was too handsome for his own good, thought Lynn, as he drifted round the counter towards her.

The boy's off-hand arrogance was too much at the end of a harrowing day with her Dad. "Only if you know oats from corn," she answered, surprising herself.

"Which are you in need of?" he asked with a broad smile.

Hello Mr Charm. Lynn was unsure what was behind the smile. His skin had never endured harsh winters, the toffee-brown eyes had experienced no suffering. She abruptly realised he was used to girls looking at him. "A two pound loaf, please."

"Wholemeal, rye, buckwheat? Seeded?"

"Just a plain, simple loaf." She hadn't washed her hair in ages.

"Sorry, we're out of plain and simple today. Something else to put in your basket?"

"I don't like floury."

"Hey-ho." The lad tipped his head, acknowledging her reply. "We have a special today. A poppy-seeded malt for the same price as a plain and simple. Only one left."

Lynn had noticed the proprietor glance at the lad. "Only one seeded? Are your mice bunged up?" The boy frowned perplexed. "Sorry. It's to do with a nasty shop in Maidenhead," she explained.

"I knew I hadn't seen you in here before. I'm Nicholas. Nicholas Middleton. Mr Scowl over there is my father and owner of this store. Welcome to our 'umble emporium . . . er?"

"I'll take the loaf, thank you., One stone of potatoes please." She'd be gone in the morning.

"Will we be seeing you in here again?" asked Nicholas, sauntering to the sacks.

By the time Nicholas's father, Timothy Middleton, had finished with his customer Lynn only had four items from her list. But she had learned Master Nicholas had lived all his life in Reading, had an elder brother Richard who was doing wonderful things in the army, his mother ran the Kennet Koffee House next door, the only such place outside London. The young lad made buying provisions almost enjoyable.

"I'll take over serving this customer, Nicholas." An ample woman had entered through the archway. "Don't you have things to do in the stockroom?" she said as a command.

"Plenty of time. My mother, Dora," said Nicholas with a flourish to Lynn.

"Doretta. But it's Mrs Middleton to customers. You'll be from the barges no doubt," she said, raking Lynn from face to toe and back to hair, her mouth curling at the threadbare clothes. "We don't give tickets to strangers."

Lynn jingled the coins in her hand. Mrs Middleton brusquely served her, at the same time ordering her son to get into the stock-room and urging Mr M to shift himself with the day's book-keeping. Lynn heard the Kennetside door open and before it had shut the bossy woman had rushed to it.

"Mistress Turner! How delighted we are to see you this evening. My, how pretty you look in that dress. It so becomes you. Don't you think, Nicholas?"

"Very. Good evening, Mistress Olivia."

Lynn turned to see he was addressing a striking girl, perhaps a little younger than herself but with a complexion and composure Lynn had only seen behind the windows of fine carriages. She saw this Mistress Olivia and Nicholas made a beautiful couple although, she noted, his natural ease had deserted him. His mother was worse, one second gushing over the girl, the next almost returning to serve her.

"Are you so busy you cannot greet me properly, Nicholas?" asked the girl.

"Yes, Nicholas. Greet Mistress Olivia properly," echoed his mother.

Nicholas went to the girl and kissed her on one then the other cheek. "I am sorry dearest Olivia. One has to be polite to customers, especially a new customer."

"Of course," said Olivia, in a tone that let him know he was never again to ignore her in that manner.

For the second time since entering the Stores Lynn was surveyed, picked apart item by item from her burly build to her worn clothes. For her part Lynn saw only slender perfection. Mistress Olivia had yellow-gold tresses piled high on the crown and cascading down a swan's neck to her shoulders. Light brown eyes under carefully plucked eyebrows and soft shaded orange-red lip-paint gave a soft pastel effect floating on the delicate canvas of china cheeks and high forehead. She wore a russet dress, too fussy for one so young thought Lynn but more costly than all the clothes Lynn had ever owned put together. Olivia stepped towards her, giving her skirt a small flick with her wrist, sufficient to hook Nicholas's attention to a peekaboo trim ankle.

"Papa told me this very morning a small barge had departed Maidenhead worked by a man and his daughter. Would that be you?" She spoke at Lynn without blinking. "I believe the *ancien* vessel is called Barge Jeannie."

"That be my Dad's," said Lynn as steadily as she could. The pretty lips had spat 'Barge' at her.

Olivia had turned away. "Mrs Middleton, you do realise this creature is from the barge about which the whole town is talking? I have heard on my way here they have the audacity to use the Abbey Backwater for a berth. I hope you were not about to trade with them in view of their abominable purpose. Perhaps you did not realise?"

"I most surely did not and I thank you for telling me, Mistress Olivia. Nicholas did not think to ask. As for you, you scab – get out! Out of my store."

"I have money to pay," said Lynn. "Look."

"That's Judas money. Be off, you job-stealing hussy."

"What d'you mean?"

"Don't play innocent with me. Taking away our jobs and acting like nothing's amiss."

"But I —"

"Out!"

Lynn looked towards Nicholas who stood transfixed.

"The likes of her are liars from the day they are born," said Olivia, stepping aside so the proprietress could hustle Lynn to the door. "They plead ignorance to our face then knife us in the back."

Lynn reckoned the sharpest knife was behind Mistress Olivia's ivory teeth. Her blade flashed again. "Don't you agree, Nicholas?"

Nicholas hesitated. "Yes, Mistress Olivia. I agree it is terrible what they're planning. What they are going to do. It seems we'll all be out of business on Kennetside."

"It seems?" yelled Mrs Middleton at her son. "We're all for the

Poor House because of her and her likes," she screeched and pushed Lynn to the door.

"I don't know what you're on about." Lynn's voice was drowned by a stream of insults from the stout woman. Some coffee drinkers, drawn by the commotion, had appeared at the archway.

"Please stop that, Mother," said Nicholas, with little conviction. "There's no need for a scene. I don't think Lynn realises what she's involved in."

"The hussy knows fine well," said Dora Middleton. She gave Lynn a mighty push through the door. Lynn tumbled on to the stone slabs of Kennetside. A few seconds later her empty pannier added a cut cheek to her bruises and grazes.

Olivia turned from the spectacle to Nicholas, pinning him to the spot with her look. "The trollop is called Lynn, is she?" she asked. "That is very familiar of you, Master Middleton." She brushed past him, sufficiently close he could not miss her perfume, and glided directly to a personable man with sympathetic eyes leaning against the column of fenders. "Sir. Would you be the gentleman who is newsman for the Reading Courant?" Frith nodded. "I am Mistress Turner. My father is Mayor Robert Turner. May I take a little of your time and speak with you?"

"I'm sure a little of my time will be well spent with you," answered the newsman. "When would it be most convenient for you?"

"Now, if you please."

"Sarah!" yelled Mrs Middleton over the heads of the men. These she set about brushing back into the Kennet Koffee House. Her instructions filled the room. "Two chairs for the corner, sharp now. And two demitasses as soon. Three chairs." She smiled confidently, standing beside Mistress Olivia and the newsman.

Kennet Koffee House, Kennetside

Three men at the table next to Frith's are in such furious argument one has knocked over his coffee. Frith isn't yet ready to be alone with himself after the hours in West Hill that passed in only minutes.

"It's plain as the warts on your ugly face," says the Butcher to the Perruquier. "Short blokes have to stand on tiptoe so —"

"Not if the stool is high enough," interrupts the Apothecary.

"Every pillory has a whole set of stools for use by dwarfs to giants, does it?" scoffs the Butcher.

The Apothecary winces. Frith knows the pale man from his visits to the Courant to check the advertisement for his Litholytick Drops, which 'soften, relax and dissolve, thereby curing the dismal effects of the Stone and Gravel'. Frith doubts the man takes his own medicine.

"He kicks the stool away," continues the Butcher. "Hangs himself he did. But we'll never know if he did it from reason or stupidity."

"No my good fellow, that was after the blighter died." The Perruquier is half-standing now. "Not six months back I held a wad of fine hair in my mouth while working the corona of a superb Lexonic periwig for a certain gentleman, when my door clattered open and, thus startled, I near swallowed the wad. I know how easy it is to choke to death. I say this John Guiney was so pelted by mud and rotten things about his face he choked."

"I know how easy it is to choke creatures," says the Butcher.

"I still say he suffocated from too much liquor." The Apothecary is on his feet.

"The fool kicked his stool away," says the Butcher, standing to tower over the other two.

Looking through the archway connecting the Koffee House and the Provisions Stores, Frith has a passing curiosity why Mrs Middleton is bothering to serve a shabbily dressed girl. He returns his attention to the arguing men. Frith composed the item for today's Courant. The pillory about which they are so knowledge-able and impassioned is at Charing Cross in London. Frith is sure these men have never travelled beyond Reading. He wonders if Mr Hyde was right, people prefer their news at a distance so they can condemn or condone without responsibility or intervention. The thought makes him more dejected about his quest for a local story.

"Even so," continues the Apothecary tenaciously, "the first cause would be suffocation which may have led to him hanging himself."

"Or choking from rotten foodstuff."

Frith recalls the final line of the article 'This miserable man left behind him a poor wife and two children'. The man's crime was perjury against persons charged with treason. Frith knows it is likely he took money or was threatened by the King's agent to give false evidence in the treason case. But this strawman was uncovered, himself tried and sentenced, and likely the same agent kicked away the pillory stool to ensure eternal silence.

A very pretty girl enters the Provisions Stores and Frith notes how she is instantly the centre of attention. Voices soar like startled gulls above the arguing threesome. Mrs Middleton is shouting of throwing the drab girl into the Poor House. Frith steps to the archway as the commotion catches the ears of the coffee drinkers. He sees the shabby girl hurled from the Stores to land awkwardly on Kennetside and he winces sympathetically feeling the grazes she collects.

Frith is aware he is being addressed by heavy perfume around a lavishly trimmed russet dress. He recognises the value of this contact in the Mayor's house. "I am sure my time will be well spent with you."

To his surprise Mistress Olivia wishes to talk then and there. Mrs Middleton bosses the activity about him. He is returned to his corner table, others squashed away from it. He senses the coffee drinkers behind his back are straining to catch every word. No woman enters the Kennet Koffee House, only Mrs Middleton and the Dame de Comptoir, Sarah, are ever allowed in the room. This is a special dispensation from the high-handed proprietress.

Frith cannot but notice Mistress Olivia's soft youthful curves when she collusively leans forward and hunches her shoulders. He knows from Sarah of the girl's mother Millicent, a beauty with the pick of any gallant, but who married the steady, portly Robert Turner. She is not presently linked with any man, such that every man's name is in the speculation. Frith has met Millicent Turner, who can look away to leave a memory of blue sparkle. Her daughter stares directly at him, confusing Frith if she is a brazen-face or an ingénue.

"My father is deeply concerned about this new waterway," Mistress Olivia says softly.

"The Kennet Navigation," prompts Frith, who has to lean close to catch the girl's words.

"He represents the trades people and merchants who fear greatly for their livelihoods and families."

"Forgive me Mistress Olivia, why is it you telling this to me?"

"My father confides his greatest fears in me. A man in his position has to be a statesman and impartial yet support the cause of those looking up to him. I am speaking to you in total confidence you understand."

Mistress Olivia has eased forward in her chair and Frith can feel her skirt against his leg. To remove his leg would draw attention, but the girl is so engrossed in speaking of the Navigation she appears not to have noticed the contact. She is nervous speaking to him for her eyes flutter round the room and her voice sometimes drops to a whisper.

"My father and the Aldermen expect at least half the businesses to close."

"Did the Mayor say how he came by these figures?"

"I don't understand when he talks so," she says with a helpless shrug.

Frith wants to be reassuring. "The town will adapt with time. One thing I have learned is that nothing is fixed. Life is about dealing with, hopefully successfully, dealing with change."

"A man of your intelligence, Mr Frith." She has suddenly spoken too loud and quickly reverts to the shy girl in a lowered voice. "You can adapt, but these people cannot."

"Would not the waterway bring more trade to Reading than it will take away to Newbury?"

"Barges will pass straight through this town. The alehouses will shut, the inns will follow. My father's timber wharf loads five barges each week. He says that will drop to one."

As he notes down the figures in his pocketbook a soft hand settles on Frith's fingers. Warm breath brushes his ear.

"In confidence please, I beg you." Her curls tickle Frith's neck as she draws even closer, her hand still covering his. "That ugly girl in the shop just now is taking a barge to Newbury, the first to use this new Navigation. You saw the fear and anger. Common folk like Mrs Middleton can never change."

Mistress Olivia is on her feet and brushing past him before Frith realises he should be standing. "As you say, nothing is fixed," she says over her shoulder across the tables of the Koffee House. Framed by the connecting archway she turns to Frith, amusement dancing in her eyes. "Has anyone told you what a handsome man you are Mr Frith? There is much to be said for an older man."

Frith's nod hides his smile at the girl-coquette. He looks up to admire the receding young figure and is jolted by the look on Master Nicholas Middleton, wounded and crushed. It darkens when the gliding russet passes him without pause or word. The young man turns to Frith a face distorted with jealousy and hatred. Frith looks away to the blank page in his pocketbook. He wonders what he has learnt of the Mayor's views on the Kennet Navigation compared to what he has discovered about the Mayor's daughter.

from Mistress Olivia's diary

I deemed it courteous to inform Nicholas of my expedition to London. What is the point in going if my beau is not yearning and worrying after me? When I asked Mama for the chaise to take me for a visit to my expectantly-betrothed, she railed against the idea of her daughter being out in the darkness. Her real concern was for me to put Lousy and Podgy to bed while she drove the maids ragged to complete the laundry for it had been a day of mishaps. It was a small matter to change her decision. I observed that in not telling him, Master Nicholas would be in her company all morning asking as to where I was, for how long would I be away, and all manner of questions to tax her patience. Mama has little time for the Nickel-piece as she calls him.

Wishing to show my Nicholas what the gentlemen of London would be admiring that he appreciate me the more upon my return, I wore my lightweight tuft-taffeta in rich russet with bone lace edging to the narrow tucker. The lace matched that of my three-quarter length chemise-sleeve ruffles. I slipped on a pair of tiny shoes over stockings of a lighter shade to be of winning effect.

Entering Middleton's Provision Stores I stood an insufferable age while the young master fussed round a ragamuffin. My first glance had mistaken her for a sack of some heavy earth crop until her jaw dropped the moment she beheld my fine looks. This person I was waiting on had for a head a potato, with two maggot holes and the gash of a spade beneath, topped with filthy wild shoots. It distresses me to sully the pages of this diary with even the briefest description of that other creature but I promised my diary I would be fully truthful.

I stood several minutes before Mrs Middle-gone entered and toadied towards me with apologies for her son's discourtesy and rightly appalled by her son's rudeness towards me. When he did condescend to greet me it was not how pretty I looked, nor how elegantly I was dressed, nor how delighted he was to see me. Marry-come! He informed me this other thing was a customer.

I appraised Mrs Middle-gone this unkempt vagabond came from the despicable Barge Jennie that would see her into the poorhouse. She immediately set about the rewarding sight of ejecting the trollop, as do maids with the morning slops into the street kennel.

How did I know of the reprobate? Through my cleverness. I had learned of the Kennet Navigation from Papa's confidences to Mama about its effect upon commerce in Reading. It will carry the trade and job of every person in our town to Newbury. Those rats, father and daughter on Barge Jennie, were to be the first voyagers along this new waterway. I had deduced the sloven in the Stores being too slothful to have earned her coins through honest work and too ugly for whoring must be the said Barge-bilge.

At the peak of this entertainment of two roly-poly sacks lumbering towards the shop door, the person who is enamoured of me, failed to speak up against the Barge-bilge. Moreover, he referred to the potato-face by her familiar name. Efackins!

This did make me think the trollop had offered him, in lieu of paying for her provisions, a trip up her navigation. Being of the male gender, Nicholas would have considered the offer to dally in her kennel. It was therefore important for his future I showed Master Nicholas Middleton where his heart truly lay. In that respect it was fortunate the newsman from the Courant was to hand and I had wit how to use his credulity.

It was simple to seduce the newsman for I have noticed many an older man is readily besotted by my youth, vivacity and beauty. I took him to be around forty years of age but not gone to fat for it. Indeed the physique of a younger man and the seasoning of his age was a tempting combination especially as I discovered he had some wit. Though not handsome he did not give offensive. It did not take me long to make him think of things other than what I was saying to him. When I modestly looked away to encourage his ardour the greater, I was delighted to see Master Nicholas greatly enraged.

I would dwell more on the weaknesses of men, young and old, and what I desire for lover and husband, though I am thinking of late these may not be the same man. But I am to London and must be fresh and alert for the sites, the capital gentlemen and purchasing a new dress without Mama's supervision.

A dawning dusk

Lynn's grazes were light compared to some bangs and cuts she had suffered working Barge Jeannie. What hurt most was the uncalled for hostility. And the humiliation in front of strangers. In front of Nicholas Middleton. What did she care about lily-livered Nicholas? Her pride had been bruised by the Kennetside slabs. She had stumbled down a small step and ended on hands and knees. The woman hadn't thrown her down though it looked that way.

There was not a soul on Kennetside at dusk. Why had she let the Middleton woman throw her out of the Store? Lynn could have easily freed herself and walked out with dignity. It was being taken by surprise at the nastiness, the sudden deep animosity. Her reactions were a step behind what was happening because it was so unexpected. Unwarranted. The day had been thoroughly upsetting starting with the abusive Maidenhead shopkeeper, then her dad's sullenness, the Reading wharf men and now this latest. She wondered if the morning's sour encounters had set her mood to which others responded.

Lynn started up the earth ramp to the wooden bridge. It had a nickname according to Nicholas, that fickle creature who changed tack with every girl who passed by. To think she'd been taken in by the patter of no more than a salesman. Lynn silently laughed at herself. Mistress Olivia's pretty looks and sharp mind will tame that eye-rover. They deserve each other.

Two large, hefty fists rammed into Lynn's shoulders and sent her reeling down the ramp. She hadn't seen the man. She'd been daydreaming, not vigilant as she should have at this time of day. Lynn kept her feet as she reeled backwards down the slope. Before she could properly balance herself a fierce punch sunk into her kidneys. A second attacker had slid from the shadow under the bridge. Lynn had no breath to shout. The first man had followed her down the ramp and swung his fist into her stomach with the force of a cudgel. Lynn buckled.

"Take that back where you come from," he spat, then spun her round and round until she wobbled from giddiness. His accomplice hurled his bulk to slam her against an upright of the bridge. She yelped when her head jerked back into the rough timber.

"Damn you!" he shouted in her face. "Starvin' our kids." He drove his knee into Lynn's groin. "Damn you!" She felt her knees start to go and forced them to stay straight. Lynn knew from exper-ience if she went down it would be a kicking next.

"Gerroff!" Peter Darville stood square behind the two men.

"We ain't finished," said the one pinning Lynn to the stanchion.

"Leave her or I'll summon the Militia."

"They'd join in," scoffed the other.

Peter twisted his shoulders and the stone-dogs scythed through the air. One iron claw hit the lout's head, a second claw broke his cheekbone before hooking his neck. Peter jerked on the chain and the man was torn off Lynn like bark from a birch, hands clawing at his head. The other stood staring. Then under Peter's glare, he shouldered his bloodied partner and hobbled off.

"Best get you back and tidied," said Peter, unable to look at her.

memoirs of Sir George Crockmore

There are matters of importance and there are matters of impatience where the latter mostly endeavour to confound the former. So it was upon my return to Southcote Hall from a most concerning Friday last, the 16th inst. In the Metropolis I had encountered Maxi at St James' Palace, who complimented my new periwig before inviting me to his chariot for a short turn. He was privy to particular information he wished to impart without fear of eavesdropper.

For my part I enlightened Maxi regarding a most pleasing whore I had taken the previous night. The strumpets of Covent Garden are filthy, ignorant and unrefined, so my surprise was profound when this one asked, "Would Sir like me to play the recorder or the flute for his entertainment?" It transpired she meant not a musical instrument but mine own, upon which she proved an accomplished flautist. It led me to ponder the price to which a gentleman might stretch for a strumpet with more than one skill and bedded in tasteful surroundings.

Maxi insisted we drop by Leicester House, much spoken of in Court and Civil circle. This plain building is the arbor around which revolve the malcontents of our Kingdom, the hub of dissension with spokes radiating into the fields of painters, poets, playwrights and politicians. The Prince of Wales, being banished from George, His Royal Majesty's Court, has established Leicester House as His Divisive Court, assisted I have no doubt by his wife.

Caroline of Brandenburg-Anspach proved a charming lady and of no small intelligence for a woman. Alas though, her house is ridden with Parliament persons. I nodded to Townshend, who would be better engaged on matters of State, and his cousin Robert Walpole, without doubt intriguing reinstatement to the position of Chancellor. I fear the Kingdom is to be governed by this Norfolk squirearchy who will have every Englishman turned away from expanding trade to growing turnips.

Where is the monarch to apply his levelling hand to the extremes of Parliament? The king has attended fewer and fewer Privy Council meetings, and fewer invariably turns to none. I fear one of these Parliament backbiters will elevate himself above the others, for does not every politician ply his public service trade solely as the means for personal ascendence? Such men are glib of speech, else how do they fool the public, and silver-tongued, else how do they evade the consequences of their ineptitude.

Concluding the pleasantries at Leicester House I hurried my coachman Henry to Sam's Coffee House in Change Alley. Acting upon Maxi's earlier information, I completed my financial business to great reward. I then took the Bath Road westwards, giving considerable thought to worries for the governing of our Kingdom.

I turn now to the matter of impatience that confounded any further important deliberations. Before Henry had pulled up the horses at Southcote Hall, Mr Robert Turner was descending the steps. The mayor had been waiting in agitation for an hour or more. He is a man of genial countenance that belies a worrier nature. I have noted his skills are as a trader. Indeed, one with a hawk's eye to a gainful chance, for he has added distributing coal to his timber interests along the River Kennet. The man has no strategic capacity, for which guidance he turns to me.

On this Friday afternoon he bore the fears of the traders and innkeepers as to the ruination of their businesses due to the Kennet river being made navigable for barges. I affirmed at length my sympathy for his and their predicament. In response to his concern that the smallest incident could boil the resentment to violence, I reminded him of his duty as mayor to preserve order in the town. I suggested he take precautionary measures and to this end enumerated his options, for the man was beyond lucid thinking. Foremost he should ensure by word of mouth that violence will not be tolerated. The Aldermen's Watch would be notified to be extra vigilant and report immediately the smallest congregation or disturbance. With his consent I, in my capacity of King's Justice, will inform Captain Hawker of the Reading Militia he is authorised to follow any commands the mayor deems requisite to quell any disturbance. Finally, and we pray for its avoidance, he has the authority to read the Riot Act, introduced by our late monarch, which will summon from Guildford the Yeomanry of the Lord Lieutenant of Surrey.

At this Mayor Turner grew ashen. I assured Mr Turner his distin-guished status would ensure the town folk followed his words and his lead. I extemporised that in this great country there has always been recognition of protestation to which I added, even a mayor could be party without jeopardising his position. I later came to regret this eulogy on freedom to a man of such narrow vision.

Before I dismissed Mayor Turner I proposed, without revealing the reason, the present might be a propitious time to sell the stock I had previously advised him to purchase. He thanked me for the suggestion but declined to act upon this advice saying he had no need of the cash. It is thus the small mind makes small profit.

As if this were not sufficient of impatience for one day, Cook presented herself to speak with me. This was at the time she ought to be preparing supper and titbits for my evening guests at my regular Friday cards soirée, and as such I adjudged the matter of some urgency. Cook was, as she put it, "at my wit's end with worry and weariness and can't go on, Sir". Cook abandoning my kitchen is as calamitous as the King abandoning his Privy Council.

As is often the case, what appears inconsequential over here proves of value over there. The topic that lanced shivers of fear through the eminent chatterers at Leicester House was not the persisting threats of Jacobites and Spaniards, but the alarming increase in servants' wages compounded by a narrowing of what each servant was prepared to do. Maxi had been obliged to take on a laundry maid after his new house maid declared laundry was not within her remit. Remembering this, I therefore authorised Cook to engage a local wench who was clean, trustworthy, diligent and obedient. The girl would be paid three pounds per annum and receive board and lodging at Southcote Hall. I reasoned a new cook would cost me five pounds per annum extra, and demand a kitchen maid to boot. Cook knew three likely girls and engaged Beale's eldest before Sunday was out. This new acquisition has come with the additional benefit of offering a whore's pleasures without a whore's price.

Thus my memoirs are roundly brought up to date as of this Monday. My final act of this satisfactory day is to write to a Mr

Frith. Articles in The Courant about local dignitaries would be an adventurous departure for Mr Hyde, and his newsman is right in approaching me first. However, I shall pen a letter declining the interview as I seek neither vainglory nor notoriety. I am a quiet man with modest needs.

Catherine's note of Monday 19th September

A week! What do you think would happen with us if we had a whole week together? All right, I'll just get up off the floor. Again, Mr Frith! I didn't think you'd put me there twice in one day. I know you proposed it as a wild thought but I so long for it to be real I can hardly breathe.

I rather like your plan for what we do together. Our <u>work</u> together, Quillman! We may well need to agree aims. Just talking about it would be exciting. We also ought to ask ourselves some questions from time to time on what we are doing. Oh, things like: Have you enjoyed it? Would you do it again? And, would you recommend it to a friend? What would you answer to that, my darling Quillman? And we should ask ourselves things like: what ways could it be improved? After all, it's mutual first-hand learning. So, are you enjoying our learning? Discovering our harmonies, matching our rhythms? I'm still talking about bringing my drawings and your words together! Just that, Quillman.

I didn't collect any of your letters until you left here and I went to pick up Beattie. They were a lovely surprise. I've been tearing out words from your 'Like What?' tale (is it true?) and sticking them to the sticks, if you see what I mean. The jagged strips of paper sit well on the bits of wood. They are smoothed and rounded by their weathering and match the curves of your handwriting. I clutch them together in a sheath then let them scatter to make a different story with each cascade. A different composition, as you would say.

Why aren't you here to drop our sticks with me? It seems an awful long time since the surprise of kissing you on Thursday and strangely much longer since my parlour floor this morning.

Maybe tomorrow we will pretend it is night time, disrobe and climb into your bed. Then mid-afternoon we can get up for breakfast. It would be Heaven to have a real night with you. What would that make a whole week together? Seventh Heaven. Everything is possible with us, Quillman.

A late explanation

Underlying her physical pains, Lynn was annoyed being so easily caught out by her attackers. That would never have happened round the London docks. Why here, in this foreign world? She would have preferred it to be herself tending the wounds caused by her carelessness but her Dad insisted on helping. Lynn conceded it was easier for him to soak off the hair-matted blood at the back of her head and it kept him occupied. She felt cold and had started to shake. Her Dad heated a malt drink on the tiny stove in the aft corner of the cabin. They hadn't spoken on the walk back for he feared an attack on Barge Jeannie while it was unguarded, urging his hobbling daughter to more haste.

Lynn started to unfold her hammock, silently praying for the earliest start in the morning away from this nasty town to the safety of the Thames. But she needed to talk. She wanted her old Dad back again. "I didn't know we still had those stone-dogs," she said over her shoulder.

"I'll do that." Her dad took one of the hammock rings from her. "You sleep on the bunk tonight."

"I'll be fine."

Peter held the ring and didn't budge until his daughter sat on the bunk. Lynn tried again. "When was the last time we had ballast for cargo?" She watched her dad unroll the canvas of the hammock and almost drop it. "I remember big marble blocks. Greenwich weren't it?"

Peter pulled across the free end of the hammock but he missed the hook with the ring. "Dammit! Can't do nothing right." His shoulders slumped. "You could've been killed," he snapped at her.

Then he spoke to the hammock. "This all were my fault."

"It could have happened by London Bridge as here."

"I should've made you stay at Maidenhead."

"You need me on the barge."

"I need . . ." He paused. "This river's been fighting me since your Mam . . ." He held the limp hammock. "I've let her down. I've let you down. No good as a bargeman, worse as a Dad. You shouldn't have come."

She'd never heard him this bad. Lynn couldn't stop her voice rising in protestation. "Yes I should! Jeannie's my life. It's all I know." Lynn couldn't stop her anger. "You should've told me what this trip was about. Why didn't you? I've a right! I'd have known what to expect."

"No you wouldn't," he shouted back. His voice dropped. " I didn't. Lord save us, what have I done?"

Lynn eased him on to the bunk. "Tell me." She hooked the hammock and quickly, fighting the sharp pains, climbed in before he could protest. "Why do they hate us here?"

In laboured sentences Peter told his daughter first what she already knew. The mounting unpaid fees had made him a debtor from Greenwich to Great Marlow. His reputation for drunken unreliability lost them many cargoes. This morning he had been given the chance to clear all his debts. Peter had shut his mind to what this windfall may entail, not asking questions, not looking for a catch in the contract.

"This River Kennet has been made navigable for barges right through to Newbury. They've dug it out, deeper, wider, put in cuts and locks. That's where we're headed, Newbury. Hoskins man said the navvies, the blokes doing all the digging of this navigation, they should have the last lock done by tomorrow."

"Why was I thrown out of Middleton's Stores? And attacked? And the horrid wharf men?"

"This new Navigation along the Kennet River will take away all the trade from Reading."

"The attack wasn't to rob me?" asked Lynn.

"It's us robbing them, that's how they see it. The Navigation will take the jobs to Newbury."

"No wonder they're upset. We mustn't do it. It's not fair."

"Maybe so. But if I don't get this cargo to Newbury and another back down, it'll be us lose everything. They'll take Barge Jeannie from me."

A chill of emptiness came over Lynn. She had been born, raised and had lived and worked on Barge Jeannie. Her Dad could do nothing else. She recalled the fear behind the fury in Mrs Middleton's eyes, the hatred in the voices of her attackers. "But all these people in Reading, their families."

"If we don't sail it some other barge will. This Navigation's here and it can't be undug. There's been money put into it and riches to be got from it. For some. The folk of Reading are going to have to realise that. There'll still be trade here. Some'll be lost, no one can guess how much." Her Dad became thoughtful. "I nearly lost you tonight, my Beaut. That's too much to lose. You're worth more to me than anything in the world. Far more'n this old barge. We're going back."

"We can't lose Jeannie. I couldn't face that," cried Lynn. "It was all puffed foresails in the Stores and a pair of hotheads under the bridge."

"You're making light now."

"They won't come looking for trouble from you again."

"There's plenty others. Mind, I don't know what I'd do without Barge Jeannie. She's our Jean's boat really."

"Then we'll do it for Mam. I'll rouse Davey first thing and we'll be off."

"Davey's only hired to Reading. And the horses."

"I've still got those shillings. I'll get fresh horses."

"There'll not be a horse in Reading to be had. Not for us."

Lynn felt defeat pressing her chest, and all the hatred pressing as she remembered faces from her attackers back to the sullen keeper at Blake's Lock. "Dad, you said the Navigation is newly dug?"

"Easy big enough for a barge. And straightened with cuts."

"All the locks will be new? Won't they all be like Blake's Lock? All chamber locks."

There was no reply from Peter for a minute. "It's upstream, but the Kennet's not a fast river and Jeannie's snug-loaded. D'you reckon you could coax Hermond to the job?"

"Yes," said Lynn, masking her worries about her forty year-old closest friend. "He'll know it's to save Barge Jeannie."

"We'll cast off at dawn," said Peter. "Be clear before anyone knows. That way there won't be any trouble."

A heavy rain

A light easterly carried Barge Jeannie along the Kennet once she had turned from the Abbey Backwater. Lynn stood on the fore-deck, slippery with drizzle, firmly holding Hermond's bridle and softly talking nonsense. It kept her calm as well as the horse. She could see people in the distance on High Bridge, their clogs clattering more noisily in the early quiet. A couple stopped to peer downriver at the barge.

Nearing the stone bridge, Peter lashed the tiller then dropped and slewed the yard with its sail. He was expert at judging their approach to bridges, lowering the mast just before the arch. The breeze gave them a good momentum and Peter was loosening the forestay when the rotten fish hit his back, splattering stinking flakes across his jerkin.

"Go back, you Devils!"

The yell from the High Bridge was followed by more, then rotten carrots, hard turnips and slimy cabbage. Hermond shied and Lynn threw her arms round his neck. She had to keep him still at all costs. She wanted to help her Dad free the forestay so the mast didn't snap against the bridge or snag under it. She wanted to go aft and push the barge faster with a shaft. Lynn counted a score along the parapet. More were joining them. The hail of abuse and rubbish worsened.

Lynn watched in horror as a woman tipped bloody intestines and offal over her Dad and then let go her wooden bucket. It smacked onto his neck and shoulder blade. He staggered and Lynn heard the rush of rope through the block. The mast crashed onto the cabin with a mighty thump, bounced once, and settled. It was suddenly dark. Lynn could hear the rising commotion on the bridge above as echoes all about her, everywhere. Hermond was on the brink of bolting. She tried to find the level tone in her whispers for him.

Her Dad stumbled aft, his palms stripped raw from when he had tried to hold the rope. "Forestay'll take too long to fix," he called. "Unship Hermond soon as."

Doing anything would be relief. Lynn hated watching but she was unable to help her Dad as he leaned against a shaft to pole the barge forward. Lynn could feel the pain in his raw palms gripping the wood. It was taking an eternity to clear the bridge. She heard a deep voice through the hubbub overhead.

"Rotten veg won't stop 'em. Cussed job-thieves. Stop 'em proper!"

The cry was picked up and the mob were chanting: "Stop 'em proper. Stop 'em proper."

Lynn heard a solid thud by her feet and watched with disbelief and shock as a cobblestone skittered along the deck. The next hit Hermond's flank. He twitched his quarters and Lynn pulled hard at his bridal. She glared up at the bridge and there among the horde she saw Nicholas Middleton, his arm in the air and yelling with the rest of the crowd. She ducked as a cobble arced towards her head.

Stones came more frequently. Lynn was hit on her hip. She stretched for the small tarpaulin and threw it round herself and over Hermond. Jeannie's bow was turning to Kennetside and against the current was quickly coming to a stop for all Peter's effort with the shaft.

"Here Mayor, you show 'em." The coarse voice soared over the jeering rumpus. Lynn heard a sharp groan from her Dad followed by a chilling cheer from the mob. Blood poured down his right cheek and Lynn watched in dismay as he slid to the deck. Another stone hit Hermond below his eye and the horse slithered across the deck to another cheer.

Lynn smelt his fear. The chances of him going overboard were increasing by the second. She dare not let him go to tend her Dad, still groggy on the afterdeck. She knew Barge Jeannie would drift back to the bridge and closer to the stone throwers. Lynn threw off the protective tarpaulin, grabbed the coiled tow-rope and hurdled herself onto the horse's back. The stone throwers stopped to watch. Lynn concentrated on the two feet of Kennet between the deck and the grassy bank. She had only unshipped Hermond when Barge

Jeannie was securely moored.

Lynn gripped the Shire's collar and kicked him forward. He stayed put. She kicked again as a jeer rose from the bridge. She leant along Hermond's neck and pleaded in her familiar whispers. He took a tentative step forward. This will be disaster, thought Lynn, knowing the lightly laden vessel would be thrust away from the bank when the weighty horse pushed off.

"All or nothing, Hermond," she whispered, then let out a high, sharp "Yilp!" Hermond took a big stride, a second, then he leapt. There was nothing under them. There was no sound in Lynn's ears. She sensed the horse's hind legs scrambling for a purchase in the soft mud. "Go, Hermond," she yelled and heard a louder holler go up on the bridge.

"Bastards are getting away! Stop 'em."

Lynn slapped the horse's flank to swing him. "Right, right," she was urging, and suddenly his back lurched up and he was on firm ground. Her Dad was shouting. She saw the mob were scrambling down the bridge ramp on to the river bank. Lynn slid off and urged Hermond quicker. The tow-rope lifted and Hermond was halted. He took the strain and stepped on. Only then did Lynn dare look back again.

Barge Jeannie wasn't angling to mid-stream. Three brawny wharf men were aboard and wrestling with her Dad. Lynn dropped the lead reign and ran back. She saw the four men topple into the river. As she raced closer she could see the wharf men forcing her dad's head underwater. Lynn screamed as she ran, watching them hold her Dad's head under the surface. Bounding onto the barge, she snatched up a hitcher and jabbed the metal point at the nearest man's back. He fell away with a howl. Before she could thrust at the next he grabbed the end, and girl and man were locked in a grim tug-of-war.

A powerful arm encircled Lynn from behind squeezing the breath from her. She dropped the hitcher. "That's no way for a lass to behave," said a gruff voice in her ear.

"Nor's that." She nodded towards the men in the water and kicked back at her captor's shins. He side-stepped still pinning her to him with his arm. Lynn felt a pistol at her right temple. "Don't try that again." The gun exploded by her ear. Her heart jumped into her mouth and she felt the side of her face burn from the powder. The man had fired in the air and, with everyone's attention he snapped orders. The wharf men begrudgingly dragged her Dad's limp body to the bank.

"Captain Teon Hawker of the Reading Militia, Mistress."

The man was unusually close-cropped with a few day's dark stubble on his jaw. Cold eyes were set deep under heavy brows and Lynn noticed a gold ring through his right ear, then the black sash across his chest.

"Me and my men be at your service," he gave a derisory awkward bow. "Welcome to Brewery Gut, as we call this stretch of the Kennet."

"Thank you," answered Lynn formally. She wanted to ask why he hadn't stopped the mobsters earlier or why he had waited until her Dad was drowned. "I must see to my Dad," she said and ran to where the louts had dumped him. Relief flooded through her hearing him spluttering and coughing the river out of his lungs.

As she tended him Lynn noted a dozen men with black sashes drive back the subdued onlookers, not sparing their fists and sword hilts. Captain Hawker swung the flat of his broadsword against scurrying backs, occasionally drawing blood.

correspondence of Sir George Crockmore

from Sir George Crockmore, Southcote Hall
to Henry Martyn, Esquire.
The Company Secretary,
The Kennet Navigation Company, Burgus House, Newbury
2nd September

Sir,

I have been led, from previous correspondence with your good self, we are in concord regarding the benefits to many from opening the River Kennet to regular trading traffic between the towns of Reading and Newbury. It is a magnificent undertaking, and a fine demonstration of the ability of Man to tame Nature. Your senior engineer, Mr John Hore, is to be commended.

I was among the first to embrace your project and have been instrumental in encouraging to participate those parties of limited vision and reticence. Without the cooperation of every landowner along the length of the waterway you would have not one navigable river but many short sections, the one not attainable from the next and thereby unworkable in the full.

At my own initiative I secured for you much of the land needed for Mr Hore's locks and for the towing path. We now stand on the threshold of this great engineering feat being brought into pecuniary returns.

It is an appropriate moment to reflect upon two great truths. The first: any endeavour incurs expenditure. The second: agreements between gentlemen are to be honoured.

This first you anticipated, raising capital through the issue in London of stock in your Company. I would remind you the declared allocation of said capital was, in part, to recompense those who are directly affected by the construction of the River Kennet Navigation. I am creditor to your Company for no small amount, comprising lease payments against my own property along the River Kennet, purchase on your behalf of other riverside stretches, various and sundry gratuities, billeting of your labourers, supplying cartage and storage, etcetera.

I have detailed the total in previous correspondence to your Treasurer. This reimbursement for expenses and charges from your Company has been due some number of months.

I draw your attention to the second truth. Your Treasurer did promise in writing to me, this debt would be cleared before the engineering work was complete. This has not been the case.

It pains me to pen a missive such as this and I trust its very receipt will instil in you the gravity by which I deem the matter. This undertaking of the River Kennet Navigation Company portends a prosperous future for those who are touched by it. It *would be inauspicious for this venture to be tarnished with a dishonourable debt at its outset.*

I leave the matter in your hands for an expeditious resolution.

Yours, etc.

correspondence of Sir George Crockmore

from Henry Martyn, Esquire
The River Kennet Navigation Company
to Sir George Crockmore, Bart.
Southcote Hall, Berkshire
7th September

Sir,

I am in receipt of your letter of 2nd inst. and relay my profound distress upon reading its contents. The River Kennet Navigation Company is indeed endeavouring to benefit landowners, commerce and the general populace. Your exertions on behalf of the Company are highly regarded and appreciated, as is the more direct support you have undertaken.

Let me assure you that every last farthing of your expenditure and fees against the Company will be reimbursed. I am confident of this claim on the grounds that this very day Mr Hore has confirmed to me the last lock at Colthrop has been completed and all that remains for the River Kennet Navigation to be fully workable is for the adjacent embankment to be built up.

On the second issue raised in your letter, the Treasurer is a fellow to whom I would entrust my life savings upon his word. I venture to suggest a misunderstanding may have arisen between the Treasurer and your good self. He could make settlement of your debt only when the Third Issue of stock was taken up. If this point was absent from the Treasurer's letter it was an oversight for which he humbly apologises.

The Company has clearly been negligent in keeping you

informed regarding the Third Issue. This, I am sorry to report, has again been delayed. I am sure a worldly person as yourself will be aware of the fever raging these past months. All, from Royalty to boot boy, are buying high yield stock in overseas schemes with the intent of speedy riches. This mania has removed funds available for other, more sound investment. The Board is of the opinion these enterprises will soon peak, releasing funds for solid and steady investments. This, I submit, is the reason the Company has not cleared its debt to you.

The opening of the River Kennet Navigation will herald a fine revenue from which you Sir, will be a preferential creditor. Upon this you have my word. Directors of the Company have already undertaken negotiations with the Mayor of Reading as to the benefit the town may accrue as a result of the increased trade from the new waterway. The Mayor has stated he will use his position and influence to champion among the citizens of Reading this creation of wealth, thereby allaying fears to the contrary. I am assured the protestations will be quickly resolved and the Company is optimistic many willing barge-masters will soon be operating.

Sir, I trust the foregoing reassures you as to your reimburse-ment in the imminent future, and of the trustworthiness of the Board in the manner by which they conduct their business.

I have the honour to be, Sir,

Your humble and obedient Servant

Yours, etc.

Kennet Koffee House, Kennetside

"My usual, Sarah," says Frith. "In a demitasse," he adds. The newsman's grin evaporates on seeing Mrs Middleton enter from the Stores. He had hoped to check for any letter and be on his way as he is already late after his soundest sleep in weeks. Tuesdays are quiet at the Courant but Frith's hopes lie away from the print room today. "Where is everyone?"

"Licking their wounds and boasting about how they got them," answers Sarah. "Don't tell me you missed it all."

"All what?" asks Frith.

"You'll have to make it up."

"People will still believe it if is in print before their eyes," he says. He realises he should be paying attention. "Missed what?"

"Biggest excitement round here for years." Sarah leans over her counter. "I'm telling you the truth when I say half High Bridge is in the river and they still didn't sink that rotten barge. I'll show 'em throwing when I gets down the Fair. I'm sharp on the cock-shy. I got an eye for which ones to aim at, though what you do with them coconut things is anyone's guess."

Frith experiences the unease of realising something has happened he should have known about. "How many were involved?"

"Hundreds. They got the old bleeder a good 'un and a couple of the lads had him underwater until they got pulled off."

"It sounds a very unfair fight."

"They're unfair first. It's what they deserve. I'll be out of a job coz of this Navigation. Sneaking upriver like rats caught out by sunrise. Going under High Bridge was a red rag to a bull and they got the cobbles, plenty of them."

"Stoning people is the right course of action, is it?" asks Frith.

"Rightly so. We had the Mayor up there chucking bricks like a good 'un. And what's-his-face, the Recorder chap." Sarah's voice is raised seeing Frith's doubts. "Don't go all po-faced with me, Mr Frith. Those Barge-bums knew what they'd get they if they went on."

"Stoned, then death by drowning, did you say?"

"Our men didn't get the chance to finish him off."

"My Nicholas was furious." Mrs Middleton flicks her hand as if Sarah were an annoying fly, indicating to her Dame de Comptoir to busy herself about the tables. She stares up to Frith's face, holding his attention. "I am so proud of my Nicholas, up there on the bridge, next to our Mayor. He went down to the barge and it took Captain Hawker's men to stop him. Are you not noting this down for your newspaper, Mr Frith?"

Frith taps his temple to indicate where her information has gone, then sips his coffee as he lets it fall out.

Mrs Middleton continues. "Typical Robert Turner. Gets himself right in the middle of things on the bridge but as soon as he's not the centre of attention, he stops everything. I've never seen my Nicholas so high with emotions since his tantrum days. Mistress Olivia will be in no doubt about his loyalties now."

"Had she been concerned?" asks Frith.

"Not in the slightest," retorts Mrs Middleton. "But you know young girls, not much confidence in themselves, not the savoir-faire of us worldly women. Their beau merely has to glance at another girl and they are at a loss for themselves."

"You mean the girl from the barge?"

"My Lord, no! It was her monstrous ugliness and disgusting clothes that had my Nicholas not believing his eyes she would dare enter an establishment such as our Stores. Her and her devious father won't be back. Only a bargemaster from Bedlam would risk going against our wharf men. Our town merchants will see there are no cargoes. And another lot I'll be pleased to see the back of is that shifty trouble-making lot digging the Navigation."

"The navigators."

"Nothing but trouble since they came. Every week it's the same. Here, take a look at yesterday's Courant."

from the Courant, Monday 19th September

Two Fires

It is heard from the Countryside of Berkshire, That on the 10th Instant, two Persons making misuse of a Pistole at Beenham Stocks, (within eight Miles of this Town) set fire to a thatch'd House, which burnt with such Violence that only Three Houses were left standing in the Village.

On Saturday last it is said a Person melting Tallow in a Farm-house close by Kennetmouth, by Carelessness set fire to the House and it was burnt to the Ground.

———

"Go on, read it properly," demands Mrs Middleton, after Frith's glance at the paper.

"No need, I composed the item."

"In that case, you composed it wrong. Ambrose Darrel is so mean he wouldn't give you the time of day though you be right next to St Giles. Melting tallow! The man's a magpie, busy only between dawn and dusk so as not to burn money in candles. You need to get your facts straight, Mr Frith."

"It was the navigators who burnt down Darrel's farm?" suggests Frith.

"And destroyed a village."

Frith is patient. "Navigators don't carry pistols."

"I wear a plain dress in the Kennet Koffee House Mr Frith, but I put on bows when Mr M takes me out. I'm telling you that burned village is too close on Colthrop for it not to be them. That's where they're working, if you call digging a ditch proper work."

"The Kennetmouth farm is a long way from Colthrop and Beenham Stocks," persists Frith.

"We have horses these days Mr Frith, to help us travel long distances quickly. Likely it was the same gang who started throwing the stones at High Bridge."

"I understood it was town people."

"My Nicholas said it was faces he didn't recognise."

"Why would the navigators —"

"Why?" shrieks Mrs Middleton. "Because they can't stand no one doing well for themselves. Ambrose Darrel is a freeholder, good land too, them riverside meadows. Them navigator people are spiteful, being never amounting to more than the mud on that man's doorstep. They burned it down out of pure cussedness. He's done for now, can't afford to build a new farmhouse, though good-ness knows what he did with the money he didn't spend on candles. Me and Mr M have two boys to bring up. I tell Mr M to put up his prices but he's too kind, too generous against his own family towards these town folk. By all that's just, my Mr M should be Mayor. Between you and me, he was kind to the wrong people and not generous to the right pockets. And I'm the same, keeping

Mrs Kempster out of pity. She should be chivvying that wharfinger, not chattering. You'd think he hasn't a job to go back to."

"He might not with the Navigation opening for trade. Whereas you seem calm about your future."

"That's my Mr M for you. He has plans. Very hush-hush, but we may not be running the Stores and Koffee House much longer. Not when Mr M's little venture comes about."

"What would that be?" asks Frith innocently.

"You see how I have to do Mrs Kempster's job, yet again," she says, and bears down on the wharfinger.

Frith's demitasse is empty and he knows he should get to work. "I'm pleased you didn't get involved in the riot and avoided injury," he says to Sarah, who has returned behind the counter now Mrs Middleton has moved from it.

"You wouldn't catch me in ten miles of that bunch of strong-arm hot-heads."

"But the Reading Militia were present."

"Them's the ones I'm talking about," says Sarah, with an exasperated look. "Them black-sashes was itching to plough in. Had to wait until our Mayor was scared he'd be remembered for allowing a public drowning. Then they was like a pack of hounds who'd lost a hare but found a hind. Folk couldn't get away from the barge coz of others still pouring off High Bridge, so they got cuffed and trodden and sabre swiped. A lot of blood."

"Nicholas was unharmed? What of Mr M?"

"You have a right sense of humour Mr Frith, that I'll say about you. Mr M only goes where Dragon tells him. I can tell you this in confidence, don't pass it on, but him and her were having their own riot this morning. Mr M wanted Dragon to hand over her jewellery so he can raise more cash for this scheme he's got. Dragon wasn't having it. You'll get it all back with a mountain of cash, he says, which sort of gets her interested. Always squawking how she hasn't got two pennies to rub together, whereas I know she's got a chest of sovereigns all rubbing together when she opens it to count them."

"Where's the barge now?" asks Frith, heading for the door.

"On its way to Hell, and I don't mean Newbury. We've seen off those Barge-bums. It's all over bar the cheering." Sarah sees Mrs Middleton is occupied and slides an envelope across the counter. "Hope this is cheering for you, Mr Frith."

Catherine's first note of Tuesday 20th September

I didn't tell you I had a long talk with Mary after the alehouse widows had gone. "What happened to the newsman?" she asked, and I said, oh well, you know, this and that. "Well what? He sounded interesting." Well he was. I mean he is. "And?" The thing is, Mary, I was looking for a friend, a kindred spirit to work with. I wasn't looking for rescue. "And what did you get?" I get these lovely letters. They began as beautiful pieces of writing to work with and now some are for me. I'm starting to know the man through his letters. "That sounds very nice. What's he like?" I thought there could be this closeness, this intimacy of working together. I have got that, I really have. But there is something else. I wasn't expecting that to happen.

Then she tells me off! "Catherine, you can't tell other people how to feel and you can't plan how things turn out. Is it nice?" It's wonderful. "Do you feel guilty?" I was sure I would, certain I ought to – but I don't. I have very intense friendships. I can't do lukewarm. And this is very, very intense. It's for me and my newsman and no one else.

So, Quillman. You and I, naked in your bed in a few hours. In your bed! Is that all right? I wonder how you'll make love given this luxury of privacy and time. I wonder how I will make love with you.

Do you think one behaves differently in different circumstances? We must – colours are changed in different light, they alter when placed next to other colours. Does it seem I set the pace? If you knew how unusual it is for me to be doing so when it comes to intimacy and making love you would not believe your ears, your eyes, your everything!

Is this all right? I've no idea how we go about this. I'm trembling with excitement, nerves. Last week I was asking only for a kiss. I thought, just one kiss, just one harmless kiss.

I have stage fright. I've never minded being neither beautiful nor the owner of a gorgeous body – except sometimes. I always feel I'm far better clothed, or in the dark. It will be fine. Just as soon as I stop trembling. One long naked kiss will dissolve me entirely. Promise to revive me if I faint?

A handy handcart

Hermond's nastiest cuts were on his withers and right shoulder, worsened by hauling then holding Barge Jeannie against the ever present river current until Lynn could stake a makeshift mooring. She searched the cabin lockers for something to cushion his collar, deciding the only way was to sacrifice one of her smocks. Her dad lay on the bunk. She boiled a milk and barley drink for him after which his violent shaking stopped and the bleeding from his head wounds eased.

"Best move on," he said, painfully lifting himself off the bunk. "Slow's better 'n not at all."

"Hermond's badly chaffed. It'll pain him. You're nowhere near fit."

"I'll decide if I'm fit." He reached under his bunk and pulled out a flagon. "Pour this on Hermond's sores. Watch for his kicks, but it'll numb him to get us clear of this God-forsaken place. He's all we've got, Lynn. The forestay block shattered with the whip-back. It was old anyway. Like this barge. Like me."

Lynn closed her ears. She knew where this talk led. "This old smock will make things easier for him," she said. "Any dead weight can go over the side to lighten Jeannie. You first." She was saddened her Dad didn't raise an eyebrow. "You rest awhile."

"You can't steer a jolly-boat up the Estuary without hitting Sheppy," he said, making for the tiller. "You see to the horse, he'll do anything for you." The daughter did as she was told.

Two hundred yards ahead, Lynn could see a few figures leaning on the wooden railing of Seven Bridges. Where was the Reading Militia to protect them? The brute who'd attacked her last night had said the Militia would join in with them. Perhaps they were not so much keepers of the peace, rather enforcers of the peace getting enjoyment from wading in to a one-sided fight.

The brandy made Hermond smell more like an ale dray horse than a barge horse. He took up the tension in the rope, snorting white clouds into the persistent drizzle. Lynn patted his muzzle and encouraged him through the stabs of pain, despite the brandy. She wondered if it might not have been better to pour it down his throat. The thought of a drunken Shire was as amusing as it was alarming.

The catcalls from the bridge jolted Lynn from her thoughts. There were nearly a dozen men and women taunting and spitting. A woman hurled a large carrot that bounced by her feet, and Lynn dreaded what would come next.

"That's right neighbourly, Elizabeth Groves." The voice above was soft and unhurried. "Giving good food to those in need." It belonged to a shortish ruddy-faced man about sixty. He had a small handcart but his passage from St Mary Butts across the bridge was blocked by the small crowd.

"They're taking the food from our mouths, Adam Carpenter," the woman snapped back. "Them scum's thieving the jobs from our menfolk."

"If you could prise the jug of ale from your husband's fist he might hold a job long enough to be thieved of it. Even as we speak he's in the Bear." The woman scowled for a few moments then strode away up Bridge Street on a mission. "As for you Jonas Reeve, is this barge likely to sail up chimneys and clean them instead of you? Will brides ask for a barge at their wedding instead of you? This is foolish and you know it."

Like rain over baked ground the group seeped off the bridge. Adam Carpenter stepped down to the river as Barge Jeannie cleared from beneath. Peter Darville stiffly disembarked to shake Adam Carpenter by the hand.

"I am indebted to you, Sir."

"I did what any good citizen should do." Adam walked to Lynn who had remained standing by Hermond. He tapped the horse's right hind leg and held its raised fetlock. "This needs re-shoeing, probably the others too. He was carrying it."

Lynn was chastened this stranger had found her neglectful of Hermond. "I thought it was his cuts."

"Could be," said Adam looking at her. "Didn't see his wounds, just his gait. So I could just as easily have been wrong."

Adam's humbleness was a balm to Lynn's wounded self-respect. But he was right about the shoe. "Dangerous thing," he mused. "A little bit of knowledge, especially when you tack on a whole raft of assumption. A whole barge in your case." He laughed and Lynn noticed her dad smile.

Adam tutted and sighed as he examined Hermond. Lynn agreed the horse should be rested. Her dad was keen to get through County Lock a few hundred yards ahead. Then the river turned sharp left and they could moor by the oyster beds out of site from town folk. He said he could make a new block for the forestay and they could sail on. Hermond's shoe would have to wait.

That wasn't good enough for Adam. "Lucky for you it's my shopping day today. You can stop at my place for supper. Rest the horse overnight. I've still got the anvil and the tools will be somewhere. Long time since I practised as a farrier. It might take a week to find them." Lynn wasn't sure if he was teasing. "I could do with the company," he said, ending any protest.

Adam lived at Rose Kiln, at the top of a wooded river bank. Barge Jeannie was to pass his small jetty then turn into Foundry Brook. After a quarter-mile there were enough willows to hide the Spanish Armada, according to Adam. Tomorrow they'd have to bring Jeannie out stern first, but tomorrow was a long time away.

memoirs of Sir George Crockmore

This morning I sent word with Henry for Mayor Turner to attend at his earliest. The man must have located Pegasus in the town stables for he arrived before I had dismissed my tailor. Mr Turner was obliged to wait some tens of minutes, which I hoped he would put to good use reflecting on his dawn activities.

The tailor is a blind buffoon. He had brought for my approval a sleeved waistcoat with four cartridge pleats, and in a colour from two seasons previous. The man avowed the pleats added status. Why then did he not shirring one hundred pleats, I asked, speculating again on acquiring a property in London where tailors are as sharp as their needles.

I was therefore in a disgruntled mood for receiving Mr Turner and, in retrospect, was too scolding. My dressing down of the mayor was exacerbated by the audacity of his defence in asserting I had sanctioned his action "to lead by example" upon High Bridge. I replied I had stressed observance of the law when I spoke on the topic of protestation. His foolishness had overwhelmed his reason and, in joining the stone throwers, had brought his office into disrepute. I made clear that interceding on his behalf could jeopardise my good name. It was instructional to witness how far the man was prepared to demean himself to preserve his situation, and to fend off what was in fact no threat. He is a man worth cultivating, for he is unresisting at taking my advice.

Assured he would retain his prominent position in the town, Mr Turner vowed to apprehend those responsible for the recent surge of robberies from the houses of local gentry and to bring them before my good self in my judicial capacity. I suggested to him that the completion of the Kennet Navigation would remove the itinerant workers, believed to be perpetrators of the crimes. He agreed, but asserted the thieves should not get away with their law breaking. I concurred, suggesting Captain Hawker be given a wider brief for his Reading Militia. This would require additional funding from the public purse. I was dismayed to learn the folk of Reading think little of their Militia's effectiveness, and resolved to place before Captain Hawker the issue of elevating their standing by making an arrest or two.

The mayor then made an observation astonishing for him. Citing the recent burglary at Viscount Arthur Harcourt's, he asserted the few objects stolen, being the most valuable, indicated the thieves were too learned to be labourers. I postulated some informed antiquary may be engaging the disreputable navigators to be the agents providing objects for his business at minimal cost.

Mr Turner's departure from Southcote Hall left snags in my mind to which I gave thought during the morning. The completion of the Kennet Navigation will mark a cessation of some activities and the initiation of others. I anticipate the house thefts from fine people, many with whom I am acquainted, will lessen. Also, it would be propitious for the Reading Militia to prove their value. Finally, the Kennet Navigation has engendered hostility and violence from the traders and merchants of Reading, which is likely detrimental to the operation of said waterway.

The afternoon brought welcome satisfaction. Sidney Levenson, Esquire and Whig member, visited with some money and other bills, having ear of my visit to Sam's Coffee House. The man enshrines the values of the duplicitous politician: advocating equality among others while he expedites advantage to himself. Levenson champions the riff-raff be taught by the poorly qualified while his child has the best in private tuition. This Mr Benevolence was mortgaging, for the acquisition of my remaining stock, his two tenant farms and the elegant house he acquired marrying a shrivelled-face spinster with elderly parents. Such is Levenson's avarice he paid far above the London price for my stock while he mocked how overly cautious I was in selling.

My thoughts subsequently drifted to wives, and last Friday's soirée in particular. At the poque table, after the ladies had retired from the whist foursomes, Henry Woodroffe declared his tens high full hand and claimed the pot. With my hand restraining his hastiness I showed my queen high full hand declaring, "The lady is well played tonight."

I savoured the dolt's dawning grasp of my words. In the frenzied last bidding, the fool put up his wife Martha, for one night to cover my fifteen guineas. The others were dubious the price so high, and haggled her tumble-worth. This bargaining revealed much about the intimacies of the Woodroffe bed chamber as he would have it known. I have discovered in the past to my dismay, his wife a cold fish.

After further mirth, I declared Woodroffe's stake revoked, stating Martha has a full house of principles with a misère of passion. I have given him one week to redeem his IOU for fifteen guineas plus five in penalty. The priggish Harcourt declared he would rather wager his house than offer the Viscountess. This had the double irony that as he spoke his house was being emptied and his wife was being filled in an upstairs room of the Winning Hand Inn. I had a mind to exact fees from Lady Harcourt for keeping her husband occupied on a Friday night, but she is of such agreeable deportment my still tongue today shall enjoy lively activity anon.

Catherine's second note of Tuesday 20th September

I can still feel your lips all over my body. If I were tissue paper, could I slip under your pillow at night, slide out and kiss you to just before your awakening? Your teasing chimera, wrapping you in your dreams, unfolding you to near wakefulness.

You said you can only be who you are – well, as you are is very fine with me. You're unconditionally Heaven. There is a simmer of joy when you're not with me that boils when we are together.

Do you want to book shop on Thursday, before my house? Better if you come to me first, as I have Beattie to collect later from her tutor. What time? Make it early so we have longer. So you can get to the shop this time! What appetite shall I feed?

The grocer asked for his money today. Is it only one month since our first walk together? It must be longer. Quillman, thank you for being so 'sympathetique.' I do notice. You don't crowd me. You leave gaps.

I spoke a while ago about introducing change into my life. It sounded dramatic but it's not. It's about living a life instead of just getting by. You know, when you are racing down hill you can let your legs run with you. It's a great feeling. But when you start to climb and use your legs, there is a kind of energy, a surge of responsibility. Last October when I began on the Saint Mary project I felt I needed to redraw myself, find who I was. I was two stone heavier than I am now. As big as those Church women! I had let myself blur, like sopping watercolours, muddied. I'm a competent mother for Beattie. I do my etchings with skill and some knowledge. And passion. None of that is recognised. Most hurtfully to me, not by Eliot. He refused to come to the opening of my biggest-ever project. I was so let down by that. He should have been proud of me.

Bother, he's dragged me off what I was writing and I haven't time to copy the page before he comes home.

I'd pushed what I did and how I did it somehow distant. I'd wrapped myself in layers of hiding. I think a lot of women do that. Not deliberately, it would be better if it were. Just laziness of convenience, a personal dishonesty.

So. I decided to make changes, starting with my appearance. I didn't want to become attractive or sexy, despite what you so believably tell me. I wanted to be more nimble, to pull back to my own kingdom. To occupy my skin. I haven't stopped eating, just a change of attitude. I'm still shrinking. I am disappearing and I am emerging at the same time! Emerging as me. It was a part of other changes. Taking off layers made me more responsive to all kinds of things. Unlooked-for outcomes. I felt more sensual, more sexual, and more exposed. But only in my head. Or so I thought. But maybe one shows it without knowing.

I wanted to find what I need 'out there'. I think it's unreason-able to expect to find everything in one other person. It's important to be alert to those special people, not to set condi-tions, restrictions. I have found you. Quillman, my lips are bruised and grazed. I press them together and think of you.

Anglers Tavern, Kennetside

The landlord's wife at the Anglers Tavern is a pie lover and that love is baked into every one of her creations. The crust is dry and crisp, the juices under the lid rich with flavour, and she uses good quality meat.

The delight of a slice of mutton pie for his supper competes in

Frith with childlike joy over his letter. Under the crust of his skull it is a mixed-meat filling, his mind savouring the delicacies and designs. Frith pictures the landlord's wife lauded in her tavern in London. Maybe she prefers here in Reading, at the hem of the town, its quiet welcome the reason he chose it. Before he knew about the pies. He recalls talking with the Mayor's daughter, the Navigation, Mr Hyde, and the High Bridge so peaceful when he walked over it just now. He had wanted a letter. Unreasonably so soon after being with her, but his heart wanted it.

"Gloating over your latest conquest?"

"Master Nicholas Middleton, if I am right." Frith offers his hand to the young man standing by his table.

"You'll receive my hand as a fist," threatens the lad.

"That is preferable to receive it clasping a dagger. Take a seat and tell me, what is my latest conquest?"

"I will not sit with you, Scoundrel. Are you for salting my wounds? Is she of so little importance that she is already forgotten by you?"

The few drinkers in the taproom have suspended their talk on hearing the young man's outburst. The mention of 'she' hooks their interest, for when a woman is between two men they will jump up in duel. Frith inwardly sighs this is his second public conversation involving Mistress Olivia, in as many days.

"She means everything in the world to me," adds Nicholas, more balefully than challenging.

Frith wonders how the lad came by that expression. Perhaps the sentiment is more important to him than the substance. Nicholas Middleton is tall, lean with thick black hair and fine features. His brows dip slightly to give a thoughtful rather than pugnacious appearance. He is the one to have a string of quickly forgotten conquests, not Frith. But Frith does not believe that of Nicholas Middleton. He senses a kindness in the lad, and his conviction is strong enough that Frith decides to take the time to lay aside the boy's upset.

"Is Mistress Olivia your betrothed?" asks Frith.

"Yes. No. We are courting and now you have turned up and —"

"Seduced her?" Frith asks lightly. "Was it I who approached Mistress Olivia? Would your mother have given us seclusion had she thought a mere newsman would be a rival for the attentions of the Mayor's daughter? Please, sit down. Ale?"

The ale arrives. Frith has complimented Master Nicholas on the girl he is courting, and is convincing him the newsman is not a notch-cutter when Frith's pie arrives. He inhales deeply to revel in its aroma. "I am already involved with a lady," confesses Frith.

In his chest is a euphoric glee at saying it out loud, yet with the terror he has said too much. "Ask Sarah. On second thoughts she is tactful enough to deny all. Ask your mother."

Master Nicholas smiles. "My apology. I jumped to a wrong conclusion."

"You were meant to. I am sorry to say this, Master Nicholas, but your young lady is as artful as she is pretty. She used me last night to make you jealous. And clearly succeeded. I doubt you have eaten today."

The answer is in the way Nicholas is looking at the pie. The newsman asks for a second spoon.

Frith draws out the flavour from a tender cube of mutton before speaking. "Why would Mistress Olivia wish to provoke you?" Nicholas can offer not one reason. "Could it be anything to do with the other girl in the Stores?"

"Her!" Flakes of pie-crust shoot from Nicholas' mouth. "You know what that job-stealing lump and her money-grubbing father are doing?"

Frith is listening to the lad's mother. "You didn't know that when she came in the Stores. You were attentive and —"

"She was a new customer. One always fusses on new customers. You're not seriously ... didn't you see what she looked like? Enormous. I thought she was a vagabond until she showed some coins. And now we know how she came by them – Judas money."

The pair agree there is only one thing to be done. A second slice of pie arrives with refills of ale. Frith suggests Nicholas call on Mistress Olivia and eliminate her fears. He shares his annoyance at missing the trouble this morning at the High Bridge and is rewarded by a first-hand account from Nicholas. The young man confirms there were several strangers in the mob and they were the most vociferous, the first to hurl stones. Frith deters the lad from moulding his recall into dramatising his story. They speculate, without conclusion, who hired the mobbers.

"It'll be the death of this town," says Nicholas. "The real business here is not the goods themselves, it's moving them. If the Navigation opens, barges will pass straight through. That Lynn, that job-stealer, doesn't realise what she's doing. Her old man told her nothing. I'm sure of that. But she's still a hefty barge slut taking away our living."

Frith changes the subject.

"The Reading Militia," says Nicholas with heightened scorn. "They do the easy bits, like piling into unarmed people at High Bridge. They haven't caught the navvies robbing the grand houses round here. To be fair, they did apprehend a vase."

Frith warms to the lad. "Viscount Harcourt's Faenza albarello?"

"Can't miss it when one goes to Harcourt's, the gaudy, grotesque thing. Just like the Viscount. He had a dedication etched under it."

"Difficult for a thief to sell a vase with the owner's name on it. No wonder it was recovered."

"The thief should have smashed it and done us all a favour. The Viscount's so conceited it's like the vase was made specially for him."

"He doesn't look two hundred years old." says Frith with a grin.

"He just acts like he is," says Nicholas, and they share the laughter.

A meaty rabbit

By dusk Hermond was newly shod and grazing in a small paddock behind what used to be Adam's forge. Lynn had dressed Hermond's wounds with heavy oils and stinging spirits from unmarked bottles. The horse had bridled at first then clearly enjoyed the special treatment and the attention. Adam's furnace, with blocked tuyere and brittle bellows after years of disuse, refused to cooperate. He fired the brick-making kiln, which made for a good deal of running to and fro.

Lynn never quite stopped worrying about how to repay Adam, but found herself caught up in his excitement of getting Hermond shod with an ad hoc forge and a ramshackle set of tools. For a while Lynn was wielding a lump of flat iron as a hammer, while Adam held the glowing metal with small pincers. After the first shoe had been fitted they decided it was too dangerous to Adam's fingers. He spent a nostalgic half hour finding a heavy hammer.

With Hermond four shod Adam and Lynn returned to the small cottage to find a pan of peeled potatoes. Lynn let it be known this was a first for her Dad. He argued he had once shelled peas from a pod – one pod. The second flagon of Dreadnought brandy was on the table.

"I didn't think it'd go this quick," said Peter, with a meaningful look at Lynn. "We must've only done two miles." Her dad's aches had stiffened significantly during the afternoon and making the new block had proved more difficult than he let on.

"The next sixteen should be plain sailing," said Adam. They toasted plain sailing. He set about skinning a rabbit he had bartered against some brickwork for the Broad Street butcher. They toasted the rabbit.

Adam produced a bottle of wine of dubious origin. They drank it with caraway cake while the rabbit stewed with carrots, onions and handfuls of fresh lemon thyme. They toasted each ingredient, listing its merits.

"Here's a question for you," said Adam with a chuckle. "What's too big and too small at the same time"

They tried all sorts of answers from a mountain of stew to a last breath, and then silly ideas like a door-mouse. They gave up.

"Barge Jeannie," said Adam, from over the pot of stew. "She's too big for old Hermond and too small for you."

"She's a fine barge," cut back Peter. "She's served us well. And will do."

"I've no doubt. She'll make you some sort of living. But you'll have seen the latest Thames barges, a hundred tonnes at least, five crew. Soon you'll see what size they've built the locks up the

Kennet Navigation. Your barge will be like a lone pea in a pod. They're looking for big barges up and down these waters. More efficient."

"There's room for all," said Peter.

"Depends if you want to scratch an existence or make a comfortable living." Adam vanished into the dark outside. Lynn thought the brandy and wine must have rushed through him but he was soon back wielding a red-glowing poker. He dunked it in the wine, making it sizzle and steam. "What a good stew really needs is burnt wine with it," he pronounced.

When they had helped themselves, he continued with his theme. "You have to keep your eyes open to what's happening around you. I'd still be a smithy if I hadn't."

"Nothing wrong with being a smithy," said Peter. "It's a good trade, skilled. There'll always be horses to shoe."

"Will there?"

"You've had too much brandy," scoffed Peter.

"I've seen Mr Savery's machine for pumping water. Not a horse in sight."

"Does it work?"

"No. But it will." Adam gazed for a while at nothing in particular. "That's not why I gave up the forge. It was too much hard work. You need to think about that for your horse. What is he, forty? There isn't much heavy work left in him."

"He's going to have to keep pulling a while yet," said Peter. "I can't afford another."

"You could hire one for each load. There again, so does another barge but they're carrying twice as much as you. You cost the shippers more per tonne. What are they going to do for their next cargo?"

"Are you telling me I need a new barge as well as a new horse? This Kennet Navigation's putting me out of business never mind that Reading lot."

"You'll make do. Or you'll adapt and do better. Same as them town folk." Adam looked across at Lynn. "You Mistress, need to watch out for your Hermond. I can see you do now, but more so.

That horse will kill himself for you if you ask him." He pushed a clinking bundle wrapped in sacking across the table towards her. "Take these liniments. His shoulder will need redressing. I doubt I'll need these again but he does." Lynn accepted it with thanks.

"That's for the horse, this is for you." Adam pulled from his pocket a tiny silver locket on a thin silver chain. Lynn dug her heels in and refused it. This time Adam would not have his way. It had been his wife Sarah's. Adam had given it to her and now, God rest her soul, it was his to give again. Who better than Lynn? When she pressed him he couldn't think of a reason why. But he knew he wanted to give it and that was all he needed.

With the locket round Lynn's neck, Adam demanded to learn more about the river and the docks at London. Peter was happy to oblige, assisted by more brandy.

from the Courant, Monday 19th september

Uniformed Brigand Act

In this Paper is inserted the following Advertisement, which (as it relates to the Blacks of this Country) we insert in our Courant hoping they'll be so wise to themselves, and so just to their Country, as to take Notice of it.

Whitehall, March

Whereas by the Uniformed Brigand Act passed in the last session of Parliament for the more effectual punishing wicked and evil disposed Persons going armed in Disguise, and doing Injuries and Violences to the Persons and Properties of His Majesty's subjects, and for the more speedy bringing the offenders to Justice, It is among other things enacted, That all Persons who since the 1st of July last have been guilty of any of the Offences in the said Act mentioned, and shall not surrender themselves before the 30th Day of September Instant, to one of the Judges of the King's Bench, or to a Justice of the Peace for the County where the Offence was committed, and make a full Confession thereof and a Discovery upon Oath of their

Accomplices, shall be guilty of Felony without Benefit of Clergy, provided that such as do so surrender themselves and make such Confession and Discovery, shall by Virtue of the said Act be pardoned: It has been thought proper to give this publick Notice thereof, that Persons under such unhappy Circumstances may be warned of their Condition, if they neglect to comply with the said Act.

———

memoirs of Sir George Crockmore

Common Man convinces himself of the actuality of the desired and, thus fooling himself, suffers disappointment. Sagacious man recognises what may be to his disliking and accepts the nature of things, or changes them into the desired. Mr Martyn is of the former. His yearning for a speedy, peaceful opening of the Kennet Navigation has him believing the hostilities will be quickly resolved. He ignores the canker that imperils his coveted fruit.

I foresee the refusal of the Reading traders to welcome the advantages of the waterway will simmer and break into boils for some considerable time. These people do not know what is best for them, which adversely affects those who have invested in their welfare. Deep surgery needs arranging to remove the canker.

This would be sufficient problem to break one man but another aggravation has presented itself. The Whigs, being like frogs from a Hanoverian spawning pond, have offered safe lily pads to every criminal in the Kingdom. These malefactors are to be pardoned by the Whigs' misguided Uniformed Brigands Act. Who are these "evil persons going in disguise" as the Bill puts it? Not just the unlawful gangs in makeshift uniform who make extortion from the populace. Is not the highway robber's mask a disguise? Is not the cutpurse's cowl a disguise? I anticipate a mile queue at my court of every villain in the county for pardon under this ridiculous Act.

This matter does recall the urgency of reappraising the Reading Militia. There is none after me with the experience, wisdom or impartiality to assume command when I transfer my industry and involvement from these rural areas to the Metropolis. Therefore, I shall encourage the Mayor to extend the parameters of operation for the Aldermen's Watch. Meanwhile, Captain Hawker on his next visit to Southcote, will be forewarned that he take opportunity to prepare his future occupation as the Reading Militia is to be disbanded.

The Captain had come earlier in the day seeking additional money for his exceptional outlay of this morning. I appraised him of the need to show the effectiveness of the Reading Militia by apprehending criminals or traitors. The latter was spurred by hearing the new kitchen maid laughing with the Captain while he waited. I severely cautioned her against such fraternising.

The subject that chafes as a burr under the saddle, is the delay in the Kennet Navigation coming into profitable business. Being a sagacious man, I have a goodly scheme to resolve it. I here record the deductions of the sharp witted mind.

Firstly I had reflected on Levenson's activities, discerning a man who distracts critical eyes by saying one thing only to do the contrary. Second, I was anticipating night sport with the kitchen maid, who had given the appearance of a lady by wearing quality material and cut. Thirdly, my thoughts on surgery had me realising that only when a patient's ambiguous shivers become the symptoms of a recognised fever can the appropriate remedy be applied. So must the resentment in the town be discreetly driven to fever, and thence cured.

Catherine's third note of Tuesday 20th September

There is always so much I want to tell you. Tonight as I work late, my coat is lying across the far chair and I allowed myself to believe it is you, half-sleeping after our hours together. Maybe my hand lightly cupping yours, or yours across my thigh, and we wander through and twine together our silent thoughts.

I lifted that feeling from the time we were in our embrace today. Lazy, tracing fingertips after we tumbled through a passion-

storm, then a glow of unquenchable embers in my core, looking at you and looking at you looking at me. Our quiet together seals us closer and our lips bond us tighter.

I carry that cherished calmness with me tonight as I quietly engrave with my coat lying on the far chair.

A cut of cloth

The sail of Barge Jeannie was raised when she regained the Kennet but it more often flapped empty of wind. Heavy low clouds gave the morning the dimness of a chill dusk. Progress was slow as Lynn with the tiller under her right armpit kept Hermond reigned back to a plodding walk. His collar was cushioned with a lining of an old fleece, an idea from Adam.

Her Dad had taken Jeannie through the first locks along the Kennet Navigation to Southcote Lock with Lynn applying windlass to the paddles and her back to swinging open the gates. She had a fright at the first, when Hermond lost his footing on the new style of bank with sloping turf. She ran up the slope to back him and slacken the tow rope. Her second scare was dropping the only windlass to watch it clatter to the edge of the chamber. Father and daughter maintained a friendly but stubborn argument: was it worse for Hermond or the windlass to fall into the lock. After Southcote Lock her Dad went down into the cabin. Lynn didn't question his uncharacteristic behaviour.

The charcoal sketch from the Hoskins wharfinger showed Lynn that Jeannie was in the straight of the first new cut by Southcote. It had a small embankment on the right side over which Lynn could see the tops of the formally planted trees belonging to a large estate and house. To her left was dense scrub and straggling willows that brushed against Hermond, and beyond that was flat land through which the old river snaked. Lynn found it hard to believe this straight channel had been dug out of the ground by the navigators with picks, shovels and wheelbarrows. Southcote Cut stretched three-quarters of a mile ahead before vanishing into the murk.

Lynn noticed a tree trunk drifting towards the barge. She lashed the tiller and grabbed a hitcher. On the prow, she was readying to jab the trunk away from the side when she saw it was cloth not wood, a longcoat. Seconds later she saw the man's head bob up on a ripple. Lynn hailed Hermond to stop, called urgently for her Dad, and hooked the barb of the hitcher into the fabric. It took her some effort while she waited for her Dad to keep the big man's head above water and stop the current carrying him away.

"He's a goner," said Peter, a little breathless. "Nothing we can do. Let him go."

"I don't think he is," answered Lynn.

"I've seen enough drowned souls round the docks to know one when I see one. We can't do anything for him. A corpse 'ud just be trouble for us."

Lynn dipped the shaft to unhook it from the coat and a few bubbles of air burbled from the submerged mouth. Lynn looked at her Dad.

The man was too heavy for the pair to haul over the gunwale so they steered him round the stern and dragged him up the bank. Lynn set about staking the barge, listening to the chuntering of her Dad as he turned the body face down and clumsily removed the sodden longcoat.

He began rhythmically bouncing on the man's back. "I've seen this done," was all he said, in reply to Lynn's alarm. Spurts of water came from the man's mouth like a weak fountain until suddenly there was a violent spluttering.

In the cabin, after several gulps of warm toddy, the man said his name was Fergus McLeish. He looked late thirties though he was aged by weather and trouble, was solidly built, strong and said in a barely intelligible Scots accent he was a journeyman.

"A Jacobite, more like" said Peter eyeing him warily.

"Aye, I tak up wi' the cause," admitted Fergus.

"An' down here spying for them. Robbing and murdering."

Before Peter had finished speaking, a six-inch dirk was at his windpipe. Lynn gasped and Fergus glared at her. Suddenly he smiled, and concealed the dirk down his gamash.

"Gin I wa', you 'n' lassie would'a be deed."

"We saved your life," snapped Lynn.

"Wa's theet to a blackguard Jacobite?" said Fergus with a broad grin.

"Point taken," said Peter, rubbing his throat and breaking the tension.

"Spying fe who?" resumed Fergus. "Yon James? He'd na step from the Frenchie boot." He paused, thoughtful of the consequences he'd witnessed of the failed invasion. "Mar? Yon Earl o' Ganging Backwards. The cause's jes a wheen o' blethers wi' chiefs like them tim'rous twa."

"What's it like in a battle?" asked Lynn.

"Lynn!" bridled her Dad.

"Tis wha' guid men turn vermin."

Fergus slowly unfolded his tale of the battle at Sheriffmuir, the Earl choosing to retreat north, and Fergus choosing to travel south. Peter didn't believe the Scot; once a Jacobite always a Jacobite. "You say fighting made you sick, so came south, and just told us you joined the Reading Militia. More fighting."

"Wha' Sassenach 'd hire a Highlander? Diggin' ditches? Theet's nay fer a McLeish. Wi' the Militia I ken I'd be fighting on the right side."

"Like on High Bridge," said Lynn under her breath. "Clubbing and cutting unarmed citizens." But Fergus had heard.

"Nay Lass. I wa' sick to ma bauchles when I keek wha' Hawker and his clan war aboot. Fergus McLeish d'na raise a hand agin those gud folk. 'Tis Hawker be the guiser."

Fergus spotted a bag of barley on the shelf and offered to cook Highland bannocks. While he improvised a griddle over the stove for the flat cakes, he told the pair of his brief time with the Reading Militia.

He had been travelling all winter and summer to be recruited in late July when he was so hungry he would have been ready to join His English Majesty's Navy. Some of the Reading Militia went on night patrols but he wasn't ready yet according to Hawker. Fergus snorted. Hawker was no leader, too self-first he reckoned. Lynn suspected the Scot was not completely open about his weeks in the Militia. What the Scot didn't say might explain why Hawker had turned against Fergus, denouncing him as a Jacobite traitor whom he will see hanged. On the run through the night, the embankment had caught the Scot by surprise.

"You can tell a tale," said Peter ambiguously.

"And cook bannocks," added Lynn.

Later she tried to convince Fergus that most people had a kindness in them. She showed Fergus the locket Adam had given her. The Scot scoffed, saying the man was merely hoping to "stir his spirtle," then rapidly apologised. Lynn felt Fergus had often been badly burned, unlike his excellent bannocks.

Kennet Koffee House, Kennetside

"You're bright and early, Mr Frith," says Sarah, surreptitiously sliding a letter to him as she stretches for a demitasse.

"Is Master Nicholas around?" he asks, pocketing the letter.

"Early bird catching the worm?" She pulls a face at Frith's blank look. "Who's to know? That lad can be in the Stores for hours and not be seen, he's so lifeless."

"You're being very unkind, Sarah."

"How come you're taking his side? Ain't that why you're here? To sort him out after him wanting your guts for garters yesterday."

Frith smiles. "Would that be the Master Lifeless who is after my guts?"

"Don't you come the clever with me, Mr Frith. It looks to me like he was more lifeless than lively yesterday, what with your lack of any cuts and bruises. From what I can see of you, that is." Sarah gives him a cheeky smile. "Perhaps Dragon told him not to hit you. Master Nicholas says and does what Dragon tells him."

"Might you not be underestimating Nicholas? He has a more open mind than his parents."

"You're wrong, Mr Frith, he hasn't got a mind, not one he can call his own." Sarah peers at Frith. "What's with the 'Nicholas'? Is there something you're not telling me, Mr Frith? That's very naughty of you. By 'open mind' d'you mean 'Nicholas' is happy over the Navigation? That's a turn-about quicker'n a spinning top."

"No, he's still against it. But he is open to thinking about it."

"Really? Nothing to do with the cat-fight in here, Monday night, I suppose?"

"There was no cat-fight," says Frith, inwardly sighing at human inventiveness around events.

"That's all the proof I need. It's that Barge-bum. I bet she opens her legs quicker than I can say trollop."

Frith is trying to hide his exasperation in case it adds ammunition to Sarah's mud-slinging. He speaks levelly. "You don't know the girl."

"If you live among rivers rats you behaves like them. Take Dunbar at the gaol, he's a bigger crook than the scum in his cells. It rubs off. That's why Dragon don't like river people in here. Lowest of the low, she says, and she should know – she was one. Bet you didn't know her Pa worked on Orf's wharf before it was Orf's. She don't spread that about too much, I can tell you. The only people Dragon wants in here are those who talk a lot about what's not important. Present company excepted Mr Frith."

Sarah suddenly busies herself wiping the counter round Frith's elbows.

"If you've finished with your chattering, Sarah," snaps Mrs Middleton from the archway. Frith doesn't have to turn to know she is scowling.

Sarah comes round the counter, whispering. "It's going to be Purgatory before Hell in here today. First off, Mr M is stocktaking and he has to 'have me' in the stock room. His words. Fat chance, but I needs to keep lively." She throws back a hideous grimace. Frith struggles to keep a straight face. "Out of there into Hell, this place with Dragon after she's had to do the serving all day."

Frith hears floorboards creak and Mrs Middleton is behind him.

"Would you be after something particular at this early hour, Mr Frith?"

The envelope rests against his thigh. Frith thinks of something else. "I was hoping to hear more of Mr Middleton's wonderful scheme to make money."

"He is a busy man, Mr Frith, with no time for coffee and idle talk. Like some," she adds, removing Frith's not quite empty demi-tasse. "Even if I was in a position to tell you, I would not. I do not want our affairs made known to the world."

"Fair enough," says Frith, standing to leave. "The talk from London is of astute, ordinary people investing for spectacular increase in return. It seems Mr M has a different scheme."

"I leave all money matters to Mr M." Frith can see the woman's indignation. "Mr M is a very astutely clever man, with an ear to what's going on. I trust him completely. That's our strength, as man and wife – trust. You're not married, are you, Mr Frith?"

"I was."

"But no children."

Frith is hurled back to Bristol, to Grace, to Childbed, the bed of deaths. He only faintly hears Mrs Middleton eulogise on her marriage, her handsome eldest, Richard, in the Army with a glorious career, an officer soon. "He never forgets to write home."

"You've acquired a painting for the Koffee House," says Frith in a desperate escape from his thoughts and a relief for his ears.

"From a very nice man. He kept running his hand through his hair, nerves you see, so I knew I was getting a bargain. When you've been dealing with tradespeople as long as I have, one gets to know these little giveaways."

Frith sees it is skilfully painted, a fine, expensive work. He wonders if that is where Mrs Middleton's jewellery was destined, but doubts it. The woman has not ceased talking.

"I'm worried so valuable a thing might be temptation to those of a nefarious disposition. Mrs Kempster knows the value of everything that does not belong to herself. I am giving thought to replacing her with a respectable woman. I am sure you've seen the way she openly flirts and provokes high-spiritedness. And she is forever tempting Mr M. He is a steadfast husband, and it irks her she can't wrap him round her little finger. One more incident and Mrs Kempster will have to go."

Frith has sidled to the door, leaving Mrs Middleton inspecting Sarah's stack of demitasses to be washed.

Catherine's first note of Wednesday 21st September

I am so restless. I make excuses to go through my parlour and stand on the spot where I took you into me. I relive that time

*with a thrill that runs up my body, and I chase it down again.
We were too hurried, too keen. Next time we'll know our
rhythms better, slow or furious, with your meaningless words
panting in my ear. But on the floor was good, and standing
there brings a tingle.*

*Twice Eliot has accused me of day-dreaming. I stop myself
shouting, "Keep out! This is my room now, my sanctuary from
you."*

*Eliot hates me for being happy. He is hostile to my work, to my
time with Beattie, and scornful of my acquaintances. When I am
bright or look good he says it is "for others" and not for him.
How can one's outlook be "for" another person? Eliot
demands that he is my whole world. To him I am some exotic
creature, this house my cage, and he my turnkey.*

*I do love my husband. I told you I love him. Not as I love you. I
love you. What a confession! The love I have for Eliot is of
compassion, familiarity, for him being the father of my
daughter. Of habit. We will never do habit, will we, Quillman?*

from Mistress Olivia's diary

I will tell of my splendiferous time in the wonderful London. The
most brilliant day her eldest child has had in her boring sixteen
years was dismissed as a gewgaw. "That's nice," said Mama. She
was more overjoyed by Lousy bowling her hoop one full yard.

Our servants are lazy and do little, but when I am prepared to tell
them at length of the delights of London for a young lady, they
have a week of chores to do in a day. Master Nicholas would listen
and be bright at my happiness then forlorn he was not the one to
make me so. But he is away on dull business for the Stores and not
there for my summons.

I turn to my faithful friend not knowing what to write first for
every moment was a whirl of pleasures and sights. Even the
tedious hours in the anteroom in Lombard Street while Papa
conducted his business was of surprising diversion. Several
gentlemen did introduce themselves and talk with me. A handsome

pair spoke of their daring in the markets and I told of Papa's wharfs and properties and that he was mayor. Whereupon the one claimed I was so naturally pretty I brightened the entire City more so than all the painted, poxed ladies of London. The second also offered his card saying he could smell on me the bucolic come to the City, the lavender-scented bush and the fruits of the cherry tree. I knew what he was about and took delight feigning misunder-standing, teasing him to more outrageous suggestions. He laid his wide-brimmed hat upon my lap, which I took to be insulting in treating me as a hatstand, until the artifice of the gesture was revealed and I replaced the hat on the gentleman's head and his hand in his own lap.

Following our most vexing late departure from Reading, with time become too short to properly complete my purchase and see everything, I nonetheless resolved not to be an ache in Papa's ear for I wanted to return to London another time. Nay, more. I had determined to live in London, not this backwater of Reading. To achieve this it was vital to be a joy to Papa.

However, I was obliged to remind him that his Princess had her own purpose in the expedition, and my stomach somersaulted at his reply. If I was willing to allow him one other matter we would stay overnight rather than put his Princess in danger from the last coach to Reading.

Papa and I took a chariot to Billingsgate, a place called the Room Land at the head of the dock, where I never saw so many ships nor so much coal being unloaded and sold. Papa was greeted by Mr Delpeck, by trade a crimp, at which title I was much taken. The merchant pointed to the dock asking, "Do you see all them hags?" I could see only muscular seamen, and he explained the coal boats are called hags. I record this to demonstrate the abundance of new things I came across.

I was pleased Mr Delpeck's knowledge encompassed the two great Exchanges containing a multitude of everyone vital from mercer to milliner. He instructed me how to bargain along the Strand. With its thousand small shops of such wares I could have filled a score of wagons. We sat for a while in an open area called

Charing Cross at a hub of streets where I observed passing lords and gentlemen, merchants and layabouts, handsome officers and silk brushing past drab. The ladies were so decorated and assured I yearned to be like them.

We strolled to a vast open place with a grand building at one end and strewn with the left-behind of the day's vegetable market. It was then filling up with the night market. Strumpets brazenly approached Papa who was comical in his refusals. His awkward way had the painted tarts think him shy and pressed him the harder with both voice and body. Our lodgings were reached in a street off this Covent Garden. Papa and I dined at an inn and everyone was keen to know if all the maidens in our town as pretty as I.

Efackins! I omit mention of the coffee-houses by Charing Cross and how they brought to mind Master Nicholas. I have never seen so many clays and reading matter, nor caught so much talk of the whole world as we passed Locket's and Man's. Those were the roaring oceans set against the village pond that is Mrs Middlegone's pride next to the tributary that is the Kennet.

This is a tedious chore for there was so much in one day I would fill a library. I remain restless from it. Papa is home for lunch so I will show how happy he has made his Princess, recalling shared memories of London. Mama will hear none of it from Papa, preferring the mindless burbling of Lousy.

A smoke signal

"Stop right there!" shouted Lynn, jabbing the metal-tipped hitcher toward the towing path.

"Do you welcome everyone like that?" asked Nicholas.

"Only rats."

"I saw no rat." Rain fanned from the brim of his hat as he looked from side to side. "You've a quicker eye than me."

" Quick enough to see you hurling stones from High Bridge."

"I wasn't."

"Liar! I saw you."

"I admit I was on the bridge —"

"Come to finish the job, have you?"

"— trying to stop the stone throwing."

"By throwing them all yourself?" Lynn thumbed to the cabin. "There's another in there saying he was on the bridge but harming no one. I saw you though, arm in the air."

"Was there a stone in it?"

"I didn't have time to get out a telescope."

"Who's this?" Lynn's Dad had emerged from the cabin.

"Nicholas Middleton, Sir," said the lad stepping forward arm outstretched. "Son of Timothy Middleton, provisions merchant."

"Who threw me out of his store."

"That was my mother. She's a bit temperamental."

"She's a bit mental," said Lynn.

"With a temper." Nicholas addressed Peter. "I came to see how you and your daughter were faring after your . . . rough passage."

"We're doing better without you," shot Lynn.

"I've brought the things your daughter, er, left behind . . . when she was . . ." Nicholas unbuttoned his coat to reveal a bulging haversack.

"Best come aboard and unburden yourself," said Peter.

As he passed Lynn he turned to her. "I came to see if you were all right."

Nicholas warily eyed Fergus sitting in the cabin, then emptied his haversack on the fold-down table. "A poppy-seeded loaf," he said, but got no response from Lynn. When Peter found some coins to pay Nicholas was firm in his refusal. "You daughter was treated unjustly and badly in our store. I don't hold with breaking the law to get one's way."

"You're giving us these from guilt," muttered Lynn.

"Enough," said her Dad.

"I'd better be getting back," said Nicholas with little conviction. "Father thinks I am out on Stores business." With quick smiles to the men he edged past Lynn.

"Does Lady Olivia know you've come a-calling?" she asked.

"I haven't come a-calling. I decided to go for a walk, and when I saw your boat I came to enquire after your welfare."

"Do you always carry a picnic?" Lynn decided four in the cabin was too crowded and stepped towards the cabin door. "Going for a walk in this rain? Are you a quacking duck?"

"I would be a drake."

"You're a rake. Did you tell Mistress Olivia you were going for a walk?"

"There was no point. I didn't know I'd come across you. I don't have to tell her everything I do," said Nicholas in a rush. "You should have been at Newbury by now."

"We should, but for a drowned bargemaster, a maimed horse, a bruised mate and a broken forestay block. That'll give you and Mistress Olivia lots to snigger about. I assume you'll be telling her?" added Lynn.

"There's no point."

"That's two 'No points' to you," mocked Lynn, abruptly turning from him. Her arm caught a small bottle of Adam's embrocation oil on the shelf. It toppled onto the stove. The top plate had been removed for Fergus to make his bannocks. The cabin rapidly filled with dense choking fumes that plumed through the door.

Lynn was pushed aside by Nicholas in his dash to get from the cabin. "Save yourself," she spluttered as she flailed around the cabin. Her hand brushed an arm and she grabbed the wrist and guided her Dad out. She dived into the cabin again, her eyes streaming and smarting. She couldn't see. A rough hand slid under her skirt, up her calf and buckled her knee. She was about to shout and kick when she was hauled to the floor. Fergus winked at her. "When th' firing starts, geet low, Lass." He pushed Lynn firmly by her rump up out of the cabin.

Nicholas nearly threw his bucket of water over Lynn. The drenched stove roared and spat, and steam plumed from the cabin. Nicholas gave it another bucket for good measure.

"You'll have her sunk," said Peter, in an effort to add relief.

"That's what I've come for isn't it?"

Lynn ignored Nicholas's sarcasm. "Run away from, that's you. It was more important to get people out."

"I've seen too many houses go up," said Nicholas. "Once they take they go fast." He snapped his fingers to show how fast but they were too wet to click.

"Houses can be rebuilt. Dads can't."

The last ribbons of smoke and steam drifted out of the cabin as Lynn and Nicholas argued who had done the more correct thing.

"It seems to me you did right by the two of you, neither the one nor t'other," said Peter. "Right thing now is to get Jeannie ship-shape."

"Wha's ya mop?" asked Fergus disappearing into the cabin with the bucket.

"There's only room for two," said Peter following him.

The two youngsters sat on the gunwale before Nicholas spoke. "That was a very unwise place to store oil. Fire is dangerous."

"This is a very unwise place for you to sit. Mistress Olivia is dangerous."

"Please be quiet about Olivia. I'm trying to help you."

Before Lynn could reply there was a shout from the top of the embankment. "You there! All well? We saw the smoke."

The sturdy man was running his fingers through his hair and Lynn sighed seeing the black sash across his chest. Her heart sank when she recognised the shaven head rising above the embankment behind him.

"The mysterious vanishing barge," sneered Hawker across the Navigation. "We've been looking for you. And an escaped traitor."

"You've found one of them," shouted Lynn, trying to sound jolly.

"Perhaps I've found both rotten apples together. You seen any strange men recently, dark hair, long coat?"

"Yes," shouted Lynn.

"Which way'd he go?" asked Hawker, with a hunter's excitement.

"He's standing next to you."

"Don't get smart with me River Tramp. Bring that tub over here, we're gonna search it for stowaways."

"We'd be happy to do that," said Peter, emerging from the cabin. "If you'd been quicker to do your job back at High Bridge we wouldn't have a busted sail and we'd be able to oblige you."

"Throw a rope. My men 'll pull you."

"There's no towing path that side. Our horse likes walking along-side water, not in it."

"Stay there," shouted Hawker. He turned to the man beside him. "Watch 'em, Quinn. No one leaves that boat." He locked up and down the Navigation but it curved before any crossing could be seen.

Nicholas stood up. "Captain Hawker, Sir." Lynn glared at him. "The Burghfield Road is just upstream. There's a bridge there."

Hawker didn't bother to thank him before he dropped out of sight behind the embankment.

"Helping brutes as well as job-stealers now?" scoffed Lynn.

"It'll take him twice as long to reach Burghfield Bridge as it would to reach Milkmaid's Footbridge downstream. That's twice as long for me to be out of your mess when he gets here."

"How do you know about the bridge?"

"I buy from the farms. This new waterway has caught me out a few times."

"There was no need to be so fawning to the thug."

"It so happens that thug is Captain of the town's only body for keeping peace and order."

"I'd rather have mayhem than that brute's idea of keeping the peace."

"He's too forceful at times, I'll grant you that."

Peter interrupted. "Stop bickering you two. We've got visitors coming, a man wanted for treason in our cabin, and a lookout across the river. You know what that means?"

"Earley," said Nicholas dully.

"Early to bed?" asked Lynn.

"Early to dead. Gallows Tree Common is in Earley."

"All I did was fish him out of the water."

"Assisting and harbouring a man on the run for high treason, that's the drop for sure. If it was anyone else but a traitor . . ." said Nicholas in a wavering voice. He couldn't stop talking. "Last Sessions, Judge Crockmore sent a man on a one-way trip to Earley for stealing eighty ells of dowlas from a warehouse. Of course, stealing cloth is far worse than high treason."

"Shut up," said Lynn. "Fergus'll have to be someone else."

"He was in Hawker's Militia," said Peter.

"It's Reading's Militia," stated Nicholas.

Father and daughter shook their heads wearily. "Hawker knows his face," said Peter.

"Then he'll have to be gone before Hawker gets here."

"That lookout knows him too," persisted Peter.

"We'll have to give him something else to look at," said Lynn, with eyes fixed on Nicholas.

Nicholas shook his head. "Obstructing justice! What next? Why don't we ambush Hawker and do away with him?"

"Now you're being silly. Come into the cabin, you're going to help."

"Absolutely not. Risk my neck for a traitor and a girl stealing my livelihood. No."

"You could have told Hawker that Fergus was on the barge. Why didn't you?" asked Lynn.

Nicholas had no answer.

A minute later he stepped from the cabin and took a deep breath. "Mister Quinn!" he shouted across the Navigation.

"Sergeant Quinn."

"My apologies, Sergeant Quinn. You recognise me? Nicholas Middleton of Middleton's Provisions. I need to get back urgently to help my father. There's a big load due in. I'm obviously not who you're looking for. May I return to my business?"

Quinn sat for a few seconds then motioned with his pistol for Nicholas to go. Nicholas loudly cleared his throat.

"Er, there is a small problem. I was walking a lady . . . who is not my fiancée. There'd be terrible embarrassment if . . ."

Quinn gave a salacious laugh. "Right-ho, you can walk the dolly home. Hold on. Let's see her first."

Nicholas leaned into the cabin and helped Lynn on deck. She wore a hooded cape hiding her face, which Quinn demanded to see. Lynn modestly pulled back a corner revealing a swathe of jet black hair across an eye. Her lips were a vivid red. Quinn laughed.

Lynn whispered in Nicholas's ear. "She forgot her reticule," shouted Nicholas. "Women, eh?"

Don't push it thought Lynn inside the cabin. The pair stepped off Barge Jeannie and walked towards Reading. "Get a move on," hissed Nicholas.

"I'm a lassie," hissed Fergus back at him. "Tha' buffoon's gidda believe it else yer lassie's done fer."

"She's not my lassie," hissed Nicholas. "We must get off this towing path. You take Milkmaid's Footbridge, I'll cut across to the Basingstoke Road. And I never want to see you again."

"Aw Hen, ye's saye hurtful to yer bonnie besom."

On Barge Jeannie, Lynn sighed. "In only three days I've lost my warmest cape, two smocks and Mam's shawl."

"Get that cochineal off your face," ordered Peter. "You three should be actors," he added gently. Then sombrely, "There's more acting to be done when Captain Hawker gets here."

Catherine's second note of Wednesday 21st September

I'm suggesting we make Thursday a mainly intimate day. Shall we do that for a change! Then we might do more work on our 'work' days. I told you I am practical.

Would this interfere with your job at the Courant – it being a working day? I wouldn't like to be composed and pressed by you! I couldn't be both, not at the same time. Pressed? I am thinking about that, and breathing hard.

So. I'm painting French ultramarine round the outside of the tissue, the burnt sienna house shape. Second coat in a minute and then I'll look at some rubbings and reorganising your words on it.

Oh, just put your arms round me.

from Mistress Olivia's diary

"Robert," said Mama, who only calls Papa by name on certain occasions. "You took Olivia all the way to London to buy her a dress, not material."

"It took longer than anticipated to sell my stocks, Millicent. That transaction was for your advantage. I had to act very quickly on advice from one who has his ear to highly influential whispers."

"That lecherous old goat Crockmore, to whom you grovel so abominably."

"Sir George Crockmore is received to The Prince of Wales' court at Leicester House. I am sure you can run up a dress for your daughter, My Dear."

"You have the time to take Olivia to London, Robert – you can 'run up' a dress."

I had to throw a tantrum that I would have nothing but a bolt of cloth to wrap round me for the fair. Papa asked Mama to find a dressmaker, at any price. Thus Mama realised immediately that in selling all his stock, Papa has cash for her Reading house. I will have a properly made dress in a cloth far superior to anything available in this town. I hope there are people of sufficient fine taste at Forbury Fair to notice.

To keep a keen ear for any move Mama might make towards her Minster Street house, I amused the brats in the drawing room. I suggested playing one of Lousy's favourites, Blind Man's Buff. As she cheats I decreed a pillowslip be put over her head and tied with rope round her middle. Thus covered I spun her round and round. She made tinny squeals of joy so I kept spinning her until she cried she was feeling sick and begged me to stop. After a few more turns I had the delight of seeing her bang her shoulder on the settle when she fell over. She complained in a grating drone of her hurting shoulder and her spinning head and it being hot under the slip.

"The knot is fast," I said. "I will get Papa. But do stop that unladylike racket." She did not, so I jabbed the stick of her bowling hoop into her tummy, which made her yelp. But the wail quickly resumed. I discovered it was not the force of the jab that put fright into her yelps and the silence between but in Lousy not knowing where the next would strike. Podgy wanted to play. He set about his sister with the stick like a woodpecker late into its nest building, not caring where he stabbed. I was almost at my bedroom when Mama rushed from the dining room to the screaming of precious Lousy. I then had the double bonus of hearing Mama give Podgy a sound hiding as I came down to join Papa.

It was vital to stop Mama using Papa's cash to buy a new house in Reading. What use would that be when I am searching for a suitor worthy of me? I was mortified Papa dismissed so quickly my suggestion to buy a London house saying London was impractical. Papa declared good profit could be made buying commercial property and land in Reading by the river. I noted this, judging it prudent not to remind him of his fears of the Kennet Navigation.

The maid had earlier returned from my errand and reported Nicholas was still absent from the Stores. She disclosed only that he had ventured to the westerly farms. However much I heeled her shins she would not tell if it was indeed to farms for harvest for the shop, or to Barge Jennie to sow a well-ploughed furrow. I will not tolerate such behaviour. Suitors shall have experience of such matters to bring pleasure to me, but they will have gained such before casting their eyes upon me. Master Nicholas must be brought to order for this baseness.

I have such cleverness in that I can see the use of one matter with another. By the time I entered the dining room my scheme to show Master Nicholas to whom he is beholden was enlarged to be a great benefit to Papa, who will thereby be more favourably disposed to my requests.

"Papa, Mr Middleton told me he wants to sell his Provision Stores and the Koffee House. I was waiting for Master Nicholas and you know how he likes to talk to all the pretty girls."

"Especially the prettiest in the whole country."

"You have said you would like places by the river." He smiled at my innocent-and-untroubled face. "He is very keen to buy that silly stuff about which you spoke to me. I have never heard the gentleman quite so excited about anything."

"Even Middleton is not such a buffoon to risk his property."

I put on my expression of I-do-not-understand-the-business-of-men which draws upon their compassion. "Perhaps his buildings are falling down because he said he had to 'put up' the Stores and Koffee House with something called collateral."

In many things Papa is as slow as a bumble bee but when he sees a business deal he speeds like an angry wasp. He has summoned Mr Middleton.

This may appear a strange thing for a young lady to have set in motion. However, it has many advantages for this lady. Mr Middleton will be debtor to Papa and that is the shortest rein by which to keep his younger son on the correct path. Secondly, Master Nicholas may suspect my hand and will be more in admiration and be concerned for my divers skills. Best of all, Papa's cash from his stock when loaned to Mr Middleton is not there for Mama's house in Minster Street. Thereby I have time to persuade Papa to buying a London house.

It occurs to me I am remiss in imparting my gratitude for my wonderful day in London. I shall therefore send a letter to Mr Delpeck expressing my sincere thanks for his personable and informative attention with the hope we may meet again. My one lapse of the whole expedition was being inattentive to the talk between Mr Delpeck and Papa at the Room Land, for Papa has a coal wharf and Mr Delpeck is a coal broker. Mr Delpeck lives in London.

A body search

Hawker did not check with Sergeant Quinn, who was still sitting across the Navigation, so keen was he to set about searching the barge without even a by-your-leave from the bargemaster. A mouse could not have hidden on Barge Jeannie, so compactly was the barge paraphernalia packed. For Hawker and his men that meant cupboard contents were thrown on to bunk and floor, carelessly scattered or smashed, except three bottles of wine that were carefully put to one side. On deck, two rope fenders had gone overboard and were drifting downstream along with halyards and other gear.

Hawker encouraged his men to greater enthusiasm and destruction in their search. He had made sure Lynn and her dad realised not even a poacher was in ear-shot, and ordered them to stay in the cabin. He took pleasure squeezing past her, pressing against her, one hand furtive over her body. The other hand held a pistol, ensuring Peter sat quietly.

The Militia men became bored and drifted into lazing and yarns from the inns. Hawker went on deck to inspect for himself, peering through the rent tarpaulin into the hold. He was assured by Sergeant Quinn, still puffing from his run to Burghfield Bridge and back, that every possible place had been searched. "What's this?" asked Hawker kicking the tightly furled sail. "Could be a villain rolled up in there. Open it."

Three set about untying the brails. Hawker pushed them aside. "We ain't got all day." He sliced through the brails with his lethal knife, unfurled a stretch of sail and slashed through it.

Peter was upon him. "Stop! I'll do it for —"

Hawker's pistol whipped across Peter's face with a sickening crunch. He was knocked to the deck, blood spurting from his mouth. Hawker put the pistol to Peter's temple. Lynn screamed.

Hawker sneered. "Attacking an officer of the law in the pursuit of his business."

"We can't survive without the sail," pleaded Lynn.

"He said it was bust."

"The block. Sail's fine. I was going to mend it."

Hawker turned to the three men by the sail. "Search it. Every last thread. The old fool can watch." He stepped towards Lynn with a look that froze her spine. He slowly traced a path with tip of his pistol across her bosom and between her breasts. "Then he can watch what happens to the accomplice of those who set upon law officers."

A clear voice came from the towing path. "That's a very exhaustive search you're doing, good Sir. May I enquire as to the reason for such thoroughness?"

Towing path, Southcote Cut

Frith stares at a muscular man, the close-cropped hair making his face more fierce. He has thick, square eyebrows over deep-set eyes and if he ever laughed he would look more menacing. He is glaring at Frith with a pistol in one hand and a blade in the other. Three tough louts have stopped hacking at the sail and are watching Frith.

Frith had been walking along the towing path reminiscing in his own world. He had handed the morning's London Gazette to Mr Hyde that the editor might chose which items Frith was to copy and compose. The arbitrary, mindless activity had irritated him more than usual and was the reason he was searching for the rogue bargemaster. He'd found fear of the Navigation in the town was spawned on ignorance or personal motive. None would consider it might bring benefit. Frith had thought the bargemaster might have his feet on solid ground and give a reasoned argument.

On Southcote Cut he is suddenly pitched from Arcadia into Armageddon. The spectacle before Frith shows the bargemaster is not on solid ground but in a deep mire. Frith had seen the old man half stumble towards the close-cropped thug, then fall back pistol-whipped to the deck. In a glance Frith absorbs the disorder and spillage in the cabin, the damage on deck, the shredded sail and the black sashes across the men. He recalls the drifting jetsam he passed unnoticed in his daydreaming walk. The bargemaster looks ill, his barge is ransacked and Frith speaks before he considered the consequences.

A gravel voice answers. "If you know what's good for you, you'll be on your way."

"This barge is my destination." Frith can feel blood pounding through in his heart.

"You're here. Now turn round and go."

"I came to speak with the bargemaster."

"What business d'you have with him?"

"The man you just cuffed to the floor."

"That's what I do to no-goods who attack officers of the law, and to scum who help a devil wanted for treason."

"Do you have proof, Captain Hawker?" Frith has made a guess and sees the man square-up when named.

Hawker is off the barge, standing a knife-thrust from Frith, exuding physical power and menace. "What business have you with this rat?"

"I am employed by the Reading Courant newspaper." Frith has

seen reaction before when he mentions he is a newsman. The Captain's eyes narrow with wariness, but also a seam of vanity straightens his posture. Frith talks without knowing what he is saying. "Your job must be very dangerous, I appreciate your need for caution. But this would appear an excessive use of force. Or are you looking for something a lot smaller than a man? Vandalising this barge might be considered stepping outside your terms of reference by Judge Crockmore." Hawker's head twitches at the mention of the aristocrat and Frith thinks how to make best use of this slight clue.

"Through my employ, I have heard your name and work often mentioned by Sir George Crockmore." The newsman sees the Captain's sharpened interest and lets him assume he and Sir George have often spoken. The exchange brings to mind Frith's letter to Sir George, and the newsman decides his best course lies with the Captain's vainglory.

"I am writing profiles of prominent local people for the Courant. I think it excellent for the people of Reading to know about the man who risks his life to defend their safety."

Interview with Captain Teon Hawker at Southcote Cut

Courant. In your own words, what is the function of the Reading Militia?

Hawker. We do all that's needed to squash trouble, keep the peace.

Courant. Does that mean you have to resort to violence yourselves?

Hawker. Comes with the territory. A villain swinging a sword ain't gonna stop for a parley. Slice your throat more like. We're in the firing line, gets our hands dirty. Like at High Bridge if that's what you're meaning. You ever faced a mob with stones and picks? Been in a real battle? Thought not. You gotta show 'em you're tougher and rougher. That's the language people understands.

Courant. I see.

Hawker. Doubt it, unless you done it.

Courant. Why do you do it? Risking your life for others.

Hawker. That's it, isn't it? For others. Without me around there'd be law-breaking everywhere. What's the point having laws if the scum aren't made to keep to them?

Courant. Where do you stand with regard to the Aldermen's Watch.

Hawker. That bunch of bucket-boots! Takes the whole troop to hold down a whore or nab a dipper. Did you see the Watch on High Bridge? You didn't even see their heels.

Courant. So the Reading Militia are admired for what they do?

Hawker. Only when it stops the loggerheads losing out. For instance, that barge geezer. It was me who saved him from being drowned but I get no thanks for that. The loggerheads hate him so they hate me for rescuing him. That's the job. I don't do it to be liked.

Courant. You do get paid?

Hawker. I run a professional Militia. But you couldn't keep a dog on what we're given.

Courant. I assume the stipend comes from the town. You report to the Mayor?

Hawker. Turner tells us day-to-day but on big stuff I deal with Sir George, man to man.

Courant. Sir George Crockmore?

Hawker. That's him. It was him set up the Reading Militia. Better under the court than the town hall he says. If you'd met that bumbling clod of a Mayor, you'll know why. Me and Sir George understand one another. We're both after the same thing and the way to do it.

Courant. A big thing at the moment is the break-ins at grand houses. How goes the hunt for the culprits?

Hawker. Them navvies is slippery as the bog they come from. That operation has to be hush-hush. You understand, Mr Newsman?

Courant. Very clearly. What about yourself? What age are you?

Hawker. Twenty-eight

Courant. How long have you been a Captain?

Hawker. Pretty much as long as there are soldiers to lead. The men trust me coz they know I'd do anything that I ask on them. And do it better. First sign of trouble I'm at the front.

Courant. How long have you been in command of the Reading Militia?

Hawker. Three year.

Courant. Was your predecessor of the same mould as you?

Hawker. A useless streak of nothing called Corsby. It was me showed the men he was fleecing 'em left and right.

Courant. How did you do that?

Hawker. Found what he'd thieved in his pockets. So naturally they wanted me to lead 'em.

Courant. Naturally. Where did you get your military training?

Hawker. Life's my training. Did my basics in His Majesty's Navy. Got pressed when I was fourteen. Best thing that could've happened to me. After five years you're tough or broken. I ain't one for being trampled.

Courant. I had assumed your rank was an Army one.

Hawker. Don't assume nothing about me. One minute I'm this, next I'm that. Keeps me ahead of the loggerheads and villains.

Courant. What of the future?

Hawker. There's always a need for a man like me. Law-enforcing is a job for life.

Courant. What about your private life? Do you have a family?

Hawker. The job's too hard on 'em. I couldn't put a girl through that.

Courant. A man of your daring must have quite a choice of the ladies?

Hawker. Too many, But no complaints there, mind you. And never no complaints from them either.

memoirs of Sir George Crockmore

I am not given to magnifying the effort I apply and the worth of my endeavours but my intention in these memoires is to record a true and full account of the life of a Shires Baronet. All must be included though one's spirit is fatigued after a testing day. Would that these jottings were for a son who might read and learn of his father and the nature of this Kingdom.

During the morning and early afternoon I presided over my court, listening to the guilty plead innocence or such circumstances as would justify leniency. These wretches would be sufficient distress for a Saint yet my burden was heavier with the urgency of matters of State. I refer again to that Whig contortion, the Uniformed Brigand Act, and the necessity for me to be about the palaces of power in London to exert my skills and talents in the lobby.

In these days of London Fever, the difficulties of childbirth and bringing infant to adulthood, of pestilence, disease and fire, all of which conspire to do away with life, it appals that the Common Man acts to abet those agents of the Reaper. It has been my duty this day to pass sentence of death upon twelve. I cite here one or two as example against the likes of do-gooder Levenson. These people through foolishness, avarice, lack of moral rectitude or absence of self restraint, have a predisposition to foreshorten their lives.

The first case was a young woman but a few years into puberty, Jane H, who took from a neighbour's house nine dishes, ten plates, a cloak, and a kettle. The following day she walked past her victim's house to pawn her night's thievery while wearing the cloak. This was recognised by its rightful owner. For her crime and her stupidity, Jane H is given a walk to Earley without return.

She will have company on the gallows of Susannah W, guilty of stealing a silk handkerchief value 2s 6d from the pocket of a gentleman in Gun Street. The woman took up accusation against a constable of the Aldermen's Watch for using her ill when apprehending her. She being a wildcat, I dismissed her charge, making it clear her sentence would have been transportation but for her calumny against an officer of the law.

My humour was more tested by a later case that revealed the existence of a vile and reprehensible Molly House on the Basingstoke Road. Mark T, a deviant from Newbury was guilty of buggery with one Thomas S. The place was discovered as the result of a vicious quarrel between another Molly and Thomas S, who shouted out in rage of their disgraceful secret. Such backbiting shows the base nature of these creatures. I ordered them sentenced to death separate from other hangings and gave instruction to the Aldermen's Watch to seek out all other Sodomites in the Basingstoke Road with utmost haste.

The afternoon session was overtaken by time wasters. Lewis J, a weaver of St Giles' Parish was indicted for deflowering and carnally knowing against her consent Rebecca R, aged eleven years. She was apprenticed to him and deposed he threw her upon the bed and put something into her. I determined the girl had no understanding of an Oath and therefore what she said could not be accepted as as evidence. The accused was acquitted. The case extended to an hour because of hysterical outbursts from the mother of the girl. I despatched her to the gaol for contempt of my court, and ordered weaver Lewis J to be guardian of the girl pro tempore.

A testing day as I have noted, but I was inflamed beyond reason upon return to Southcote for tea to find the workmen had made a hotchpotch of the lawn arrangements for my Michaelmas Ball. I have summoned them for immediate explanation and remedy.

Editor's office, Reading Courant

Frith is thinking about different ways to write his interview with Captain Hawker. There were questions he should have asked, supplementary ones he didn't. He has been out of practise for four years and, as such, is reasonably pleased with the material he obtained. Especially when he considers how vulnerable he was out in the uninhabited countryside.

"And this for page sixteen," says Mr Hyde, carefully putting down the quill in its accustomed place after wiping and inspecting the tip.

Frith reads the paragraphs in the London newspaper that his Editor has outlined.

"Are all nineteen ships lost? " asks Frith prosaically.

"They have not yet arrived. That is what is reported."

"Is this comprehensive enough for our readers, Mr Hyde? Should we also report we have as yet no account of the coach from

London being arrived at Maidenhead?"

"Do not be flippant, Mr Frith."

"It was sarcasm. This is no-news. Putting it in a newspaper makes it news prompting false conclusions."

"That is not our business. We print facts. People buy the news-paper and that is the end of our responsibility. Facts are easily identified, such as this for page sixteen."

Mr Hyde is stalling before plucking up the courage to deliver a disfavoured message. He has had Frith's piece on the Navigation since early morning. Frith has been in Mr Hyde's office for five minutes and knows what the smooth-faced implacable man will say about the piece, and that makes him annoyed. The editor knows how important it is to Frith, yet delays. The newsman feels irrational anger bubbling.

Frith reads Mr Hyde's note concerning a stolen silver tray of Reverend Collins that has been returned. "Found where?" he asks. "At the end of a rainbow? What else was stolen? How long ago?"

"There is no need to dwell on the worrisome aspects of the theft. We shall concentrate on the recovery."

Frith reads on to the end. "We are not concentrating on the recovery, we are concentrating on the Reading Militia. You accord them three commendations yet there is not one detail about the tray."

"The policy of this newspaper is to publicise and promote those who by their efforts keep good order and moral rectitude in the town. The Reading Militia have been unsung for too long in their dangerous endeavours as law-keepers."

"By coincidence, I had the opportunity —" Frith stops himself from telling Mr Hyde about his interview. He had been mulling the position his interview would take: the Captain Hawker who spoke of his mission to look after the people of Reading, or the brute who Frith saw enact his duty on a weakened man and his daughter. Frith realises his Navigation article castigates the Reading Militia for their tardiness in suppressing the riot on High Bridge. He is out of kilter with the Courant's abrupt tack in editorial policy.

Mr Hyde is waiting for Frith to continue. The newsman decides he might as well thrust himself on the poisoned quill.

"I had the opportunity to present you earlier with a piece about a local issue."

"Ah yes, your opinion of the new Navigation."

"The opinions of town folk, from labourer to Mayor."

"The opinion of the Mayor is hearsay, you will agree? As to these other opinions, our readers already hold them, or do not wish to know about them."

"They ought to see there is another side."

"Another side? What you have presented are opinions. Where are the facts?"

"You tell me. All the hatred and anger and fear is based on speculation."

"To which your piece is whip and spur."

"It gives both sides of the argument in a level-headed way."

"As you have said, the Navigation is not being discussed in any rational way."

"So we should set the example."

"This does not do so."

Frith looks his editor in the eye. "You never had any intention of publishing my piece."

"To be candid with you," says Mr Hyde in what for him is a stern voice. "So that you do not take it as a personal rebuttal, for you could be a good newsman —"

"Could be! I was in Bristol where I was allowed to be."

"This is not Bristol, Mr Frith." Mr Hyde steadies himself before proceeding more levelly. "To my point. The Courant has no intention of publishing any piece on the Navigation while there exists a concern about unrest and violence."

"The Courant has no intention? You, you mean."

"No, the newspaper has its proprietors."

Frith lets that fact drill through his anger. "You're telling me the proprietors set the editorial policy? Not the editor?"

"Only in the broadest outline."

"Mr Hyde, it is demoralising to spend all one's time copying the clippings from the London newspapers as chosen by one's editor, but it is demeaning to learn one's editor is being told what banal rubbish to select."

Before Mr Hyde can answer, Frith strides out of his office. He continues without slackening through the press room, into the street, and through the next doorway.

An open gate

"This may be an out of the way spot," said Peter as they cleared up the mess Hawker and his men had left them, "but there's more folk out and about here than along the London Strand."

"Captain Hawker and his ruffians aren't folk," replied Lynn on the brink of tears. Her home, her whole life had been violated and she had been powerless to do anything about it. If she thought about the lout's hands groping over her body it was as the scrabbling of a rat caught on ice: his desperation, her coldness.

It took the pair most of the afternoon to get Barge Jeannie shipshape. Lynn had dressed the pistol-whip across her Dad's face, but he was carrying a pain he wouldn't talk about. His forehead was hot. Lynn couldn't bear to watch her Dad struggle with the effort of clearing up, neither could she stop him. As a diversion she rode Hermond back to Southcote Lock to collect the jettisoned gear, finding most caught against the gates.

Peter wanted to press on, arguing Hermond had rested. The sail would need days of mending. Lynn had to agree with the reasoning, but also for her strong wish to be away from Southcote Cut.

Dusk was pulling down fast as Lynn saw Sheffield Lock over the long reins, the nearby wooden swing bridge of the Theale track and a tightening bend of waterway beyond. "What about mooring here?" she suggested.

Her Dad came slowly out of the cabin. "Aye. We'll take the lock in the morning."

They hadn't eaten since Fergus' oatcakes so Lynn used his improvised griddle to fry potato and onions. She watched her father numb his pain from a bottle of brandy that had been concealed in the false ceiling of the cabin. Its access was from behind the once gaudily painted name board.

Lynn could not sleep though the night was still and the rain had eased. She heard a nightjar 'churr' its way overhead and a distant owl. A brushing sound along the barge brought her instantly alert. It came again from the hull, but Lynn knew noises could seem in one place though in fact be far from their source. She held her breath to listen, dreading the creeping footsteps of the Reading Militia or wharf men. Barge Jeannie listed a fraction to starboard.

"Dad!" She tipped herself from the hammock. "Wake up! We're sinking!"

From the aft deck the barge clearly listed from the bank and Lynn fought the silliness of her eyes that Barge Jeannie was sitting higher in the water. Who would want to steal the cargo? Lynn was at the midship hatch about to drop into the hold and check the hull, by the time her Dad appeared on deck,.

"Leave it," he called. "Look bank side."

Lynn saw a swathe of wet mud over a foot wide along the bank.

"Bastards," said Peter with venom. "They've drained the pound. It'll be that miller back away. I'll sort him."

There was a creak beneath their feet. "Go make sure the cargo's fast. She shouldn't tip if it don't slide."

Lynn chose to ignore her Dad when he picked up the stone-dogs and clambered to the towing path. Nearing the tall grey mill she could distinguish the water rushing from the Navigation Cut into the old river Kennet. Her Dad swerved off the towing path and through the bushes following a very shadowy trail until he almost fell onto the weir. The water cascaded through, rushing by the millrace into a swirling mass that darkened into the distance. Peter crossed the narrow planking on top of the weir.

"Hand paddles," he observed. "Every one of them missing."

Lynn stared at water racing round the stout upright slides, between each of which should have been an oak board with long handle. Her hopes flooded away with the water. She had believed once they were through Reading they were clear of nasty people. Then another relief in Southcote Cut when Hawker had finally left them. But a dozen Hermond couldn't move a grounded barge. And what if the Navigation bed wasn't flat?

Lynn had to stop her Dad making things worse. He was hammering at the mill door with the stone-dogs, shouting for the cowardly miller to show his weasel face. She stepped cautiously on the narrow planks, reaching for the next solid slide until she was across the weir. Lynn caught her Dad's arm and was shocked when he doubled-over gasping.

Lynn spoke to the door. "Hello. Mister Miller. My dad is very upset. I'm sorry if we frightened you. We don't want to hurt you. We only want to get our barge afloat. Please close your weir. Please." Lynn sensed there was someone inside and persisted. She kept coaxing.

A small face appeared at a window. He was bald with a dark rim of hair, a pointed nose and tiny eyes too far apart. A harvest mouse thought Lynn. She resumed her pleading, standing several feet from his door to win his confidence. As a young girl she had done the same with Hermond. Her Dad squatted on the ground coughing through noisy breaths.

"Please Sir, please close your weir."

"Can't."

"I'll do it. Where are the paddles?"

"Gone."

"Washed away? Is the weir broken?"

"Yes."

"All we have is in our barge, Sir." Lynn remembered the greatest fear of millers. "Our barge being grounded is a disaster for us, just like if your mill caught fire." She saw him flinch. "Not us. Heaven strike us down, Sir, should we think of such a thing." Lynn started to suspect it wasn't she and her Dad who terrified the miller. "Has someone threatened you?" His wide-eyed silence proved her correct. "They opened the weir? Broke the paddles?"

The isolated miller, living alone, had been visited by a gang of men late that afternoon. He gave Lynn a small comfort. The river wouldn't drop much more, it wouldn't drain dry through the weir. Nevertheless, Barge Jeannie was firmly grounded on the mud at Sheffield Lock.

Saracen's Head Inn

"You look like you lost a crown and found a farthing," says Sarah looking up from the cat's cradle of fingers round her sweet cider.

Frith pauses at the Petties Snug. Sarah pats the bench beside her. Perhaps with the mood he is in a downcast Sarah is better than a chirpy Sarah.

"I still have my crown," he says, dropping heavily onto the seat. "But someone said it was a worthless nothing."

"If I'd listened to the things people said about me I'd have topped myself before I was born. 'Specially sodding Dragon."

"I work for a half-blind, puppet-mouse," says Frith into his ale.

"She nearly had me in tears this afternoon."

"No. He's a puppet-flea on the backside of a mouse."

"The Lord rot her tongue."

"He's scared of controversy."

"Calling me a whore."

Frith takes in Sarah's set jaw. They both take a swig. Sarah speaks first. "Ain't we a right pair of pansies in a rainstorm? You first, Mr Frith."

"I put forward an article . . . you wouldn't understand."

"Thanks," snaps Sarah. "You sound like Dragon saying I'm thick as two sacks of meal."

"It's me who's stupid, Sarah," says Frith more buoyantly. "I'm outraged my article on the Navigation was spiked. Two minutes in here, with real life on the faces of people slap-bang in my face, and my concern is trivial. Just words. What right have I to be upset because Mr Hyde wouldn't print my words?"

"That's as clear as the ale-glow on your face, Mr Frith, and you can't see that either. Coz you care about it, that's why you've a right to be upset. Not what you wrote, the thing you wrote about's what you care about."

"I don't particularly care about this barge. The issues, maybe." Frith takes a long gulp then addresses his jug. "Being really honest? I care a lot about the article, less about the issues. I care about me."

"A barge isn't that easy to cuddle. I bet there's been people you cared about," says Sarah softly. "Care about," she adds quickly.

"It's painful when the woman you love is —" Frith jolts himself from the confessional pull of his ale. He looks round the inn filling with evening drinkers. "You can't force the other person, else they become what you turn them into and not the person you first cared for. But she has other cares, of which one is one – of which I am one – maybe the greatest, but the others can be obstacles to yours . . . and I've got myself confused what I'm talking about."

"Makes you easier to understand."

"Thank you," says Frith, lightly. His mind is leaving the Petties, drifting to intense understanding conveyed in so few words, to the sensation of his fingertips over her skin, to West Hill.

"Now you can hear about my day. Bleeding Dragon called me a whore. And my gentlemen made it worse shouting about Mr M having his stock checked, and Mr M's whore-room. I'd made sure boxes and bags was between me and him, and dodged his other tricks like – could I check again what was on the top shelf – and I walk straight into Dragon's fire-breath. I'm a Jezebel, a brazen hussy."

"Didn't you correct her?"

"No Mr Frith, I took it because that's what I gotta do. Fuming inside I was, tears in my eyes, but I weren't gonna let Dragon see them. Do you know why? Because I care. I care like nothing else about my little Bron and Ben, about my Mum. If I don't have a job the lot of them'll starve. O yes indeed, I was busting to land her one and give Dragon some home truths, but I didn't. D'you know what Touchy-Timothy told me? He's gonna be so rich he can keep two women. You might be able to keep two, says I, but you'll never get two."

"His get-rich scheme Mrs Middleton won't talk about?"

"Dragon don't know about, more like. She never knows what's what. Huffs with pride when Mr M is called to the Mayor's, but it's to deliver his provisions. Mistress Olivia comes visiting all prettied-up and Dragon reckons the girl's besotted with her Master Nicholas. her Master Richard's in charge of His Majesty's Army, and His Navy. Her son's a lazy, bottomless tar-pit for their money.

I read his last letter. He was after fifty pounds. Demanding it, no less. Half that could keep me and my kids for ten years. But I have to put up with her husband in the stockroom and her mouth in the Koffee House."

Frith is smiling when Sarah pauses. "Feeling better for that?" he asks.

"Are you for that?" she mimics, pointing to his empty jug. "If I was you, I'd have another. And seeing as you're going to the bar, you can get me a refill."

Catherine's last note of Wednesday 21st September

The dung has hit the rafters. Eliot found your letters. He has burned everything. Where are you? I need you to hold me and shut out the awfulness. Don't come to the house. Don't contact me. Please.

Round-room, Saracen's Head Inn

The barmaid is peering at Frith through the hatch with its shelf that serves as the bar for the Round-room. It is jovially rowdy this evening. At Frith's expense.

"Don't you think you've had enough, Sir?"

"He don't think," bellows from the window table Frith has just left.

"The young lady is perfectly correct," slurs Frith thinking hard about making the words sound as they ought. "I've had enough ale. Give me a brandy." In Frith's mind the argument is closed in his favour.

"I'm not sure that's a good idea after what you've put away. Sir."

"Are you not the serving wench? Then serve me a brandy."

"Everything all right, Mary?" asks the landlord from behind her.

"Mary, Mary, is being contrary," chants Frith through the opening, this time aware but not caring his voice is too loud. "Becauth Mr Frithed is mightily pithed."

Mary scowls and places her palms on the bar in defiance. "You've had too much."

The landlord approaches. Mary repeats her concern. Frith repeats his request. "I have money to pay," he adds. Frith delves in his pocket. His finger catches his kerchief and coins cascade to the floor. The drinkers in the Round-room watch the newsman grope on his knees until he stands up with a pleased grin. "Money!"

"He can stand. Serve him," says the landlord, returning to his regulars.

Frith speaks to the barmaid's back "That is an example of how our new commercial world works." She finds a reasonably clean glass and goes to the brandy barrel. Frith speaks louder, "So long as I have money the businessman will sell to me what I don't need, what I shouldn't have, and not give one jot if it kills me. Provided he makes a profit."

"Shut up and finish your story."

Frith turns towards the voice, somewhere from among his previously unknown companions sat round the window table. He stares blankly at them. A ruddy, knurled face reminds him. "The Three-Kick Contest. The stuck-up London lawyer shot a duck that fell on a farmer's land and both said it was theirs."

"The old farmer challenged him." This new voice spoke out of so many jerkins and scarves Frith shivered with cold just looking at him. "They'd kick each other in turn till one gives up. Remember?"

"Course I remember," says Frith. "I was awaiting your complete attention. Creating a dramatic hiatus."

"Just tell us the bloody story," says the closest to Frith, jabbing him with a finger.

"The old farmer has first go," says Frith, instantly deciding to enact the story. That will get him away from finger thrusts and give him time to remember the ending. "Mister la-di-da London lawyer thinks the challenge is easy won. He'll kick the frail old git into the next field when his turn comes. The farmer gets down from his cart." Frith theatrically steps over a chair. "He's wearing great clogs, toes with metal caps, and one swings right in the lawyer's groin." Frith drops to his knees clutching his privates in agony. "Before the lawyer has time to feel the torment in his testes a second kick digs into his midriff." Frith slides doubled-up across the stone floor knocking over a small table.

The landlord is suddenly at the doorway. "Any fighting, you're all out."

"He's acting," says the man in scarfs.

"Acting the fool," says the landlord, turning his back.

Frith is raising himself to all fours when his mind is in Catherine's parlour, her body underneath him. He holds in a sigh that yearns to break free.

He hears shouts. "Get on with it!"

"The third kick is square up his big fat —"

A boot slams into Frith's backside sprawling him across the floor. Belly laughs fill the Round-room. He has jarred both knees and scraped one hand, but doesn't feel any pain.

"You weren't acting it good, so I helped you," says the man standing behind Frith.

"Thank you," says Frith. He takes a gulp of brandy. "Could you fetch a cow-pat? For realism because that's what the lawyer's face landed in." Frith has to climb across the table to squeeze back into his window seat before he continues. "The lawyer heaves himself out of the mud and dung, sorely aching in vital places. 'Right you old churl, now it's my turn,' he says." Frith swigs his brandy, savouring the vapours in his skull. "The old farmer smiles. I give up, he says. You can have the duck."

Whoops erupt from the table and jostling re-enactments start. Frith is aware the content of his stomach is preparing to leave him. He hasn't time to get round, over, nor under the table. He stands on the bench and opens the window to vomit into the street.

"Shut the window after you," he hears behind him. Strong hands are on his backside and his legs and then the howls of laughter are somewhere in the distance.

His body takes a bone-shaking thump followed by violent shudders. It is a lot colder in the street. Don't worry about me, he thinks slumped on the ground but has no time to dwell on it. Acrid bile burns up his windpipe and spews from him. Swinging strands of yellow saliva dangle from his face but all he feels is his throat, scraped raw by a score of pitchforks. His body doubles violently with another retch. He shivers, groans, is aware of the stench cloying his nose. Frith rolls back to sit against the wall and vomits a lapful.

He wants Catherine. He wants the Navigation piece published. He doesn't want to vomit again. He wants to talk about important things. He wants the street to stop spinning. He wants to be in the remotest part of remoteness with Catherine. Frith topples sideways.

from Mistress Olivia's diary

For this evening I arranged a recital in the drawing room, being of two musicians: myself with recorder and Mama at the spinet. I had suggested this to Papa, that I might show him the benefit from engaging my music teacher. Mama was disinclined to participate, for she is loath to be seen doing that in which she does not excel. For this principle I do admire her. Nevertheless, I pleaded for accompaniment and Papa insisted she do this one thing for her eldest child. Thus she sat at the spinet and tapped out some notes and a chord or two.

I spent the whole afternoon preparing and the response I received was worth all the effort. Especially from Master Nicholas whom, as I had anticipated came calling, no doubt lectured by his scold of a mother about his earlier absence. He was obliged to make small talk with Papa and Mama and amuse the brats until I felt it right for me to enter the drawing room. His eyes popped from his skull and through the recital his squirming could not conceal his manhood filling his breeches.

Mama was predictable. "Olivia, what under Heaven are you wearing?" The expression crosses her lips mostly when she feels eclipsed. I explained it was the current fashion along the Strand and at Charing Cross drawing Papa to my support.

"Reading is not London," she huffed.

"No Mama, but you have often contested we should live by the highest standards and not by those of our neighbours."

"One of those standards Olivia is to ask before borrowing from someone."

"I am sorry, Mama. You were so busy with little Lucy I wished not to disturb you. Besides, I wanted to surprise you." She could say no more in front of our guest but as she stared at my ensemble her eyes glazed and her cheeks flushed slightly. I am sure she was recalling the times she wore the garment.

This afternoon I had taken my finest Flanders gown of lawn, a dark hazelnut colour, and cut it clean up the front. I ordered the maid finish the edges with lace and hitch up the back of the skirt. I selected which of my patterned petticoats would be best revealed. Some months previous during an excursion into Mama's closet, I had noticed a stomacher hidden away at the very back of her garderobe. I retrieved the heavily embroidered corset and replaced its gaudy red ribbons with ones resembling gold. The maid had sewn neatly for the gown fell in an even, deep-V to my waist, revealing much of the stomacher. I was obliged to pad this with stockings under my bosom.

"That is very daring, Mistress," said the maid.

"The mantua is day wear in London," I said, and applied the finishing touch of red-gold colouring to the upper lids of my eyes and accentuating my tresses which did flounce well. This I had seen on the ladies in London but never in these dull streets. Thus I entered the drawing room to stunned admiration.

I noted the effect on Master Nicholas of each inhalation before I began the next bars on my recorder. Though it was a simple rondo, Pourquoy donc by Susato, I declared I had played it too poorly. This second time I set about the cadences with fortissimo, which deep breathing did send the head of Master Nicholas spinning. When Papa and Mama allowed us a few moments of private discourse my beau erupted with praise and glorification.

He then remarked, "Sweetest Olivia, you surpass in every quality every young lady in this town. How can I be worthy of you?"

I was suspicious of this uncharacteristic outburst and of its intent. To know more I lamented the afternoon had been a torment for me without his company and not knowing where he was. How I yearned for him during those hours he was away doing goodness knows what. "And with whom," I said pianissimo.

I could see unease jangling him and anxiety behind his eyes. Before I could stretch him further between his discomfort and his desire for me, Papa returned. Master Nicholas promptly asked Papa if he may be my escort to Forbury Fair this Saturday. I dallied before accepting. I will abide by the agreement provided Master Nicholas proves his unconditional devotion.

Upon the boy's departure Mama ordered me remove and return her garment. After I left the drawing room I heard Papa tell Mama he could not recall her wearing the stomacher. Mama's answer was annoyingly inaudible. I swear no red-blooded man could forget Mama wearing such a garment, especially when it was adorned with scarlet ribbons.

memoirs of Sir George Crockmore

I was kicking my heels in agitation awaiting the belated arrival of the contractor for the lawn arrangements, when Mr Hyde paid an unexpected late visit.

A highly meticulous nature serves him well as bookkeeper but poorly as chapman or raconteur. In this instance, his pursuance of correct protocol proved advantageous. He brought an article put forward this morning by his newsman, and after perusing the opening paragraph, I ordered him to destroy the inflammatory document the instant he returned to the Courant office. I instructed the editor that such pieces would rouse angers and passions and in very short time lead to disturbance and riot. Therefore I strongly advised the newspaper carry no information or opinion on the River Kennet Navigation. Thus was one potential calamity nipped in the bud.

The second will take longer. Though vexing my full wrath on the incompetent contractor for siting the principal marquee grossly out of position and incorrectly oriented, it will take the morrow for correction and catching-up. I must oversee their work, else I have a marquee where there are no Ball guests and ball guests where there is no marquee.

Thus am I unable to journey to London on important matters of State until the next week, as there is scant point in going on a

Friday. After this arduous day I must compose myself for the writing of a score of letters to people of influence, that we might scupper this confounded Bill and its amnesty for all villains in His Majesty's Kingdom.

When the candles burn low and splutter their last, I shall call for a hot malted milk with a glass of port, and command it brought to my bed chamber by the new kitchen maid.

Wakeman's journal – 11:00pm

So close! Then pitched to the blackness beyond stars.

"Don't come to the house."

I must help her.

"Don't contact me."

I have to talk to her.

Please!

Catherine never had need of "please" with me. Why now? Oh Zitkala, I want to be with her. Fly me to her. I need to help her, for her, for my sake. But how? I can't think. There's just this hurting pressure in my skull. Hours ago nothing else mattered, and now – there is nothing. Poor woman with confrontation, pain, decisions. Poor me with nothing. Should I go against her instructions? Go see her. What could I do? We are so new to each other. It's too damned soon to lose her. Ten years as Eliot's wife, as buttress to that draining kill-joy. All my love, my experience, my learning, all are useless because I must stay away.

We'll keep in touch through the Courant, her etchings for the paper. No, that'll be stopped by him. Will it? Could this be our liberty? With Beattie? Without? Take on her child? His child. Too complicated. I can't think straight. The ale and brandy are not numbing this amputation in my soul.

I'm lying on a bed of nails, bleeding from every one. I don't breathe, just shudder. Dry-eyed. She's gone fills my head. A death knell. She's gone, she's gone. Clang, clang. I can't stand doing nothing. A pulsing vice crushes my being, then I'm cold, then it crushes again.

Did she really mean don't contact me?

If she did, but I do, would that turn her against me?
Will she run to me tonight?
She did but I wasn't here.
She left. Left a note and is gone.

Wakeman's journal – 7:30am

Back at the Anglers. Back from hiding. Back from trying to catch the whispers of this new stranger. A woman I once knew but don't recognise today.

"Wakeman, I've thrown away something important."

Me? Her husband? Her child?

"I've put a powder keg in your life. In everybody's life."

She has shouldered all the blame. She wouldn't listen to my protests.

"I shouldn't have . . ."

She should, she should. She did. We did. I shouldn't have kept writing when I knew she was keeping my letters. But I wanted her to keep them, however much danger that involved.

This morning Eliot was crying in the house while we had hurried whispers through a hedge.

Catherine: "I can't come to your lodgings."

Me: "Do you want me to come here later?"

Catherine: "No!"

Me: "What do you want me to do?"

Catherine: "I don't know."

Me: "Do you want me to stay away."

Catherine: "No!"

Me: "We'll go for a ride, a long way out of town."

Difficulties fixing a possible time, where we could possibly meet. Is this what it is going to be like? All our time together spent arranging our next time together. That's not enough of her.

Our ride might be the time she says a forever goodbye to me. That's why she agreed, why she's taking such a risk. I feel sick. So much lost potential – someone who is my same species. Maybe in some future we'll rencounter. Can't think about that. I want her now. She was my salvation from my past, my joy for the present and beyond, the reason I took each next breath. She was? No, she is! She's gone. The end after forty-two days.

It is too damned soon.

A different wharfinger

Peter worried about the barge settling too firmly in the mud the longer they remained aground. Lynn worried about her Dad who had started a chesty cough during the night that he couldn't stop. The gash on his face still oozed a thick pus. He spoke as if drunk and their conversation had been laboured. After a breakfast, eaten slowly by Peter, the two had returned to the mill. Shutters were across the windows and Peter's knocking produced the hollow echo of an uninhabited building. Peter restated his opinion of this and all millers.

Through dogged persistence that in normal times her Dad would have called nagging, Lynn had her way. She set off alone to walk the thirteen miles to Newbury for the slim possibility of raising help to mend the weir, and the sure certainty of the thirteen miles walk back. Reading was not an option, it had to be the hopefully non-hostile Newbury. Besides, the canal owners were based there.

Lynn stepped out with troubled thoughts of how she had over-ruled her Dad, who had insisted it was his duty to go. At one point Lynn had gently nudged him and he fell back on the bunk. She reminded him how he had laboured getting to the bushes to relieve himself. By contrast, inside herself there was a drive to do something, not to wait for some Knight Errant to charge up. Preferably with paddles instead of a lance.

After four miles Lynn came upon a small wharf. She'd put on her most comfortable clogs but her big and little toes were already chaffed. The wharfinger was a large man who chortled every time he explained it was called Aldermaston Wharf though the name-sake village was two miles away. "Should be Hag Pit Wharf," he insisted. "Not from the diggings yonder," he added with a smile. "In honour of my Missus."

When he heard Lynn's business the wharfinger would not let her proceed. So Lynn told him of Barge Jeannie over a jug of ale and a chunk of freshly baked bread from the village. "Same as what the nobs eat up at Hind's Head," he winked. "Mind, they eat off white cloth not green grass."

She set off refreshed by the rest, the food and easy talk about things other than the Kennet Navigation. The wharfinger told her the navvies were at Colthrop, raising the embankment of the pound. It was half the distance to Newbury, and the chief engineer would most certainly be there. "Very much a hands-on chap is John Hore," he added.

Lynn forced herself to believe she would have to walk to Newbury, though Colthrop was the hope she tried to keep secret from herself. She had experienced the disappointment when dreams were used as the foundation of expectation.

memoirs of Sir George Crockmore

I was woken by a calamitous din and blinding light that left me fearful Jacobites were besieging Southcote Hall. Cook had brought breakfast, but was so brimming with fury she resembled one of her cauldrons. Foul-mouthed workmen with clod laden boots were stomping across her floor and their filthy hands were everywhere with grubbiness and mucky intentions. I feared what devastation these oafs were wrecking on the south lawn and parterre as they corrected the errors of the marquee.

Some way into Cook's tirade my reason began to function. Hercules would have trembled had Cook a mind he should not enter her kitchen and larder. I was not long in eliciting the true thorn under Cook's apron. The ovens had not been lit this morning, neither had the water been fetched and Agnes was away as a gossip during her sister's confinement. The new kitchen maid had not risen. On enquiry by Cook, the maid declared she "would rest a little longer" adding that if it was not to her liking, Cook should "enquire of the Master as to this maid's duties."

I assured Cook the girl would be severely reprimanded, promising one more instance and she would be returned to Pingle Farm with blackened references. This gross insubordination left me appetite for but two of the kidneys.

Being engaged in bed linen duty late into the night as girl, is supplementary to the obligations to Cook during the day as maid. As she entered my bed chamber last night with the warm milk and port, the girl was at lip with being woken. I cupped my hand across her mouth, for I did not relish a gutter stream in my ear while I enjoyed her. There grew a glint of entreaty in her eye that fascinated me by its falseness. I despatched her to fetch a silk scarf from my dear wife's closet. She returned with three, feigning she could not tell which was the better for the purpose in my mind that she could not fathom. I employed all, and for some good while made play on her restrained body to our mutual pleasure. Then did I enjoy her most enormously and dismissed her.

To calm myself following Cook's morning tempest, I read that which I had written yesterday. A discord regarding the content had lingered in my mind, but on review I was rewarded that my keen sensibility had again proved reliable. Indeed the memoir was of an angry mind and not that of an unbiased judge and I was initially inclined to burn the pages and compose them anew in a more compassionate frame. My sound sense came to their rescue for the Court records will show, when I wear the robe and wig, I am the instrument of that office, the impartial arbiter of justice. The pages in these memoirs will show a man with sagacity and compassion, responding to the battering and elevations of life, a member and leader of Mankind.

Wakeman's journal – 11:45am

Back in my room and the shaking starts. Should have had a slice of pie downstairs but too desperate to get to my hideaway, to be away from others and suffer the awfulness in private.

I am safekeeping our work: two pictures, the sticks, some sketches. Scraps Eliot didn't destroy. Petty Bastard.

On the rack now. Held it together during our ride. Strong for her. Keeping our work for her. Until the day she can retrieve it.

My guts want to be sick but nothing comes up. I want to shed tears, but my eyes just squeeze shut and the dry shuddering sobs are all I have.

A coach and horses

The towing path returned to the south bank at the Wickham Knight footbridge. Lynn waited for a herd of cattle to amble over. The farmer was happy, which Lynn took as a good omen. He explained this new footbridge saved him the mile and a half round trip to the road bridge at Woolhampton.

Such was Lynn's mood that the Rowbarge Inn looked like a yawning but friendly devil, with its tall chimney stacks for horns and open door for gaping mouth. A man hurried from the dark interior as Lynn anticipated a glass of sweet cider. "Hello Mr Frith." Another good omen, thought Lynn.

He was so startled he spilled both tankards of ale before resuming his scurry towards a small copse. Not so good an omen, Lynn corrected herself, to have been snubbed. A few throat wetting minutes later Lynn followed the route taken by Mr Frith. She soon crossed a rickety footbridge where the Kennet rejoined the Navigation and stepped briskly along the longest cut of the Navigation towards Colthrop.

Gabriel White acted his usual at the sight of any young woman be her pretty or plain. The rest of the navvies joined with catcalls, whistles and rough remarks, especially when Lynn eased past the dray loaded with turfs. The massive horse reminded Lynn of the young Hermond, inquisitive about the new, and she paused to stroke his head to a background of more fruity comments.

The calls stopped immediately Lynn shouted she wanted to speak with a director of the Navigation Company. The navvies were used to trouble presenting itself in many guises. When Lynn mentioned she was from Barge Jeannie there was silence. Suddenly the navvies whooped and cheered, raced to her across the drained pound as fast as the gluey mud would allow. Gabriel wanted to shake her hand but desisted seeing the layer of mud on his. Lynn was overwhelmed.

Gabriel sent his men back to work and escorted Lynn to the lock, pressing her for details about Barge Jeannie. She glossed over them, thinking ahead about what she needed to say to the Company gentlemen.

The lead navvy introduced her to John Hore, the chief engineer. Lynn was expecting a man as big and muscular as the navvies but he was short and skinny with quick darting eyes. He wore a three-quarter coat with waistcoat, the only concession to the muck being sturdy shoes and leather breeches. Gabriel, claiming he knew everything about grounded barges, followed Mr Hore and Lynn to a track where a coach stood, its thills empty of horse and harness.

Humphrey Devereaux stepped from the travelling office, his bob wig completely out of keeping with the surroundings. Devereaux ignored Gabriel and apologised excessively that his fellow director Mr Martyn had just left. "Such an enormous distance for a person to walk," said Devereaux. "Particularly for a young lady alone. How brave."

Lynn remained quiet and waited for the gushing to abate.

"You say your boat is aground as a result of a weir malfunctioning." He reached into the coach but it was Hore who located the map he wanted.

"Deliberately broken," said Lynn as the Company men peered at the map.

"Such a pity Mr Martyn is not here," said Devereaux with a high-pitched laugh. "This really is his territory. In all seriousness, as senior director of the Company, effectively our Company Secretary, these issues are under Mr Martyn's jurisdiction. It is his forte."

"Where is he?" asked Lynn.

"As I said, he was here. You barely missed him. I fear he is about his own business which could take him to Newbury, to Oxford or even London. I have never known him be away more than three nights."

"Three nights!" spluttered Lynn. "Can't you do something?" Gabriel bit back a smile.

"My, you are a forthright young lady," he said as if seeing Lynn for the first time. "To the contrary, we shall see what can be done to have your boat under way again. Mr Hore?"

"Simple enough. Staunch the weir, let the pound refill and up she floats," said Hore. Gabriel nodded his agreement.

"Excellent," said Devereaux. "The first task then, is to find some person to negotiate with the miller with a view to agreeing either our men working on his weir or himself undertaking the necessary repairs. We do not want to be charged with trespass. It must be understood to be at the mill's cost. We do not own the weir, Mistress Darville," he added before Lynn could interrupt. "It is not our property and we therefore need permissions."

"But you'll be making it good!"

"What if a man was injured during the course of the work?" continued Devereaux in his even pace. "More importantly, what if other property was damaged? Who would be responsible? However, I jump the gun. Do you see how it would be so preferable for Mr Martyn to be involved? It is likely this miller is a tenant, in which instance our dealings will be with the landowner. Do your charts say whom that might be Mr Hore?"

Hore did not look at the map. "Sir George Crockmore."

"Oh dear," sighed Devereaux, displaying for Lynn the most sincerity in anything he had so far said. "Oh dear. I fear under such circumstances there is very little I, or indeed anybody, can do. We must await the return of Mr Martyn."

"I'll go and talk to this Sir Crockmore," said Lynn with pent frustration.

"You will not! I will have you apprehended here and now if you persist in such an impetuous idea." Devereaux caught the look on his chief engineer's face. "Sir George Crockmore has threatened to take the Company to the Debtors Court for monies unpaid," he explained quickly. "We do not dispute his claim but at this moment in time we are without the requisite funds to settle with him."

Gabriel coughed. Devereaux scowled at him and continued. "We have great plans to raise extra capital but it is unfortunate so much investment money is pouring into seductive overseas stock. Therefore our priority is to complete the Navigation for trade as soon as possible, which means ensuring our work force is content." His look begged no dissent from Gabriel. "More importantly, not to ruffle the feathers of creditors to the Company."

"You can't do anything," said Lynn.

"If only you could have had your mishap further along the Navigation."

"Mishap!" Lynn strode away from the imbecile. Hore and Gabriel caught up with her at the lock. She turned on them. "If he wants the Navigation trading he shouldn't leave barges stuck in the mud."

"Mistress Lynn," said Hore softly. "Please do not attempt anything foolish. If the Company's debts are called in by its creditors the Navigation will be foreclosed – including all and everything in it. I will speak with Mr Martyn the instant he returns."

Gabriel spoke to Hore. "We could dig a side pond at Sheffield so the lock discharges less water down the Navigation. That should keep the miller happy." He turned to Lynn. "That would give Mr Martyn something to bargain with."

"We should have done that on every lock from the outset," said Hore, expressing aloud what were clearly deeply held beliefs in him. "The water management would have been a good deal simpler and a lot more efficient."

Gabriel and Lynn could hear the fervency in his voice.

"The Board refused. Too costly. Profits before principles."

"You can't speak to the miller about anything," said Lynn, "he's run away. Looks like you'll have to talk with this Sir Crockmore."

Hore stood looking into his lock, slowly shaking his head. Lynn stared too for a short while then made up her mind leaving the engineer with a promise she would do nothing rash.

The navvies tried to force their lunches on Lynn to win a change from their gobbled routine. She chatted with them but under the lightness her thoughts were on her failure to get the weir mended. Then on her Dad alone for too long, and Lynn was suddenly in a hurry to leave.

A hundred yards along the towing path a loud pistol shot made her jump, and two more cracked out. Lynn dived low into the bushes, the words of Fergus after the stove fire having flown through her head, her heart thumping in her ears. The navvies were yelling abuse as they dived for cover. Lynn heard a rattling accompanied by the pounding of heavy hooves. She looked out from her hiding to see a terrified horse charging towards her. The dray careened behind with its wheels skittering dangerously close to the edge of the cut. Turfs jolted off the dray in its wake. She had a choice. Stay in the bushes with a possibility of being hit by the hurtling dray, or sprint into the drained pound and pray that wasn't where the wagon lurched from the towing path. It would drag the horse to injury, probably fatal, as well as her.

Lynn stepped onto the towing path, faced the horse and flapped her arms. The navvies yelled at her to get out of the way. "Quiet!" she bellowed with such authority they did. She called to the terrified horse. He was only a young Hermond Lynn told herself as she clacked noises, shouted the calming sounds she had learned with Hermond. She waved her arms more vigorously and stamped her clogs to break into the horse's vision. The pain from rubbed toes and blisters shot up her ankle. Lynn emitted a piercing "Yilp." The horse saw her. Another "Yilp." He tried to pull up. She knew the horse didn't want to trample her but the momentum from the dray propelled him forward. Lynn didn't stop shouting to him, commanding and coaxing. Hooves slithered along the packed earth, clouds belched from nostrils and the dray slowed. Two yards from her she looked straight into his frightened brown eye, grabbed a rein as his neck went by and hung on, half running, half dragged, whispering to him, guiding him straight so the shafts wouldn't slew them both into disaster.

Horse and girl were panting heavily by the time the nimbler navvies got to them. Lynn was shaking violently. Then she was rattling inside a firm cage of strong arms. Men told her she was stupid, brave, amazing. Gabriel explained they'd had their work disrupted quite a bit near Reading but this was the first time pistols had been used. He was pretty sure the shots had been fired above them, a warning.

"If we'd lost that dray and the horse it'd ha' stopped us a day or more," said Gabriel. "No work means no pay. We owe you, Lass. First light the morrow we'll get horses from stables in village and come fix that weir." There was a rumble of agreement.

"And that miller," added Lee over his shoulder.

"I promised Mr Hore I wouldn't do anything rash," said Lynn.

"Won't touch the miller," said Gabriel, more for his men's ears. "Fixin' his weir ain't rash. Asides, it weren't us made the promise to Mr Hore."

Lynn set off back to the grounded barge and her Dad. Gabriel shouted to her. "We'll be with you early morning. Have a kettle going. It'll be chilly."

Half a minute later she heard a horse gallop towards Reading. Towards Sheffield Lock. What wouldn't she give for a horse to get her quickly to her Dad with her hopeful news.

Wakeman's journal – 12:30pm

Catherine was nervous, terrified of being seen. For a long time she couldn't say anything at all. Then it was nothing about us or our work or of herself. I grew angry at her. Why is she letting this happen to her? Where has my defiant woman gone? She doesn't counter Eliot's calumny.

"When Eliot maligns you, imagine I am behind you, my hands round your waist holding you against me."

She found her tender smile. "Then rolling your thumb over my nipples. If I turned up at the Anglers and you were out, I'd set up camp inside your room."

Our paintings and sticks, her letters to me, are stored here in my room. A reminder we are being separated, rent piece by piece. I refuse to accept that. It's one strand plaited into an unbreakable rope joining us. This is torment.

memoirs of Sir George Crockmore

I returned from inspecting the repositioned marquee to the unexpected presence of Captain Hawker. He bore information, the source of which he was loath to reveal, that a mob of navigators were to march to Sheffield Mill at dawn intent upon destruction and mayhem. This news demanded a clearly thought response. I decreed the Captain should make the Reading Militia available to assist Mayor Turner, as they had at High Bridge. A preventative measure, I insisted, as the navigators themselves were unlikely to instigate any fray requiring forceful suppression. Only if word of the march reached the ears of the Reading wharf men would there likely be trouble.

That part of our exchange having achieved much, I turned to an issue that Captain Hawker is unable to grasp. Without mentioning my particular concern, I described a change in the climate of opinion regarding the agents of law enforcement, and repeated my pronouncement of a few days previous that the Reading Militia must be more demonstrably successful. He replied they had nearly caught a Jacobite traitor. My rejoinder that one hung traitor is worth a score slipping the noose, was not the wisest considering the Captain's excess of both temper and hubris. He ranted of having many irons in the fire and would not give them up until all were red hot and hammered into shape.

I noted the words of the Captain before steering him to less confrontational issues such as the rewarding days ahead of patrolling Sheffield Mill and Forbury Fair. For amusement I gave caricature to the pretentious upstarts attending my card soirée tomorrow evening, particularly the vain Henry Woodroffe who would wager his wife on a weak hand.

from Mistress Olivia's diary

It was hap this morning. Mama lost her poise in front of Papa who left the house fuming and pained. Through tear-filled eyes Mama told the uncaring man he will find his belongings removed to the guest room until he adjusts his ways. This was too dangerous a ploy by Mama for she gains much influence when they retire to their bed chamber. Also, Papa is stubborn in seeing through his business stratagems and he seldom relents. The flaring into anger and tears could be a tactic by Mama, which to her credit is one she rarely uses. A lady can cry too often.

The fun started when Mama probed Papa about purchasing the house in Minster Street. The more vague Papa's replies the more relentless was Mama's questioning. Papa had to admit he had no money for a new house.

"You have converted your investments into cash," said Mama.

"And used it to repay those who loaned me the money to invest with the addition of their interest."

"The moneylenders gained from your dealings and you made nothing?"

This was an excellent point striking at Papa's pride. I knew Papa would not be forceful to swing the argument to his favour as he loves Mama to silliness. Neither could I argue on his behalf for Mama would then recognise me as her rival in some way. I prayed that Papa had shaken on his deal with Mr Middleton for then it could not be undone no matter how much Mama cries or chides.

Mama let self-control fly from her mouth, for her harangue was fierce. It is not a method I would employ. It is clear Mama is earnestly set upon a new house in Reading. I must make my case well for a house in London, and do so before Papa's loan comes due.

I tried to console Mama after her morning quarrel and be ear to her worries but she dismissed me abruptly, only taking comfort from Lousy who is getting far too much attention. Mama was unaccountably nervy seeing me enter the drawing room for our recital last night and later when the two of us were alone was sharp demanding the return of the original ribbons. Parading these emotions on her sleeve may be due to her monthly courses but she is usually not so badly affected. The stomacher is again out of sight in the garderobe but the scarlet ribbons are so well secreted I could not find them. I must investigate this further as I sense it may offer some advantage to me.

Wakeman's journal – 1:00pm

I'm eating broth from downstairs. I should have been sharing it with her. Can't taste it. How strong can I remain? Catherine said she had to find what was left of her marriage. I said: "You have to be whole-hearted in your search." How noble! How deceitful to my heart. I added, "Perhaps nothing of us for . . . six months?" What a stupidly grand gesture! Thoughtless generosity that will bankrupt my life. A separation of six months! I'm giving her up to Eliot.

Her friends had asked over the years, "What about you Catherine? . . . You need to do what's good for you." Will that persuade her now? She's in shock. Nothing is familiar to her, she no longer has way marks.

"I'm not normally like this" she said.

"This isn't normality," I said.

All morning riding along the paths, keeping away from roads and turnpikes. I waited for her with two horses on the far side of town. We followed Holy Brook in silence, gradually emerging into a swirl of agitated words nearing Woolhampton. She shook in terror at going in to the Rowbarge, of being seen. All the ride, listening to her crying, her lament to what has been lost, to her future that she cannot perceive but she knows will be dire. A ride to plead with her, to persuade, to think for her through the blizzard in her head. She has to see her futility in staying put. But she's retreated into herself, frightened. I fear the comfort of the familiar to her, her living stupor with Eliot.

Eliot: What will you do?

Catherine: I will pull up the drawbridge.

Eliot: What will he do?

Catherine: He will do what I ask.

Eliot: How do you know?

Catherine: Because.

I finished it for her, the words she wouldn't say aloud. Because I love you. The words burst out, taking me by surprise. When I first read her desperate note I was pierced by Catherine's agony before feeling my own loss. Did I? Or is that what I want to believe of myself? I want her. She's gone. I hurt fearsomely.

Eliot had asked if she was prepared to give me up. Then another question, in the continual bombardment, before she could answer the first. She'd been slow to reply. Catherine said she didn't want to lie. I cling to that.

Her ten year limbo of marriage is brought to a crisis. Don't let her sink. She is strong. No she isn't, not now. She's with him now. He's corroding her will with tormenting questions, suffocating her with his hurt. She didn't want to lie; keep hold of why, Catherine.

I have to stop. I must go to the Courant, be doing something.

I've packed away the pieces of our vibrancy. "I'm not returning these to you," she stuttered. "You are keeping them safe for me." Do we both believe that? Don't ask. Don't put the sticks together just to see, just to stab my heart to see how much it is hurting. Don't read anything of ours. Put them away. They are only things.

In the trees near the Rowbarge. "We can't go back to get home. We have to go on." Did I or did Catherine say that?

Editor's office, Reading Courant

Frith is not disposed to speaking. A pail of hot ashes sits in his chest and there is a consuming deadness in his head. He moves because he must, without volition. He cannot arrange choices so as to make a decision. He recalls the smallest detail while swathes of time vanish. He doesn't care a jot what Mr Hyde might say to him, he doesn't care a jot about the job. He cares about one thing. He doesn't know what to do about it. He doesn't know. Immobilised in mind and body and that frightens him.

Mr Hyde has been finding it difficult to express what he must. "I am disappointed in you, Mr Frith," he finally says. The editor repeats himself, so uncharacteristically it piles more hot ash in Frith's chest. He has let down another person.

"I estimated you a fine newsman and this has proved the case over these past few months. Your compositing has been quick and accurate and you have an excellent eye for layout. But of late your standards have slipped."

Frith has no answer.

"I took you to be an honourable man, one who knew his duties and his obligations. In this you proved my judgement correct," continues Mr Hyde, addressing the ordered top of his desk. "Until this past two weeks. You have left work supposedly on business errands but I have noted your absences being too long for their singular completion. You have left on some task in the after-lunch and do not returned to work."

Mr Hyde pauses expecting a rebuttal or reason. None comes. "Do you have an explanation why you have only this minute put in an appearance today?"

Frith does not care to share it with Mr Hyde.

"Well?"

"It was a personal matter." Frith is expecting his editor to release him from the Courant, and what would that loss matter by comparison to the loss of Catherine.

"Personal." Mr Hyde peers at Frith. "Do you know what has upset me more than anything about your behaviour? You did not have the confidence in me, or even the decency in yourself, to tell me of your problems. This is not a workhouse. I had thought you could have done that little thing of warning me, and agreeing when to make up the hours. I try to be a reasonable employer. Your absconding without notice hurt me, Mr Frith. I see that surprises you. I know you think I am a nit-picking plodder, but I do have feelings."

"I do not doubt it," says Frith, taken aback by this self disclosure. "My absence this morning was about my feelings, my passions."

Mr Hyde looks a wearied generation older than Frith though under ten years between them. "The article you submitted on the Navigation," says Mr Hyde in his business tone. "It was a well written piece, for its kind. There was a powerful sense of indignation."

Frith is confused by the sudden change of subject, the praise. He cannot put two thoughts together to link into one idea.

"That was the reason the Courant could not publish it, the passion in your beliefs as to what was right and what was wrong. The piece was too affective. Passion may be the whip to set the horses a-gallop but clear-headed control, accompanied by stamina, are required to keep them charging the full course. You were so embroiled that you omitted important voices from your arguments such as the Navigation owners."

"But they are in Newbury," replies Frith, defending this attack on the integrity of his work.

"Had you asked to make the journey, you would have learnt the present policy of the Courant is not to publish articles on the Navigation."

"Therefore, asking would have been a waste of breath."

"For the Courant, yes. For a well-balanced article on a topic in which you are keenly interested it would not. I could have pointed you to outlets other than this newspaper."

Frith cannot put into place what he has just heard from the editor who is staunchly loyal to the newspaper and its proprietors. It makes no sense to him. But this morning he has not the will to bother thinking about the inconsistency.

"I could have suggested additional directions to look, pertinent to the barge's voyage."

The newsman remains silent, bewildered, awaiting an explanation. The editor's hands steeple under his chin to signal the end to what he had to say. "In the long run, passion can whip things into action; but perseverance is needed to achieve the desired result."

"Passion cannot be opened and shut like a stable door," retorts Frith from the pain flailing his insides. "Passion bursts through doors and leaves them swinging on their hinges. Passion drives perseverance."

"On that point we disagree, Mr Frith."

Frith does not know if he believes it himself.

memoirs of Sir George Crockmore

In the mid afternoon Mayor Turner paid me an expected visit. His nag was in a lather, more from the man's corpulence than from the canter. It would be a conservative opinion that declared Mayor Turner alarmed. He was hopping in agitation and I had to send for a brandy to stop him bringing on a sea queasy in me. The Mayor had word of a pitched battle the morrow at Sheffield Mill between navigators and wharf men. My surprise was not in what the man was saying but in how quickly the encounter between the two factions was established and how speedily the Mayor had come to hear of it.

I suggested this trouble was worse in the rumour than in the reality, adding I had primed the Reading Militia to be present as a safeguard. This did not remove his fears, so I proposed that if he expected violence he should make request to the Lord Lieutenant of Surrey to dispatch a troop of his Yeomanry. I had recognised

Sheffield Lock as the opportunity to put into play my cogitations on fanning the latent resentment of Reading folk into a fever and thus terminally abate it with the surgical remedy of the Yeomanry.

To my considerable annoyance Mayor Turner declined this advice, suddenly taking the opposite tack by agreeing with my first supposition the alarming news was hot air. I had not taken into account the vanity of the man. Summoning the Yeomanry would be seen as his lack of authority over his citizens. Using this weakness against him, I postulated his reputation would be ruined should events prove more than the Reading Militia could handle. The Mayor said that was unlikely as the good citizens respected the expedience of the Reading Militia on such occasions. I thought it wise to retire from the argument and let the Mayor follow his course. Alas, I am not in a position to notify the Lord Lieutenant, however discreetly, as the request must be from the injured party.

Before Mayor Turner departed I aired my deliberations that several victims of the house thefts had been my guests at cards on their luckless evening. Further, it would not require much brain to lay in wait each Friday and note the coaches that turned into my drive. The Mayor was impressed by my reasoning. To his enquiry, I named my guests for the following evening, noting Henry Woodroffe was boasting a princely addition to his collection of fob-watches. Mayor Turner declared he would arrange a hidden guard on Woodroffe's house. I reminded him the Reading Militia will be at Sheffield Lock from dawn, remaining there until peace is assured. Thus he agreed to instruct the Aldermen's Watch for the evening task, authorising them to bear arms.

Duke Street, Reading

People flow past Frith as he drifts unseeing down Duke Street towards High Bridge. He had not noticed the afternoon passing. If he tried he could not recall anything he composed. Then again, he has not the will to recall the slightest thing. He snorts at his ostentatious thought of walking straight into the River Kennet and staying on the bottom without trace.

A hand taps his shoulder and he slowly turns into Sarah. Her cheerful face irritates him. "What are you doing here?" he barks.

She tilts her head. "Hello, Mrs Kempster. How are you? I'm well, thank you."

"I was surprised to see you." Frith tries a smile. "Sorry."

"No wonder you've a sore head, what you was putting away last night."

Frith stares without voice, unwilling to correct her. Sarah links her arm through his, and with a tiny nudge they walk, out of step, down the street. "If you'd been to collect your letters you'd know why I'm here. Dragon lets me get up at the crack of dawn, sort the kids, mum, get myself presentable, rush to the Koffee House for her to tell me I'm sacked. Couldn't even give me a lie-in."

Frith utters sympathetic noises but Sarah has a lot more she wants to tell.

"The lad who helps said he'd had an earful of screaming women and he's off to a proper coffee house in London. That set Dragon off worse'n a clamour of rooks coz she thinks the Kennet Koffee House is a cut above London ones. One day of being the 'Dragon de Comptoir' and she'll have me back. You don't see if I'm right."

"There's always someone else," says Frith ruefully.

"Not with my know-how of getting gentlemen to spend more of their cash. Learned that working in the Saracen's. Dragon'll not take a tenth what I do when I'm giving them some sweet talk."

"You're convinced Mrs Middleton is desperate for you?"

"Sure as horses pull carts."

On the crown of High Bridge, Sarah lightly asks, "You'll be asking after you friend Master Nicholas?"

"How is Nicholas?" asks Frith dutifully and ashamedly.

"He's turned right moody these days. Glum, he was, hearing that cussed barge was grounded and rotting. Dragon gave him a full face burn for not being pleased with the news. Silly boy. Do you men never learn?"

"No Sarah, we never do. Especially when it comes to women."

"No more letters?" asks Sarah tenderly.

Frith does not answer. They stroll along Kennetside in silence. Sarah gives Frith's arm a tiny squeeze.

"Shame, Mr Frith. You were so perky after you read them, almost human you were. What I say is there's no point crying over spilt milk, not for long anyway. What's meant to be's meant to be, even if it ain't right. Take my sodding Thomas. Took off when my lad was four and little Bron was two. Now that ain't right in anyone's book, kids should bind you. Then again, marriage isn't all its cracked up to be. Marriage is just like a pig in a poke. You never know who you're in for till you've tried it, and then it's too late. Like buying cake from Matthew Preston. When you bite into it you find it was last week's. The Aldermen's Watch should have him up before Judge Crockmore. And those navigators. You know they've taken to throwing bricks and shit at the Kennetmouth farms. Not farm shit either. And stomping their boots all over the kitchen gardens. Forget I said the Watch – it took four of 'em just to nab little Dorothy Clay. She hadn't eaten for three days and they done her for stealing a bit of Preston's stale bread. She won't survive the crossing to the Indies. First puff of wind and she'll be blown overboard."

Pieces of what Sarah has been saying bounce round Frith's head: what's meant to be, Nicholas, the Kennetmouth farms. "She'll be chained below decks," he says, with a shiver from memory of his time in Bristol. "The girl will be ravaged by every prisoner that can get to her. They'll have to wait their turn until the crew have plundered the human cargo. If that doesn't kill her, starvation or ship fever will. It'd have been merciful to have hanged her."

"I see the Mr Frith we know is back with us again," says Sarah, reaching into her pocket. "Wish me luck. Here, I rescued this for you before I was chucked out this morning."

Frith's blood drains from his face seeing the phantom envelope. He doesn't notice Sarah leave.

Catherine's third note of Wednesday 21st September

I agree, this is a good way to work. Were you asking me? Do you want a progress report? I hated leaving you on Tuesday. I've soaked this note with my perfume to torture you because you're not with me.

I think our work is going well. We had to start somewhere and it's very hard to start. So we have started by drawing on themes from our past, and pieces perhaps already finished. We have used them to build a frame of familiarity. Did I write that? How smug! Drawing bits of our personal maps, not running blind into a wood. It's hard to make a huge personal investment in two seconds. We could sketch our working relationship in charcoal, then blend-out the edges. This is as I see it, happening in a very unwitting way.

I could see that I wasn't going to be bullied by you. I saw you had purposeful impatience and eagerness. Do you like that, Quillman? I can relax when I take part in creativity with you. I am so enjoying the playfulness, a sort of intense and precise recklessness. I can't describe this physical feeling of creativity. It is physical. Then, I'm a sensual person. That's what comes from being not so good at using words – vivid sensuality!

Anyway, I would rather let this run on a little toward the picture-with-words idea, and maybe more plaster pieces later, with other bits, a collage. What have you done with your cast? I dare not write what I've done with your hand! It was creative in its way.

You're right that in time we can look back at our pieces and perhaps then see a theme, rather than be driven by an imposed theme. Things will emerge and we will remain alert and responsive. I don't want to fake it and produce something I know I can do without raising a drop of perspiration. I'm talking work! Does this make sense?

Oh Quillman! What have I done to you? Are you wasting away? How much thinner are you? Do I have to be extra careful not to crush you now? It's such early days. You don't have to feel afraid. Think how cross I'll be if you found a raven-haired, chestnut-eyed quill-cutter to fall in love with. Half my age and half the bother! And with pert breasts.

The husband thing. Some difficulty there. It's sad. I've been making the effort for so long I've run out of energy. There is nothing more I can do. My attempts . . . anyway. He has been the reason, I suppose, for the thinking about myself that I wrote about. It was not deliberate, I thought, only a way of redrawing who I am, scrawling myself.

So, I didn't plan this. If I had wanted to find this, I wouldn't have known where to look. I am rather shocked by whatever it is between us. This tenderness, among other things, is very moving. Aside from that comforting warmth you are such a furnace for me that my body goes . . . never mind!

Wakeman's journal – 8:00pm

At the Rowbarge she asked: "What if I'd turned up on your doorstep at midnight?"

"I tried willing you to come. I stayed awake."

"We both had fantasies about all kinds of outcomes."

She knows my dreams are her dreams.

If she stays with Eliot all that it is gone. The futility, the waste. Damn! He's using her caring nature to shackle her to the marriage. She props up his self-doubt and is squashed into anonymity. Be strong Catherine, for yourself.

Listen to your closest friends: "What about you, Catherine?"

Listen to me: "What about us?"

Damn it! "What about me?"

Scared to leave the Anglers tonight in case she needs me. In case she comes here. Oh, what happy problems that would bring. If she did, she'd wait. I ought to go out. I do not want be with myself. Out, to not think. But I can't pretend happy. And this is a private pain. No one will know of it, no one will ever know of her-and-me. I gave my solemn promise to protect her name while she decides. After she decides? Oh Zitkala, not that. What is there to decide? It is so obvious. It was destined to happen, we were meant to be. The cage was killing her spirit and she knew it. But we needed longer to build our foundation.

A crowded path

A steaming infusion greeted Gabriel White and the navvies when they dismounted from two and three a horse near the listing Barge Jeannie. Lynn handed round the mugs filled with nettle tea, instructing the men they would have to share them. In her turn Lynn was told bluntly to stay with her Dad. She was glad of the excuse to get out of helping at the weir, not wanting to break her promise to Mr Hore whom she believed would do something. Also, her Dad was worse. He had a soaring temperature and forehead constantly damp with perspiration. His wounds were not drying and most worrying, he did not have the will to get off his bunk.

Gabriel lead the score of navvies to the weir. He didn't know what he was going to do with so many but every one of his team had insisted on helping Lynn. The weir was missing eight central paddles through which gap the water now sedately ran into a lake that stretched the half mile to Sheffield Bottom. The towing path from Reading ran along a spit of land between the new Cut parallel to the winding river, with the unoccupied mill standing astride this neck of land. A search of the buildings had produced just one new paddle so Gabriel knew the miller hadn't squirrelled them away. Gabriel sent the men back to the weir to thoroughly search the shrubbery, reasoning the vandals were unlikely to carry off the heavy timbers. Repairing broken paddles was easier and quicker than fashioning new ones.

He was tossing over the idea of damming the weir with grain sacks filled with mud and be blowed to the miller, when he recognised from down the towing path the sound of many feet and the level mutter from a throng of voices.

A band of determined men were striding along the path. Most were carrying some form of weapon improvised from their daily life: staves, shovels, pitchforks, two sickles that Gabriel could see from his vantage on top of the weir. He reckoned there were over fifty men. The navvies could get to their horses and be away in time but what would happen to Lynn and Peter. He picked five navvies to stay at the weir and grouped the rest at the planking that carried the towing path across the culvert.

"We've no quarrel with you," said Gabriel, firmly. "We're here to mend the weir."

"Maybe so," said a solid wharf man at the front. "But we have quarrel with you and we're gonna fix you." A swell of support rose round him. "You clod-shifters is doing us from our jobs."

"What about th' miller?" asked Gabriel, pointing to the weir. "Your handiwork's done him from his job."

"How come?"

"Busting his weir."

"Weren't us. It's you pieces of shit we've come to flush away."

"The weir bust itself, did it?" Gabriel felt a gentle prod in his back and grasped the sturdy bough handed to him. His men behind him had been busy. "Ain't got the guts to admit what you done?"

"Calling us cowards? Damn all navvies," said the wharf man rallying his mob. "You're scum." Cries of scum echoed after him, then of thieves, child snatchers, house torchers and every crime they could think of.

"We ain't got time for any of that nonsense," said Gabriel trying to deflect their fury. "We're breaking our backs for fifteen hours a day."

Out of sight from the confrontation Lynn had stepped on to the bank by Barge Jeannie to sit down after applying a fresh poultice to her Dad. She found the tilt of the barge unsettling. It was stable but what the mind can reason the gut often refuses to accept. Like Nicholas Middleton. She'd seen the last of him and good riddance. Voices of challenge carried to her from the weir and her stomach lurched.

Gabriel continued to argue his case. "Thieving? We're too busy digging mud."

"Digging our graves," answered the lead wharf man. Other joined in. "Graves for our starving little 'uns." "Taking away our jobs." "Taking our women." The clamour rose. The Reading men were firing up themselves to attack. Gabriel tightened his grip on the bough behind him.

Lynn climbed the rise to the lock to see what was happening at the weir. Cresting the mound she saw the too familiar ugliness of Captain Hawker sprawled along the boom of the head gates. Sergeant Quinn with half a dozen Militia men lounged nearby.

Lynn was inflamed. She broke into a run. "Why're you sitting here? Can't you hear there's trouble at the weir." Hawker stood. Lynn raced on. "You're supposed to be peacekeepers. Get in the middle of that lot," she shouted into his face pointing back to the weir.

Hawker grabbed Lynn's arm and spun her round him. "You're going in the middle of that," he snarled, releasing her down the turf slope towards the lock chamber. Lynn screamed and grabbed for the first thing to stop her slide, hooking her hand through the leather cross-sash of Hawker's scabbard. The Militia leader's neck was yanked sideways pulling him off-balance. The two tumbled and slid down the wet turf, over the edge and splashed into the timber-lined chamber.

Gabriel heard the scream. The navvies turned as one and started running towards Barge Jeannie. A great cheer lifted from the wharf men who they set off in pursuit with weapons ready.

After he hit the water Hawker yelled in panic until his mouth filled with the brown slurry. He wildly flailed his arms, incoherently cursing Quinn to rescue him as he desperately scrabbled for anything to cling to.

"Stand up you silly man," Lynn smirked. "It's not five feet deep. Unless your dancing is digging a trench."

Quinn and the others broke into laughter when Hawker stopped and stood chest high in the water. They ceased laughing the instant they saw the wrath blazing from his eyes. Lynn knew she had to get out of the chamber before Hawker got to her. Her skirt was heavy in the water and her feet slipped on the mud. She thrashed towards the head gate with its ladder. She was two strides away when Hawker pincered her wrist in a grip tight enough to break every bone.

"Boss!" Quinn yelled from above them.

"Captain!" snapped Hawker.

"Captain. There's a gang of navvies coming."

"Best let me go." Lynn winced at the tightened grip.

"They's bent on trouble. We gotta go," came the receding voice from above.

"Stay put!" commanded Hawker. "Shoot 'em if you have to." Hawker pulled Lynn away from the ladder. "Stop 'em any ways you can till I gets out." A pistol shot echoed round the chamber as he scrambled up the ladder.

The navvies had stopped at the crest of the lock. Gabriel saw Lynn's bedraggled hair appear over the edge. "Are you all right, Miss?" he called.

"Shut up," snapped Hawker dripping into a pool of water round his boots. He could see the navvies' faces hardening at the same instant remembering his pistols had taken a soaking. Before he could reach for his broadsword he heard the victory whoops of the chasing wharf men. Gabriel and Lee looked at the Militia with several pistols among them, then back at the mob of armed Reading wharf men. Those at the front had slowed but the pressure of bodies behind kept edging them forwards.

Two shots went over their heads.

"You can all stay exactly where you are," commanded Hawker. He had spotted some tethered horses and was scheming how to get himself away and let the two mobs fight it out. "The rest of my men will be here any minute," he lied. He heard a cantering horse behind him. The only coincidences he had ever known turned out bad for him. He wheeled, hand on sword.

"Good morning, Mister Mayor," said Captain Hawker.

Robert Turner surprised himself that morning. He stood on the lock gate and addressed the truculent mob and the incensed navvies. He knew it wasn't great oratory but it was effective. First he sympathised with his Reading citizens then with the navvies going about their work. He reminded them all of the Act of Parliament that had enabled the Kennet Navigation to come about and had accorded boats the right of passage. It was the law of England.

Damaging the weir was a criminal act and it had to be repaired. The pivotal moment was when the Mayor threatened to read the new Riot Act. He told his audience it would undoubtedly bring the Lord Lieutenant of Surrey's Yeomanry from Guildford who would cart many of those present to gaol. While the Riot Act was in force he reminded them, every inn and tavern in the town would be closed. That was enough and the Reading men dispersed, grumbling their way back along the towing path.

"What happened to the girl?" the Mayor asked Hawker.

"Fell in the lock," said the Captain calmly. "I jumped in to save her."

"Brave fellow," said the Mayor. "Altogether an excellent day's work. It could have been very nasty but for your intervention."

"Thank you, Mister Mayor. We do our best. Got information there'd be trouble so we had to get here fast." Captain Hawker casually indicated the tethered horses, noting the Mayor counting them. "Rest of my troop's in hiding, for the surprise should they be called on."

"Tactics. Very good, Captain."

"What with having to pay for information, a set of clothes, the horses and you know these thieving ostlers treble the cost for a nag when they sees you're in need."

"I understand. Put in your claim to Sir George and I will vouch-safe it."

The edge was taken from Hawker's pecuniary cheerfulness spotting Lynn walking with the navvies back to Barge Jeannie. Something Sergeant Quinn had mentioned gave him a distasteful feeling he'd been duped by the little bitch at Southcote Cut over that Jacobite carrion-feed. Now this humiliation in the lock. Captain Teon Hawker could be very patient when revenge is the target.

from Mistress Olivia's diary

At breakfast I was upbraided for staring slack-jawed. It was Mama's fault for she was doing nothing but coo and fawn to Papa on his return from Sheffield Lock. Papa believed her flattery was genuine and snuffled like a lapdog. She said Papa is the hero of the town using many more words than I can bother to write here. Marry-come! All this simpering and adoration only one day after she evicted him from their bed chamber.

It took the maid but five minutes to return Papa's belongings from the guest room. This reinstatement was for no giving of ground by Papa that I could see. The eviction from her bed was a token by Mama and I begin to see the game she plays. At one time she is Madam Wronged and the next she is Lady Loving such that Papa does not know if he faces forwards or backwards.

By the dessert Mama's unctuous concern had turned to the danger to which Papa had exposed himself and the calamity it would be to Mama, to his daughters and especially to young Robert Junior had he been injured or . . . She let her voice trail away. The scene was so tenderly sweet I near sicked up my custard pudding. Papa was so smitten by the solicitude he held her close to his chest and for once Mama did not break from it.

I saw Papa put some guinea coins in Mama's hand saying it was a little extra pin-money to spend on herself and Podgy, upon whom he dotes far too much though he be the son. Mama does not need telling twice to spend money and departed the house quicker than it takes to pull the drawstring of a purse. She instructed me to look after Lousy and Podgy to which I replied that was impossible as I had my dance instruction. The maid was therefore redirected from her household duties for the afternoon leaving me to reflect upon the events of the past two days. I had to concede Mama has scored a victory towards her new house. Mama has regained Papa's adoration such that she can do no wrong.

Wakeman's journal – 11:00am

My anxiety did not lift until we walked round the lake. Catherine's hung over her like a noose, a noose that was Eliot's halter on her. The still water of the lake heard the first serious talking of what we would do in these next days, next weeks. Please not months. Impulsively I jumped in front of her, took a comic pose. She found her smile and stepped into my arms. Lips on lips. Instinct.

She eased me away. "That is all very well, but could you do it properly?" Her noose was fraying, light coming into her eyes. Leaning against a tree we kissed our passion, a mindless few minutes intense touch. Then she squatted in the bushes. The thankful return of a little normality.

A smaller craft

Lynn had changed into her last smock. One was sodden with mud from the lock, one reeked of Hermond and Adam's liniments, the third was wherever Fergus had discarded it. She found Gabriel studying the weir.

"We could dam it," he said. "Owner 'll squawk before level's up an inch."

"We can not upset the gentleman landowner," said Lynn, trying to mimic Mr Devereaux and gesticulating across the Cut. She noticed a small boat approaching from downstream. The steady rhythm of the rower reminded her of someone. As the boat drew near she hailed to Adam.

He had seen the Reading men pass Kiln Lane like a long hedgehog bristling with pitchforks and indignation. "I couldn't leave my bricks to chase a load of brick-heads," he joked, after enquiring of Lynn and her dad. "This boat belongs at Aldermaston Wharf. Could you take it when you get going? Feel free to make what use of it you can."

Lynn didn't believe the lightening boat had any connection with Aldermaston but she went along with Adam's insouciant help. Off-loading part of Barge Jeannie's cargo would lessen her draught and make unsticking from the mud more likely. They could get under way sooner and Lynn knew that was Adam's unspoken offer. Gabriel said the men would transfer some of the cargo to the light-ening boat after they'd exhausted the hunt for the paddles. Staunching the weir was the priority because Barge Jeannie wasn't going anywhere without water, neither part-laden nor empty.

A few minutes later there was a shout of jubilation. An undam-aged paddle had been found. It indicated the other paddles had been neither carted off nor destroyed. The men scoured all round the area but no more of the six-foot timbers turned up.

"That's two," reported Gabriel to Lynn, turning his attention to figuring the best way of getting a cauldron of coal out of the barge's hold and lowered onto the lightening boat. "Not enough."

"I'd have expected them to be dumped together," said Adam.

"We've near uprooted every bush, except those under the lake," said a navvy. "Before you ask, a couple went in the water but no joy," added a second.

"They would float," said Lynn thoughtfully. "The rush from the broken weir would carry them to the other side."

Gabriel's face fell. "That's a big lake and the far side is sore overgrown. Mr Hore can't cover for us being away too long."

Lynn was surprised to learn Mr Hore knew about his workers' expedition and satisfied to realise she had rightly judged the man's integrity. "Can you stay a little longer?" she asked Gabriel. "If your men can lift Adam's boat onto the lake it'll follow the current and we'll easily see anything washed to the other side from the water."

"A good job we didn't rush to unship your cargo," said Adam with a smile.

"The day is getting better by the minute," said Lyn registering the sun on her face.

"Don't count your paddles too soon," said Gabriel not convinced by Lynn's plan.

They found five paddles in short time. Three navvies dammed the remaining open flute of the weir while the rest off-loaded every sack they could get their hands on: salt, raisins, beans, tobacco and more salt.

"I suggest you stay clear of rough water," said Adam, looking how low his boat sat in the water. "We don't want the Kennet Navigation turned into a salty soup."

"I'm praying I can stay clear of rough water," replied Lynn. "I don't want us turned into soup."

The navvies rode off with promises of meeting upstream. Lynn didn't need telling it would be a long time before the pound filled. What if Jeannie was stuck fast in the mud? Being lighter lessened that risk. Adam and the navvies had asked nothing of her for their help and kindness. She watched them part their separate ways, her heart open with gratitude.

Lynn turned her attention to her dad. Through the hours of the day she nursed him as best she could, pushing from her mind the black thought of what fever could hold her ever healthy Dad so tenaciously in its clutch.

Wakeman's journal – noon

Catherine wasn't there. I stalked the disused Lodden Court Estate for an hour, worrying, fretting, fearing the bad then worse. Driving myself to the horizon of sanity. Was I at the right place? I checked her note every half minute. Does she think somewhere else is where I believe this to be? Can she not face me? Has Eliot stopped her? Have I missed her? Am I at the correct place? Round and round.

She galloped up, scared, hot from the riding, hair bedraggled, rigid grin seeing me, hands trembling. So beautiful. I held her, deep breaths against my chest, her body contoured to me, warm breath on my neck. We walked. Gave her brandy from my pouch. Irrelevant talk, her friends, sister. Not us. The gravel crunching under my boots. Then it came. Along with tears.

She had ridden to Yedda's Herbary north of the town. My alarm it was for a potion to take her forever from her misery. Stupid. She's strong. She was. Will be. Has to be. By Lodden Lake she produced a small parcel. White poplar bark mashed with a mule's kidney. Eaten, washed down. She nearly vomited, forced it down, face staring across the unruffled water. Another packet held a paste of alkanet to smear inside her.

Eliot forced her last night. "What are you trying to prove?" she'd asked. Years of never touching her then Bastard rapes his wife. He cried afterwards. The hypocrite begged forgiveness through his sham tears. "I can understand why he did it," she told me.

I don't want her to understand.

"It's about possession," she said.

Exactly! She's a thing to him, to the Bastard. To Erebus – that's who he is. I want her to feel violated by this Erebus, this personification of darkness, for her to hate the physical abuse. Not be understanding and forgiving. She saw my anger, and I was the second man in half a day she had to calm. Damn me. We walked round the lake, sat straddled a fallen tree trunk, facing, talking about other things.

The knowledge of what Erebus had done to this woman burned like acid. I wanted to touch her with tenderness. Knees to knees I lifted her skirt, placed my hand on her inner thigh. Couldn't read her look. Slid my hand, turned it, cupped her in my palm, let my fingers gently stroke her, soothing her intimately. She let me, passively, allowing this for me. Suddenly an awful thought. Was this my possessiveness? Was I another man violating her? She hooked her legs over mine, opening herself more to me, then unfastened me and her hand curled round my cock.

She rode off in a flurry of fear for what she was returning to, where she might have been when asked. Erebus questions her about every minute she is out of his sight. I wanted her to say, "I've been for a potion to kill the semen you forced into me." She won't. Nothing resolved, only a small piece of my world reassured. Missing her is intense.

A fruitful visit

Lynn looked out through the cabin door. "The day has suddenly got a lot worse," she said to her sleeping Dad.

"Good day, Mistress Lynn," hailed Nicholas from the towing path.

"Hush!" she hissed. "You're too late for the fight. Or was it your plan to be there but miss it?"

"I've brought back your clothes," said Nicholas ignoring her sharpness and speaking quietly.

"You can leave them there. Goodbye."

"Do you realise what I did for you and that Jacobite?"

"What you did for yourself. You couldn't get away fast enough."

"That was a long, slow walk with a traitor."

"I didn't ask you to come a-calling."

"I came to see how you were," said Nicholas, calmly.

"You said you decided to go for a walk."

"Today."

"We're fine. Just giving Barge Jeannie a day's rest on the bottom of the river."

"Is your father better?" whispered Nicholas.

"He will be when you've gone."

"Look, I heard you were grounded —"

"Two days after everyone else in your poxed town. I thought your Kennet Koffee House was the sewer for all the nasty news."

"And came to see how you —"

"Was that after breakfast with Mistress Olivia?"

"If you must know, I haven't seen Mistress Olivia all day."

"I don't want to know," said Lynn huffily, annoyed that she was a little bit pleased with the news. "And now you've paid your respects you can enjoy your walk home."

"Very well, but I'm not carrying this lot all the way back again." Nicholas slid a haversack from his shoulder and with a flourish tipped the contents over the deck. At Lynn's feet were bread, smoked meats, a few ounces of cheese, potatoes and turnips, a pigeon, olives, two small cakes, a bag of dried currants and two round reddish things that Lynn vaguely recognised.

"You can keep your food," she snapped, and kneeled to collect up the items but was soon dropping as many as she gathered. Angry frustration had swelled in her. She hurled one of the soft round things at Nicholas. "Go away!"

Nicholas caught it. "This is for your Dad. There's an idea about that if a person eats one of these oranges they'll recover from London Fever."

"He doesn't have the plague!" shouted Lynn. She glanced in terror she had woken her Dad.

"I didn't mean he had," blurted Nicholas. "Prevention. That's what I meant."

"How could he have London Fever? No one comes near us. He doesn't have it." Lynn stopped still with her fear.

Nicholas climbed on board and began picking up the food. When he had gathered it all into the haversack he noticed Lynn still squatting motionless, her back to him. He bent down, lifted and turned her, held her, soothed her shudders. "I'm sure he doesn't. Like you say, how could he have caught it? It's just . . . a lot of little things . . . a cold, the stoning." His voice trailed off.

Lynn buried her red eyes in Nicholas's chest so he wouldn't see. She wanted him to go away and take her confusion with him. She liked being held by him, feeling the rise and fall of his chest. She could visualise the smooth features of his face. Lynn pushed away Mistress Olivia's betrothed. What would he want with her, plain, big, graceless? Oh yes, one thing.

"I need to check Dad." Nicholas followed her into the cabin. "Thank you for the food," she said. "We have plenty. We don't want your alms."

"I don't want you dead."

The rapid reply was clearly the first time he'd spoken to her when he hadn't thought out what he wanted to say. Lynn believed he meant it.

"When was the last time you ate a proper meal?" he asked. He waited for a reply. "If you have to think about it that much it was too long ago. Your Dad's deep asleep. You and I are having lunch over in Theale Meadows. Find something to sit on."

Lynn found herself pleased someone else was saying what was to be done. She realised the burden she'd assumed since her dad had been ill. Since her first step yesterday morning to Colthrop, instead of it being her Dad going for help, she had been making all the decisions.

These thoughts came to Lynn as the two were walking from Barge Jeannie over the new swing bridge and up the lane that led to the small hamlet of Theale on the north of the river. They passed Hay Fields farmhouse and soon came to Holy Brook, more a small river than a brook thought Lynn. They ambled through a lush meadow beside the clear flashing water. The sun had dried Lynn's hair to an unsightly mess. Nicholas had explained the ploughed field on the other side of the lane was Withy Farm where the Clemson's didn't bother anybody and didn't like anybody bothering them.

When they settled on the grass Nicholas produced a bottle of cider from the inside pocket of his jacket, but he had nothing about him with which to get past the cork stopper.

"One of us will have to go back to the barge," said Nicholas, making no move to stand up from the tarpaulin Lynn had laid out for them.

"It wasn't me who forgot a cork-puller," said Lynn.

"If I wake your father searching for one he'll get an awful shock, thinking I'm robbing him."

"Not half the shock you'll get if he thinks you are."

Nicholas sat for a while. "Oh, very well."

He was thirty yards from her when she called out. "Look what I've found in my pocket." She held up a small piece of horn into which was folded a blade and along the other side a thin awl.

"You little tyke," he shouted pacing back to her. "You knew you had that all along."

"It's Hermond's. He got it for his twenty-fifth birthday. I only look after it for him."

"Give it here," said Nicholas, grabbing playfully.

"You have to promise not to break it." Lynn stepped out of reach.

"I promise." He lunged.

"And to give it back." She dodged his hand.

"I've had enough of this," said Nicholas turning back to the tarpaulin. "If you want some cider stop playing silly games."

It was the first light-heartedness Lynn had enjoyed for weeks, She was irritated Nicholas had so quickly ended it. She returned to his stiff back on the tarpaulin. He whipped round and grabbed her wrist before she knew what was happening.

"Got you!" he exclaimed.

Lynn cried out. He let go sharply, then gently pushed back the sleeve to see the finger-shape bruises round her wrist.

"Hawker," said Lynn.

Nicholas put his lips to the bruising, then holding her arm he eased her to the grass and delicately stroked his fingers down her forearm across her hand and back again. Lynn told him about the episode in the lock He cupped her arm and continued stroking with his palms. His hands were soft. She took a quick glance at his face that was absorbed in what he was doing. What does he make of my labourer's paws, Lynn asked herself. Nicholas was holding her hand in both his. He looked her straight in the eye.

"Lynn. You are quite remarkable."

Her body froze yet her heart was thumping. No one had said that to her. Her hand was in a furnace but she wanted to leave it there. She had stopped breathing.

"Maybe, but I still need to eat." She saw his gorgeous smile and wanted to lean into it. Nicholas helped her to her feet. She had been foolish. An ox can be remarkable in its way.

Nicholas prised the cork from the bottle while Lynn laid out the food. They drank from the unmarked bottle of last autumn's home fermentation. Jelly-knee strong thought Lynn, then didn't think about it any more. They ate and drank and ate. She spat out the orange until Nicholas explained she was supposed to eat the inside not the skin. Nicholas peeled the second orange and magically split the inside into fleshy crescents that he pushed between her giggling lips. She held one by her teeth its end sticking out like a cat's tongue. He bent over her to bite it in half and she was being kissed. Orange kisses.

She wanted to pull him down into her mouth. Nicholas rolled on top of her and hugged himself to her. Sighs slid out of Lynn's mouth between meshing lips. Her whole body was calling for him. Nothing else mattered but for this rapture to continue. Don't stop. Lynn held Nicholas tight against her. They did a complete roll across the grass. One hand found her breast, caressed, pulped, began teasing her nipple. She felt his other hand reach for the hem of her skirt and she eased her leg a little for him. Her groin yearned for him to touch her. Somewhere in her head she knew she should not let him. I don't want you dead, he'd said. She believed. He was the harbour after years in the foggy estuary. They had nothing in common. I don't want you dead. She angled her hips for his hand. Lynn floated into the blue sky, she expanded into the clouds with nothing stopping her.

Suddenly the meadow's hard ground was pressing her back, short grass stalks sticking into her flesh.

Nicholas had abruptly rolled off her. His hand still clasped hers, flesh in lifeless flesh. Lynn wanted to ask him what was the matter but she didn't want to hear the reason. She would have given herself to him, had wanted to. Would she? She didn't know. When he had her skirt above her hips and he unbuttoned himself would her upbringing have made her tell him no. Her skirt above her hips, the idea sent a shiver thrill up to her chest even then, in the eerie silence, side by side. Why didn't he say something? Lynn's head was whirling. There was a rising anger at his silence mixed with apprehension filling the emptiness of her draining body. She had mistaken him. He had seen how ugly she was.

Nicholas spoke. "I couldn't. Not with you."

Lynn shut her eyes squashing back tears. She had an urge to punch him and punch him again until her fists hurt more than her heart. Her leg twitched involuntarily from her desperation to flee back to the barge, from still wanting to feel his touch.

"I want it to be right with you," he said at last. "This isn't."

He was lying to make her feel better. He was being sincere. He said it to make himself feel better, not guilty.

"There's something I have to resolve first. Then . . ."

She knew immediately what it was. Outrage at him flashed through her for bringing Mistress Olivia into their meadow. Then a fury-jolt and Lynn felt the knot tighten. The pretty scorpion in Reading was why she had been floated high then dumped back on the ground. Nicholas being honourable be damned. Lynn had wanted him. He must have sensed that. This meadow was right with her. Damn Mistress Olivia for humiliating her.

They lay for some minutes and Lynn's hand slowly revived its receptiveness to the touch of Nicholas's. At one point in their lunch Nicholas had stretched out and plucked a buttercup, holding it first under his chin then under hers and pronouncing, "We both like the same thing." He had given her the single yellow cup on its thin stalk.

Lynn pulled the flower from her smock. "The buttercup closes its petals when the sun leaves the sky." Immediately she wished she hadn't said it. She saw the hurt in Nicholas's eyes. He had taken it wrongly. Nicholas leaned across and gave her a gentle kiss on the lips.

Lynn lay on the tarpaulin picturing Nicholas as he walked away. She was too exhausted to work out what truth there was in anything he had said, if his leaving made her happy or made her sad.

Wakeman's journal – 4:00pm

I was filled with future hope from Lodden Court, believing in that time with her there was nothing else in the world. Now Catherine is drawn back into another life, which I choose to believe is a mire for her. I must to pull back from tearing myself apart, or from acting rashly and destroying any hope.

"I have to clear up my mess." Did that mean she's going to continue in it? Please no.

"It'll be a lot of work with Eliot and I'm not sure I want to do it." Then don't. I didn't say. Can I keep a lifeline for her?

"I need to make a decision about Eliot. Then we can decide about us." My practical woman. Have faith in intuition. I beg you.

from Mistress Olivia's diary

I adore visiting the Kennet Koffee House and have no qualms about entering a gentleman's place for it is merely the business of my unlikely-to-be-mother-in-law. Mrs Middle-gone's coffee shop is a tawdry imitation of those I have seen in London with much inferior customer. Upon entering, the consternation on the face of Mrs Middle-gone lifts my heart and I smile at her agonized predicament. The foolish lump thinks I smile in fondness for her and this adds to the delight.

Today she washed the floor with her tears and polished it with her hot wails of lament. Her grovelling over the disgraceful conduct of her shameful son was pathetic, making me the more resolved to ridicule her. No sooner had the thought occurred than I saw a chance with Mrs Middle-gone's pointless remark about some ragged cut of cloth. I asked what she planned to wear for the

Forbury Fair and soon we were ascending to her dressing room, though henceforth I will call it the distressing room so offensive to the eye was its décor and contents.

I told Mrs Middle-gone I would be truthfully blunt. She had to make the most of what little Our Lord had given her for a figure. The "little" being of contour not of volume for the woman is twin to the sacks of goods in the shop, shapeless and short.

Her garderobe displayed her ignorance of fashion but had some items useful to my design. I ordered her to cut the top from a heavily brocaded dark maroon dress and sew it to the skirt of a cream coloured light linen with a cross-hatch pattern. I explained this, with the broad belt I had in mind to hang loosely across her belly, would have the effect to an observer of splitting her body in north and south to make her shortness appear not as such. (She would resemble a garish dumpling for that is my plan for this odious, pompous ignoramus who is mother of a hurtful son.) Thus I advised a dark choker, if she can find any neck in the folds of fat and chins. To show off her tiny ears I suggested she buy the biggest earrings in town.

It was a shame the maroon dress had not a stand-up collar to heighten the effect of choker and earrings but the garment was tight fitting and I opined an extra pair of darts and double lace edging could make her bosom outstanding as is the London fashion. (For bawds in the alleys and galleons under full topsails in the river.) She will cut short the sleeves to slightly above the broadest part of her arms thus displaying their magnificent form. (Her forearms are such she could kill a cow by strangulation alone.) Mrs Middle-gone flourishes her boorishness with a ring on every stubby finger and I said larger pieces of her coloured glass would heighten the effect.

Finally, she is to buy the highest pair of shoes she can find, for this is all the rage and will increase her height. (And increase the spectacle of dumpiness.) She was concerned they would cause her to wobble. That was the intention I said, so men do a double-look. (Before they double-over with laughter.) I urged the higher the shoe the better to keep her attire immaculate as I expected Forbury field would be sodden. (With providence the mud will add a side-slip to her wobble. I fear for the stalls at the Fair when her buttocks start swaying like a pair of loose-roped hogshead.)

Satisfied with my work I departed the Kennet Koffee House looking forward in one respect to the morrow and the sight to be seen at the Fair. Another will be witnessing Master Nicholas shrivelling with eyes popping in aghast amazement at his mater. These are small relief from my other discomforts. Mama has been tardy and not severe with the seamstress over my dress. In addition she has been astute in her management of Papa's goodwill towards her.

Kennetside

The stone plops into the Kennet. Frith watches the ripples, trying to spot where he can no longer see the outermost ring.

"Kicking stones is for kids, Mr Frith," chides Sarah with a smile. She keeps a watchful eye back into the Koffee House.

"Kicking myself," Frith replies gloomily. "Into the river." There is another small splash.

"Wanna hand?" asks Sarah. It raises no response. "Coming in for a coffee?"

"You don't drink the 'nasty bitter muck' I notice."

"I serve it." Sarah waits a moment. "I told you yesterday I'd get my job back. That's where I was headed when I met you."

"Well done. I suppose I'd better be heading to the Courant." A flat stone skitters across the flagstones.

"You should 've been in here earlier. That'd have cheered you. We had the older Beale girl, from Pingle Farm, strut in. Bold as brass right into the Koffee House. Mind, she's common as muck and wouldn't know about not stepping into the place. Pretty thing, but showing far too much of herself out of her smock, if you ask me. Dragon lumbers forwards, with maiming in her mind, when the girl slides two sovereigns from her tiny wrist-purse and asks for eight ounces of ground coffee and two cakes of chocolate. You could hear Dragon's claws scratching along the floorboards at the glint of gold. I learns this Penny has a position up at Southcote Hall and has mighty high opinions of herself. 'I see you noticed my lace cuffs,' she says, by way of casual conversation that's about as casual as smack round the head with a frying pan. 'Sir likes me to wear 'em.' I reckons either she's had her hand in Sir George's strongbox or he's had his finger in hers."

"You have a salacious mind, Sarah," says Frith mildly.

"Have I?" There is a questioning pride. "Well that's more mind than she's got, her thinking how she's special and Sir George is gonna look after her."

"He might. I heard he's childless," says Frith, absently.

"He got through three wives coz none of 'em gave him a son. Perhaps he reckons if she don't breed a farm girl will be easier to get rid of, like a farm animal."

"And a slanderous tongue," says Frith, tilting his head with raised eyebrows in caution. He has stopped kicking stones.

"My tongue's nothing like as cutting as the next young madam. The Koffee House was more like a ladies' parlour this morning. Dragon explains to Mistress Olivia that Master Nicholas is such a kind boy, a thoughtful boy, and he's gone out to help a friend. Dragon goes on like this for a couple of hours all the time making herself a bigger and bigger fool. Mistress Oily very quietly asks, 'Would this friend be a trollop, massive as a sow and a flabby face like the back-end of a barge?' She sounded just like her mother in full venom, dripping the poison tiny drop by drop onto the cut. 'Tell your son I will be second to no woman, especially a harlot of contemptible breeding. He will call on me, if it is me he desires, to offer to escort to Forbury Fair. I might accept his plea, or I might not.' What happened then had me in stitches but for it being so mortifying. Dragon started begging. You'd be amazed what Master Nicholas has promised to do and him not there to know it."

Frith is amused by the picture in his head. "Did that placate Mistress Olivia?"

"Nothing could stop Dragon whining on. 'When you become a wife you'll realise we women have a ragged cut of the cloth.' Before you can crush a coffee bean Dragon's leading Mistress Oily upstairs to get the girl's advice on what to wear to the Fair. You could have knocked me over with a foreparte. I'll tell you, there's nothing Lady Oily likes better than telling people what to do or what to wear. Did I tell you I bought a new foreparte. Silver thread an' all. Mum's at the needle now. With her tipple of gin. Probably sew it to herself as well as the dress and I'll have to go to the Fair with her in tow."

"It'll be company for you," says Frith, a yearning burning down from his heart into his gut. Longing to have Catherine on his arm for others to see, to witness his joy. To have that opportunity. It cannot be.

"I've enough company, thank you Mr Frith. I have three beaux to escort me."

Frith can see why, in her sudden glow. "Good for you, Mrs Sarah. Be a spring butterfly, fluttering from one to another. Delighting but never settling."

"That's nice. Thank you Mt Frith. Dragon goes on how I've turned her Koffee House into a knocking shop and the Watch'll close her down. They should close down her mouth first, but they ain't got enough men for that. She's always on, 'I kept my door locked until I was married.' That ain't difficult when no one's knocking. We all know how old Richard is and how many months shorter when Mr M was shackled."

"Why do you put up with her?"

Sarah shrieks a laugh. "That's my Mr Frith, asking questions when the answer's plain as a pikestaff."

The noise brings Mr M from the Stores to scurry Sarah back to the Koffee House. He is scornful of Frith not at work in his newspaper place, if you can call what he does work. The contempt bridles the newsman into keener questions.

"I'm the success I am because of three things," puffs Mr M. "Hard work, keeping my nose to the grindstone, and having an ear to the ground."

An image of a contorted Mr M passes through Frith's head before he asks if that is how Mrs Middleton is able to buy fancy paintings for the Koffee House. What does Mr M buy for himself.

Mr M is cagey. "A business man's cleverness is to hold his cards close to his chest and play them at the best time. My present little venture is not for your newspaper. Also, I would be obliged if you didn't quiz Mrs Middleton about my affairs."

The newsman points out he didn't have to. "Your good lady volunteered you were telling her the other day that Mayor Turner had wind of a get-rich-quick scheme and the two of you were going into partnership."

"Who said anything about partnership?" says Mr M quickly. "Everything I have I got by my own hard work and sharp thinking. Turner only heard about the scheme through the nobs he meets being Mayor. And getting that position was more through good luck than his talent. It's my ear that's close to the ground and I've been using Robert Turner to hasten my plans. Robert and I are neither partners nor rivals. We are business men."

"Is it a sound scheme?" asks Frith.

"A sure-fire winner. If only I had more cash I could fill chests with the returns. How big is the world?" he asks rhetorically to Frith's quizzical look. "We're finding out how big it is and finding how to make money from it. This scheme will last for many life-times." He is indignant when Frith asks if he had thought about using Middleton's Stores to raise more cash. "I am a highly successful business man, not a stupid oaf. What man would risk the roof over his head? Now, if you don't mind, the store doesn't run itself. I have work to do."

Before Mr M is halfway across Kennetside, he turns. "Perhaps you ought to think about hard work and getting your ear closer to the ground. That way you might have caught our brave men seeing to those navigators and that barge this morning at Sheffield Mill."

Dismay floods through the newsman. He tries to keep it out of his face and voice. "Was anyone hurt?"

"Word has it a couple a hundred were in the fight. Our Reading Militia kept the two sides apart and told them to go home else all the ale-houses would be closed. Threats like that would be enough to start a riot, not stop one. We had word yesterday from one of the Militia the navigators were heading on a rampage. Ear to the ground, Mr Frith," scoffs Mr M.

"Why would the Reading Militia stir up the wharf men?"

"Would you want to face a hundred thick-head, thick-arm navigators wielding picks and shovels? Seems like a good move by
Captain Hawker, getting plenty of men behind him and sending the
scum packing." Mr M disappears into his stores.

memoirs of Sir George Crockmore

The more one does the more one can do. This adage could well be
the Crockmore motto when I am raised to a title. It matters little by
what means great works are achieved, only that they come to glorious fruition. Since dawn I have strived for the happiness of my
Michaelmas Ball guests, dealing with florist, draper, butcher,
vintner, sword master, carpenter, again the marquee contractor, and
labourers in want of guidance how to smooth the ruts in the Bath
Road. My staff have lost all capacity to organise the minutia of
their tasks. Even Henry who, though he brought to my attention the
sodden condition of the drive and the delicate shoes of the lady
guests, was equally aware of the matting in the north-west cellar,
but could not put the two together in his head.

While waiting upon the music master that I might instruct him in
the latest selection of dances, I amused myself with a reversal of
being overseer. It was I who took orders, bowed low, stoked the
fire and straightened the bed linen. I obeyed, in the most servile
manner, my Master, who was not as such Master but Mistress. The
maid, for the sake of our charade, ordered me to address her as
Madam Penelope. The girl had proved herself a willing slave
yesterday, and this morning was splendid as a demanding disciplin-
arian. I could never correctly comply with her commands, such
was her changeable mind and imagination. In the playing I was
well sated.

It came about in the study when, reflecting on my Michaelmas
Ball preparations, I stated I was weary of making every decision
for every person. The maid made bold to suggest she could relive
me of that burden for an hour. A few minutes later Madam
Penelope entered the study wearing a black satin gown, a favourite
of my second wife Eleanor. Madam Penelope filled it far more
favourably. She wore beneath the satin a body of whalebone that

thrust up her bosom as no red-blooded man could resist.

Seeing desire in my eyes, Madam Penelope forbad me look upon these luscious mounds. She leaned the better to tantalise me as I sat on the rush seat chair, her stern face a warm breath from mine challenging me not to let my gaze drift down. Having failed this first of her tasks, Madam Penelope declared she must punish me and had me kneel to watch her remove the cord from the window drape which she put to exquisite cruel use about my body and limbs. There followed a prolonged delirium as I failed to satisfy her commands, from the manner of addressing her, to taking into my mouth each toe in a sequence she had in mind but did not disclose. Every failure was punished with the cord.

The joy continued as waves until I was naked before her though she had discarded not one item. Such was my craving that lashing me to kneel more upright, she did drag the peep-toe of her shoe down my chest, abdomen to my groin and I expended into the air. Then did she permit me close, pressing my face into her satin panel and the aroused nature of that which lay beneath.

In the relaxation I intimated I had plans for the girl should she prove herself through the grooming I was bestowing upon her. She responded with an unexpected remark, which in the after light may have been a continuation of the play-acting. She queried if her grooming in learning to tease yet avoid being taken was for handling the nobs at my Michaelmas Ball. Reverberation from the immediate minutes of Mistress Penelope and her bosom filling my vision did conduce a sudden fury in me. I know well these gentlemen of London, who would force her upon a hint. I held my agitation unobserved. This was a mistake for the maid then mentioned Captain Hawker had spoken with her and how his ruggedness made him a handsome fellow.

I subsequently realise the maid, or Mistress Penelope as she still acted, was teasing me, but my concern for her blinded me to her clumsy coquetry. I warned her in no uncertain fashion that to continue receiving my grooming for greater things I demanded absolute fidelity. I wanted no bastards under my roof, and emphasised this by wielding the fire poker from which nearness she felt the hotness. I dismissed her, charging her not to let tears despoil the satin gown.

Before the arrival of the music master I thought on the disadvantageous nature of marriage. The gentleman puts up his wealth as proof beforehand of his protection and maintenance of the woman, yet the woman need put up no proof of her fecundity. I am thrice deceived by wives in this way and shall ensure not a fourth by confirming the belly be full before confirming a ring on the finger.

Wakeman's journal – 6:00pm

"I won't just up sticks and move in with you." A rent in the thunder clouds! The idea remains in her. A possibility. She was talking about a measurable time. The six months I'd said yesterday. Separation, evaluation. Why not three? One? A week, a day? The more time with Erebus the more she will sink back, her energy burned up with the effort of being with him.

A sudden punch in my gut. There stretches ahead an empty, dead six months, and Erebus with Catherine. Wearing down her willpower with his laments and pleading. Reverting to the familiar. Erebus sleeping with her. My pain is acute.

My fist is rattling the table. Concentrate on the positive. What positive? My greatest love is gone.

Erebus was staring from across High Street at the Courant most of the afternoon. I wanted to punch him for his selfish, suffocating obsession that causes pain in someone who cares for him. Except he would use the bruising to win sympathy, and more ruinous understanding from Catherine.

from Mistress Olivia's diary

Mr Augustin Wybourne should be named Mr Gruesome Wishbone. His skinny legs dangle under a bony stump of body. He is ugly even for an older man, made hideously so because he dresses as a beau, chortles as a fop, and cavorts as a creaky youth.

I informed him Papa had taken me to London and I was to be instructed in the latest dance in fashion. This he was reluctant to undertake without direct instruction from my parents neither of which he could find about the house. I asked if he thought me a liar to which question there is but one answer from a hired person.

Rather than teach a dance à la mode he expounded on the etiquette of the Dance at Court. As this will prove of use to me when we are housed in London I note the kernel of what he said.

Courtiers are expected to learn four new dances every year such they have at least twelve dances at the ready. I declared this was no arduous matter for me with which Mr Wishbone concurred. He recited the favoured suite of dances: Branle; Courante; Gavotte mostly in round form, which I must learn to do particularly well as I would dance with a succession of gentlemen, and Allemande. Finally the Minuet, this being the unrivalled queen of dances.

Mr Wishbone began teaching me variations of the opening *Danse à Deux* as it allows everyone in the Court to judge the rank of the dancers and the quality of their dancing. He concentrated on instilling control and precision, poise and refinement, and these I exhibited with excellence.

I discovered the Minuet is special in that the dancers face each other and for this reason he refused to teach it to me. This vexed me intensely but he was steadfast in refusing me.

As a concession, before resuming the *Danse à Deux* he coached me in the Plié. I kept my body and head upright while lowering my gaze, bending my knees as appropriate to the status of the lord or gentleman before me. This did require matchless balance with which I am thankfully blessed.

At table this evening I remarked to Papa and Mama it was a shame I could not show to them my progress in the dance as I had with the music. To their enquiries as to what I was being taught I spoke at length on the *Danse à Deux*. Yet it was upon a brief mention of the Minuet they alighted. I said I had been learning it for some time in the Italian form. Mama had not heard of this so I demonstrated with Papa. I stood so near that our tummies touched and made such close turns that his hand brushed me inappropriately for a gentleman. My final deep Plié allowed my loose gown to curtain little modesty.

Mr Gruesome Wishbone will never again teach me. What are

wishbones for but to be broken? My next instructor shall be more accommodating to my requests. Though I chastise myself for not foreseeing a second and greater gain from my stratagem. Papa reprimanded Mama for allowing so vile a creature under his roof. Did Mama not take up the charlatan's references, demanded Papa. How could she abandon their beautiful, innocent daughter without chaperone to a lecher while she spends money on fripperies. Mama is in great disfavour and her new house a thousand miles removed.

Lodgings room, Anglers Tavern

One door with latch, one window under a sloping ceiling, three floorboards that creak. One bed with piss-pot under, one bachelors' chest, one gate-leg table with bowl and jug, one curtain across the corner, one hanging rail behind. His knapsack, his satchel, his pocketbook, his pencils, his quills. Frith surveys his estate.

He is sitting cross-legged on the floor. His back is arrow straight, hands lying palm up in his lap. He wishes he had the calumet, drawing in the smoke so he could ascend with the bald eagle over the Mohawk mountain Zitkala. From there he could appreciate the unimportance of Man. But he could never grasp the essence of the Land the way the Chief and Elders could.

This evening in a small town in England, his heart realises what his intelligence has long been telling him – why Angeni said he could not remain with her. He believed he had found Heaven in a woman who embraced the Earth. Frith pictures Zitkala with its two massive shoulders either side of the spearhead peak, as if a bird about to take flight. For the Mohawk it did take flight. But never for Frith. He gives up pretending the small sparsely furnished room above the Anglers' Tavern is a native longroom.

Standing now, he shuts his eyes and attempts fall-down-dream. He wasn't much good at that either. He did the falling down but it came from disorientation rather than trance. Frith tries to push his mind into the black sky, anywhere that is away from his body.

But he cannot. He remembers his small sister collapsing on the boat crossing the Great Ocean, the weeks in Boston waiting for her to die, the Indenter shipping the family to Pennsylvania. Did he desert them? Or did he break free from the slavery that awaited them? It has been over twenty years without knowing.

If his first great passion and love Angeni was Heaven, his wife Grace was the angel. Frith knows he will always be bitter he could do nothing. It has been six years since his angel died in childbirth, following the path taken by their cherub. He hears his wife's screams at the dead thing from her womb, her howls fading to a bleat. His lamb. Over a few hours he watched his child, wife and faith shrivel. Every week the newsman sees 'Childbirth' in reverse type every week: 17 Childbirth, 9, 22, 11. Small deaths. Massive loss. Faceless figures.

Frith hooks his thoughts to the two turtle doves that have been at his windowsill every day since he first saw Catherine. Softly cooing, rubbing necks and together every day. He doesn't allow himself to think they existed before that awakening day he met Catherine, not in previous summers. He only remembers their history starting when his life rekindled. He is sure that was the day they fluttered up and down together with wings a blur of greys as they hovered and played in the air and made him laugh aloud at their antics.

It had been an early morning standing before the great mountain that he had tried to lift into flight. It had crashed on top him with Angeni's heavy reality of who they each were. And now burying him again in the despair of extirpated joy. Frith falls down with a heavy sigh on his bed. He knew which way he was falling. He was cheating on fall-down-dream.

A short candle

The whirligig inside Lynn was slowed through busying herself on deck mending the sail. Her Dad roused and grunted something under his breath when Lynn presented him with a slice of salted beef and potatoes on his platter. He poked at the potato for a while then gave up in favour of a large shot of brandy.

Perhaps he knew the beef had arrived today, thought Lynn in the awkward quiet of the cabin. And who had brought it and, in his imagination, at what price. Perhaps her Dad had picked up on her bursting desire to tell of the afternoon, to examine it, to assess it by speaking of it. She knew she could never tell her Dad.

Lynn brought two of the rent pieces of sail inside the cabin, lit a tallow candle and settled on the drop-down seat by the stove.

"Why're you wasting good candles?" asked her Dad gruffly from his bunk. The brandy had been regularly topped-up.

"We need the sail for when we get back to the Thames," said Lynn.

"If we ever do. Do it in daylight."

"We'll be under way tomorrow," she said levelly. "You're not well enough to steer Jeannie, so it's got to —"

"I am well! I've been steering this barge for —" He coughed violently. He waved Lynn away from him.

Nothing she did that evening was right by her Dad. She let his spats dissolve into the next silence. Her eyes were getting tired in the poor light and she rested the sewing on her lap. An untouchable wave rolled through her and she could feel Nicholas on top of her.

"You got something to tell me?"

"No?"

"I know you have." She had never been able to lie to him. "You lain with that gangly useless boy."

She thought quickly how not to answer. "The one who brought us the food?"

"Poison food. Why'd he do that if he's not after something in return?"

Lynn's mouth tightened. "The one who saved our necks when Fergus was on board?"

"His neck. Who fished that Jacobite scum on board? I warned you. And I've warned you about boys. What'd he do to you?"

"Nothing."

"What d' he do?"

"Nothing."

"I'll beat it out of you, so help me."

He couldn't. She couldn't bear to see him fail. "We ate lunch."

"What else?"

The joy flashed back to her and she was too slow answering.

"Trollop!"

"He loves me." Where did that come from?

"He loves one thing."

"I love him."

"Now he's had that, he's gone."

Lynn froze for a moment. In her head she knew it too likely and be true. The pretty scorpion had her sting in Nicholas, they were both of the town, both beautiful. All evening she'd been ignoring the obvious. "He's honest and decent, and nothing like the barge boys."

"So what's he see in you?"

She couldn't answer. She remembered an echo. "He told me I was remarkable."

"Lads'll say anything to get under a girl's skirt. How many times have I told you?" Her Dad's face was red, spluttering out the words.

"Nicholas is different." Why was she picturing Olivia in her fine dress with her delicate face.

"Tosh! I've warned you countless ... warned you ... and now . . ." He looked straight at her. "You're no daughter of mine."

"Dad!"

"Just like your mother. She was the same."

"Stop it!" shouted Lynn, covering her ears.

"Whores, the pair of you."

"Don't you dare say that!" Lynn stood. "Not about Mam!" She carried on shouting incoherently, drowning from her ears the stream of hateful, vile talk from her Dad.

In a flash of clarity, as if she was another person listening in, Lynn heard herself yelling at her Dad. She ran from the cabin into the night.

Wakeman's journal – 9:30pm

"I want to disappear into a cave," she'd said. "Be buried under a stone."

Yet Catherine has been with me both days since the discovery of our love. I must never forget the risk she takes to be with me.

Much more I'm sure than she reveals.

I am confused why I know this through reflecting on the other women I dearly loved. Why I value it so dearly. Angeni and Grace gave me a quality of themselves. Then they were gone. There must not be a third. I cannot trust myself after another such deprival.

A real wretch

Lynn ran up the lane and stared into Holy Brook, coughing up sobs. In the dark meadow the buttercups were closed, rejecting her. She could not face returning to Barge Jeannie, or be on her own this late in the hamlet up the lane, yet she had a drive to keep moving. Lynn entered the ploughed field.

Concentrating on stepping across the clods kept her thoughts grounded. Too soon her feet adapted to the terrain and her mind took up its harrowing. What had her Dad meant? He was wrong. Mam was not like that. Dad was right about Nicholas. All too keen to get away from the meadow that afternoon, away from her, away to Mistress Olivia. She sobbed. For a brief time she had believed in a future.

Lynn followed Holy Brook into a dense copse. Why now had she let herself be reckless with a boy she wouldn't see again? And one she knew in her gut she could never wed. She'd blocked that from her mind, let herself believe a handsome boy was in love with her. Fooled by a silver tongue and the golden smile of a shopkeeper. Had she wanted to be fooled? What did that make her? Not like her Mam. Jean Darville had principles firmer than barnacles on a hull. Dad was wrong about Mam. He was delirious with fever and brandy. But she had lifted her skirt for a moment's madness in a meadow far from London. Dad was right about his daughter.

"What have we here?"

Lynn's heart froze when she placed the gravel voice. She turned to flee only to face Sergeant Quinn with a leer splitting his face.

"Come looking for us?" said Hawker. "And we'll both come for you." The two chortled.

"My Dad's just —"

Hawker's fist hit her jaw sinking Lynn to her knees. He pushed her face into his groin. "Hey Quinn, look how keen she is for it."

Lynn pulled away and Hawker jerked his knee into her face. "Oops. Dangerous down there." He grabbed a handful of her hair and hauled Lynn to her feet, twisted her round, dragged her and flung her on a grassy patch at the edge of the copse. He threw off his coat and ducked out of his scabbard. He stood over her.

"You may as well have it too," said Lynn trying hard to sound confident. It was the first idea into her head and wasn't sure at all where it would lead.

"I'm going to," said Hawker not pausing from unbuttoning his breeches.

"The cure's not that painful, but it could mean —"

Hawker kicked her legs apart. "You ain't poxed. Likely never had a man."

"Last one this afternoon." She said it too eagerly.

Quinn spoke. "I wondered what that pretty shop boy was up to."

"Now you know. And what he's taking back to Reading."

"Won't be to the Mayor's filly," said Quinn. "She cut his reins yesterday."

"So the jilted lad found the first trollop to ride," said Hawker with bitter malice.

His words hurt Lynn more than his fist or knee had. There had been a tiny place in her that believed Nicholas really cared for her. That was crushed. Nicholas had used her out of spite against Olivia.

"No!" she cried out.

"Tell you he loved you?" smirked Hawker. "This is the only thing he loved." He had unfastened the last button and was opening the flap.

"There is no point going on," sighed Lynn, ripping up some green leaves and bracts near her head. "Oh! Here, will I set up my everlasting rest." Hawker was stopped momentarily. "And shake the yoke of inauspicious stars from this world-wearied flesh. Eyes look your last!" She pushed the handful into her mouth.

As she spoke she was recalling the young actor on the makeshift stage the one time she had been to a proper play, and praying she sounded anywhere near as convincing as Romeo. Lynn chewed, swallowed, and grabbed for more. "Purest of woodland poisons, bring back pure happiness in death." She doubled herself imitating a spasm, forced saliva through her lips, clutched at her stomach and pretended another violent convulsion.

"Put the cow out of her misery," suggested Quinn.

"And lose our fun?" answered Hawker, breeches half way down his thighs.

Lynn felt a real pain in her guts, sharp and violent. Genuine panic distorted her face. Had she swallowed something that was poisonous? That hadn't been a pretend convulsion.

Hawker's exposed manhood took the full splatter of Lynn's spewed vomit. He leapt back and tripped. Lynn was up and running for the trees spurred by the fear she'd be caught before reaching Barge Jeannie. She could hear Quinn's boots crashing behind her.

Lynn remembered her stomach had felt weighty all evening from the smoked meats, cheese and olives. The rich food she never ate. It had been worsened later by the tension in the cabin. She hurtled through the copse, slapped and scraped by the undergrowth, with the acrid taste in her mouth of bile mixed with oniony wood garlic.

While Hawker quickly sluiced his lower parts in Holy Brook he was vindictively aware this was the second time that day he had been soaked because of the barge bitch. He caught up with Quinn at the edge of the copse.

"Gone," said the Sergeant. "Dunno which way."

"I'll have her," vowed Hawker.

Lynn could hear them below her. She had seen a tall beech tree draped with mistletoe in its upper branches and made a decision. Now her heart was beating like a drum, her breath rasping loud enough to be heard in London, and she concentrated on calming both. It pushed aside the dread she had made the wrong choice.

"Not tonight, Boss. Early on was a bad omen."

"Stuff omens. What was those sodding Watch doing there?"

"Dunno. Anyhow, he deserved to get knifed, creeping about like that."

"I need to think about that. The barge bitch can wait. We know where she'll be."

The two had retraced their steps a few yards when Lynn's footing gave way with a loud rustle. She had been standing on a vine of mistletoe, not the tree's bough, and now it rapidly gave up supporting the extra weight. The ground beckoned her forty feet below. Lynn threw good sense over her shoulder and pitched out into the night air, arms wide to embrace a massive hang of the evergreen. The mistletoe unwrapped and tore from the supporting branches, swinging Lynn in a wide arc until her back thumped against the trunk of the tree.

"Look who's dropped in to see us," said Hawker turning to the noise.

Lynn dropped the last few feet from where she was hanging to her mistletoe swing and ran. She ran for all she was worth across the ploughed field, screaming for help as best she could through desperate breaths and her acid raw throat. She was gasping for every lungful and her feet slithered into the furrows and kicked against the lumps of earth.

Hawker caught her half way across the field.

"You ain't getting away this time," he spat at her. His eyes were wild. "Cut up over lover-boy, are you?" He unsheathed his knife. Lynn's free hand went to her front pocket. "You will be."

Lynn jabbed the long sail-needle into Hawker's wrist, pushing it with her thimble through sinew, past bone and out. Hawker roared and dropped the knife. He gripped her forearm like a mantrap. She had enraged him, not escaped him.

There was an explosion behind her. Hawker and Quinn instinctively ducked as Lynn heard a soft whoosh above her head. A man stood at the edge of the field reloading his blunderbuss.

"Clear off!" he called. "Next won't be in t' air."

Lynn saw two shapes scuttling back towards the copse. She turned to the distant man.

"Good Sir, thank you. My attackers have fled." She walked tentatively towards him. "If you will allow me to the lane I can be on my way." He held the gun ready but waved her on.

"There's cattle rustling round these parts," he said by way of explanation when she drew close. "More so since them navvies been around."

"I'm not a navvy," she lamely quipped, quickly adding: "Nor a cattle thief." Lynn thought it wise to tell the farmer what she was going to do before she did it. "If you will, I'm going down the lane to my barge. It's moored there."

"Ah-ha! You're the troublemaker from barge," said the farmer waving his blunderbuss at Lynn. "Crazy rabble and pistol shots this morning. An' I seen what you was up to in my meadow after. Now you're taking more lads in the woods. Ain't one man a day enough for you? Be off. We don't want your kind whoring round 'ere. We's respectable. Off! Quick, before I change my mind."

Lynn broke her walk into a trot. She didn't have to look back to know the man stood in the lane, blunderbuss ready, making sure she kept moving far from his land.

A friendly field

Lynn was woken by grassy breaths clouding her face. "Good morning, Hermond," she said and began scratching his muzzle. The horse's bobbing head gradually edged back the cloying cobwebs from yesterday that were binding her mind. There's nothing like a good cry she reflected, especially for oneself.

Last night, Lynn had not wanted to add her shaking hands, tumbling tummy and wobbly knees to the accusations her Dad would throw at her followed by the blame she knew he would eventually heap on himself. She heard his wheeze with each out breath as she collected a blanket and tarpaulin before walking to the pasture she had found for Hermond. The last thing she remembered was the sound of Hermond steadily grazing close by the bower she had made for herself.

Having walked Hermond back to Barge Jeannie, Lynn dithered on the towing path not knowing what to expect from her Dad. She was worried how ill he was yet she harboured a lingering anger at what he'd said about her Mam. She stepped on to the gunwale and it dipped slightly. Barge Jeannie was afloat.

They were quickly under way with the briefest of necessary exchanges. They both shied from talking of anything, however trivial, that might lead to disagreement or of anything that might recall the previous evening. Lynn worked the locks and sat on the foredeck repairing the sail as they moved along the pounds from Sheffield Lock, through Hosehill Lock into the Ufton Cut. She hoped her other sail needle was turning septic in Hawker's wrist. In front of her was a devotedly weary horse while behind a withdrawn, weak man slumped across the tiller. Her Dad clipped the gate of Tyle Mill Lock. If Lynn thought the barge drifting too close to the towing path she shouted back a question only caring that some answer came back and Barge Jeannie corrected its course.

from Mistress Olivia's diary

Stupid and more stupid. I am furious with myself for being so careless. I raged exactly as Mama had done at Papa though I had seen how she lost that engagement. This morning I slackened the reins on my emotions and Master Nicholas Middleton bolted without being brought to his knees with penitence.

Worse still. He has refused to comply with my demand he never sees the Barge-bilge again. It was a thinly disguised excuse that she will be up and down the river and in his father's Stores for provisions. Up and down indeed! Why did that expression spring from his lips? If I could be bothered she would be bobbing up and down the river as a bloated carcass and a hazard to any other rogue barge. If he is sniffing round the trollop's keel that will be his downfall. But there is no way I will tolerate that until he knows I have finished with him and he is mortified at what he has lost. Do men want to sow their oats so desperately they'll plough any muck? Or is it that he sees his mother in her? They are both frighteningly large and hideous.

Our discourse had started well in that he was apologetic. Too effusively such that I suspected he had again seen the Barge-bilge. I showed him how distraught I was that he had denied me his company, reminding him how lucky he was to have me as his almost-betrothed. He agreed with enthusiasm I was the prettiest girl and the most sought after match in Reading. Only in Reading, thought I? This spurred me to note the Barge-bilge was not in the town. I spoke with too little forethought, "I ask you directly, have you been with this trollop on her barge?"

"No, Olivia, I have not been with Lynn on her barge."

Lynn! Marry-come! Nicholas Middleton will burn to ash from my fury for using the slut's name so familiarly. I noted his eyes were too steady looking into mine, his reply too evenly paced. Alas by then my anger had melted my shrewdness. Only after we went our ways did I realise he was reciting my words back to me with something else not fully said. He was able to answer my too precise question with a too precise denial.

This awareness was absent when I continued headlong, "If you wish to escort me to Forbury Fair you must promise never to see nor speak to that trollop." Master Middleton refused to make the promise on the lame excuse I have already noted.

For the second time I had put to him a question that allowed me no room for manoeuvre should the answer be not to my liking. I had snared myself for I could not slacken my demand and thereby weaken my position in future confrontations.

He blustered for some time that he has to deal every day with maidens as customers in the Stores or on the farms. His protestations were repetitious without moving towards my request, so I told him to leave me and only present himself when he had come to his senses.

In a few hours I shall have the mortal embarrassment of being at Forbury Fair as a little girl with her parents after last year being on the arm of the most handsome boy in the town. No doubt I shall be questioned by the uncivilised. I will reply Master Nicholas is bewailing his mistakes and stupidity.

Wakeman's journal – 11:30am

Ten had just chimed and I was waving, half-calling hello, to a startled Catherine as she approached Yedda's Herbary. I knew she'd be buying emblems for a garland her daughter will wear to Forbury Fair. Beattie was not with her. Was that deliberate? Hoping for and giving me the chance to be alone with her for a few minutes. The wise woman of Sonning Common kept herself to herself. Has she witnessed our scene before, a repeated pattern to her, each time unique for the lovers?

I had started by telling Catherine she must cling on to the woman I love. A sigh of relief from her, I had recognised her as a person. These past days she has been mother, possession, adulteress, nurse, negotiator, harlot, cook, comforter. Yesterday night Erebus said, "I've something to ask. You don't have to reply. Do you miss Frith?" She didn't reply. She finally said such questions did no good except to fuel her husband's feeling of being hard done by. Erebus sulked. She felt wretched for speaking her mind. It was back to how it had been with him.

Erebus told her he'd waited outside the Courant and watched me, did nothing, and hurt inside. She hugged and comforted the Darkness. I shouted that's why he told you about watching me, you stupidly sympathetic woman! I threw my arms in the air, ashamed of my outburst. She hugged me.

Why do I add to her burden? Add to the "unrelenting anguish" under her own roof. "I'm under observation every moment." She's not sleeping, is questioned in the middle of the night, and strains to keep some façade in front of her daughter. Hounded by him until she begged, "Have you no compassion?"

We drifted round the beds of herbs, autumn birdsong in the air, took a walk up an overgrown track. It was many, many steps before I felt her relax a little then soften into my embrace. She has been forbidden by Erebus to see me, speak to me, have anything to do with me. I felt the familiar physical strength flow between us, a strength that had restarted in our talking and the brushing touches round the herb beds.

We allowed ourselves to look up a little, not to events but to attitudes. We are so good together. I made her laugh a few times and later she caught me with some teases. "Is this what you want, Quillman? A woman who says meet me at such-and-such and you jump to it." The mirth in her voice. Her birdsong. I looked at her all the time, listened to every word, yet can remember so few. Only the sensation, the tenor of her words. Suddenly her arms round me. We are breathing as one.

Then someone at Yedda's. "It could be one of my neighbours!"

"What is the chance of that?" I ask. But no use, she is panicked to be seen with me. We no longer have lingered disengagements.

A sideways hoist

In the silence of their own thoughts Lynn and Peter brought Barge Jeannie to Aldermaston Wharf to be greeted with warm hellos from the wharfinger. Lynn returned from taking Hermond for a short break in a pasture to find Adam's lightening boat emptied and stowed on the wharf. The wharfinger had effortlessly transferred the sacks from the small boat to Barge Jeannie with his hoist.

"Best thing I ever bought," he claimed proudly. "After the wife." He had seen her approach from the house and made sure she heard.

"He's going soft in th' head," she retorted. "Last week I weren't above his wheelbarrow as best." She put down a tray of cuts and ale for lunch. "Anyway, I ain't a woman who can be bought."

"That's true. You'd drain the King's treasury."

The Aldermaston pair kept up their banter through the meal, setting a bright mood and drawing Lynn and Peter into it. The wharfinger was clearly proud of his new hoist. "Why break your back when a machine can do it for you?"

Peter was wary. "If it took three men to unload what one can do with a hoist, what happens to the other two?"

"They do something else," came the quick reply.

"What if they can't?"

"No such thing as can't. Lazybones talk."

"There's only so many jobs," grumbled Peter.

Lynn wanted to say there had been no such job as a wharfinger or a lock-keeper years and years ago but she let the men talk as it seemed to do her Dad good. She found herself talking about clothes with the wharfinger's wife who was curious how Lynn coped and did she buy the latest fashions when she was in London. The woman was plainly dressed in a light brown serge with a white cambric apron yet Lynn felt her enquiry was genuine and wasn't looking down on her own worn shirt and soiled skirt. The woman spoke of the big Forbury Fair at Reading and how "misery guts over there" wouldn't take her. Her husband replied he wouldn't walk the "old nag" a ten-pace for fear people see her and be terrified to death.

"Such a shame you'll miss it," she said to Lynn, as the two worked the paddles of Aldermaston Lock just upstream from the wharf. "It's such fun and the boys will be full of high spirits."

Later along the long cut towards the Rowbarge Inn, Peter suddenly spoke. "You haven't had much women's company a while, my Beaut." He waved aside her protestation. "I heard you talking clothes and the like with the Missus back there. It ain't fair on you. You should be courting by now and I stopped you with the up and down the river, never stopping nowhere. I was trying to do my best by you. You know that don't you?"

There came a rambling penitence for all the things for which he had to be sorry though she kept telling him he had no need to be. But he didn't speak of the one thing Lynn wanted him to take back. Of her Mam he spoke only about his ache for Lynn having to go through the months of watching her die and her absence for the growing girl. It was awkward and one-sided but her Dad was talking and Lynn was thankful for that.

Wakeman's journal – 12:30pm

The women in the butcher's shop this morning were comparing hands. "I had the longest fingers," Catherine said with a laugh. She began massaging my hand with them, strong, firm but also gentle, exploring. My hand was the clay she kneads. She has sturdy ankles, not the sinewy calves of petite women. A cleft on her upper lip, a nest of wild black hair, rough-cut short. The gnarls of work hands. This is the woman I love and that makes everything about her beautiful. My Goddess of love and art and sentiment.

Angeni, stunningly pretty with white eyes inquisitive and playful from her tan skin. Grace, with her poise and serene elegance. Catherine, beauty in the eye of the beholder. A commonplace saying, but they once held truth, were meaningful. Where there's smoke there's fire. Or ashes.

I have this glow inside from being with her for an hour at Yedda's. Not the kiln heat after Lodden but the powerful lasting warmth in a rock after having lain in the sun.

"No – promises," she said.

"No – saying we will do this or that," I said.

"No – it will be forever," she said.

We are realist romantics. Nothing lasts; adapt or perish. I am exhausted. I told her I'd sent my love last night through my open window and bounced it off the full moon to her. The bliss of these memories, breathing her fragrance on my hand.

Forbury Pleasure Gardens

By middle afternoon Forbury Fair is well under way when Frith wanders to the ground. His shoes are quickly sodden and he takes the grassier route to what appears to be the most popular attraction, judging by the length of the queue.

A woman of breathtaking features with high coiffure that cascades down a slender neck is speaking punctiliously. "You are the Mayor, Robert." Her eyes pin the portly man who wears his chain of office. "These people should be honoured for you to visit their exhibit."

"I cannot take advantage of my office, Millicent."

"Then why have the position? Offer to pay the man double."

"That would start a commotion."

"Do something, Robert."

Frith sees Mistress Olivia scowling nearby, rocking from one foot to the other in sullen boredom. She catches sight of Frith and her face lights up.

"This is Mr Frith," the girl is saying to the crone taking the money at the tent. Olivia has dragged Frith to the front of the queue. "He is senior newsman on the Courant newspaper and will be writing of your exhibit. If it should prove worth writing about."

"Be sure it does," answers the woman proudly.

"The Reading Courant is the most influential newspaper in the whole of Berkshire and beyond. Mention in it will serve you very well throughout the county at every fair. However, Mr Frith is a very busy man."

"I can't let no one —"

"And this is my father, who is Mayor of Reading," interrupts Mistress Olivia, spotting her parents approach to find out what she is up to. The four are soon shepherded into the tent.

They pass an assortment of misshapen creatures in clear bottles, and weird animals that are badly stuffed, before arriving at the star attraction, the Grotesque from the Country of the Great Mogul. A wry curl settles on Frith's lips as he looks at two adolescent girls in the cage. They wear a lacy pink dress that does not sit well under the Oriental faces that stare torpidly forward. The showman proclaims the Creature has one body and he is itemising the four legs, two arms, two heads.

"Prove it," challenges a young housekeeper earnestly. It has cost her a good portion of her wages to get in. "Could be cuddling each other in a clever dress."

The owner pulls down the top of the dress. Frith is startled by the young nakedness, then queasy on seeing the four nipples then troubled noticing the distortion of the shoulders and the sides where the bodies meld into each other. The owner is bouncing and squeezing the small breasts to prove they are genuine.

"They got two down-below?" shouts another woman, provoking a burst of coarse comments.

"Indeed they have but modesty forbids." The owner plays the catcalls and whistles for a minute then, little by little, raises the skirt, exposing more of the legs of one girl then the other.

"They can take two blokes at the same time. Double the fun," caws the woman to wild yelps. The dress is flung off and the girls stand immobile in front of the baying and gaping crowd.

"The ill-bred woman comes into her own at the Fair," says Millicent Turner. The four are standing outside the tent. "More impudent and shameless. Come."

The family set off for the Most Ferocious Beast on Earth Tamed by Man and Fire. Frith smiles to himself at Mistress Olivia dragging behind, clearly fascinated by the Grotesque. A compact man with black wavy hair holds Mistress Olivia in brief conversation. Frith knows the man from somewhere but it eludes him. He can see the man is a stranger to the Mayor's daughter. At first she is indignant then for a split second fury distorts her features before she recovers her composure. Frith can only hear the odd word: "Navigation" and "be growth." The girl slips some coins from her wrist purse into the man's palm. He must be a navvy thinks Frith, with information to sell. He wonders if Mayor Turner has a private plan for the waterway that is contradictory to his public proclamations and if he employs informants within the Company.

Frith drifts away from the amusements, cajoled from left and right to ride in the flying coaches, swoop on swings, to view puppet shows and tumblers. Frith knows the best drolls in the kingdom would not be able to make him laugh and he does not want to be confounded by theatre shows.

By the time Frith reaches the trade area of the Fair he has been approached by three whores and one clumsy pickpocket. The Brewers' marquee dominates the Fair with wholesalers and retailers vying to offer samples. He passes the astutely positioned Pye-Powder Court dispensing it's summary justice to the misdemeanants, fining them sufficient to pay for a month of the Aldermen's Watch.

After a jug of amber Frith is sampling a stout when he notices Captain Hawker quickly leave his ale to chase a delicately pretty girl. Frith watches the lovers with ironic amusement. He sees Hawker grab her upper arm from behind and spin her onto his lips, powerfully holding her while they kiss. She slaps him for her public embarrassment and skips off. Frith rips his thoughts back to the sickly honeyed ale he is sampling.

Some while later he beholds Mrs Middleton with the same appalled shock he viewed the Grotesque. She is on a regal procession among the trinket stalls, handing this and that trifle for purchase to a trailing Mr M. He waits for his wife to move on and hands back the object to the stallholder with a resigned shrug. Mrs Middleton is expounding in volume on whatever comes into her head be it a bauble or a passer-by. She is the gaudiest pudding Frith has ever seen, and the gabbiest. Her face is puce from the several constrictions about her, compounded by her exertions in stumbling upright. He follows the Middleton couple purely for the spectacle, his eye unable to rest on any one garment spread round the woman before another asserts itself. Frith has a pang of pity for Nicholas.

In a confrontation of contrasts Mrs Millicent Turner is cornered by Mrs Doretta Middleton in the clothier's section. The refined lady is picking at cloths with expertise, judging their weight and fall, the finish and feel of each.

"This is nice, don't you think Mrs Turner?" The bedecked Beetroot is holding a brilliantly striped worsted.

"Lovely," answers the lady through a tight-lipped smile and dead eyes. "A cantaloon. I wondered if you might favour a woollen Scarlet. There is a bolt in chartreuse green on the stall over there."

"I had considered that, but —"

"I do understand your dilemma," says Millicent Turner in a deadly even tone. "A serge would suit you better, being so much more durable. The Scarlet is so dratted expensive a cloth."

"You mistake me, Mrs Turner. It was the colour I dallied with. The cost is neither here nor there to me and Mr M. I wonder about the colour against my pale skin."

"The stall man has other colours to pale against your skin, Mrs Middleton."

"Perhaps you would —"

"Mr Frith!" exclaims Millicent Turner from several yards away. "A word in your ear if you please. Do excuse me Mrs Middleton."

Frith finds his arm taken and propelled away. For the second time this day he is a pawn in the designs of a Turner female.

"Are you aware Mr Frith, this is properly known at Saint Laurence's Fair?"

"Presumably because of St Laurence's church just over there."

"You will have noticed the sizeable presence of ale and cider makers, brewers in general. This dominance developed over the years and it so happens the patron saint of brewers is Saint Laurence. A happy coincidence." Millicent Turner looks over her shoulder. "A very happy coincidence. Thank you Mr Frith for your availability at the right moment."

"I am delighted to be of service to so elegant a lady. At any right moment, Madam," he responds.

"I shall keep that in mind." She pauses. "Mr Frith."

Frith registers how he felt drawn to her by the way she said 'availability', the breathiness, the cadence, the slight tilt of the head and the slowly shuttered eyelids of Millicent Turner. He is furious at himself for enjoying the momentary flirtation. He has betrayed Catherine. Before Wednesday he would have told Catherine and she would have teased him where a man's motivation resides. Before Wednesday he had motivation in his life.

He nods to the puffing Mayor Turner as the husband sets off after his wife. Frith calls out, "You have left your daughter behind."

"The little Princess has returned home that the nanny for her brother and sister might have opportunity to enjoy the Fair."

"Kind girl," says Frith soberly, for he would not have expected Mistress Olivia to deny herself the Fair. On reflection, he would not expect sacrifice from any of the Turner family.

He turns away and is looking into the eyes of Catherine twenty yards away. His heart lurches, his guts clench, his body is transfixed. Hers too; he knows this. Their love darts between their eyes. In less than a second her look turns to terror and she whips her head away to shepherd a young girl with corkscrew black hair. A man with pointed chin, a slight hunch and drooping shoulders sees them move and follows. Frith can see the gap between his Catherine and her husband as they stroll away. He has an urge to be in that gap between Catherine and Erebus, keeping them apart.

The recognition and their silent exchange happened and was over so fast. Frith is awash in hopeless melancholy, drowning under it, bitter at everyone around being frivolously happy, the senselessness of him being unhappy. Isn't it better for two to be happy than four to be sad? Catherine doesn't look back. He knows she dare not yet he feels a loss at her not doing so.

Frith walks briskly to a gap in the hedge bounding the nearest side of Forbury Gardens, squeezes through and darts behind the concealing foliage. He marches at a brisk pace for the Anglers Tavern. Catherine will be on edge knowing he is at the Fair and he hopes fervently she saw him leave.

Wakeman's journal – 8:45pm

One hour of reaffirmation this morning at Yedda's of what we have, of what we do not ever want to lose. Us, our work together, a life together. Then at Forbury Fair our hearts joined across an unbridgeable void. Oh to be as the Grotesque, inseparably one.

Perhaps not. Better being individuals who can come together and savour it anew. As this morning brought confirmation in the holding, the kisses, eventually tender, after overwhelming passion. I was trembling. Catherine was jittery. Entirely us as one. Abruptly she became another woman. "I have to make him strong. So he doesn't have to lean on me." What about you? "I'm not being fair to you." You are in the long term.

Where did her sudden change of mood come from? She won't answer when Erebus asks "How do you feel about Frith now?" Every time he asks he is slicing my lamb to see where she bleeds. Leave him, Catherine! Not easy with a trunk packed with guilt? You can do it. Remember there is no such thing as a clean break.

from Mistress Olivia's diary

My new dress was ill finished, fitting here and there on a whim with a neckline for an ancient spinster. I had strained words with Mama after I refused to wear the hideous thing, both of which upset Papa. I offered to wear my Van Dyke dress with part-pleated back though when it was bought for me it was already decades out of date. I looked like Papa's little girl, which pleased him.

We meandered from stall to stall without entering any, which annoyed me. What was the point trailing my parents and not see the exhibits. Mama and Papa disputed outside what looked to be the most popular tent and I made good use of the newsman to gain us entry without queuing.

Everything in the tent was tedious and fake grotesqueness for the gullible. Eventually, the showman lowered the chemise of the two girls joined at their bodies causing my tummy to do a somersault of revulsion. Yet I could not take my eyes from them. I registered a tightness across my own chest as I gazed upon theirs. A desire came upon me to pinch one nipple to see if one or both mouths gasped. When the showman suddenly stripped them fully, I swear a flush swept down me. To my shame, thoughts entered my head of the kind voiced by the lewd riff-raff around us.

Upon leaving the tent I was approached by a rough looking man who had taken advantage of my parents having sped on ahead. He introduced himself as second in command in the Reading Militia and that he had some information of interest to me. I immediately knew what he was after and tried to recall how much small coin I had in my purse.

"I been patrolling the Navigation," he said, which I thought too grand an activity for what he may have likely been about. "Keeping an eye on that rogue barge." I did not show any interest. "We think they's helping a Jacobite."

"What has a Jacobite to do with me?"

"That's by-the-by. I was in that Koffee House the other day," he said. "On a matter of business," he added against my doubting look. "I learned from the busybody her son is betrothed to the mayor's daughter." He left the statement hanging. I stood surprised the boor had recognised Mrs Middle-gone for what she is.

"I am daughter of Mayor Turner," I affirmed, "but her son is merely courting me."

"Fact is, forgive me saying this, Mistress, the lad's acting like he's not courting you at all."

"Pray tell me what you mean by that. You are defaming the son of a reputable Reading merchant."

Sergeant Quinn recounted to me the young Middleton hailing him from the accursed barge. "I saw with my own eyes, I don't like bringing you such news, Mistress Turner, but I seen the barge lass and Young Mr Middleton together another day when the two sidled into a field by Sheffield Lock and lay together."

It is a gnawing thing to have a suspicion, but it is a relief to have that suspicion confirmed though it be contrary to one's liking. One can take action with confidence upon knowing facts. It shall be my pleasure devising how to act upon this information to my utmost advantage. The father of my twist-mouth deceiver is in considerable debt to Papa. But I am frustrated that swaying Papa to call in the loan will give Mama her Reading house. I need to think more upon this before initiating anything.

Wishing to abate the churning inside me I insisted we go to the amusements area. One merryman was mildly comical, the acrobats and contortionists were passable, and the ferocious bear slept. The trick riding was so poor I could do better after less than an hour's tuition.

My mind had returned to the question of my next conversation with Master Middleton when the slack-rope dancer began his performance. I heard the jolly music and looked to see. My heart jumped into my mouth such that I could hardly speak to urge my parents to the show.

The Amazing Acrobatic Angelo was so beautiful my breaths came in short bursts, if at all. When he nearly fell off the rope I cried out in horror and he looked straight at me, for we were at the very front. His gaze went as a red-hot poker through my core, which was already a gooseberry fool. I could not take my eyes from him. His coal black hair lay strangely flat on his head, the triangular face had big almond shape eyes and his lips were luscious with red paint against a white mask. The slender body danced on the rope with extraordinary grace and rhythm. When he bowed to the audience his last was for me and he smiled directly at me. I felt heat where respectable young ladies should not.

A favourable current

The past eight miles had been mostly new Cut with very little flow of water. Hermond had kept a steady pace after working hard past the Rowbarge Inn against the river current. In the river water Barge Jeannie made slow progress and Lynn enforced frequent rests for the tiring horse.

Newbury was three miles upstream, temptingly close to avoid laying up for another night but stopping would be a chance for Lynn to finish repairing the sail. Her Dad had taken to his bunk so Lynn had to tiller. She wanted to be walking Hermond, chatting to take his mind off the pull, to take her mind off needling memories.

If Nicholas cared at all he would have come out to see her today, after yesterday. For all he knew they were still grounded at Sheffield Lock and under threat. If he could afford a coat like he wore yesterday he could easily afford to hire a swift horse to ride to her. But today was the big fair and no doubt Mistress Olivia would be in her finery and Nicholas would be drooling after her like a puppy trying to impress with clever tricks. Unless that awful Sergeant Quinn was telling the truth. Which was most probable for how would he know anything to make it up? Then Master Middleton will be hunting down another girl at the fair.

It had taken well over an hour to cover a mile of river and Lynn gave Hermond another rest. With the man comes the mother thought Lynn with a quick smile at her escape from a lifetime of that prattling snob Mrs Middleton. Lynn waited until Hermond took the strain of the tow rope then slipped the mooring warp so Barge Jeannie didn't drift downstream and give the horse a jolt.

The son of that dreadful mother had been on the High Bridge throwing stones at her. She had only his word he was trying to stop them. Wasn't he wonderfully effective at that, thought Lynn cynically. Clop, clop, clop. She looked at the struggling Hermond, aware of the wound on his neck. Barge Jeannie was snug loaded or they'd never have made it this far. Instead of crying unfair why can't the store boy be like Adam and take advantage of the Kennet Navigation. He was small-minded, couldn't see an opportunity if it fired a broadside at him. But could she? Like her Dad, she'd scorned and dismissed Adam's point about Barge Jeannie being too small.

When Lynn decided to abandon reaching Newbury and moor for the night at Ham Lock she realised she had fully taken over as bargemaster. She hadn't even asked her Dad's opinion never mind his permission. The thought did not please her. Her Dad lay in the cabin with sweat trickling down the deep creases round his mouth that used to be folds of laughter.

Hermond stepped on towards the lock. Master Middleton could turn lock-keeper, collecting lockage fees. But there would be no women passing through for him to seduce then set aside. With her dad normally at the tiller, Lynn would run ahead and set the lock. Having to make a temporary mooring first had slowed their progress through today's locks. Lynn peered at Ham Lock ahead with a thankfulness. She was nevertheless dismayed the navvies had been negligent and left the tail gates open. Barge Jeannie glided into the chamber.

"Hurrah!" The cheer startled her. Men clambered through the bushes onto the towing path. Lynn recognised Lee first, then Gabriel, who gave her a crushing hug, and Sandy, Pick, Mogger, Burrer, and Cully with One-eye and a score more who swarmed over the barge.

"There's a right royal welcome for you in Newbury," said Gabriel.

The men dressed the mast with ribbons and roses, dripping bunting down the forestay, backstay and every shroud. They added a nest of mistletoe tied to the truck. Lynn looked up at the green crown and shuddered from the echo of her close call with Hawker.

"Where I come from mistletoe means – I overcome difficulties," said Gabriel. "That's you."

When Lynn heard the Mayor of Newbury was to welcome them personally she insisted she had to tidy her hair to a backdrop of ribald jeers as she disappeared into the cabin. But she was embarrassed on her reappearance by the whistles of approval. Lynn was wearing her one and only dress. She had never thought there would be occasion to wear it when, as they left Aldermaston, the wharfinger's wife had tossed it on board. "We can't have you with only working smocks," she had shouted. Lynn remembered the wharfinger hadn't said a word, just smiled at his wife. No matter she didn't have any petticoats but the simple dress was of the softest material Lynn had ever felt next to her skin.

Hermond had been unharnessed and he sported large rosettes and autumn flowers woven into his groomed mane. Lynn was sure he was as self-conscious as she was. The navvies picked up the tow rope and pulled Jeannie. At Greenham Lock Lynn started to feel the excitement of the arrival. She squirmed when Mogger gave his version of a familiar song, taken up by the gang towing Jeannie.

There was a youth, a well-beloved youth,
Who dug the Kennet yon:
He loved a bargee's daughter dear,
That lived in Islington.

"I know it ain't true, but that's the song and it rhymes," shouted Mogger, and then resumed singing loudly.

Yet she was coy and would not believe
That he did love her so.
No, nor at any time would she
Any favour to him show.

But when his friends did understand
His fond and foolish mind,
They sent him up to fair London
An apprentice for to bind.

And when he had been seven long years,
And never his love did see:
Many a tear have I shed for her sake,
When she little thought of me.

Mogger rubbed both eyes with the backs of his hands prompting great theatrical sighs from the navvies, who began the song again.

Approaching Newbury Lynn helped her Dad to the tiller. The navvies pulled the barge into the Basin, which was crowded on both sides and with the Mayor in full regalia at the head.

Lynn didn't remember much about everything that happened or what was said, it was too overwhelming. Gabriel later explained the pair were guests of the town with a room and food at the best inn. One thing she remembered was the deafening cheer and applause when she stepped ashore off Barge Jeannie. The other thing she could not forget was helping her Dad on to the wharf and seeing him collapse at her feet.

Side Bar, Anglers Tavern

Nicholas mutters into his ale. "What a damned Fair."

Frith mutters into his. "What a damned affair."

Man and youth snort to themselves.

"Woman?" asks Nicholas.

"Yes. Woman?"

"Yes."

Frith gazes at the yellow ceiling, hands behind his head. "In us we have two ages of Man confounded by the problem of Man."

They are lost in their reflections, only them in the tavern.

"I didn't go to the Fair," says Nicholas.

"Avoiding someone?"

"Olivia. You?"

"I went. Left smartly."

"Avoiding someone?"

They swig through another silence.

"She was there with her parents," says Frith.

"Oh."

Frith doesn't pursue it. "The Turners met your parents."

"So there was some entertainment."

Snatches of other encounters of the day drift through Frith's mind. He forces away that of Catherine before it can tip him into a maudlin pit. He pushes into his mind visions of Mistress Olivia at the Grotesque tent, the Reading Militia on the barge, Sarah in the Saracen's, Nicholas's father, Mr Hyde, Hawker kissing the girl. Catherine at the Fair.

"Before Woman," says Frith flatly, "I was going to write a groundbreaking article that would make the Reading Courant the most talked about newspaper in Berkshire. I would be the newsman other editors would court."

"Good dream. Article on what?"

"The Navigation. It wasn't groundbreaking because it wasn't based on any firm ground. Opinionated twaddle. What intrigues me are men like your father and Mayor Turner. They'd never have existed years ago, they'd be either serf or aristocracy. Now there's this new breed."

"Write about that," suggests Nicholas.

"No story." They sup. "Before Woman," repeats Frith, "what were your plans?"

"I'm twenty and destined to take over my father's businesses. I know less about them than I know about the art of the physician. I am to marry Olivia, to take . . ." He put down his tankard. "Actually, I didn't have plans. Everyone else had plans for me. I didn't have plans for me. Do you find that sad?"

"Lamentable dear boy. How about after Woman?"

There is a long silence during which Nicholas peers at the table. "I have one plan, to make a plan." Frith toasts the excellence of Nicholas's reply.

"After Woman for you, Mr Frith?"

"I don't know yet if this is After Woman," says Frith, mentally crossing his fingers. He realises he has let their conversation slip from their unspoken agreement of not dwelling on the painful. "I interviewed Captain Hawker the other day. He is an intriguing fellow, and the Reading Militia."

"Intriguing and inefficient."

"They have inordinate trouble catching these navvies believed to be burgling the grand houses."

"The Militia make their own mayhem" says Nicholas in a lively voice. "It would have been comical but for one of the Aldermen's Watch being stabbed. He died."

Frith questions Nicholas about the failed robbery and bungled arrest at Henry Woodroffe's house the previous night. He learns both the Militia and Watch lay in wait for the thieves who escaped in the confusion between the two groups.

"I've heard some more stolen property has been returned," says Frith. He is dismayed because he doesn't care that he has missed the newsworthy event of failed robbery and a fatality.

"Only the rubbish items," says Nicholas. "The silver, jewellery and valuable items are never found. Drab pictures by unknown painters and sentimental trophies is what the Militia recover."

"If a Watchman has been killed that should make people sit up."

"They're already sitting up about the Navigation," replies Nicholas. "What's a dead Watchman when their livelihoods are about to be flushed down the river?"

In the silence Frith detects the lad has sunk into his nest of doubts. "We've done Before Woman and After Woman is hopeless. What about Without Woman?"

"That needs another ale," says Nicholas.

"Brandy?"

"Better."

from Mistress Olivia's diary

I had been expecting an eternity of boredom at the Fair but my head still spins from the experience such that I cannot sleep. The only calmative for me is to write down as much as I dare, hoping none see the candlelight in my room.

These words are written long after the ink has dried on those preceding, for my head soared off the paper for some uncountable minutes. That must stop. It is necessary I complete what happened this day for it unnerved me.

I really, truly did intend to return home allowing nanny to go to the Fair. On the way I found myself passing through the amusements area and noticed the slack-rope had been taken down and the dancer nowhere in sight. I was strangely downhearted.

"Have you returned to see me?"

The voice was the higher pitch of a boy rather than older, which dismayed me for the rope-dancer's body was of a sinewy, lithe young man. The notion flashed through my head he is a castrato foregoing his manhood for his profession. I did not know how I felt about that. All this raced through my mind as I delayed the moment of turning my head. When I did Angelo was staring intently with the hint of a smile that sent a shiver through me.

"I had hoped to see you perform again," I said forcing my voice to sound normal.

"On or off the rope?" He beamed mischievously with his eyebrows lifting in quizzical exaggeration. The effect was to dazzle me with his eyes. I fought to keep a composure for my chest was rising and falling like a wafted sheet. I saw he took in this sight.

"On the rope of course."

"Of course." He had approached so close, had there not been a slight chill in the air I would have swooned. "Will you permit me to offer a beautiful young lady a command performance?"

I recognised the moment immediately. There have been others in my life where I had the choice to step forward into the uncertainty of either hazard or happiness, or step back and remain in the humdrum. No other of these critical moments was anywhere so thrilling as this offered. "If it matches the quality I witnessed earlier," I answered. "Dance on, Sir."

With too wide a grin I thought, Angelo led me from the bustle of the amusement area. With every step I wondered what I was doing yet each pace glided easily to where he had the slack-rope.

There was a canvas spread across the grass upon which Angelo laid the thick rope. He sat me on a chair and removed my shoes with such delicacy as I have never experienced from any shoe-fitter. I have the sense this minute as I write, of his hand sliding a little up my calf so he could coax off the shoe and his hand gliding down and drawing along my foot to the toes. I was re-shod in pumps with ankle laces and very soft soles. In consternation I real-ised I was to be giving the performance.

I concentrated hard on what Angelo told me to do. How to feel the rope with my instep and toes as I walked along it and to do quick half turns without stepping off. He was delighted by my balance and I progressed to small jumps, landing on the rope without looking. I confess that many of these ended with me wobbling to left or right and each time he was there to steady me. I declare none of my falling was deliberate. After some while my feet and ankles began to ache from the unusual effort asked of them. I did not express this but Angelo saw and stopped the instruction, pouring on me compliments on my ability and grace.

At that point he gave me a small card saying should I wish to take up rope-dancing it would be his privilege to teach me. First I must learn a little of tumbling. Angelo showed me how to fall without hurting myself, this being the only acrobatic I could attempt wearing a formal dress. I found this unnatural for instinct-ively I wanted to put out my arms only to experience a sharp pain in my wrist. Angelo's long fingers soothed scented oil into my wrist and forearm.

He stood behind me as I let my knees collapse to tumble. On the fourth attempt my concentration lapsed and I thrust forward my hands. Before I knew what was happening Angelo had encircled me with his strong arms pinning mine to my side and had somehow turned me about to face him. He held me tight and looked into my eyes with such intensity my whole body froze and melted at the same time. Except my mouth, which opened in a tiny sigh.

His lips were soft, moist and relentlessly moving against mine. I was losing my thinking and pushed away to be free. He held me firm. His hold was not brutish and I sensed he would release me had I pushed harder. Instead, my pushing transformed to pulling.

His hand slid off my shoulder and traced across my breast leaving a trail of yearning. It stroked down my side and clasped my buttock, briefly but so deliciously I tremble now at the sensation.

"Life is full of surprises, my delicate flower," he whispered.

Angelo took my hand in his and guided it to his thigh. At this I tensed for, exhilarating as his caress and kiss may be, I would not be a trollop for him. He reassured me and drew my fingers to press them against the join of his legs. I gasped. There was nothing there. I pulled away my hand in shock. He held me but I was flooded with confusion.

"My given name is Angela," he said softly.

At first I was without comprehension my mind functioning as a coach with no horses. Then it came to me and I was utterly repulsed and disgusted and mortified. I leapt from him and ran. Angelo, or Angela or whoever, did not restrain me or chase after me. I ran home. I needed to be somewhere familiar, somewhere safe. I stopped to be sick along Friar Street but nothing came up except a wail.

I do not know what to make of the episode. It is repulsive, it is frightening. It was luscious. No! It is wrong. I can taste his lips. Her lips! I smell the acrobat's make-up and sigh softly when I recall her hand run down my side. It is awful. I must imagine a handsome officer doing the same, crushing me against his uniform, his deep voice in my ear, his keenness pressing against me.

Angelo lives in lodgings in Wellclose Square in a district of London called White-Chapel. The Amazing Acrobatic Angelo. Angela. I have instructed myself to put her card to the flame of the candle.

Sunday 25th Newbury

Wakeman's journal – 6:15am

Woke at five-thirty from dreams of preparing to decorate an old house that I didn't recognise. Many people there, my father too, waiting for an agreed start time a long way off. I found a tool to make the job easier. So pleased I could help with the project.

Awake, I can sense the excitement, the urgency, associated with this tool but cannot recall it, cannot picture it. That is frustrating me, knowing the tool in my dream but not in this room.

The landlord mentioned Alford had human turds smeared throughout his kitchen one night last week. His wife has gone to her sister's, away from all their troubles. Catherine suggested I look into the Kennetmouth goings-on. After I look into the burglaries. Much happens everywhere, and also under the surface when one starts looking deep. All I see is the glance at Forbury Fair from my beloved. Beloved? What an airy-fairy word for the passion, desperation, longing I experience.

I have frequently looked through this lodgings window. Today I registered, for the first time, the white willow bordering the field. It is being choked by ivy that encases its trunk and winds along every bough. There is something in that beyond the obvious. What did the woman of Lanercost say they represent? She sat at the foot of the old Celtic cross to the fury of the Augustinian monks who shooed her away and their pupil back to his Latin texts.

Hedera, ivy. Its folklore meaning is marriage. Salix alba, the white willow. And that signifies ... mourning. How true that I should notice it today. No, that's weeping willow. The old woman said to put a picture in your mind to help remember. Salix alba, sail alba, sailing albatross. Freedom! Ha! Here through my window is freedom being strangled by marriage.

I vow the beautiful white willow will be released from its ivy fetters before dusk.

memoirs of Sir George Crockmore

My Michaelmas Day Ball this year surpassed all others. I broadcast this neither as immodesty nor to inflate my prestige. My important and influential guests were profuse with praise at the lavishness: for Cook's masterpiece with the geese, for the afternoon entertainment, and for the splendid music. The success was the result of my endeavour and expenditure, governed by my detailed preparation and attention to every detail. Such achievements do not happen by chance, as many men vouch in exculpation of their laziness.

The kitchen maid, charged to replenish drinks and snacks of those idling round the marquee during the afternoon activities, had taken a needle to her smock. Several gentlemen tried their hand upon her, only to grasp the September air after the zephyr swirled away from reach, favouring me with adoring looks. This gave delight to the ladies who had intrigue to discuss.

Much mirth and great tongue wagging came about when Lady Elisabetta was at the butts coincidentally with the young widow, Baroness Anne. Having walked to retrieve her shots the baroness was pierced through the thigh by an arrow from the bow of Lady Elisabetta, who claimed to have been startled at the moment of loosening her arrow and was altogether distraught at the mishap. Baroness Anne was hastily conveyed to the house and soon took coach to London. There followed whispered bespattering that the fine archer Elisabetta had hit a gold on her intended target. Both ladies are enamoured of the same Count who plays a merry game of setting one against the other. One guest, a plain wife, made suggestion that Baroness Anne would then be at home offering her wounded thigh to the attentions of the Count. Very soon after, the comely Lady Elisabetta had a sudden pretext to return to London.

Another rivalry emerged between the finalists in the fencing, who were at daggers-drawn before the en garde. So entrenched was the determination of each, that the gambling proved equally ferocious. As host I offered to act as stake-holder, taking bets on first blood, second blood, cuts to head, arms and chest. Out of this charitable act I gleaned funds to clear the account of the marquee contractors should I decide to settle their account.

I am of the belief that needs engender invention. With no Mistress of Southcote Hall there was the rankling question of whom to seat at the head of the dining table. The Duchess of Mont-fern was the most elevated of my lady guests and thus she must be head-seated, though she bears a visage I did not wish to look upon for the duration of the banquet. However, I could not expect her to perform table duty. This quandary had brought me to the invention of a Carver, a person with the requisite skill with the knife hired in for the evening. This was the talk of the dinner, and will be for some weeks hereafter I have no doubt.

This morning I took a light breakfast with my guests, giving orders for the laundry maid to be sent to me the instant she returns from church. The Duchess had craved my ministrations before she retired. She had ordered a supper to my bed chamber that was comprised of a bowl of burnt wine, a cake of chocolate that she unsparingly grated into the wine, an almond flummery and a lemon syllabub. She instructed me in the manner by which they were to be consumed. This was by smearing each comestible over appointed portions of her body and displaying my delight in devouring them therefrom, at times feeding her from my mouth. During the course of her passion she pronounced the preparations thus rubbed into her skin did revitalise it. For my part I consider she has left such remedies too late.

I could not determine if the cause of my later disgorgement lay in the sugariness of the foodstuff or the unclean, furrowed platter. I experienced no pleasure of my own but caused the Duchess much writhing with delight. This is to the good as Gertrude has the atten-tion of the most influential ears in Court and commerce. To protect her modesty, the bed linen shall be discretely laundered.

Wakeman's journal – 9:00am

My landlady was bewildered by my burst of activity, attacking the ivy as if it were a French patrol snooping round John Churchill's camp at Ramillies. She did not enquire when serving my breakfast. She is canny, I am the fool. The ivy is not Erebus. Even if I manage to cut it all down that will not cut Catherine free. Mindless hard labour, however absurd and illogical, finds me the oblivion I crave on this empty day of the week. The two interviews I have arranged are as two dandelions in a ploughed field.

When a runner of ivy brushed my arm it was Catherine's touch at the Herbary. When we were sitting she had absent-mindedly taken my wrist and gently brushed my finger tips along the inside of her other arm. I knew what she was sensing and let her have control of my hand and arm.

I draw my fingers over my skin and recall the smooth cool of hers and the gentle yet enlivening stimulation we gave each other.

from Mistress Olivia's diary

"Did you seek out the Barge-bilge after you promised not to?" I pressed the hand of Master Nicholas Middleton on the Sacred Book and told him if he tried to remove his hand or if he failed to answer it would be confirmation of his perfidy. He started some long excuse about delivering provisions. "Did you walk with her to a nearby field?"

He could not mask his surprise. Thus I knew my informant had not lied. A rage flared through me and I was about to scream at him in front of the High Altar when I recalled my previous loss of composure when questioning him.

I had dressed to advantage with my russet silk-shag, allowing three twists of hair to fall against the shoulder even though we were for Church. I noted with amusement Mrs Middle-gone grandly receiving the smiles from the congregation, failing to see how they were laughing at her. I nodded to Master Middleton and quickly looked down for I believe this is a fetching gesture of mine. I was not surprised he agreed to return with me into St Mary's after the service to admire the decorations of flowers.

"Did you bundle with this Barge-bilge in the field?" There was a mumbled yes.

"Did you swive with her?" Master Middleton went red but vigorously shook his head.

I spoke as forcefully as I dare in the sacred place without drawing attention from outside. "How much did she charge you?"

He found voice not for himself but in vindication of the slag's good name. Efackins!

"Why are you saying these things?" I asked suddenly breaking from Madam Wrath into Mistress Wronged. "It is hurtful to learn you have gone with another. And on top of that to defend the harpy, it is just too much." A tear came to my eye exactly at the right moment. "You have speared my heart with your betrayal. Not content with that you shred my heart with every word you utter defending the harlot."

I continued thus for a brief while then took to shuddering with great sobs. Finally I sank to the stone floor under the crucifix of our Lord leaving the twist-tongue at a loss how to comfort me. Everything he attempted made me the more wretched.

When I heard a church official enter I made a great effort to collect myself and with a lace kerchief to my eyes walked out of St Mary's with Master Middleton trailing hopelessly.

I could be a great actress. But this morning's performance is not sufficient. Any suitor of mine shall keep his undivided attention to me. It is my prerogative to turn from him. Master Middleton has by no means suffered enough for his waywardness.

Interview with Reverend James Collins, Grazeley

Courant. I apologise for disturbing you on your busiest day, Reverend.

Collins. Please don't concern yourself. Saturday is busier what with preparing today's sermon and the evening Service. Plus as every day, my flock to shepherd. You mentioned you are employed by the Reading newspaper. Might I be named?

Courant. The editor may not include my article, for reasons of policy. Should it be published your name can be withheld.

Collins. Oh – I see.

Courant. Though having your name in the piece would give more credence to the article.

Collins. I see that. Very well, I agree. Not for myself you under-stand, it is for the enlightenment of others. You intimated your visit is to do with this dreadful contagion of burglaries.

Courant. I gather the vicarage has been plundered by the thieves.

Collins. I would hardly say plundered aptly describes the crime. We of the cloth live modest lives. For the thieves to pick on this vicarage must indicate they are very desperate people. Such crime on one's doorstep was a tremendous shock. Not in the loss of the items taken for they are but chattels of our life on Earth, but through the intrusion into one's home, one's sanctuary. At the time this struck me as a personal violation, and I admit to you I gave way to anger. With the Lord's help I put that behind me.

Courant. Perhaps the Lord's help was present in the return of the stolen property. May I see it?

Collins. To your left, on the dresser.

Courant. A very fine tray. So heavy. Silver? The chamfered corners add elegance.

Collins. It is splendid, don't you think? The proportions have a wonderful perfection to them and there is a pleasing absence of fussiness. That young man who made it is a master silversmith and will surely make a name for himself. Turn it over and you will see his mark.

Courant. LA?

Collins. Paul de Lamerie.

Courant. There is also a dedication engraved. I take it this tray is a gift from your parish?

Collins. My previous incumbency. The gratitude of my flock expressed in temporal form. It was a small hamlet located in the grounds of a great house. I was pastor to the titled family. Though I know it is against the teachings of our Saviour to venerate material objects, I cannot forbear from the memories I associate with that tray.

Courant. It must have been a great relief to have had it returned.

Collins. Indeed it was. I would have willingly paid ten-fold to redeem it.

Courant. You paid the thief for the return of your property?

Collins. Goodness me, no. It was returned by the Reading Militia. A charming soft-spoken gentleman with thick black hair who explained they had come across it in their hunt for the thieves.

Having been told of the expenses they had incurred in its recovery, and how any contribution I might offer goes towards the upkeep of the Militia, I was more than happy to give a little.

Courant. How much?

Collins. Gifts are a private matter between the giver, the recipient and Our Lord. It was nothing like the value of the tray.

Courant. You refer to thieves not thief. I presume the Militia told you it was a gang?

Collins. They did. Though they only confirmed what my house-keeper saw when she left the vicarage that night. It was somewhat later than usual and she was startled by three strangers in the lane. Being aware of her vulnerable situation she hurried on as quickly as she could.

Courant. Can we surmise these men stayed in the lane until they saw you had retired to bed?

Collins. They had broken in before I returned. I had been out from the early evening at the personal invitation of Sir George Crockmore. He invites local persons of importance or upstanding in the community on a Friday evening for an intimate soirée. I would stress that I do not indulge in the games of chance that are a regular feature after dinner. I am present for sociable reasons as well as private discourse concerning spiritual welfare.

Courant. You said items were taken.

Collins. I gave a full list with valuations to the commander of the Reading Militia when he called to investigate the break in.

Courant. So I have a more full picture for my article could you make a list for me?

Collins. I have a copy in my escritoire.

Courant. That is a handsome piece of furniture.

Collins. Walnut. Do you see the feather-banded drawers? Each has a moulded divide. I insisted the insert be of the highest quality leather, hoping that writing upon it may produce the highest quality sermons.

Courant. This list of missing items is quite lengthy.

Collins. A few bits and pieces. Tokens of appreciation.

Courant. Still a significant loss.

Collins. Nothing so great as the de Lamerie tray.

Courant. Mostly silver items?

Collins. Some fine porcelain as well. However, it is the sentimental loss that eclipses the monetary. Especially the silverware.

Courant. They too were engraved?

Collins. Only the tray. On reflection Mr Frith, I think it wise not to publish a list of the stolen items. There is no need for the parish to know the private affairs of its vicar.

Courant. May I include details about the recovered tray?

Collins. Perhaps not.

Courant. How about a "treasured item"?

Collins. A "small cherished item" would be best.

Wakeman's journal – 11:00am

This hacking and tugging labour drives cogent thought from my mind. Good. It is mechanical. Good. In part symbolic, in part numbing, in part a belief I am doing something for Catherine that isn't words, in part frustration, in part anger. I am nothing but parts yet all these parts add up to a longing and emptiness.

I found the ivy had completely encircled the trunk from the ground to its first branches. A coarse, abrasive girdle of wrist-thick aerial roots sucking out life and strangling beauty. So thick and clinging that my hands were ineffectual. I vowed it would be done, this crazy, uncelebrated mission for Catherine. Borrowed the land-lord's ladder and a saw. The ivy will be sawn, pulled, cut, levered and ripped from the willow. The choking ivy will be burnt.

memoirs of Sir George Crockmore

The smiling faces of my guests this morning erased yesterday's disagreeable finale. I console myself there are harsh things to be undertaken here and now that the days after may bear more plentiful reward. I cite the pinching out of a side growth that the stem of fruit be greater.

In this frame of mind have I been considering Mr Newton's recent *Principia* where he declares every action has an equal and opposite reaction. I disagree. Effect is not drawn from a single cause, discounting of course the church's *Causa Causans* of but one God. If a man's action were from a single cause it would be effortless to predict him, and his behaviour arrested before it manifests in extreme practice.

Having fortuitously tested the smoked fish and found it barely warm, I excused myself from the informal breakfast to seek the cause, being most perturbed when Cook flung her apron to the kitchen floor. The dozen guests staying for the hunt would be sore hungry after their exertions should Cook walk out. I asked Cook had I not treated her fairly, and was she not known as my most valued servant. It was to my advantage to raise her indebtedness, and she replied in the affirmative. Adding, she had been valued until these recent days.

The new kitchen maid has taken to behaving as Mistress Designate of Southcote Hall. She addresses Cook as if Cook were her servant, and obliging all staff to address her as Penelope. Cook's resentment ignited this morning on finding the hunters' pies not prepared. The maid had skived to the Fair yesterday, had arisen this morning just in time to attend Church, where it was noticed she sported a gold neck chain. I was more enraged by this souvenir than a catalogue of misdemeanours in Cook's kitchen. Taking action, as is my aptitude, I suggested Cook devoted her skill to the pies while Agnes complete the breakfasts without the smoked fish. Cook was left in no doubt the upstart maid would be severely censured, her wages revoked, and dismissed unless she proved unequivocally apologetic.

When summoned to me, the repentant maid did not deny visiting the Fair, but claimed she bought the neck chain with an advancement against her wages. At this revelation I vouched to verify her story with the bookkeeper, and she pleaded earnestly I should enquire also of the chain seller who would remember her. I doubted the rascal would be found, for the chain was base metal made to look golden. The maid confessed meeting Captain Hawker, swearing on her life resistance to his entreaties as I had bade her. By then the girl was in tears, flinging herself before me in abject pleading, which did some way satisfy me. But I recalled how much she is actress and competent in the art when her mind is set to it. I lectured her again, then despatched her to Cook to grovel for forgiveness.

This interview had occurred in my ante room, which also serves as a small library and reading room. To compose myself before engaging with my remaining guests I settled to read. After a few pages a soft tapping on the door disclosed a contrite maid wearing the smock that had delighted my guests. The little girl, for that is what she had become, whimpered how naughty she had been and whispered in short breaths the only way she could believe herself forgiven was if her Master were to mete some punishment on her.

To assuage the girl's desolation, I bent her over the side arm of the twin chair-back settee and lifted her skirts above her back. Her magnificent firm buttocks were as a dream after the nightmare I had endured the previous night. Tantalus knew nothing of the temptation before my eyes and I could not resist reaching out to caress the creamy pears against my palm and thrill to their gyrations in my hand. I smacked her hard across the right buttock and was rewarded with a tiny yelp, a heat in my hand and a firming member. My second smack was more fierce and better placed, making her backside quiver from the blow. Her yelp encouraged me to set about reddening both her cheeks with right and left hand until she began uttering low moans.

Then came a rapidity of carnal desire from I know not where. Uppermost in my mind was this happening was consequence from the wiles of the actress. This thought drove me to push my member without pause at her arse and, at her shriek, to thrust it forcefully. To muffle her howls each time I gave her my length, I pressed her face into cushions, and continued so until I was fully satisfied.

Such was the maid's reparation. I argue my reaction was not directly the outcome from the action or cause, of her begging. It came from the myriad of causes in her, in Cook and within myself, the sum of which lead to the event. Thereby is Mr Newton proven false.

Wakeman's journal – 3:00pm

Each ivy tentacle I rip from a willow bough worsens my agitation over Catherine. That is a surprise for I expected it to lift as each bough of willow was freed. On what is this bilious agitation founded? Not knowing? This pointless exercise of hacking ivy? I must get on with my life, try to find an island of calm normality.

How can I compete with a man who leaches sympathy from a woman? Who succours himself through weakening her. Saps her compassion. I can't steer her, beg her or push her towards the values she must adhere to as an individual. She has to find them. That is impossible while she sees herself only in relation to him.

A bleeding physician

Since Saturday evening her dad had said nothing Lynn could understand. The Mayor had ordered his private physician to examine Peter once he was carried from the wharf and made comfortable at the Malt Wagon.

A kindly looking gentleman arrived two hours later and set about examining the patient. He prodded the dark blotches on the skin holding a candle close to see the colour. "Excellent, another bruise," he pronounced with each groan from Peter. He inspected under the arms and round the groin.

"I find no indicators of Capital Fever," he announced to the landlord, who had watched the whole examination with a worried look from the doorway. The physician explained his morbid joke. "London Fever. It comes from our capital city and it is a capital illness as in bringing death."

"That's a great relief, Sir," said the landlord. "If he brings the plague to my inn that's my death warrant. I'll be closed down by the authorities never mind having no lodgers or drinkers. Burn it down, they might."

"What's wrong with my Dad?" interrupted Lynn.

"Nothing for you to be worried about."

"He won't die?"

"We all die. I shall return the morrow and administer cures and restoratives to delay the inevitable until its due time."

The landlord brought a bowl of beef stew with dumplings, a jar of ale and told Lynn not to worry. "It's paid for by the Mayor."

The room was ten times larger than Jeannie's cabin yet Lynn felt oppressed and hemmed in. She dozed in a chair through the night listening to the wheezing breaths of her Dad and wondered about the fair far away in Reading.

The physician reappeared after morning church. The landlord presented him with an ale and whisky chaser. "On the town," explained the landlord with a wink.

"Double fees on a Sunday," replied the physician, and the pair toasted the town treasury.

The physician asked Lynn many questions. Several she could not answer, such as what colour was her dad's urine, his stools. He prescribed a term of bloodletting to drain the ill humours that had provoked the fever. He advised twice daily visits for a week.

The kindly man turned sour when Lynn insisted she would be taking away his patient the next day. The physician was the more qualified to know about fevers and their cure. Inferior practitioners churned the ill humours through the body with hasty letting. He could not credit Lynn putting her dad at such risk by removing him from his knowledgeable treatment.

Lynn itched to be away from the smoky room with its badly drawn fire and stench from the street. Her dad needed to be in the only place he was happy. He had lost hope after the death of Mam, living whole weeks in alcohol. On this trip with Barge Jeannie he had regained a part of his old self. Lynn stood firm against the physician, on her instinct, fighting the part of herself that bowed, through a lifetime of its application, to male authority.

As instructed, Lynn did ensure her Dad stayed face down with one arm dangling over the side of the bunk so the heavier humours would collect into this arm. The physician returned in the afternoon, persisting for his double fees, and made two lengthy cuts down Peter's forearm. They watched Peter's blood run into a basin on the floor. After the physician had finished his second ale, the flow stopped, and he pronounced the gross humours expelled. He cautioned only some had been removed but Lynn was adamant about departing the next day. She nursed her ashen Dad alone through Sunday night.

Interview with Blaydon Thurgood Esquire, Ufton Nervet

Courant. When was your painting stolen?

Thurgood. I have told everything to that brutish Captain. Ask him why don't you?

Courant. Captain Hawker is concerned with the crime, I am interested in the personal side. A theft from one's home is a loss in many senses.

Thurgood. You are indeed so right. I was distraught.

Courant. I should think so. I gather it was painted by Peter Lely.

Thurgood. The name of the artist is neither here nor there. It is only to assure a good rendition by a skilled craftsman. The subject is paramount. You do know it is called Ladies of the Thurgood Family. A magnificent portrait of my two younger sisters. I was overwhelmed how the artist captured their delicate beauty. But the thought of some lewd lout's coarse hands . . .

Courant. When was it taken?

Thurgood. Oh, that infamous day! For once I was ahead at the table, not much, but compared to my previous ill-luck a penny is as good as a guinea. I was so happy . . . and then when I had returned home to find a bare wall . . . there . . . where my adorable sisters should have been. I plummeted faster than Satan from Heaven to Hell.

Courant. But your spirits were resurrected with its return. Why have you not rehung it?

Thurgood. It has no frame. I am awaiting a new one.

Courant. Why would the thief go to the trouble of separating a Lely canvas from its frame and keep the frame?

Thurgood. The frame was full-yellow gilded in pure leaf, very costly. My painting was so well known, by such a renown artist it would be impossible to sell, so the Barbarian removed it from the frame. It was providence the Reading Militia found it before the elements could ruin it.

Courant. By any chance, did you pay a fee for its recovery?

Thurgood. Absolutely not.

Courant. Nothing?

Thurgood. If I had, it is none of your business. I may have offered something to the running expenses of the Militia, such was my gladness. I forget.

Courant. May I view a work of the great Peter Lely?

Thurgood. It is not at its best without the frame.

Courant. Agreed, but a unique masterpiece is always worth seeing. If I may?

Thurgood. I am sure you will fully appreciate it however it is presented. It is just here.

Courant. You keep it in easy reach.

Thurgood. See, the girls are still radiant.

Courant. They are very pretty ladies. They look so . . . young. You say they are your sisters?

Thurgood. The taller on the right is Gloriana and the other with the lute is Honbria.

Courant. When was this painted.

Thurgood. It was five years ago when I commissioned Mr Lely.

Courant. Commissioned? Only five years ago?

Thurgood. Honbria is the baby of the family.

Courant. The painting shows her fully a young lady. As is her sister. Those are daring necklines for demure young ladies.

Thurgood. It was my suggestion. It is the fashion.

Courant. Indeed. The luxuriant folds and sensual colours of their dresses emphasise the paleness of the skin and the very direct gaze of the sitters. Would you agree? Mr Thurgood?

Thurgood. What? You are knowledgeable about fine painting.

Courant. Merely describing what I see. I am enlightened Mr Lely signs the canvas L-i-l-l-e-y.

Thurgood. He is a Dutchman.

Courant. That would explain it.

Thurgood. Now you have seen the painting I am sure you have other important matters demanding your attention. I am expecting visitors imminently.

Courant. I do apologise for taking up your time and am indebted to you for allowing me to see this Lely. I can see how the rendition of your sisters must make you proud.

Thurgood. Indeed it does.

Courant. I will leave you to your imminent business in hand. Do tell Mistress Gloriana and Mistress Honbria, when they arrive, I am sorry to have missed them in the flesh.

Thurgood. Goodbye, Mr Frith.

from Mistress Olivia's diary

How to exercise sufficient punishment on Master Middleton confounds me. My parents are rooted in Reading like two ancient oaks. Papa continues to believe he is not in need of a London property. Mama replied a vigorous no when I casually asked if she would like the delights of London, saying she has no reason for London shops on her doorstep. This is false excuse. In this town she is renown for her beauty and being wife to the leading citizen whereas in London she would be one of many with faded looks and her fashion years out of date. She fears being reduced to a pleasant looking woman whose pretty daughter receives the handsome suitors she once could command.

It is my glittering future that is stagnating in this backwater and that sorely vexes me, more so than that irritation Master Middleton. I have not had word back from Mr Delpeck and that is irritating.

With these thoughts scorching my mind I sought out my little brother and sister. After sending away nanny on some errand I showed Lousy how twisting both my hands in opposing direction round her forearm did give her a mild burning sensation. I let her practise on my forearm and was a little taken aback by the strength she drew from her skinny limbs. When I suggested she include her brother in the game she grabbed Podgy's flabby arm with glee. I cupped my hand across his howling mouth claiming he was pretending and chided him for being a poltroon. His flailing arm caught Lousy on the cheek incensing her to such a madness she set about him with admirable vigour. I let go of Podgy that he might defend himself with determination.

When Mama is denied what she has set her sights on she is

disagreeable with Papa. She refused to raise her voice never mind her hand to the girl brat for applying tortures to the boy brat. Mama declared her husband's son must have started it and Papa replied in a sharp voice the identity of the torturer was as plain as a pikestaff. Mama told him never to use that tone of voice to her.

I fear Papa will soon succumb to this wearing changeableness in Mama, that he will seek relief by granting her the Reading house. Then there is Master Middleton to make suffer more for crossing me. I am blocked from every arena of progress. Even with my skills in . . .

I shivered thinking about it. My mind had dallied on the kiss from the slack-rope dancer. Was that from a delight in the sensation or from it being illicit? But I didn't know it was a heathen act at the time. I stop myself for that avenue of thought must be blocked. Then I feel the softness of moist lips against mine. Her moist lips

It matters not a jot. Angela could be anywhere in the Kingdom. Perhaps she has found a girl almost as pretty as me. Oh! She will return to London while I am stuck here. I wonder what White-Chapel is like. She did not say what is special about the punch served at the Three Nuns Inn. Does she go there attired as boy or girl? How are her lodgings furnished?

I am so blind! I have my mind set on a certain thing believing it what I want when it is but a means to what I really desire. I do not want Papa to own a house in London – I want to dwell in London. I can dwell in London in lodgings. And such bliss with no Mama to undo all I attempt or choose to wear. And no brats. It is altogether an ideal solution.

Again I am blocked. Mama and Papa will forbid it unless I lodge with a chaperone trusted by them. Someone who will spoil all my comings and going, who will restrict my enterprises, who will tell tales to my parents. We have no family in London who could be persuaded to be more amenable than a chaperone. I have no acquaintances there. Marry-come, my life is one of a succession of problems.

memoirs of Sir George Crockmore

As my guests walked the horses through Blagrave's Estate, gay in amiable witty conversation, the absence of any culinary aromas gave me concern there would be no lunch at the lodge. My Michaelmas Ball had so quickly had the crest knocked from it. I soon eschewed these dispirited thoughts, for a man of diverse talent will savour the high moment for its own worth.

Cook had excelled herself with a bountiful spread, including a variety of pies still deliciously warm. The maid had maintained diligent silence, thereby achieving much in convincing Cook of her repentance. My relief seeing the voracity with which the hunters attacked the food was a fortifying preparation when I came to deal with my evening visitor.

Captain Hawker hardly allowed himself to be announced before he filled my receiving room with his pacing, fulmination, threats to my person and accusations against my integrity. All these I withstood without offering him one word upon which he might spark a brawl, though I stood within quick grasp of the bell cord.

I slowly unfathomed there had been a mêlée in the grounds of Woodroffe's house. The outcome was minor cuts and bruises to some Reading Militia and Aldermen's Watch with one of the latter succumbing to a fatal knife wound. The Captain's rant on the single cause was as mistaken as are Mr Newton's ideas, there being several causes for both groups being present at the same location.

Waiting upon the Captain to complete his slander against my person allowed me to orchestrate my response. I was candid in saying the Mayor speculated there might be a burglary at Woodroffe's on that Friday night, and I anticipated he would inform Captain Hawker. The Mayor utilising the Watch is confirmation of his and the town's disfavour towards their Militia.

I quickly moved the topic to the rising antagonism throughout the Kingdom against coteries of constables, that being my phrase of the moment, as understood in the Uniformed Brigand Act. I reminded Captain Hawker they had failed to bring to trial any villain for several months. In the unfriendly glare of public and parliamentary scrutiny, it was clear the Reading Militia must disband. To my dismay the Captain refused point blank, declaring his men had a vital purpose with much more to be achieved. He then spoke loudly and wildly, threatening to destroy me along with himself should I proceed with my intent. This is the foot soldier commanding the officer! Such attitude indicates a mutinous seam in Captain Hawker.

It was essential to distract the Captain from the topic, so I informed him the infamous Barge Jennie was set to return the morrow accompanied by a hoard of navigators. Their employ on the Kennet Navigation being ended, a trail of mayhem, looting and destruction is their likely purpose, to which the wharf men will undoubtedly respond. Captain Hawker could be the salvation of the town and the Reading Militia held again in good favour. I postulated the merchants' area would be vulnerable to plundering by other bands of navigators approaching along the Bath or the Oxford Road. I was rewarded to see Captain Hawker recognise where his duty lay.

My remaining duty of the evening is to draft a brief letter for delivery by night messenger, then order my chastened kitchen maid deliver her gratifying supper.

Wakeman's journal – 7:00pm

"I found a small place to hide," she said. "A tiny place deep inside me. Away from everything."

Through telling me Catherine let me join her in her hiding place.

"I am damaging everyone. I'm having to be duplicitous. Never with you, Quillman, because of what we have."

I sensed that link between us from our first meeting and became more sure each time we were together. She didn't have to say it. Not at this awful time. It sounded ominous rather than reaching out to hold on to me for support. I know it is the latter. How do I know? Do I want it to be our truth, therefore I believe it is?

Did I really sense something very special between us at our first meeting or am I believing that because of what has happened in the forty-two plus some days since? What did I write at the time?

Wakeman's journal of Tuesday 9th August

Following her visit yesterday to the Courant, Mr Hyde suggested he, Mrs Lampry, myself and young Jake partake of the Saracen's Head. I had been pleasantly agitated from the instant I saw Mrs Lampry. In the tavern, she did not talk to me, yet it was as if the two of us were waiting for our private conversation. Her mirthful eyes spoke to me, though she faced the person whom she addressed. First with Sarah who talked lengthily about her mother, then the two women swapping experiences of working in the Saracen's at different times. Next some chap who thought he could impress Mrs Lampry with his knowledge of painting. Mr Hyde asked a little on her stay in London and they spoke on their common acquaintances in Reading.

This morning there was a note from Mrs Lampry accompanied by a small print of a Japanese cat. What did she mean "not enough time – or perhaps too much other was going on"? I am reading between her lines, have underlined phrases. I am making words take on special meaning. What I am doing is ridiculous, fanciful. Yet her note was sent to me, not the editor, and that must be significant. As significantly meaningful as ending her note "Catherine".

Catherine's note of Tuesday 9th August

Thank you for making my visit so nice, <u>so engaging for me</u>. I feel it went well. Many things I do have to be done quickly, and I feel I don't have time to work through ideas properly. Do you ever revisit ideas? I sometimes return to themes. Maybe because a <u>new experience</u> has given me <u>a different insight</u> into what I'd thought I'd resolved and sometimes it's because I had left too hurriedly to work on something else.

Oh yes, yesterday. I felt <u>we didn't have enough time</u>, or perhaps <u>too much else was going on</u>. I wanted to follow up your ideas about mixing words and paintings <u>with each other, mingled</u>, not abutted as in cartoons. Anyway, it deserves some discussion and perhaps we can do that via letters or maybe <u>us getting together</u> for a meeting.

I enclose the print I mentioned in Mr Hyde's office, plus a
curriculum vitae of my work as an engraver as I realise I
hadn't done that. But I didn't want to do too much too soon!!!

Wakeman's journal of Tuesday 9th August continued

This note is a straightforward thank you. Assuredly, but for the
twisting of my guts from the moment Mrs Catherine Lampry
entered the composition room. I was elevated by her presence,
made sure I sat next to her, heard little what Mr Hyde said, but felt
throughout my body the woman sitting next to me. I took every
excuse to turn and look at her. I made certain she would deal with
me, not Mr Hyde, on any etchings or cuts she might do for the
Courant. She is exciting. Was that her enthusiasm for her work?

Around forty? Hard to judge with her compulsive brightness. She
can be girl or sage. She had Mr Hyde smiling, and taking us all into
the Saracen's. Wild frizzy raven-black hair, deep dark-brown eyes
and a big enveloping smile generous with the bold lip paint. Solid,
not flabby, shapely body and wonderfully big hands, bigger than
mine and flecked with ink and paint. Her thrilling eyes drawing me
into her. In what I write in this journal entry am I underlining parts
of my memory as I did with the words in Mrs Lampry's note?
Picking out what my heart senses, highlighting the carefully placed
ambiguities?

Was my underlining quill guided by intuition? That rainbow eel
of mischief.

Wakeman's journal – 7:00 pm continued

I want her so ardently it bleaches all else, dissolves my concentration. The irony lances me that, since Erebus discovered us, we have
been together longer and more intensely. Catherine wants me to
keep writing letters. She will read, then burn them.

The bonfire in the field is now embers. I am the one still burning.

A note handed to Sir George Crockmore

*Mr Darville wee Bargemen of Redding thought to acquaint you
before 'tis too late, Dam You, if you work a bote any more to
Newbery wee will Kill You if ever you come any more this way,
wee was very near shooting you last time, wee went with
pistolls and was not too minutes too late. The first time your
boat lays at Redding loaded, Damn You, wee will bore holes in
her and sink her so don't come to starve our fammeleys and our
Masters, for Damn You if you do we will send you short home
for you have no occasion to come to teak the bred out of Oure
Childrens Mouths. Take warning before 'tis too late for Damn
You for ever if you come wee will doo it.*

memoirs of Sir George Crockmore

Mayor Turner gushed with the calamity that had befallen many of
the town, recounting how persons stood bewildered in the street or
wailed unceasingly of their woes. One vile wretch had taken his
own life, leaving his family to suffer the shame of his suicide while
struggling through their lives paying off his debt. I obliquely
enquired after the Mayor's own position and congratulated him for
embracing my advice of the previous week. He asked how I knew
the South Sea Company stock was to collapse. I stated the quality
of what one knows derives from the quality of who one knows.

The Mayor was too full of pernicious glee, listing rivals who
faced the Debtor's Prison, for me to embark immediately on the
matter for which I had summoned him. The parochial man is obli-
vious of the widespread repercussions, whereas I have applied my
sagacity beyond the immediately visible. There are to be had for
picking many ripe windfalls from this South Sea tree that has been
shaken to its roots by the wind storm of Mammon. The morrow I
shall do profitable business in the Capital. My action is not imitation of the scavengers who glean from the bodies of fallen soldiers,

for these investors are felled through their own volition and greed-blinded stupidity. The Mayor concluded with most pleasing news that the populace, in want of a scapegoat, are laying their misfortunes squarely on the Whigs.

I then acquainted Mayor Turner of the troublesome barge and its squadron of navigators, hell-bent on trouble, showing him the note, but not disclosing how I came by it. The barge attaining his town trailing destruction, bloodshed and deaths would see Mayor Turner the scapegoat, as his office is granted the information and authority to ensure peace. I argued the extent and numbers involved were too great for the Reading Militia and Aldermen's Watch, and he must request a Company of the Yeomanry. The Mayor nodded agreement and I dismissed him that he may hasten to pen his letter.

Thus I discharged my responsibilities to the town, its environs and all citizens through the proper channels that have been through the centuries so strenuously established in this great Kingdom.

Wakeman's journal – 10:00am

Mary had told her, "Leave him. Right now. He's killing you."

Brother-in-law said, "Get out from him, you dozy cow."

Catherine told Erebus, "It's over. It's empty."

His answer. "You are an adulteress. I have done nothing wrong."

She was silent, defeated.

She saw only the result, her adultery, not the cause, him. Why won't she leave? Catherine had taken her note to Sarah's house. I bless Sarah for passing it on to me so quickly. Why won't my love meet me today? It's been three eternities of daylight since I spoke, touched, kissed her. Tomorrow is too long to wait until I see her.

"It takes two." His accusation was another bludgeon to her. He quotes my letters to her. Erebus has memorised them. He read them and read them until he was blind with hate and could read no more. He didn't burn them in a rush of hurt anger. He schemed how to use them to wound her for ever. He made her watch him burn them. The Darkness pulls down Catherine until she vanishes.

Five minutes. Anywhere. She can do that even if Erebus is home ill. Another ruse to win her pity, another tether about her. Is she that crushed? Why can't she leave him?

Am I failing to do something? Am I not saying the thing she needs to hear to make the break? Catherine was resolute, "I have to decide about my marriage. Then we can decide abut our future." One, two – practical. I have to let her decide, otherwise I am no better than Erebus, dictating what she is to do, what she is to be. Damn it! She hasn't control of her life. Have I shown her where the reins are? She won't let me put them in her hands. Do I take over? Do this, come here, say so-and-so. That's not the woman I fell in love with. Not the woman I want to be with.

A free board

"A few of us want to come with you," said Gabriel.

"If you don't sing all the way." Lynn thought a dozen navvies would keep Hawker well away. Once past him and then past Reading she wouldn't ever come near that town ever again. Once past Reading Jeannie would belong to her Dad again, that's what he had said. The men's company would keep her mind occupied.

Newbury merchants had vied to get their cargo on the first barge down the Kennet Navigation. Lynn looked from the stern at the deck cargo draped with burly men. That morning Gabriel had received a letter about work to be had near Great Marlow to build a water mill for the men of Temple to help them beat out their brass plates into ornaments. A change from mud he joked. Hermond was released from his duties as navvies took turns on the tow rope. It was easier as the current was with them. Most walked alongside with no freeboard for them on the fully laden barge.

Lynn talked to her Dad through the open cabin docr, convinced he looked much better than yesterday. Sometimes he would reply with a feeble grunt. Gabriel encouraged Dicky to start up a song. After the first round Mogger took it over with his own version.

O where ha' you been, Lord Randal, my son?
And where ha' you been, my handsome young man?
I ha' been to Berkshire; mother, make my bed soon,
For I'm wearied wi' digging, and fain would lie down.

And wha met ye there, Lord Randal, my son?
And wha met ye there, my handsome young man?
O I met wi' a barge girl; mother, make my bed soon,
For I'm wearied wi' digging, and fain would lie down.

And what did she give you, Lord Randal, my son?
And what did she give you, my handsome young man?
Hot tea and a smile; mother, make my bed soon,
For I'm wearied wi' digging, and fain would lie down.

from Mistress Olivia's diary

I believe Our Lord was moved by my cries of woe in St Mary's. He strikes down his enemies and hearing my eloquent plea He has struck down mine. The Middletons have lost every last farthing and much more they did not have, and are poor and they deserve it for siring so obnoxious a son.

Mama considers the acquiring of money beneath her dignity and wished to hear nothing of this South Sea Company thing until Papa said that was where he had invested all his cash. She had the vapours until Papa assured her he had sold in good time through quickly acting upon informed advice. Mama then lost interest.

"Mr Delpeck told me he had bought stock," I said to Papa after Mama had retired to comfort Lousy. I am thinking lately she gains more comfort from the brat than she bestows on it. It continues to intrigue me why Mama never rebukes Lousy.

"Mr Delpeck was clever like you, Papa," I continued for I sensed Papa was proud of his stock dealing and yearned to tell someone. I deemed it sagacious not to remind Papa it was I while playing with the soapy water who had spurred him to act, so I listened awhile. Papa's view is these bits of paper are only valuable while every-body believes they are worth something and want them. It was then time to steer his talk to his loan to the odious shopkeeper.

"If I understand what you have told me Papa, there is every reason this stock stuff will continue to be worth less and less because fewer and fewer people want to buy it now." I furrowed my brows to heighten my dramatic pause. "So all the money you gave to Mr Middleton is gone because his bits of paper are worth less and less each day."

"Princess, I didn't give the money to Mr Middleton. I loaned it."

"But he has no money to pay you back," I said using my terribly-concerned-and-fearful voice.

"If he cannot repay me, he has to give me his Provision Stores and Koffee House."

Having confirmed what I'd suspected about Papa's deal with Mr Middleton, I thrust my knife into the Middletons. "He is such a silly man Papa, he will likely sell them so he can give you back a bit of your money and no one wants to buy business here when it is all going to Newbury because of the Navigation, so he will sell them for very little and you won't get back hardly anything of your money," I said in a frightened burst. "And poor Papa cannot buy such a well placed property on the river in the middle of Reading because you loaned all your money to Mr Middleton."

Papa was amused at my limited understanding and told me what I knew. Mr Middleton's properties were worth ten times the loan.

I sent out my very-fond-of-you sigh before I gave my knife a final twist. "You are such a kind man Papa. Mr Middleton will be eternally grateful to you." I waited for Papa to ask as to what I meant. "By not asking for your money back today you are giving up the chance to get back in the form of properties ten times what you loaned. You are especially generous letting Mr Middleton keep your money when his son has been so nasty and horrible to me and cannot be trusted."

This was the right moment to tell Papa about Master Nicholas Middleton, the Barge-bilge and my informant from the Reading Militia. I saw the effect of my blade immediately.

"Will all the Middletons have to go to the Poor House?" I asked to confirm my hopes.

My mind is so deft that while busy with one idea it tackles another. I told Papa I must now look elsewhere to find a match. "I am a burden to you Papa," I said. "All I do is drain your empty pocket when Mr Middleton has lost all your money. I shall find myself a small employ to pay for some of the clothes I will need if

I am to make a match as befits me and will do you proud. If I am to be a gentleman's wife I have need of a lady's raiment."

As I expected, Papa would not hear of it but saw my need. He agreed a monthly pin-money. This I shall husband, not to gain a husband but to gain lodgings in London. Every woman must have a private income that she is not beholden unto any man.

Press Room, Reading Courant

"It is really that bad?" Frith is pacing across Mr Hyde's office. The editor's placidity is exacerbating his newsman's concern. "The stock is not worth the paper it is written on?"

"That is not strictly the case. The value of the stock has decreased significantly."

"It has plummeted," says Frith, sweeping down an arm for effect. "When I passed the Guild Hall just now it resembled a bee colony with the queen stolen. I saw Mr Middleton in such a state I feared he would throw himself into the Kennet."

"That gentleman has always been prone to histrionics."

"Self-aggrandisement. His wife is the Madam of Melodrama."

Mr Hyde raises an eyebrow. "I trust such hyperbole would not garnish any piece you wrote for the Courant."

"Yes I can, and would keep it out of an article on the stock collapse. If we pull the Bill of Mortality list and —"

"No," says Mr Hyde, firmly. "There will be nothing in the Courant concerning the South Sea Company." There is a tense pause. The editor speaks. "Giving our readers partial information is more dangerous than giving them none."

Frith is scornful. "Ignorance is bliss?"

Mr Hyde unexpectedly steps round his desk to talk very quietly to Frith's ear, away from any chance of Jake overhearing from the press room.

"It is very serious," says Mr Hyde with a solemn face. "The South Sea Company debacle is of a hundredfold greater magnitude than any strife the Navigation may unleash."

"The speculators and investors who jumped on this get-rich whir-ligig have suffered a setback. Probably a temporary one."

"You are riding your affiliations as if on a donkey in a circus ring Mr Frith, when you could be galloping a cavalry charger."

"Metaphor is the deceiver's smoke screen, Mr Hyde."

"Your point is taken. But listen. The aftermath from this financial catastrophe will touch the whole country. And I do not mean in a geographical sense."

"I can envisage gentry buying stock, perhaps with money they haven't got." Mr Hyde gives an affirming nod. "The aristocracy?" Mr Hyde raises his eyebrows as affirmation. "Peers of the Realm? Royalty?" asks Frith incredulously.

"It is so rumoured. To the very top. Neither was it honest trading in the stock, for as the share price had less and less relevance to the real value it seems the South Sea Company directors turned to propping up the façade through bribery, goodwill payments, and underhand dealing. Two of the auditors are suddenly deceased. Those who have reputations to rescue will rush to cover up corruption, while others will rush to unearth it. The Kingdom is on the brink of civil turmoil and this newspaper must not be used as a coach and four by anarchists."

"Hyperbole, Mr Hyde? What do we actually have? Some people who had wealth have less. Some great family names may be ruined. We have an absentee monarch – good riddance to him. We have ministers of government who are corrupt, incompetent, avaricious and ignorant – throw them out. We have a church selling happiness in the hereafter by impoverishing its flock in this world."

Mr Hyde gives a deep sigh. "In a calamity such as this, who is it will suffer greatest? Not those with the cushion of estate or connection. None of those groups you cited will be irrevocably set back." The editor pauses, debating with himself. He sighs again. "It has come to my attention that Mr Middleton, and no doubt many more like him, have vested everything they own in the South Sea Company stock. His is not a temporary setback."

"He has the Stores and Koffee House."

"He has nothing."

"Mr Middleton told me . . ."

Mr Hyde slowly shakes his head. "He has proved as irresponsibly greedy as our leaders. His only comfort is that his stupidity affects fewer people."

Nicholas's dreams of Before Woman whistle into Frith's head and he strides to the door of the press room. Mr Hyde calls after him. "You cannot do any good there unless you have several thousands of pounds to give away. The best thing you can do is print the Courant as usual to maintain some sense of normality for our readers." Frith is hovering. "You also are in debt to the Courant for at minimum a half day. We are already behind on the final folio."

Frith is locking-up a forme on the imposing stone when the street door swings open. A solid well-dressed and groomed gentleman of around sixty strides in with an eagle scan round the room. "Mr Hyde. Your office."

"Immediately, Sir George."

After what Frith deems sufficient time he steps softly to the back of the press room and scrutinises a hanging sheet of drying print. The editor's door is shut and inside the two men are conversing in soft voices. Sir George Crockmore is doing the talking.

A few minutes later Sir George leaves the office at his brisk pace, gives a slight nod of acknowledgement to Frith accompanied by a fleeting inspection. The street door closes and Frith enters Mr Hyde's office. The editor speaks before Frith can ask.

"Sir George came on the matter that is, and will be, on everyone's lips for months, if not years. Do you now appreciate how consequential this matter is?"

"That the most prominent man in the area comes to tell you what to print?"

"To offer advice in his judicial capacity as Crown Judge for Reading. He advised the policy I outlined earlier. The Reading Courant must not be a pamphlet for agitating unrest or provoking disobedience. Sir George assured me he has not lost one farthing by the collapse of the stock and thus his words are without prejudice. Shall we publish our newspaper, Mr Frith? The one that the law-abiding, God-fearing townsmen wish to read."

Wakeman's journal – 2:00pm

Every conversation I have with another person is betraying Catherine. Why? Because I am not speaking to her. Because nothing I say has meaning. All I do is without purpose. What I say to others has no relevance to my true existence. I can tell no one. I promised.

Erebus made a promise to his wife, "I won't do this to you any more." Liar. He continues to bleed her resolve, tying his wife with her guilt and with his calculated helplessness. Bastard.

A direct course

The wharfinger's wife at Aldermaston refused the return of her dress, especially when Lee and One-eye raved how pretty Lynn looked wearing it. It warmed Lynn she had gained a large protective family so far from the familiarity of the London docks. Her happiness was tinged with knowing they would soon separate. She did not allow that to mar the day.

Lynn looked in the cabin. Her Dad's health had not really improved since returning to Barge Jeannie, his slight lustre was from being back on his boat. The letting cuts had become sticky with a greenish yellow cast. Lynn poured brandy on his arm before winding a cotton rag round it. More brandy went down his throat.

They passed where Foundry Brook joined the river. Rose Kiln was hidden behind bushes and trees and there was no sign of Adam. Lynn's stomach was tightening from knowing there was a mile of the reach before the Kennet Navigation curved into County Lock and then the town. She had with her a band of strong men but that would make any violence more wholesale and fierce. The navvies' had stopped singing.

Jeannie rounded on to County Lock, a broad space with its weir and towing path on the north bank. Lynn remembered the awkward crossing for Hermond on their outward journey but it was simpler for her towing men. They could see no one about and both sets of gates were properly closed. The only odd thing was the bare earth on the sloping sides to the chamber.

A couple of men raised the head gate paddles and all waited for the half-empty chamber to fill. The men swung the gate booms and

Jeannie glided into the lock. Cully had the windlass but he was having a problem raising the tail gate paddles to lower the water and Barge Jeannie with it.

"You should stick to your shovel," said One-eye taking over, but he failed to turn the windlass. With three of them on the handle it jolted then came more freely.

"Unseasoned wood, likely swollen in its runners," said Cully, opening the paddle fully and setting about the second.

Lynn's ears told her something was wrong. She joined the men at the tail gate and looked over the side at the untroubled surface of the river. It remained so after a similar struggle raised the second paddle. Barge Jeannie remained high in the chamber. Lynn stared in disbelief. There was a splash and she caught sight of two bare feet disappearing into the chamber waters.

"Burrer's our otter," said Gabriel. "Had to be the number of times he fell drunk off locks and bridges."

Lynn told the men on Barge Jeannie to tie her fast as she'd only looped the ropes and didn't want Burrer to surface into a shifting barge. A dark brown scalp rose from the water by the gates.

"This be where turfs be," spluttered Burrer.

Before Lynn could blink, boots and shirts were off as men jumped in with loud whoops. Some clung half-submerged to the gates, passing up the sodden turfs to those on the side.

"Stop!" yelled Lynn. "Close the paddles or the flow will drown you soon as sluice's clear."

Gabriel paused for a reflective look at Lynn then set to with the windlass. Over his bobbing back Lynn spotted a small group of men coming along the towing path from the town. Another larger throng followed.

It wasn't long before the rim of the lock was a wall of onlookers jeering and gobbing at the navvies who struggled in the chamber to clear the underwater turfs blocking the gates. The more they cleared the harder it was, for not only was it deeper but the weight of turfs had compacted the lower ones. A wharf man slithered from the rim of the lock, grabbed a sodden turf, and hurled it at Sandy who was leaning over the chamber. It caught him on the shoulder and he toppled into the water. A cheer went up and wharf men scrambled down to the pile of recovered turfs.

Pick made for the wharf man who had thrown the turf, landing his fist on the man's jaw. He'd seen it coming and feinted with it but his return swing was from off-balance and missed Pick, almost spinning himself into the lock. Fists started flying, knees, elbows, anything to do damage to others along the narrow strip by the chamber. Lynn had hurried to the cabin and taken up a poker. No one was going to touch her Dad. She looked at the raucous cockpit that had minutes ago been tranquil. Now it was a confusion of fighting men.

A salvo of musket shot rang out. The fighters became statues. Mayor Turner stood on the tail gate holding on very tightly. Flanking him were half a dozen of the Aldermen's Watch, each with a musket. Three were re-powdering. There was undisguised hate in the eyes of the Watch men, speculating which navvy had knifed their colleague last Friday.

"The next man to perform any act of aggression will be shot," said the Mayor. Arms fell to sides and throats were released. Robert Turner's chest relaxed a little. "This is the second time I have stood on a lock to address warring factions. I will not tolerate it in my town." Three more of the Aldermen's Watch arrived bearing muskets.

"You navigators have come to Reading looking for trouble and have provoked a gross disorder." The wharf men were easing away from the navvies leaving them clustered at the edge of the chamber. "I am therefore authorising the arrest of each one of you navigators and barge people." The men of the Watch trained their muskets on the isolated group, fingers itching for one to make a run for it.

Four Watch men approached the navvies and began herding them through a narrow corridor that had opened in the crowd round County Lock. The navvies were cussed and spat on by the walls of scowling, jeering faces.

Lynn had listened to the Mayor and the sight of her friends being led off to gaol spurred her along the lock. "You can't do this!"

"I can. I have. We had warning your gang was coming hell-bent on making trouble. So it has proved."

"It was them started it," cried Lynn, pointing to the wharf men. "They jammed the lock —"

"If you associate with that kind you should be prepared for the consequences," continued the Mayor ignoring what Lynn said.

"They wrecked the lock. They're vandals. Put them in gaol."

"Do not tell me what I should do. Insolence like yours is the seedbed of disorder. Take her to the gaol. Every one of them, as I have ordered."

"Not my Dad."

"Not one agitator shall be lose in my town."

"He's ill. He's too weak to walk."

"Get your brawn to carry him."

Mayor Turner refused to inspect the condition of Peter Darville. Lynn organised for her Dad to be shouldered by Mogger and Dicky, following the other navvies over the footbridge across Holy Brook and the short climb to the gaol.

Mayor Turner called to the leading Watchman. "Give word to the turnkey the prisoners shall have no visitors." After a pause he added: "Especially the girl ring-leader. She is definitely to have none whatsoever."

Lynn gave a last look back at Barge Jeannie and saw the gloating Mistress Olivia at her father's side.

Wakeman's journal – 3:00pm

What did she mean? "I'll be happy for you if you found someone else. It would break my heart but I'd be pleased for you."

Testing me? We don't do that unless we're teasing and what opportunity do we have for that now? Today's Courant is published. Be with me. Walk though the press room door. Zitkala! Don't you know just how completely you and I are an us? Your voice constantly in my head saying, "We do this, talk, cuddle, kiss. We can do this a long, long time."

I can do nothing this afternoon except write to you Catherine. It's the only way to be close, to pretend to be talking to you. My head putting words into sentences that all say, be with me. The altern-ative is to be screaming aloud I want you, with me, now. This letter is about me not for you. Start again. I must get away from thought.

Kennet Koffee House

"Dragon's upstairs wringing the last drop from a bottle of gin," answers Sarah to Frith's enquiry about Nicholas Middleton.

"To cut a long story short," she says, handing him the demitasse and settling in the chair at his corner table, "Mayor Turner strides in saying how Mr M, who hasn't been seen all morning, owes him a cartload of money and if he don't pay up sharp Middleton's Stores and the Kennet Koffee House belong to him. Gives Mr M until first thing tomorrow, does our caring Mayor."

"So the Navigation wasn't the big threat to Mr M's livelihood," mumbles Frith. "His avarice was."

"Now Dragon's his biggest threat. First she near hit the Mayor, then she hit the roof screaming about 'your insane effrontery, Robert Turner'. Then it dawned on her he was serious and she hit the gin."

"Has Mr M reappeared?"

"Wouldn't discuss nothing with nobody. Whereas Dragon wailed to everyone that all she prized was lost, her Koffee House, Richard's gallop to being the next captain-general of the King's army. On and on."

"Master Nicholas?" asks Frith, earnestly.

"Another how-d'you-do. Master Gutless only turns on his father saying the idiot's 'obsessive greed is a canker rotting the family'. Where'd he get that from? I wonder, Mr Frith? Anyways, Dragon bites her son's head off for being disrespectful, and then Master Not-So-Gutless tells his mother she's 'an avaricious, envious gannet'. Ever since then, the only time she shuts up her cater-wauling is to down another gallon of gin. 'I am ruined. I am disgraced. My family is falling apart.' That's when Mr M took a swing at Master Nicholas."

"What!" exclaims Frith. "Was he hurt?"

"You'll never guess. The boy stood there and took the punch.

Poof! Mr M stood dumbstruck. His son looked him straight in the eyes and said, calm as you like, 'Does that make you feel better?' He said nothing else. Magnificent he was. If I was his mum I'd have been right proud of him. Instead, she's calling him all the names under the sun, then blaming him and her useless husband for her undoing. 'I am ruined.' The selfish cow."

"Where is Nicholas now?"

"Gaol probably," says Sarah, dispassionately.

"What!"

Sarah wipes unseen crumbs from the table then smiles. "Said he and was off 'to help a family who really needs help'. It don't take putting two hitches together to know which tow rope he was hoping to shorten."

Frith hears about the fight and the arrests at County Lock. He puts his head in his hands.

"Sarah," he says wearily, when she places a hand on his shoulder. "You have witnessed how the collapse of the South Sea Company has destroyed people, families. You know the Navigation is causing distress and anger and fear across the board." He looks into her kindly eyes. "Today I have been setting type that reads, 'The most material News this Paper has, is from Pyrmont, That His Britannic Majesty has done drinking the Waters, and intends to set out for Herenhausen the 26th Instant.' That Sarah, encapsulates my completely nothing, useless life."

"Poor Mr Frith. This might cheer you up," says Sarah sliding a familiar envelope to him from her skirt before she greets the new customer. Frith can smell the familiar perfume at arm's length. It fills his head with a hurricane of fear and hope, a rending dilemma of desperation to know the contents and not know what Catherine might be telling him. He dare not open the envelope in the Koffee House, in public.

memoirs of Sir George Crockmore

I pride myself that I am impartial and equanimous towards those delegated to enact my designs, be such plans grand or minor. This day I am obliged to delve deep to find any benevolence towards

Mayor Robert Turner. His lack of action was in contempt of my directive to him that he summon the Yeomanry and a dereliction of his promise to me.

His parochial head has been embroiled in personal financial matters. I chastise myself for entrusting a bold scheme to a modest mind. Even so, I can see an irony: the man does nothing when action is needed but, when action is unavoidable, the man chooses the wrong action.

The mayor's unilateral arrests sends a signal to every barge-master that to ply the River Kennet Navigation is to end in gaol with cargo pirated. In itself this is a significant setback for the Navigation Company. Second, the hostility to the River Kennet Navigation has been endorsed by a civil authority. Third, the Reading Militia will fervently resent being spurned in favour of the Aldermen's Watch. Fourth, the town is now obligated to feed a full gaol of prisoners. Point number five, the charges against the prisoners will be dismissed, for the accused were pursuing their lawful passage along the River Kennet Navigation. Mayor Turner has brought about a fistful of setbacks for naught.

The fifth point I imparted to Mr Hyde when he brought this week's Courant, after inducing the editor to share his concerns over a glass of Rhenish. He has been obliged to reject several written pieces from his newsman on the grounds of them being incitements to unrest among the citizens. I praised Mr Hyde for withholding the South Sea Company item, agreeing it is wrong to gloat and profit from the misfortunes of others. The editor had been relieved when the newsman, clouded by some distraction, had secluded himself after their altercation. The affray at County Lock would have spawned another unacceptable article, stated Mr Hyde, so keen was his interest in the River Kennet Navigation.

At this I acquainted Mr Hyde with the Act which authorised the bringing about of the River Kennet Navigation, and which guarantees by law unimpeded passage along it. This I plainly stated, is the unequivocal defence of innocence for all those incarcerated from Barge Jennie. I exhorted Mr Hyde to make that information generally known, accompanied by the fact the owners of the River

Kennet Navigation have power therein to ensure compliance by request to the Lord Lieutenant for dispatch of his Yeomanry. Mr Hyde understood my message, allowing me to retire more peacefully for an early start the morrow to London.

Barge Jeannie, County Lock

"Permission to come aboard?" asks Frith into the dark cabin. He has sensed someone is on board. Frith has walked from the Anglers Tavern to County Lock in search of his quarry.

"Stand fast and identify yourself," says Nicholas.

"Before Woman."

"Step aboard. How did you know I was here?"

"I picked the least likely place to find you and came here."

"What was the most likely?"

"The gaol," answers Frith.

"Dunbar wouldn't let me put a toe over the threshold."

"Didn't you offer to bribe the turnkey?"

"With what?"

"It wouldn't have succeeded," says Frith, settling in the cabin. "Mistress Olivia promised Dunbar a guinea over the bribe of anyone wanting to speak to the prisoners. Done in the name of her father, she said. Looks like she got away lightly at a guinea. Then again not. Dunbar will lie to her about the vast bribe you offered. Will she check, I wonder?"

"Why would she do that?"

"Mistress Olivia is an astute young woman with people, and also with money."

"Why would the Mayor want nobody talking to the prisoners?"

"Mistress Olivia offered the bribe. I doubt Mayor Turner knew anything about it."

It takes a few moments. Nicholas looks up. "Lynn? Ridiculous. Olivia never had serious intentions with me. I realise that now I am not worth a farthing."

"She would wish to be the one to cut you," says Frith. "It would be her worst nightmare to be seen bettered by a girl from a barge."

"Olivia hasn't been bettered," snaps Nicholas.

"What are you doing on this barge?"

"Stopping further acts of lawlessness. That's all. Being a friend."

"Where's the horse?"

"Stabled."

"A very good friend."

"Who can't pay the stabling fees. Damn the man!"

"You can't blame Robert Turner for what happened to —"

"Not him. Damn my father. He tried to be more wealthy than the Turners. He brags he knows about business when all he knows is sacks and sailcloth. Mother is worse, goading him for not being Mayor, doesn't own a wharf. Now he doesn't own a bed."

The outburst is absorbed into the still waters and the night. Nicholas continues in quieter voice. "I completely blew up at them this morning, just let rip. My parents for Heaven's sake! Then I just could not stand being near them with father whining apologies, mother blaming everyone but herself. I didn't learn what had happened to Lynn until I got back. When it was all over. I wasn't there to do something."

A wave of compassion for the lad fills Frith. It has been a long time since he felt such a forceful, unselfish caring. It transforms to a vision of Catherine in their moments of carefree bliss. He forces those thoughts away before they manifest in his physical collapse. He concentrates on the lad with him, how he must feel about the collapse of his world.

While Nicholas trawls paths of hopeless speculation on his family, Frith rummages in his satchel and flicks though his pocket-book. For the first time in days his thoughts are sharp as freezing water. "I am going to step outside this circus ring and lead a charge," says Frith, arousing the lad's curiosity. "The plight of Lynn and the navvies is not going to be resolved within the boundaries of this town." He finds the page. "According to Mr Hyde, an Act of Parliament grants freedom of passage along the Kennet Navigation. Lynn and all the rest of them are in gaol illegally. The owners at Newbury need to be notified so they can call on the Lord Lieutenant to intervene. My Navigation article spells out how Jeannie has been harassed."

"I need to stay on the barge to guard it," says Nicholas.

"That's understood," says Frith absent-mindedly, for he is fired by his plan. Action will lift his mind from Catherine, at least for a while. "At last Mr Hyde has been useful."

"He's very useful in his way, otherwise Sir George wouldn't have employed him as bookkeeper for twenty years. It surprised everyone when he quit."

Frith derides his editor's incompetency, then entertains Nicholas by recalling his Sunday interviews. "When the thieves realised they couldn't sell the silver tray they could have dumped it anywhere."

"Or melted it down for the silver. That'd be only a fraction of what they'd get for a tray."

"A lot less than the owner might pay for its return," says Frith. "Suppose one of the Reading Militia was in with the thieves. I kept coming across a man with wavy black hair."

"Sergeant Quinn. Hawker's sidekick."

"Second in command? That's the deal! Has to be. He makes sure the thieves don't get caught by the Militia and pockets the recovery fee for anything they can't sell."

"But it went wrong at Woodroffe's," adds Nicholas.

"When the Aldermen's Watch were involved." Frith is thinking. "Their unpredicted presence threw Quinn's scheme awry. That's worth investigating."

"First things first?" prompts Nicholas.

"Yes. Our friends in gaol," says Frith.

Wakeman's journal – 1:15pm

Such enveloping happiness. Walking through Nipper's Grove woods with Catherine, talking and touching, kissing. We'd done that from the first moment together, along the bridle way, then into a fury and a stillness on a bed of newly fallen leaves. She had been too repeatedly violated under her own roof for me to enter her, too bruised to absorb me. Yet retrieving the glorious sensations of her body against mine, mine against hers, with sounds that are not words to a chorus of birdsong.

Hearing her. "I'm dealing with so much – from wall to wall to ceiling." Hurting with her. "He touches me all the time, always wanting to hold my hand." She offered her big hand. We were both clinging, then I was running my fingers over her hair, tracing her face, cupping her breast in my palm. "He forces me every night." She placed my hand under her skirt, pressed it against the place usurped from her and she looks into my eyes. Her invitation. Neither of us blinked.

"I'm not with his child." Absolute conviction. She slid my hand up to her belly. "Although the idea of . . ." and a collusive twinkle lit her eyes. We agreed it would be the wrong time, wrong reason. I felt my presence brush through her womb. Maybe I wanted unreason, but I let a shiver of hope of some distant future make do for this time.

The teasing had returned over a girl in the baker's I said had given me the eye. It would mean nothing written here yet it was another beam of sunlight on us in Nipper's Grove. "I've never kissed a man so much." Nuzzling her neck and she giggling with mirth at my fundamental pleasure. The smell of fern. Nature stuck on her bare back. Tight in our embrace, willing us tiny, tightening, so we become inseparable, became one.

Crouching low and hushed while some riders went by. Reading Militia, crouched lower. Cradled in my arms, silent, still. Decorating each other with twigs, leaves, creepers and creating our private mystical rite. Breathing the same breaths.

Beattie is very attached to her daddy. She cries when he castig-ates the mother for his wife hurting him, her being selfish, her infi-delity. He never questions the cause. Catherine walks into her parlour, to be with me where we once were. Erebus is quickly at her side, sorry for hurting her, holding her hand, begging to be held. Catherine sees Beattie in the doorway – the Darkness has consumed her again.

Sunlight through the trees made a necklace of silver pearls trickle down Catherine's cheek. She sat up. "I can't think of a world without you." A huge smile. "I'll turn up on your doorstep one day and find you're married again." Forced laughter. I didn't deny or agree. She didn't expect a reply, nor a lukewarm platitude. No saying that we will do this or that.

I helped her on her horse. "I'm not strong." She looked down at me. "I have to do what's best for Beattie. I have to." Her back was as rigidly upright as a flagpole. Catherine wasn't breathing. "I don't want to do this. I have to. I can't ask you to wait for years. But you have to remember this. Please. You have to. Always, always remember you have been loved."

I couldn't move. Panic. Here was the void of Darkness swal-lowing me. A crushing pressure collapsed my ribs. Screams in my head that could not get out. I don't want to have been loved, I want to be loved. I stood motionless, voiceless, without will.

Journaling it is the only thing I am able to do. Every word written flings me back to Nipper's Grove, numbing the present by flooding it with the anguish and torment lived through again, and again. I don't want to have been loved! Don't leave me with only the past. I want the future. Our future. Our love.

A closed peephole

Yesterday the black-red bricks of the gaol stood in contrast to the white stucco walls of the Sun Inn next to it. The prison resembled the salient of the old town wall with the same impregnable purpose. Inside was dim with the only illumination from a couple of torches by the turnkey's post. Five stout wooden doors rein-forced with iron each pierced by a tiny sliding peephole, faced the slabbed central area off which a stone staircase lead to cells on the upper two floors. In each cell daylight could only squeeze through a tiny high window.

The stench hit Lynn first: shit, vomit, piss and fear. Then the echoing noises of keys jangling on iron hoops, doors slammed shut, the turnkeys banging their truncheons on everything and anyone, the angry voices of the navvies and whining laments from the cell already occupied. The turnkeys were not short of voice either ranging through abuse and curses for the inmates to complaints about absentee masters. How were they supposed to guard so many? Who was going to pay to feed the scum?

The navvies had been crammed into three cells, each with its scattering of straw and a piss-pot. Lynn, her Dad and the two who had carried him were in the end cell. Dicky took a truncheon blow when he pulled away the turnkey's hand roving over Lynn's body.

The thick-set, paunchy chief turnkey – Mister Dunbar, Sir, as he insisted on being addressed – amused himself loudly speculating the punishment for his prisoners: hanging for the leaders, transport-ation for the rest. They'll be his guests for some time before they knew their hanging date. And no money to feed so many. Dunbar eventually wearied of his own voice and absence of imagination.

It had been sleeping by shift overnight but none slept. Lynn had listened to the scrabbling claws of the rats. Her Dad had lain silently but for his wheezing, his head in her lap with eyes closed or staring vacantly at the blackness above.

In the morning a boy from the fifth cell was ordered to empty the piss-pots. Dunbar threatened he'd personally break the ten-year-old's neck if anyone caused any trouble. A bucket arrived at noon with thinly flavoured warm water and bread so stale it wouldn't soften after a soaking. Some of the men wondered who could help them. Lynn knew from experience there was nobody in this hostile town.

Editor's office, Reading Courant

Mr Hyde sits collected behind his desk. "Your article is poorly reasoned. The few facts are unsupported and the rest is conjecture."

Frith does not register the editor's displeasure. He is battling the annihilation of his other world, every breath rasping his lungs. He does not want to be here, nor anywhere, neither does he know what to do. He suddenly recalls standing on rocks by a shore, storm waves pounding, water breaking over him, getting soaked, knowing he should move away. Moving away to be frozen by the wind is as bad as getting more sodden.

"What do you have to say for yourself?" asks Mr Hyde.

Frith pulls an answer from one word he heard from Mr Hyde. "It is a speculative piece."

"If you mean your ideas were theoretical, then better to have discussed them with me than waste good paper and valuable time with this fabrication. We can all sit at our desk and dream up wild stories, such as this possible double-dealing by one of the Reading Militia. If the Courant printed everything that was possible it would be wide open for suits of libel."

Frith wants to be moving, walking. He doesn't care where. "I apologise for wasting your time. The piece was written in a hurry."

"It should not have been written at all." Mr Hyde pitches the sheets into the waste basket. "This is the third piece you have put forward, each has been worse than its predecessor. Am I to suppose my remarks have the opposite effect to what I intended?"

Frith shakes his head. Nearly forty and being told off like a child. What saddens him is knowing he deserves it. What unsettles him is that he doesn't care.

from Mistress Olivia's diary

"We women have a ragged cut of the cloth," I reminded Mrs Middle-gone and heard such a gin scented burp it would have felled an ox at fifty paces. "Can you be sure your Nicholas has run off?" For this solicitation I was rewarded with a river of tears. The woman is a farce of misery and the more she drinks the more entertaining she becomes.

She wailed for the twenty hundredth time, "I raised him with no help from that useless lump of a father. I am made destitute by that useless lump of a husband and deserted by my ungrateful son."

The merchant himself batters the ears of every customer, blaming all his misfortune on Turncoat Turner, as he calls Papa. So urgently do the customers wish to leave that the Stores has made no sale. I express my sorrow to him how his pockets are empty of coins for a single ale yet his wife empties bottle after bottle of gin. He berates her and she curses back and the bear-baiting is revitalised again.

Thus far I have sacked the serving boy so Mrs Middle-gone's drunken clumsiness as server is merriment to all. I have overseen the woman burn her repulsive painting and to ease her suffering I have restocked her gin cupboard. A disappointment is the absence of Master Nicholas Middleton to witness his lamentable parents.

I have warned the Dame de Comptoir as the Froth-head fancifully calls herself, to stop her chit-chat with the customers. If the men wish to converse with a lady it shall be with me, though there is not one of the rag-bag bunch with whom I would chose to speak. The newsman loitered with the chirpy Froth-head until I reminded her of her duties. I asked the nosey newsman if he knew the whereabouts of Master Nicholas Middleton and from his evasive answers deduced the pair have formed a friendship. I suspect this rootless Noseman encouraged my deceiver to the recklessness that resulted in my great anguish.

These observations must be well presented to Papa that he might the sooner turn both places into warehouses and turn the Middletons into the Poor House. Mama is cross every day knowing the Stores and Koffee House have ruined her plans for a grander house in Reading. This is my extra reward.

Papa now declares to all that the Kennet Navigation not a threat to commerce in Reading but potentially a benefit to those who can grasp the opportunity. I need to ensure he concludes that acquiring this advantageous site on its bank was through my timely assistance. That he is indebted to me.

I was pondering this, when four flamboyant gentlemen requested demitasses of coffee. Mrs Middle-gone denounced them as vagrant actors, troublesome ne'er-do-wells lowering the tone. One of the gentlemen asked was that not the pot calling the kettle black, which inspired all four to wittily mimic the woman's affectation of speech exaggerated and slurred by gin. The gin-bladder puffed to great indignation, wobbled and sat with a thump into a chair. Two of the four gentlemen rushed to the assistance of the stricken chair.

This endeared me to them and I encouraged the four to converse with me. I warmed to their eyes upon me and put forward girlish answers to their earnest questions. One asked why such a pretty maid was languishing in the backwater of Reading when she abso-lutely must be in London. I said that was my heart's desire and lamented the impossibility of fulfilling it. To end the vexing issue I asked of their travels.

One by the name of Valentine Prince spoke of a place called Mesopotamia beyond the seas and the mountains, a land where Arabs live in ways different to us.

"In 1712 when barren Anne ruled her barren land we four made an adventure to the Orient and there I came as close to death as this." He brushed his nose against my nose and surprising me with such intimacy caused me to colour.

"We had performed at a place called Al Basrah and set off in the cool of dawn on the humped horses they use across the desert region to the next village. An old Arab was our guide as we trekked at a steady pace. In the early afternoon our guide suddenly leaned to his side and fell dead to the ground. We had no chart and only meagre water rations. We could not retrace our tracks for the wind had smoothed them. We stared at the white hot sky with a rising terror at our doom."

Here Mr Prince paused and his eyes drifted away. I concede I had become engrossed in his tale.

"We tried to go on but dropped from our camels with exhaustion and despair. Some desert wandering Arab people called Bedouin saw us and descended when, for their own good, they should have kept trekking the ridge to the next water place they call an oasis. They distributed their rations among us, not resisting when we in our delirium demanded more. They remained with us until we were strong enough to ride. We drained their reserves. We threatened their safety and still they tended us. When we reached safety the Bedouin refused to accept any offering, even our thanks. I felt cheated of expressing my gratitude and flared into anger."

Again Mr Prince stopped which I took to be the end of his story and was about to praise him for it when he held up his palm.

"The sheikh, or headman, came close and squatting on his heels told us an ancient story of the three men caught by a sand storm. Two young men set forth from their village to walk to another across the most terrible of dry places being of fine sand and steep dunes. The wind rose into a blinding sand storm that was so fierce they lost everything they carried except one water bag. It was very old and the battering had caused the precious water to begin seeping through a seam. The young men cupped their hands, pressing them firmly together to hold the water. The storm passed and they trudged on through the heat. Each nursed his handful of life saving liquid, arms aching from the unrelieved effort."

While Mr Prince was talking I had been persuaded to put my hands together as he had explained and another of the actors Mr Hockley Barton, poured in water. It was not very long before it trickled away and I was impressed by the deeds of the foreign men in the tale.

"After an hour the two came on an old man lying by a wadi, a dry river bad. One of the young men let a few drops of water fall onto the lips of the prostrate body. The other man did not stop, saying nothing could be gained by sharing his meagre supply with a dying old man. He needed all his water for himself. Soon, the old man opened his eyes, his strength renewed. Some say he recovered his will from the drops of generosity. He pulled himself to his feet and shuffled alongside his benefactor. Every five hundred paces the water was poured from one pair of aching hands to the refreshed pair, the giver licking the dampness from his palms."

So engrossed was I that I startled a little when Mr Barton took hold of my wrist and drew my moist palm towards his grinning mouth. He speedily relinquished it when I gave him I-am-not-to-be-toyed-with fierce look.

Mr Prince continued. "The burden of holding the water was thus shared and their drinking was rationed. For the aching muscles that cupped the priceless cargo relief was always closer than five hundred paces. This pushed exhausted legs to keep moving until the pair regained the village and safety. The other young man was found lying next to a small indent in the sand where his water fell."

Mr Prince continued after a pause. "To this day said the sheikh, our people still talk about the young man and the old man who stumbled into the village. How they poured from cupped hands to cupped hands nothing but arid air. For days their hands could not be unclasped so determined was each not to spill the life of the other. The sheikh said, 'This way we survive the desert; so should each live in their desert.' Then the Bedouin went on their way."

I broke the silence. "You are such travelled and experienced actors. What then are you doing in the backwater of Reading?"

"The young lady is a cynic," said Mr Prince. "She will thrive in London."

I am uncertain exactly what he meant but it was assuredly a great compliment. I remarked Reading was a dessert without sand and asked if these wandering actor people had any way of rescuing me.

Mr Barton became animated. He outlined a ruse whereby he would take on the part of a London nobleman and make a recommendation of a lady actor friend who ran a lodgings house in White-Chapel. Upon inspection by Papa she would be convincing as a strict woman and ever watchful chaperone.

My excitement was twofold. The prospect of dwelling in London and second, the mention of White-Chapel. The actors not being desert people I agreed to pay them and the lady actor a hiring fee. Mr Barton claimed in addition a kiss from such a pretty young lady. At this suggestion the other three took on leering grins as is the way among men.

For my modesty he led me to a warehouse where he leaned against a post and pulled me to him. I closed my eyes and offered my lips as I had espied Mama with Papa. I felt him fumbling with the buttons of his breeches and I abruptly pulled away telling him with no uncertainty I was not that sort of lady.

"I said a kiss and I meant a kiss," he chortled, pushing my head down to his unmasked manhood. He proceeded to teach me how to tease it with my lips and tongue. During my ministrations to it I engaged my mind on when and how I might introduce him to Papa that the meeting seem not contrived. It was little effort from me to satisfy Mr Barton and yet remain a maiden, which knowledge may prove useful in London.

Upon returning to the Koffee House I drained the bitterest coffee and was gratified to hear Mr Barton's report. "She kisses the best I have come across." To this the others yelped approval avowing I would make a splendid entry in London.

Mr Barton has agreed to be at the Yield Hall for eleven of the clock on the morrow, where and when Papa has a meeting. It will be happenstance the two men meet, upon which the actor will ply his craft and Papa will realise an acceptable means to honour the debt he owes to me in acquiring his prized warehouses.

Wakeman's journal – 4:30pm

Did Catherine conspire with Fate by being incautious where she hid my letters? Did she want Erebus to find them and force him to do something? How can I think that? Damn Mistress Clivia!

I had promised not to tell anyone and I have betrayed Catherine. Because she betrayed me? Because she has deserted me? Olivia was compassionate on seeing me so morose in the Koffee House. She said she was keen to help a friend of Master Nicholas. My defences were demolished by heartache and my caution was blinded by her sweetness. She had some idea of the cause, goodness knows how, not the name, not the all-consuming passion of it. The cause for my abject dejection was obvious to Mistress Olivia, and she soon prised out the reason for my great loss was for the sake of my love's daughter.

"Typical man," said Olivia. "You swallow any tale a woman offers you."

That brought me sharply to my senses and, were she not a young woman, I might have rebuked the person who said such a thing.

"Your lady had her fling with you. That is all there is to it. No doubt she enjoyed it, and you. She had excitement in the thrill of clandestine meetings, the anticipation during the chase and the final delights with her ardent stag."

Mistress Olivia brushed aside my protests, albeit pathetic from the mood I was in.

"Her lazy husband finds out and the stallion within him is spurred into giving the pair a ride every night. Saying it was for the child was her way of not hurting your feelings."

Not hurting? They are crippled! I asked how could she know, it was not like that at all.

"Your adulteress made sure her husband found out about you, didn't she? It didn't take her long to decide which bed to sleep in at night. You only have her word he took her against her will. You say he has taken her every night since. Is that resisting him?"

The girl's words were cutting deeper into me.

"She isn't resisting him. She has not left him for your ready arms. Has she? What woman would abandon a house and a husband who worships her for a man with no trade who lodges in a tavern? She had a dalliance with you to give her husband a cock-crow wake-up. The rest was play-acting. And you foolish man, believed everything she said."

Why can I not fault Mistress Olivia's reasoning? It has cast me from the vast hole in to an abyss.

A man's lullaby

The noon sun had passed across the window of the cell before Lynn's Dad roused. He spoke lucidly and she convinced herself the two days starvation had broken his fever. She held him and recounted what had passed from the time Barge Jeannie arrived at Newbury to where they were now. She told him out of habit, because he had always come up with a solution to their problems.

He touched Lynn's face. "I never told you how much I loved you, My Beaut."

Lynn tried to shush him in front of Mogger and Dicky but there was no stopping his regrets what a poor father he was, yet how lovely she was despite him. "You're like my Jean, beautiful and loving and generous. You've got a quick mind and tongue, but it's never hurtful." He took quick shallow breaths for some minutes. "I adored that woman from first clapping eyes on her. Betrothed within a six-week, married in fifteen. Then blessed with our treasure." Lynn's hand registered a faint squeeze.

His mood switched. "I tried to do my best by you. The Lord in heaven knows it." His bleak words cut across Lynn's urgent talk of the future, of cargoes, recalling his friends round the London Docks. To counter his failings that he proclaimed she said he was absolutely right about Nicholas Middleton. The scoundrel had not showed his face to her since her moment of foolishness in the meadow. It was she who had not heeded her Dad. But Peter could not be deflected. "If only I'd got Jeannie back to the Thames, then we'd be set." Lynn didn't know how she would cope if he were to cry. "I've lost everything: the barge, Jean, and My Beaut in gaol." He fell silent.

"A song," she mouthed to Dicky who along with Mogger felt awkward and helpless. "Please," she implored. Dicky began a soft chanting. Mogger and Lynn joined in, filling the dank cell with a melodic murmur.

I'll sing lullaby, as women do,
Wherewith they bring their babes to rest;
And lullaby can I sing to,
As womanly as can the best.
With lullaby they still the child,
And if I be not much beguiled,
Full many wanton babes have I,
Which must be still'd with lullaby.

memoirs of Sir George Crockmore

Today's dawn chorus was not the melodies of thrush and finch but the far sweeter sound of a distressed Whig. Sir Sidney Levenson awaited me downstairs. With incomparable unseemliness the fellow gushed that his house and both farms are sunk in the South Sea. I lectured him on the prudence of being a cautious man, and watched him choke ingesting those words with which he had belittled me not so many days before. Being of generous nature I transacted with him, offering a rate of interest determined by his urgent need for cash. Against this loan I have foreclosed on two high yield farms and a lease on his house. I shall demolish the hideous building when Levenson defaults as he inevitably must, for my coup de grâce was to secure his word never to follow his ambitions to Parliament. Thus he is deprived of income in the form of bribes, perks, junkets and directorships.

My day in London has been of great pleasure, partaking of much profitable business among the flotsam of those wrecked by the South Sea tidal wave. Some quarries are not entirely snared and will require my attention in the morrow. I was espied by Maxi who heartily forbad me exert myself more in commerce for the day. He removed us by chariot to the rehoused Bethlehem Hospital at Moorfields where, for a small gratuity, we found amusement at the antics, the frenzied humours and rambling expositions of the lunatics and the possessed. A walk through the Large Gallery is to be more entertaining than several hours sitting through the theatre pieces of Mr Dryden or Mr Vanbrugh. The second floor is filled with chains and whips to control the especially dangerous inmates. This adds several degrees of excitement to the viewing as these creatures are provoked to excess by the presence of divers gentle-women who flirt between the danger and the rescue.

Maxi and I took coffee in Lockets and thence to Figg's Theatre. The entertainment was a bloody and robust boxing booth, lacking skill but overflowing with grim desperation. By the time we returned to Covent Garden the vegetable hucksters had been replaced by the night hawkers. I despatched a fine supper of London eel beheaded at my table, quaffed with a strong Malmsey. I am content to let my loins rest tonight, for Gertrude has sent word our joint speculative venture is advanced.

Wakeman's journal – 10:00pm

"You have been loved." I've been told I have been loved. Words. It's too soon to know, too sudden. It is too final. Can't write.

Near Theale

This walk is foolhardy and pointless, thinks Frith. He is alone, unarmed, no one knows where he is. He is retracing last Thursday's 'ride of despair'. It could have been yesterday or a year ago. There seemed even less purpose to sitting in his lodgings.

The night hides the pits and the wheel furrows on the track so Frith has to concentrate. The distraction offers only a lace shield to the barbed arrows from his memory. Frith is no longer certain what people mean to him, nor he to them. To her. When he thinks of Catherine his doubt of her love causes physical pain. He can banish the thought by holding one moment of untroubled joy in his mind. Not for long, for the doubt forces in and the torment resumes.

He walks on. Frith gasps seeing Grace on her blooded childbed, at the last of her vitality. "My Love, think of me if you need me." He is doing that, remembering her generosity in life and in death. He suddenly understands what she meant. Frith allows images of his past to come to him, not questioning, not analysing them. He stumbles, falls over. He smiles to himself because he has achieved a kind of fall-down-dream.

Frith realises the purpose of his walk has been fulfilled and decides he can go back to the Anglers Tavern. It amuses him he had no purpose when he set out, its recognition only arrived after he embarked upon it. In characteristic manner he refuses to return the same way. He descends along a track from Theale to the Kennet. The suspicions in his head over Catherine flare into warring Titans, and for Frith the best way to lay them is to tackle a distracting route. The towing path alongside the navigation would be too easy. He decided to follow the river.

The clods of ploughed earth make his boots heavy and his progress slow. He weaves through a dense copse to come upon the river. He reasons it is too small to be the Navigation or the Kennet. Holy Brook, but it is too deep here to be forded and Frith follows it in the expectation of a cattle crossing. The grass is waist high, bushes have to be ducked, and he soon comes upon a hedge that blocks his way. He abandons the bank to scramble through a thinner section, cursing aloud at the hawthorn on the far side.

Something very heavy smashes on the back of Frith's head.

Frith comes to with a screaming pain at the top of his cranium and drumming ache in his shoulder. He is in a barn. He is kneeling. His arms are tied behind him, his ankles are bound. The ropes cut into his flesh. His heart is pounding. He sees Captain Hawker.

"Why're you creeping about here?"

"I'm returning to Reading."

"Roads are quicker and safer. What you up to?"

"Nothing."

"Look newsman, we heard you sneaking about, spying on us."

"Why would I?" That was unwise, thinks Frith. Brain before mouth would have been better but his brain is filled with pounding hooves. "I didn't know the barn was here. Is this where you hold the property you have recovered?"

Frith has eyed the barn while talking. It is a treasure house, an auctioneer's viewing room of countless stolen items. He reasons both Hawker and Quinn must be involved in the criminal scheme, reckoning his immediate hope lies in playing dumb. He knows he won't get away with it for long.

"What do you know about the stuff we get back?"

Frith tells Hawker about his Sunday interviews.

Hawker's knife is at Frith's windpipe. "You ain't answered me. Why are you nosing round?"

Frith is sure what he says next will determine if he dies instantly. He has to convince them he is of greater value alive than dead. What are they scared of? Nothing. They have nothing to lose. Except this fraud. They'll want to keep that, if only to dispose of this hoard. Exposure is what they are worried about.

Full circle, thinks Frith. These men are most worried about being discovered, I have discovered them, quod erat demonstrandum, eliminate the cause of the worry – me. Unless killing me will make it more likely they are discovered. Frith urges his thinking off conjectures. He needs a substantiated fact to link him to them.

"You're aware I work for Sir George."

"A newsman on his newspaper," replies Hawker scornfully.

Frith masks his surprise that Sir George owns the Courant, that he is the man who dictates what Mr Hyde is not to print. "For Sir George," says Frith sharply.

Hawker's mistrust is alerted. "Doing what?"

"It's obvious," says Frith while thinking he is Sir George's dancing bear, his dupe newsman.

"We better watch it with him," says Quinn with an unease that Frith can't attribute.

"Quiet!" snaps Hawker. "He'll say anything to save his skin."

"I have proof?" Frith knows this is an all-or-nothing gamble. "Let me show you my letter of commission from Sir George."

Quinn unties Frith's hands so he can sift through the papers in his satchel. Why did he bring it on this pointless pilgrimage? Because it contains Catherine's notes. Frith finds the letter carrying the crest of Sir George Crockmore. If these villains can read they will learn Sir George declined to be interviewed by the newsman.

"You do recognise the coat-of-arms?"

"Course." Hawker casts his eye over the page.

"Doing what, newsman?" Frith breathes out at Hawker's pride concealing he cannot understand the writing. There had been less assurance in Hawker's question. The Militia man must be fearful his commander Sir George might discover their lucrative sideline. A shot of terror lances through Frith. If Hawker thinks Sir George has employed the newsman to investigate the burglaries he is dead. The only defence Frith has is more bluff.

"I'm not at liberty to say," he answers, with a steady gaze at Hawker. "A newsman can rove about asking questions."

"You said you didn't know about this place."

Frith sweeps his arm round the barn. "This is insignificant. I know what's going on. I'm not interested with this copper money, I'm chasing gold for Sir George. Big money."

"Liar," says Hawker. There is a flash of something in his eyes that Frith reads as greed confused by uncertainty. The man clearly wouldn't trust his own mother never mind his employer.

"I can tell you this," says Frith softly, so Quinn does not hear. He hopes Hawker will feel he is being given a confidence. "Why was I was at Southcote Cut the day I interviewed you?"

"To talk to the bargemaster."

"I could have spoken to him in Reading." Frith is playing poker in his head but he doesn't know what cards are in the pack. "I stopped you ransacking that barge. If you remember, I asked if you were looking for something a lot smaller than a man."

"You said it was best done in town."

Frith uses Sir George's name whenever he gets stuck what card to play. "Best done where Sir George wanted it done."

Hawker locks Frith's eyes. "There's something on that barge?"

A villain sees villainy in everyone, thinks Frith. He helps Hawker embroider the treachery. "Why would a small barge carry a part-cargo up the Navigation. That doesn't make sense,"

"Tell me."

"I am sworn to secrecy." Frith raises both eyebrows and nods at the crested letter. Hawker takes Quinn aside. Frith is tempted to embellish the tale but knows too much detail is a liar's undoing. It would make them suspicious. He lets the two convince themselves thanking Angeni and the hunting-men for instilling in him the faculties of silence and listening.

"You're lying," says Hawker. The tied man senses doubt behind the accusation. "We'll keep you as our guest tonight."

Before he can thank them for their hospitality Quinn has tied a strip of sacking across his mouth. Frith's arms are tied behind him round a roof post, and he is slid to the ground where his stretched legs are bound. His shoulder is crippling him from the blow and the gag already abrades the corners of his mouth.

Hawker shows his pistol. Frith nods. He has no desire to be fool-hardy. He has no plan. Suddenly he remembers he had a plan. He and Nicholas in Jeannie's cabin in County Lock. He curses himself, visualising the bargemaster and his daughter entombed in gaol. For how many more nights because the Navigation owners remain unknowing? Nicholas is guarding the barge and he is guarded and bound in a remote barn. Frith is dismayed with himself. If only he had done what he said he would.

A solitary dawn

Lynn shook herself from another fitful snooze. Dawn had not yet broken. The cell was cold, quiet and her Dad's head rested peacefully on her lap. The night had been long and she was weary of the grinding thoughts in her head that had prevented her from sleeping.

She realised the cell was too silent. She could not hear her Dad's wheezing breaths. A single shiver scythed through Lynn's body. She dared not move, did not want confirmed what her mind told her about the cool, motionless body in her lap.

No tears came as she sat almost as motionless as her Dad. Her thoughts found other places to visit unbidden, drawing the living man, his mannerisms she had taken for granted were as clear as her hand. The memories were warm trickles across a freezing avalanche that was burying her. Lynn felt herself receding through a place without form or sensation. A flash of his joys with her Mam, the three of them together brought a dry-eyed shudder. The weight of the past pushed Lynn deeper into the darkness of the cell. Recalling the richness of what had been against the emptiness of what now was, of what will be. It was squeezing the life out of her.

Minutes later, an hour later, two, and a solitary pigeon heralded the morning with its five-note phrase. It's repeated pure notes became a tranquillising incantation filling Lynn's mind.

The Out Barn, Withy Farm

Hawker's pistols are out. The barn door rattles again. Frith hears a hushed voice. he tries to catch the words through the pain in his shoulder and the aches in his limbs.

"It's me, Dan. Let me in."

Dan Blacklock takes a passing look at Frith. Before he can speak his face collects spittle from Hawker's snarl. "What'd I tell you about coming here?"

"It's important," says Dan, wiping his face.

"It better be."

"I been in the Bear last night and it don't look good."

"Never does," pipes Quinn. He is sobered by a glare from Hawker.

"The whole town's expecting mobs of them navvies to bust up the place to get their mates out of gaol."

"More work for us," says Hawker. "Another reason for me to call on the Governor."

"A couple of the Watchmen were boasting about the muskets they've been given."

"What're they doing with muskets?" asks Hawker. He pulls Dan out of earshot of their prisoner.

Frith has a blind compulsion to stand up, to do anything, or his limbs will atrophy from their hours of restraint. His attempts to caterpillar his back up the post don't move his backside off the earth. He thrusts his tethered feet in a fury, his shoes slip and the angled push spirals him round the post and slightly up. The success revives his strength. He does it again, and again, until he is standing. A protruding nail digs into the back of his head. He suppresses the yelp to avoid attracting the Reading Militia men from their talking. After a couple of breaths, he begins to pick behind his head at the gag. The raw corners of his mouth ooze blood.

It dawns on Frith that Dan knew about the barn with its hoard of stolen goods. If one regular member knows the chances are the whole squad are involved.

"Watch him," Hawker tells Dan, nodding at Frith. He addresses his prisoner. "I'm off for a chat with the Governor. Got yourself a better view on this side? Enjoy it. Likely be your last. Quinn, see about rounding up the men."

Hawker and Quinn leave but will soon be back, Hawker from Southcote Hall certain Frith has been bluffing him, and the Reading Militia, the gang of thieves. Frith expects the Captain would want to demonstrate his ruthless cruelty in front of his men.

Dan is anxious and takes periodical peeps from the door. Frith works the gag against the nail visualising the two hitches of the knot behind his head. The nail head snags on the material and Frith jerks his head forward in frustration. Tears fill his eyes. He stamps on his toes to take his mind from the acid pain round his mouth, a Mohawk trick. He works on loosening the second hitch, watching Dan pace the barn. Frith needs a non-threatening gambit for his first words.

"Drink!" gasps Frith. Dan leaps. "For God's sake man, a drink."

"Shut up," hisses Dan. Frith waits half a minute then begs again.

"You're getting nothing," barks Dan.

"You and me likewise," says Frith with resignation.

"What d'you mean?"

"It doesn't matter," says Frith. After a pause he adds: "You'll find out soon enough." He lets that rebound in Dan's head for a while. "They're not coming back."

"Course they are."

"The only ones coming here are the Aldermen's Watch with their muskets. It's over. The Mayor knows all about this. Why else would I be here unless I knew about it? Hawker and Quinn are half way to another county by now."

"Hawker 'd never leave his men."

"A loyal man is he?" Time for another hunch, thinks Frith, recalling the interview with an retrospective insight on Captain Hawker. "What was your previous leader like?"

"John? Good man. Straight. What's it to you? Knew where you stood with John Corsby."

"Corsby retired did he? So Hawker could take over." Frith hides any sarcasm.

"No. He was thieving from us."

"You said he was straight."

"We was wrong."

Frith can hear the uncertainty in Dan's voice. "How did you find out he was stealing from you?"

"We found the stuff in his pockets."

"You did?"

"Well . . . Hawker did."

"When?"

"After he'd knifed him."

"So John Corsby didn't get a chance to prove his innocence." Frith lets this seep in. "Hawker said Corsby was a thief. Hawker killed him. Hawker's hand found the evidence. Hawker became leader. Loyal, trustworthy Captain Hawker."

Dan peeks through the barn door. He listens.

"Why did Hawker need to take Sergeant Quinn?" asks Frith.

Dan looks out again.

"The two always visit Sir George together, do they?"

Another peek, then the Reading Militia man sidles out of the barn.

Frith hears the man's footfalls fade. How long should he wait before he starts shouting? Until Dan is out of earshot but before Hawker returns. Who will hear him? What choice has he? The ropes round his wrists and ankles are manacles. Only by breaking both arms could he get his wrists up to the nail. Frith is not that fearless.

A kohl comfort

The pigeon's unremitting call turned from a balm to grist for Lynn's mind. She vowed to herself that her Dad, Peter Darville would not be buried in a pauper's grave. It was as obvious as the cold stone surrounding her the vow would be impossible to bring about from inside the gaol. Therefore, she had to be out. Other things followed as to why she must be out. She would attend his burial. She owed it to Gabriel and his men to do something about getting their release and that could only be from outside. After the others, there was herself. Her brain was stagnating in the cell, her body starved weak. She sighed at the hopeless promise to her Dad she could never keep. Lynn tried to recall the last time he had been his old self, cheerful and opinionated.

It was at Rose Kiln. Adam – how had she forgotten him? By being wrapped in her own misery. He would have some ideas, might know the Mayor, maybe the judge. How could she get to him? Could she convince the turnkey she was a helpless child caught in men's quarrels? Hadn't she fooled Hawker with her "death before dishonour" act? Probably not, it was the real retching that had saved her. Lynn guessed the turnkey Dunbar had heard every excuse, just like the inn-keepers round the London docks as to why a customer couldn't pay just then. The Mayor had stressed the importance of keeping these prisoners securely locked up. And isolated thanks to Mistress Olivia's vengeance. Anyway, Dunbar only listened to the chink-chink of coins into his palm.

Perhaps Adam could bribe Dunbar to be her warden. Unlikely. Every idea ended beached. Adam might have an idea what could be done but only if she was able to get a message to him. Remembering the noises during the night Lynn formed a plan. It depended on early risers and drunken sleepers.

Lynn was at the peephole in the cell door when she heard the turnkey's door scrape open. It was too carefully moved to be either of the ogres. With a pounding heart Lynn hissed. The soft footsteps stopped. Lynn hissed again.

"I've something for you." Silence. "Let me show you." Lynn tried a different tack. "I'm alone with these men. Please."

The peephole slid cautiously open revealing wide, wary eyes outlined in smudged kohl, faded cochineal cheeks with two black beauty spots. She could have been fifteen or fifty.

"What you got?"

Lynn showed the woman the locket round her neck.

"Pretty," she said. "I wouldn't have a neck to put it round if I let you out."

"That's not what I want. Just to deliver a message." Lynn checked her urgency, tried not to gabble. If Dunbar woke now the whore would get a beating and he would take the locket she had had the foresight to hide.

"I ain't stupid," she said. "You get a mob of them cut-throats come and free this lot and I'm the first one they'll come looking for."

"This is for me. I can't cope with another night with them." Lynn thumbed behind her. "It's a message to Adam, you now, the brickmaker at Rose Kiln."

"That nutter?"

A surge of hope flashed through Lynn. The woman knew of Adam and she was clearly keen on the locket the way her eyes kept straying to it.

The whore spoke again. "You're stupid if you think Becky Shaw's going all the way out there. It's far too bloody dangerous for a pretty woman on her own."

Its more dangerous in the beds you work, thought Lynn. If the woman won't step outside the town to convey a message, who would? There was only one person. It was an all or nothing gamble. Nicholas Middleton had deserted her after Theale Meadow. Her note would likely go straight into the fire. But Lynn could not thrust aside an instinctive belief in some honourable vein in his nature. Maybe remorse for what he'd done might make him do this one thing for her, to appease his guilt. She mentally tossed a penny and let it fall unheeded. What other option had she?

Becky knew the storekeeper's handsome son and agreed to take a message there. That's four people in this relay thought Lynn, who had seen messages fly across London Bridge to arrive in Southwark with the meaning reversed. It would have to be written. She pictured Adam's cottage without a book in sight, not even a bible. Could he read?

"C'mon," urged Becky glancing behind her. "I ain't hanging round here longer 'n I have to."

On Lynn's instruction Becky brought a pamphlet from the wall and passed her a thick kohl pencil.

This is the barge and here we all are in prison, whispered Lynn to herself as she drew the second picture. One of us has died. Lynn choked on her whisper and stopped voicing to herself the other sketches as she drew on the back of the poster. It was too complicated but there was no chance of an explanation being passed on. No, it made sense. Anything was worth trying and this was her only anything.

Lynn pushed her life line under the cell door. "Look at it, Becky," she said, having decided to add the simplest explanation possible. "I'm asking Adam to lend me coins to pay the turnkey. That's who the message is for, Adam, with his hat and handcart."

Becky folded the piece of paper and quickly tucked it away out of sight. "And?" she whispered.

Lynn unclipped her locket and threaded it through the peephole. She tried to read in Becky's eyes if the note would be thrown away two paces outside of the gaol.

Lynn knew she had to keep the death of her Dad from the turn-keys or she would never see him again. Mogger and Dicky would go along with her. She calculated how long before Adam could get to the gaol if everything fell into line. Then calculated how long if so-and-so happened, or so-and-so did not happen. Minute followed minute bringing the morning, respectful quiet from Mogger and Dicky, greasy slop, much from her past with her parents in answer to her companions solicitous questions, and waves of certainty in the failure of her note.

from Mistress Olivia's diary

The Kennet Koffee House is a temple to tedium. The rare customer with his glum face and his dreary clothes is boorish. I would yawn in their faces but they think it the new fashion. There is fun sending the sottish Mrs Middle-gone on urgent errands only to scold her for some mistake fabricated for her return. The more rascal wharf men have caught on to this recreation confounding her with their coffee requests or over the adding up.

My keenest amusement is goading Mrs Middle-gone over her runaway son. If she fears he is become a highway robber I reassure her he has neither the nerve nor the wit being surely caught and hanged within the week. Her dread he is vagabond I discount saying he has not the guile and will be dead from cold and hunger within the month.

"During our courtship," I say as introduction to my own version and reminding her she has lost me as daughter-in-law, "your son never made one lewd overture for me to fend off. As a very attractive young lady I found this reticence unusually polite. Yet a week ago he chases the barge trollop as if to proclaim he is a red-blooded male. Was this not the same time as the Aldermen's Watch unearthed that contemptible Molly House? Perchance that was a coincidence. Though your pretty boy son often frequented the Basingstoke Road when he was supposedly buying for the shop. Who would look for a Molly under a trollop's skirt?"

There is no greater enjoyment than leading one's adversary to face their worst fear. Today it was the mother of the louse who betrayed me. Yesterday it was that contemptible ally of Master Nicholas Middleton, wrecking his pathetic faith in his adulterous woman. His dream collapsed as easily as I crumple a page from his newspaper. When Mrs Middle-gone could speak she vowed to renounce her son. This makes both sons lost to her for I read in Richard's latest letter he disowns his family as they can no longer advance his military career.

I am graced by good fortune. A poxed woman crawled in whom I learned through the Froth-head's remonstrations, is the gaol whore. This disgusting wench cawed, "I's looking for Master Nicholas. I got a message for him."

"In your belly?" asked the Froth-head, which did endear me to her for that moment.

Mrs Middle-gone let out one cry and I reassured her that her son would not have gone whoring. Most likely as a Molly, he was her bawd. To my irritation she withdrew so I could not watch her distress while I dealt with the whore. She had the affront to refuse me the message though I told her plainly I had been betrothed to the recipient. I ordered her out instructing her to crawl back to an inn of disrepute and earn her next farthing.

The Out Barn, Withy Farm

Every shout is a sand storm through Frith's throat. His mouth rasps its torment every time he parts his lips. Frith wonders if he is delusional. He isn't sure at all if he heard a woman's whispered voice.

"It be my barn," says a man.

Frith takes a steadying breath. The last thing he wants is to scare the anxious pair outside. "Help me. I'm a prisoner." He attempts to reassure them. "I am alone. Help me, please."

A weather-worn face squints round the barn door. Vale Clemson takes in with widening eyes the garishly ornate cathedral that is his barn. His wife follows like a sparrow, hopping back out, then back in to the farmer's side. The Clemson pair half listen to Frith's explanation how Hawker has been using their barn as they inspect the booty with awe.

"They warned us to stay away," says Vale Clemson, judging the weight of a silver candelabra.

"For reasons of security, they said," adds Nancy.

"Always locked fast," says the farmer. "Saw it open, just now. Thought they'd cleared off."

Frith is keenly aware Hawker could return any moment, putting the Clemsons in the same peril as himself. He has no time to question them, only to urge them to a safer place. Vale Clemson sets about untying Frith's bonds with a look set to take on all comers. Frith speaks of pistols and swords, and the couple scurry from the barn.

Frith sees that he can get away to anywhere, far away from Hawker, far away from wrongly imprisoned souls, far away from penniless Nicholas. He stands free of the post, his body remembering how to balance itself. By doing nothing he abandoned Catherine to her husband. Had he been positive he would have known for sure what their forty-two days meant. He has done a good deal of thinking through this night, mainly about his nature and how he reasons himself away from rashness. He knows that is his way.

Frith leaves the barn with one thing in mind and this means avoiding Hawker. He retraces his steps through the copse and across the ploughed field, turns down the lane towards the Navigation. It is the new route. In his pockets and under his arm he carries thoughtfully selected trophies from the Reading Militia's hoard of plunder. Frith crosses the wooden swing bridge by Sheffield Lock and strides briskly along the towing path.

A cosmetic undertaking

Lynn worried about the navvies in the other cells. Lynn worried about Hermond. Had he been taken to the knacker's yard to pay for their gaol food? Her Dad lay alongside the wall of the cell. The bell of St Giles completed its toll of the hour.

How long did it take to walk to Middleton's Provisions Stores? Or did Becky Sharp dally along the way to show off her new locket. If Nicholas Middleton had a ha'penny of honour he would deliver the message quickly. Or was he not at the store but out round the farms. Calling on Mistress Olivia. Adam would sacrifice a kiln load if he had to. Or would he? Was he away from Kiln Lane working for the butcher? Would he find a note left if it was for him? Adam was already three hours late. Lynn should be planning another way to reach him. She found it impossible to think of anything except the many disastrous fates of her note.

These thoughts were stopped by a ruction in the turnkey's room. Dunbar's voice was loud with consternation. The peephole snapped back and Dunbar shouted from a yard away.

"You got a dead 'un in there?"

Lynn went cold. How did he know? Becky had left long ago. Had Adam arrived? He'd have spoken. Dunbar demanded again.

"Yes," said Lynn, shrugging her shoulders at Mogger and Dicky.

"Dickens you have!"

A slight man in his twenties stood at the opened cell door. He wore a black longcoat, maroon breeches and black stockings. It was nobody Lynn had ever seen before.

"Go to ya work," said Dunbar with a shove.

The man stumbled across the cell. Another followed him in, a big fellow with a black flop-rimmed hat. The thin man flashed a calling card to Lynn and as quickly pocketed it.

"Valentine Prince, undertaker. At your service, Mistress." He turned to the door. "I shall be undertaking an examination of the corpus delicti —" His assistant coughed. "Gaol-keeper, fetch me hot water that I may wash my hands after examining the body."

"Don't have none," answered Dunbar from outside the cell.

"Then to the tavern. Hurry man. Unlike this corpse I haven't got all day. Beg pardon Mistress."

The turnkey locked the cell door and grumbled out of the gaol.

"Who sent for you?" asked Lynn feeling uneasy about the cavalier behaviour of the undertaker. She would fight to the death to stop body snatchers having her dad.

"Valentine Prince, actor," said the undertaker bowing low.

Lynn looked to his assistant.

"Aye, Bonnie Lass," said Fergus with a wink.

"Hold yer wheesht," said Valentine in a comic imitation of the Scot.

"Haud," corrected Fergus. He had a conspiratorial smile but behind it Lynn could see his dread of standing in the cell of an English gaol.

"Don't speak, you'll give us all away." Valentine turned to Lynn. "He'll never be an actor. A one accent man, see." He was delving in the pocket of his longcoat. "That's one gaoler out of the way. Now for the performance." He stopped.

"I am most frightfully sorry, Mistress Lynn." Valentine bowed to Lynn. "Please accept my deepest condolences for your great loss. I never knew the man but I too had a father."

Fergus' arms embraced Lynn in a bear hug. For some seconds she let herself sink into caring protection, an oblivion of thought, before drawing herself out. At least her Dad would be properly buried. Maybe they would take another message to Adam.

"It's very kind of you to do this for my Dad, but what I need —"

"Yes, yes," said Valentine, pulling from his pocket what looked to be a small pillbox. "A brilliant ruse of yours if I may say."

Lynn was baffled. What ruse? Where was Adam? He would never be party to this kind of deception and Adam knew nothing of Fergus or the actor.

Valentine continued. "Such a jape I just had to be a part of it, star performance and all that. Afraid this is the best I could do not being familiar with the real thing."

He opened the box to reveal a Burgundy red powder which he rubbed in a patch on the neck of Lynn's dad.

"Stop it!" Lynn moved to pull him from the corpse but Fergus eased her away. Mogger and Dicky squared up to Fergus but Valentine was issuing instructions.

"My idea this. A little face powder to make it convincing. You two gentlemen next if you please. Mistress Lynn, it would make good sense for you prepare yourself to scream. It must be convincing, though alas you can have no rehearsal. Stand up straight, take some big breaths, loosen the jaw, say 'ha, he, hi, ho.' The first cry must be powerful but the rest can be in a higher register." Valentine had finished covering the exposed skin of Peter in dark blotches and he hurriedly turned to the two navvies.

It was a moment of torment for Lynn. She could tell Valentine and Fergus to stop whatever they had planned and to resume their disguise to get her Dad's body out of the cell. Or she could break the law, praying no one was hurt in the process. It was against all her upbringing. But they were wrongly imprisoned with no hope of justice from this town. Fergus was risking his life for her. She had got the navvies into this mess so getting the first two out was down to her.

The group in Lynn's cell were ready and highly nervous when the grumbling Dunbar returned. As he neared the cell door Lynn screamed from the pit of her stomach. The turnkey dropped the pitcher, yelling as the hot water scalded his arm before smashing round his boots. Dunbar's curses and Lynn's screeches echoed through the building.

"Get me out!" cried Valentine. "Plague! 'Tis London Fever." He flailed against the door with the conviction of a man absolutely terrified. "Let me out or you'll hang for my murder." Fergus stood flat against the wall by the door and raised his eyebrows to the ceiling. Valentine's dramatics had the desired effect. Dunbar looked through the spy-hole at the plague-blotched body, the lesser symptoms on the two navvies, the distress on Lynn's face, the hysterics of the undertaker. Fergus needed an inch of open door and Dunbar lay winded on the cell floor. Mogger and Dicky caught the second turnkey before he reached the street.

"Quiet!" shouted Gabriel as a cheer started up. Mogger took the keys from Dunbar's belt.

"We can't do that," said Lynn. "We have to get them released properly, else they'll be —"

"You don't desert your mates," said Mogger. His face brooked no argument.

The turnkeys were bound, gagged and locked in two cells on the top floor. The prisoners in the fifth cell were released and all the doors locked shut.

"That might buy us some time," said Gabriel. "What'll buy us more is not charging out like wild men."

So it was that Valentine Prince led from the gaol a cart bearing the shrouded body of Peter Darville, followed by his grieving daughter, and a band of mourners made up of several navvies, a cut-purse, a counterfeiter and a boy. The solemn group was followed by the undertaker's assistant. The navvies who had remained, stepped out one or two at a time as confidently as bees leaving the hive on a sunny day.

Lynn was relieved to see Barge Jeannie still afloat in County Lock. Her joy was quenched when she saw its high ride in the water. "The upright citizens of Reading don't blink an eye about looting," she sighed to Gabriel. "The cargo's been taken. I've lost everything."

Gabriel was more interested in the lock gates, satisfied the turfs they had removed had not been thrown back in. "We'll soon have this cleared," he said, inviting some of his men into the lock chamber.

"What's the point?" asked Lynn. "With no cargo the contract isn't met. I might as well give up Barge Jeannie here as a mile further on."

"A lot can happen in a mile, Mistress Lynn."

"You must get away. You're gaol-breakers."

"We stand by our friends." He looked her in the eye. "No matter what."

"I'm sorry Gabriel. I know you do." Lynn chided herself as to how many times she had to be told. "It's just I'm not used to receiving such kindness." She went to check the state of the cabin not really knowing what she was going to do. Gabriel's men seemed to have decided Barge Jeannie was going on.

With no Hermond and no cargo reasoned Lynn, the twists of Brewery Gut would be tricky. Did that matter? The barge would be recognised, stopped and she'd be caught. She could leave the barge. Fleeing was not an option for the body of her dad was in the hold and Hermond was maybe somewhere. She just didn't know.

The looters hadn't bothered with the cabin and its paltry items. Lynn sat on her Dad's bunk fiddling with the familiar objects, touching them for reassurance. Fergus was telling her how he came to freely walk into an English gaol. The effort of listening brought Lynn's mind to practical matters. She fired the stove to make a hot broth.

Fergus had been minding his own business in the Sun. Next to the gaol was the last place Hawker would look for him. The local whore skips in flashing her new locket from her rich gentleman admirer. Fergus had seen it round Lynn's neck at Southcote Cut. A few strong words to the lying slut and Fergus had the locket and Lynn's note. He asked a clever-looking chap at the next table what the pictures had to do with a barge, a girl and her dad.

Valentine read it straight away. "The dad is deceased in the gaol. The boat represents freedom, breaking out of gaol. The turnkey is to be terrified helpless, these blobs are the plague, discovered when the undertaker comes with his cart. He's wearing an unusual hat, someone in disguise." There was no stopping Valentine after that.

Lynn held her breath and asked why Becky still had the note when she went to the Sun. Fergus said nobody had seen the store-keeper's son, not since the father lost everything to the Mayor in the financial shenanigans that's been going on. Nicholas Middleton had deserted her, then deserted his parents. Lynn knew the breakout from gaol had been her only option and reconciled herself to now being a lawbreaker.

Gun Street, Reading

Standing on the main span of Seven Bridges, Frith is nonplussed by the empty County Lock and the deserted streets. His heart pulls a twist when his gaze looks towards West Hill. He turns the other way to Mayor Turner's house where he will denounce the Reading Militia as a gang of thieves. He catches ear of a commotion beyond the brewery and decides to avoid an inflamed crowd while he is carrying stolen property.

Frith has just cleared the bridge when he is hailed from Gun

Street by a coarsely dressed man struggling to push a four-wheel handcart. "Over here," calls the man, with a furtive gesture to make Frith suspicious and curious.

"Right how's-your-father," says the man, reaching for the gilded mirror under Frith's arm. "Mayor's in thick of it with 'em all. Hawker should do his place. There'll be a few guineas in there, I'll bet."

The scruff lifts the cover off the handcart and slides the mirror on top of a heap of gold and silverware, miniatures and clocks, ornaments and jewellery. Frith realises Hawker's men are looting on a grand scale while the town folk are distracted on the river. He also realises the vicious Captain could appear at any second.

The man indicates for Frith to throw his second piece of evidence on to the cart. Frith notices he has a short sword and pistol on his belt. "Picture?" queries the man. "We was told no pictures."

Frith plays along with the man, who has taken the newsman's slovenly appearance and wares to assume he is one of Hawker's gang. "Do you want me to put it back?" The newsman spoke too well.

"Ain't I seen this one at the barn?" asks the man warily.

Frith's stomach drops. He puts on a scowl. "Look Hog-brain, all bleeding nobs looks the same don't they? Powder and wigs and prancing. So Sharp-eyes, can you tell Lord Nose-in-the-air from Baron Brains-up-his-bum. Can you?" Frith keeps his other evidence in his pockets. "I don't know you, do I?"

"Burkitt Took."

"How long you been with us?"

"Couple of weeks."

"That explains. I been away on a special job. Want to stay on Hawker's good side?"

"You bloody bet."

"Then shift this cart."

Took grabs the shafts and pushes forward.

"Where're you going Prat-head?" snaps Frith.

"Castle Street."

"Change of plan. Been checking County Bridge, see. We're

clearing off over the Wood, shooting up Red Lane."

"That's back to where trouble is," says Took.

"Round behind it, Cloth-ears. Use the big hedge round Forbury to hide us." Frith sees Took is not convinced. "Got a better idea, Took? Let's you and I go find Hawker and discuss his plan with him. See if he thinks yours is better."

They turn the laden handcart round and bend into pushing it towards Minster Street. A change of plan for Frith. He has to go along with it as he cannot see a way to get to the Mayor with well-armed Took and a handcart laden with stolen goods.

Interview with Mayor Robert Turner, Greyfriars Street

Courant. Thank you granting me this interview after your ordeals of this afternoon. I feel it important the events be accurately recorded for history.

Mayor. I wholeheartedly endorse that viewpoint, Mr Frith. Let me stress I do so, not because I was at the centre of the events, but that posterity may benefit from a true record of the events of this momentous day. First though, let me take this opportunity to record the town's gratitude for your quick thinking today. I have for some while suspected the Reading Militia of underhand activities and sought some agent to expose them.

Courant. Concerning the events on the river, you are custodian of the peace and good order in the town. Do you agree this was placed in jeopardy to be rescued only by good fortune?

Mayor. Not good fortune, though fortuitous timing always plays an important part. Today there were many factors at work to ensure the safety of our citizens.

Courant. Perhaps you could elaborate for me.

Mayor. It was rumours among the citizens that brought my attention to the great danger. I am able to distinguish truth from fearful exaggeration and could discount the alarm that two hundred navigators were approaching from Newbury and the same from from Oxford, as I know there are not that many in the whole county. Neither would numbers of Weybridge wharf men travel to support their arch rivals here in Reading. However, I had intelligence of a violent break-out from the gaol and could anticipate the riot I had endeavoured to avoid by imprisoning them on Monday.

Courant. Did you verify the break-out was violent? That the turnkeys had been butchered, as was widely but falsely rumoured?

Mayor. Any unprepared venture towards the gaol would have been hazardous. My strategy was to wait, ascertain the intention of the escaped prisoners and, using that time, to muster the forces I had at my disposal.

Courant. The Aldermen's Watch?

Mayor. Quite so. Alongside those brave souls, the wharf men stood by as loyal citizens.

Courant. Why did you not deploy the Reading Militia?

Mayor. As I stated, I had doubts of Captain Hawker, and therefore placed the Militia away from any confrontation in the town centre.

Courant. Allowing them to freely run amok.

Mayor. Doubts are not proof, Mr Frith. It was important not to raise suspicion lest Captain Hawker flee from justice. The rumours of mayhem had brought Captain Hawker to my door with a plan for the Militia to protect our men's backs from Newbury and Oxford.

Courant. Which attack you had recognised as exaggerated rumour. Why did you give the Militia opportunity to pillage when you suspected them?

Mayor. You do not appreciate that politics is making the judicious decision at a given moment, achieving the best compromise under the worst circumstances. My priority is the welfare of my citizens, even if that meant putting a few properties at risk. By playing to their greed I gave the Reading Militia sufficient rope that they were discovered. You effected the outcome I had hoped.

Courant. I am pleased to have been your fortuitous agent. When the barge carrying the navvies came into Brewery Gut you read the Riot Act. Without the Yeomanry, did you hope to enforce it with stones?

Mayor. I am a dignitary and respected citizen of this town, Mr Frith, with all the propriety and decorum necessary for my office. A week ago it was my passion for my town that was on display. Today it was the authority of my office.

Interview with Mrs Sarah Kempster, Saracen's Head

Mrs Sarah. I reckon Mistress Oily started it. She sees this pile of cow dung walk in and has her chucked out of the Koffee House quicker than you can say Becky Shaw. Next thing, those gaol-breakers are smashing-up the town.

Courant. I don't see the connection.

Mrs Sarah. Becky's the gaol whore and Mistress Oily didn't grab the note off her. I was this close to the note, Mr Frith. This close to stopping everything.

Courant. That close to a different story, a tragedy. However, you were at Brewery Gut?

Mrs Sarah. Me and every mother's son and daughter. No pack of navvies was gonna tear our town apart. I never seen so many wharf men fixed on what they was about. High Bridge seemed best place to get a good look but it was stomach-in-your-mouth stuff, I can tell you. It all happened so quick. One minute I was watching two barges in some river carnival, next I was in the middle of a real ding-dong. Not just fists. They was set on serious personal damage. Hated each other's guts like they was fallen-out friends.

Courant. Tell me about the barges.

Mrs Sarah. We saw that scab barge do —

Courant. Barge Jeannie.

Mrs Sarah. Yeah, the scab barge do a runner for the Thames. I gotta say, he's a good bargemaster. That's a nasty bit of river and he kept her plumb centre with little wind to give him rudder. We was cussing, thinking they'll get away with just another stoning, except our useless Mayor hadn't mended the bridge since the last time and there weren't no stones on it. We was hollering our lungs out, when out from under High Bridge comes one of Orf's barges loaded with wharf men poling it along for all they was worth. Did we cheer, never heard the like. These two barges heading at one another like one of those jousting things. They got closer and closer, then ours swung across quick to ram the scab. Willing to sink the two of them they was, but the other, give him credit where credit's due, he did the —

Courant. She, she did. The daughter Lynn Darville was at the tiller. Her father died in gaol.

Mrs Sarah. A girl? Oh. God rest the old man's soul, and hers, the poor girl. Anyway he, she, did the exact opposite of what you'd expect and swung her barge towards ours. Instead of us busting through her gunwale the two scraped sides.

Courant. Then Barge Jeannie came on to High Bridge.

Mrs Sarah. Who's telling this story Mr Frith? Our blokes were using their poles like good 'uns trying to poke the navvies off their boat. I tell you, we had the navvies ducking and dodging. One of ours caught the girl coz she was having to stick by the tiller, and that got the navvies real mad. One jumped on our barge and him and two others ended up in the river, along with Fat Jimmy. Poor oaf ain't that bright and he's so busy with jabbing his pole he didn't see their barge's clew-line until the sail clouted him. He lay across both gunwales like a sack of beans until the barges moved apart and he fell between, splash! Everyone gasped coz we knew when the barges washed back together Fat Jimmy would be crushed thinner than a kerchief. We all love Fat Jimmy to bits and suddenly this weren't some fairground show.

Courant. Have a swig of brandy.

Mrs Sarah. Thanks. If you ask me, knowing what I know now, I think that girl saved Fat Jimmy's life. She went full over on her tiller yelling at her navvies to drop the sail. It looked like she was bringing her bow into our barge to deliberately squash him. That sent our lot wild, I can tell you. Course her stern slewed out, letting our guys keep a gap poled until the barges had passed Fat Jimmy. You think something's happening, like she was aiming to squash the poor blighter, but later you realise it was something different to what you saw.

Courant. It often is, Sarah. What then?

Mrs Sarah. One of our lads got a rope round the saddle-chock before he was bundled off their barge. The the barges are tethered like two fighting dogs on a short leash. Our poles were gonna win as their sail was down, but it weren't easy, what with keeping the rope taught so's they couldn't slip it. Then the girl's barge catches the back eddy from where Holy Brook joins the river, and she does this slow turn. Just at the right moment our guys slip the rope and the scab barge swings into the shallows by Townside.

Courant. So Barge Jeannie was grounded by High Bridge.

Mrs Sarah. Next we see another mob of wild-eyed navvies charging along Townside with all sorts of I don't know what as weapons. Goodness knows where they came from.

Courant. The gaol. They probably heard the noise and came to help their pals on the barge. That was when it became frightening?

Mrs Sarah. Bloody vicious it was. The navvies on the barge were having a pitched battle with our lot on Orf's barge. This other lot came laying into our blokes piling off High Bridge. I screamed when a pitchfork went past my head, but mine was lost in all the other screams.

Courant. I thought you weren't on Townside?

Mrs Sarah. Didn't matter. Folks was fighting anybody who got in their way, pushing and shoving and clawing each other. I didn't know which way was home. Even women was punching and bashing. Shocking it was, I can tell you.

Courant. Were you hurt?

Mrs Sarah. You ain't seen me ducking and diving when I need to, have you? Quicker 'n a grebe and gone, I am. I get myself to the far side of High Bridge from the fighting and guess who I found there? Our Mayor cowering behind the Aldermen's Watch. They was doing what they do best – watching.

Courant. Let me get this straight, the fighting was on the barges and Townside but the Mayor and Watch were on Kennetside?

Mrs Sarah. His face was the colour of a flag of surrender. I could see the fighting was slog and grunt, mindless bashing each other and anyone who came near. I decided the safest place was next to the Mayor. Except it wasn't coz I heard this galloping down London Street. Blow me if Master Nicholas don't rein-up just in time not to trample His Wobbling Worship and I know the lad's a good horseman. Poor animal was sweating buckets but Master Nicholas was the one foaming at the mouth, shouting back at the Mayor what I prefer not to repeat. Then he spurs on, through the crowd like they was ducks on a village pond. We all thought he was going to muck in with our lads and do something useful for once. Oh no, he rides through the brawling, leaps onto their barge and goes straight for the girl. Blokes in his way was butter. Brilliant, I thought, take out Queen Rat and the rest 'll run. Picture this, Mr Frith, there's all sorts of nasty things flying about, women and kids screaming for all they're worth, there's blokes waist deep in the river slogging it out, and on the barge is Queen Rat and Master Nicholas having a quite chat.

Courant. What were they saying?

Mrs Sarah. You're not listening, Mr Frith. I couldn't hear my own voice for all the noise. I saw her land him one, a good haymaker. He had plenty of time to see it coming but he didn't move. Thump! Perhaps his father's cuff had addled his brain. The girl looks at him for a second and I thought here comes a second m'lad, and whoosh she has both arms round his neck and his arms loop round her waist and it was like they was Romeo and Juliet with no idea there was mayhem and blood-spilling all round them.

Courant. Thankfully not as tragic. But Nicholas did get injured.

Mrs Sarah. A pair of doves ain't gonna sit long on a branch when the tree's being shaken by a hurricane. The lad has no idea about fighting so he soon gets cracked across the head with something heavy. The girl drags him into the cabin and stays with him.

Courant. Until the end of the fighting?

Mrs Sarah. No. She shot down into the hold. By then our wharf men had got the upper hand and were forcing the navvies back along Townside. A couple of our lads set about the barge's hull with a pick they'd got hold of.

Courant. Planning to sink Barge Jeannie.

Mrs Sarah. Things was beyond any planning by then, Mr Frith.

High Bridge, Reading

After being trussed in the barn, Frith's muscles howl with pain pushing the handcart up Minster Street. Took waits while Frith checks the narrow Yield Hall Lane that curves down to Townside close to High Bridge. The noise of the skirmish echoes up the empty lane.

In his head Frith lists the options. His shouts would be drowned under the noise. Only burly Took would hear and silence him. If he ran down he would be absorbed in the crowd. He could engineer it so the handcart rattled down Yield Hall Lane where it would fall into the river, Took escape in the other direction leaving Hawker free to seek his retribution of Frith.

Twenty yards on they stop so Took can see if Broad Street is clear. Frith loosens the brake and lets the cart slip back. He pulls a circular silver platter from his pocket and, giving up his fate to the skies, he spins it high through the air down Yield Hall Lane. He flicks off the handcart's brake. "Took!" he yells. "Brake's gone."

The Militia man runs to behind the handcart with Frith and puts his shoulders to it. The handcart jolts in and out of the roadside gully and the two lose their footing on the mud. It lurches towards the corner of a building. There is a crack as the right shaft snaps against the bricks. Frith and Took, backs to the wall, jump to brace their feet against the backboard of the cart. The other shaft grazes along the wall, the handcart nearly pitches over. A wheel hits a rut and the cart stops abruptly. The gilded mirror slides off and smashes noisily on the street's cornerstone.

The pair are wedged two feet off the ground, the big Militia man squashed like a trapped caterpillar. Frith is shaking after his escape from being crushed.

"Thieves!"

Frith's heart lifts when other voices take up the cry. He sees a score or more running up Yield Hall Lane towards him. A woman waves the silver platter above her head like the colours of battle.

"We've got to get out of here," says Frith. He struggles to free himself while doing his best to keep them trapped against the wall.

The group surround the handcart and pull off the canvas. They are silenced by what they see. Frith fears an eruption of blind outrage. They came up the Yield Hall Lane already fired for a fight. The platter is wielded on high like a silver axe destined for Frith's head when he notices the woman's face.

"Mary! It's me. Mr Frith." He pleads into her eyes. "Mr Frithed is not pithed?" The barmaid recognises him. "You know what I do. By any chance, is the Mayor down there? I need to speak to him about this"

"Rat!" Frith's head is slewed by Took's punch. Rough hands circle his neck. Frith loses vision in his left eye. Panic flares from his bursting lungs. Took's assault on Frith convinces the crowd and the choking hands are pried from the newsman's throat.

The pair are led down Duke Street. Frith sees Townside ahead is thick with battling men, women diving into the shifting mass. High Bridge is solid with people. The noise is deafening. It is a pitched battle.

People become aware of the approaching handcart with its stern escort. By the time the handcart stops in front of Mayor Turner on High Bridge there is quiet. Frith has prepared what he says to the Mayor: the burglaries, the barn, Took, this handcart.

"Mr Frith, the town is indebted to you for rescuing these properties," says the Mayor grandly. "And for discovering the hiding place for the stolen goods. As to your claim the burglaries were the work of our Reading Militia, I fear you have let your imagination run away with you."

"Coz it was the damned navvies."

There is a swell of agreement with the lone voice from the crowd. Frith hears this as the overture to renewed violence. He has lived through an ocean storm of emotions over the past days and these funnel into a tornado of resentment against Mayor Turner for disbelieving him. Frith clambers on to the handcart.

"Listen! When was this stolen?" He holds up item after item

from round his feet. "This? When? These were stolen in the last hour. Where are the navvies? There, and over there. Where are the Reading Militia? Has anyone seen the Reading Militia in the last hour?"

"They are patrolling our streets against attack," states the Mayor.

"Patrolling empty streets and stealing from empty homes." Frith looks down at Took. "Take off his jerkin."

Clawing hands peel the coat from the scared man to expose a black cross-sash. "I only been with 'em a week," blurts Took. "I didn't know what they was up to. Honest. Hawker just told me to push the cart. I didn't steal nothing. It was the others."

One of the Aldermen's Watch calls out. "If the Reading Militia been burgling, it's they's who done for our mate at Woodroffe's."

The rising disquiet spreads through the throng. Mayor Turner decrees all members of the gang are to be arrested, taken dead or alive. "They are no longer to be referred to as the Reading Militia but by their true identity the . . . the Berkshire Blacks. Our trusted Aldermen's Watch will ensure the return of all property to its rightful owner."

This last declaration brings one thought to each mind. There is a surge forward of citizens frantic to retrieve their property from the handcart. Frith is knocked down the pile to the ground. He sees keen eyes inspecting objects as to their worth rather than to owner-ship. He sees the Aldermen's Watch stand powerless on the far side of the bridge.

Interview with Mrs Sarah Kempster, Saracen's Head (con.)

Mrs Sarah. Why'd you need me to tell you?

Courant. When the crowd surged to the cart, I was pushed up High Street.

Mrs Sarah. You be useless at St Giles' rummage sale. Anyway, the Mayor went into a parley with the noble Watch, pretending nothing was happening. That stopped very smart when Captain Hawker and his Militia men stroll along Kennetside.

Courant. That's where you were?

Mrs Sarah. Here's me thinking I've got myself a safe place to scoot home and along comes that bunch of evil bastards. They stop in front of Mayor Robert Turner with me like a hare between two packs of hounds. Everything went fearful quiet. We'd all heard the Mayor declare the whole bunch of them as outlaws. Except the Militia weren't around at the time to catch it. Hawker speaks first, all cocky, "Captain Hawker reporting to Your Worship that all is secure about the town." Normally you can't shut the Mayor up. Said nothing, he did. "Indeed Sir," continues Hawker, "and our timely arrival has restored peace here. A good day's work by your Reading Militia, Sir." You could see Hawker was suddenly a bit wary. Then a voice piped up, "More like a good cart load of thieving." It all happened in a couple of blinks. Hawker clocked summat weren't right, and just in case the bastard hadn't cottoned on, the Mayor finds his voice. "I presume you and your men have come to give yourselves up?" What a complete prat. The Militia was armed to the teeth and outnumbered the Watch twenty to one. All right, three to one. Hawker stalls, "Give ourselves up? What tongues have been wagging against us?" I could see his men getting ready. My back's to the parapet, the Watch on my left, Hawker's mob in front, and I'm thinking who's going to look after Bron and Ben if I gets killed. "For robbery and looting," continues Mayor Turner, like he's addressing a bunch of do-nothing councillors. Then he points to the cart and the crook you found pushing it.

Courant. Burkitt Took.

Mrs Sarah. "Who's he?" asks Hawker, all innocent. "The sneak's passing himself off as Militia." The Mayor still thinks he's in charge. "We know about Vale Clemson's barn. I order the arrest of —" Bang! My guts jumped off the bridge without me. I gotta say Hawker's men were bloody quick. Ordered the Watch to drop their weapons. Then I saw the dead man not three paces from my feet, a red pool from this bloody mess of what used to be his face. I couldn't help myself.

Courant. Your scream brought the wharf men and the navvies onto High Bridge.

Mrs Sarah. I've got hitchers and boat-hooks threshing about my ears, all the pistols of the King's arsenal in my face, and the Watch itching to get at their muskets to murder the scum who've killed two of them.

Courant. Terrifying.

Mrs Sarah. It's strange Mr Frith, I was, but I could see and hear everything clear as clear. One scream and that was it for me, all the quaking stopped.

Courant. It was a stand off.

Mrs Sarah. To start with, then Hawker's lot was backing off, offering a bullet for anyone who moved. Clear as a skylark comes this voice from behind Robert Turner, "You can't let them get away, you are the Mayor." The silly girl should stick to taunting Dragon. It was like that bit in the Bible where this river opens up a corridor, and that's what happened with the Watch. The Mayor found himself slap-bang at the front with daft Mistress Oily beside him and him making threats he can't live up to. Hawker decides he can't leave before telling the Mayor what he thinks of him. He's in full flow when we hear the clatter of hooves up London Road.

Courant. A detachment of the Yeomanry from Guildford under Second Lieutenant Wilson.

Mrs Sarah. If you say so. You could tell he was in charge soon as he opened his mouth. "The situation, Mr Mayor. Briefly." Two Militia bolted along Kennetside and the Reds rode 'em down. Mayor Turner finds his big-shot to big-shot voice, "I have ordered the arrest of these Berkshire Blacks." No one knew who he was talking about until they see him point at Hawker and his lot. "The authority under which I act is —" The officer cuts him off like he's known a hundred Mayor Turners in his young career. "My authority is the Lord Lieutenant of Surrey."

A firm hold

The pale dust-speckled sunlight slanting through the hatch fell on the shrouded body of Peter. Lynn sensed him watching her thoroughly check by touch the hull inside the bow locker. Holes were easy to find, the water came in, weakened timber not so. It was a waste of time but Lynn continued. The keel was as dry as it ever was. She replaced the last inspection board under the keelson and pulled herself up through the hatch into the blinding bright.

The quiet baffled Lynn. She wondered if she was dreaming she was still in the gaol. As her eyes accustomed to the bright, she saw concerned faces staring at Barge Jeannie. Looking round over the cabin Lynn recognised the close-cropped dome of Hawker. Her stomach turned over. Nicholas was in the cabin. On Townside she could see Gabriel, Lee and Mogger bridling in fury. Hawker obviously held them at bay with something. He was facing High Bridge with his back against Barge Jeannie's cabin. Lynn thought fast through possibilities: drop back into the hold and hide; jump over the side; stay put and leave it to the Yeomanry. Face up to your enemy and you'll face it down. That was her Mam talking after Lynn had been bullied by the Shadwell boys, the day she climbed on the towering Hermond for the first time. Lynn recognised not all her enemies were on the outside of her.

Lynn crawled towards the stern hugging the gunwale on the side away from Hawker who was occupied shouting at the Mayor. Perhaps she could startle him and hope Gabriel and Lee were quick off their marks. Lynn crouched so the cabin blocked Hawker's view should he turn round. Her heart was thumping worse than rigging in a gale. An eerie stillness fell across the crowd. Surely Hawker would notice and be suspicious? Lynn edged across the deck and saw a flutter of bright orange at the bottom of the cabin. A skirt. The coward had a girl as hostage. That explained the behaviour of the onlookers.

"It's me you really want, isn't it" said Lynn stepping forward to face the brute. She gasped at the vicious knife at the slender white neck. Hawker dragged his hostage away from the cabin to the stern, keeping his back to it so he could watch Lynn and the bridge. Lynn recognised his hostage. Mistress Olivia. Her! Lynn could walk to the bow and join the others to watch the fate of the little madam. But the girl in the grip of wild-eyed Hawker was not the composed, contemptuous young beauty Lynn had seen in Middleton's Stores. This was a helpless child paralysed with terror, her face dishevelled by tears and fear.

"This one's a better prize," sneered Hawker. He twitched the knife. Olivia shrieked. The Mayor called on Hawker not to be hasty, a horse was being fetched.

"I never learn," said Lynn looking Hawker in the eye but speaking loud that all those around could hear. "If there's something left on the shelf it's always me."

"What're you on about?"

"Two can do more than one," answered Lynn not flinching from the devil's stare.

"You want to team up with me?"

"I'm a gaol-breaker, on the run," she said more quietly. Then forcefully, "I've burnt my bridge. It's a way off the shelf."

"You're a girl with guts," said Hawker. "I'll have those guts soon as I'm shot of this lot." His laugh had a frightening chill as he lifted Olivia's jaw with the flat of the blade.

Olivia's face turned Dutch-linen white. She wailed and feebly struggled. Hawker's arm squeezed breath from her and his knife broke the skin of her neck into a thread of blood. Her scream was cut short by a more vicious squeeze from the encircling arm.

"Don't!" shouted Lynn. She could see he was on the brink of not caring what he did. "Don't kill the golden goose until you've flown. You're not thinking. She's your only shield." Lynn ignored shouts from High Bridge for her to get off the barge. "You can't cover front and back with that twig."

"Go join the clod-heads. Or I'll give the girl another necklace." Hawker pressed the blade against Olivia's windpipe with a sick smile as she squealed.

Lynn placed a bare foot against a fender behind her. "But think about —"

"Fire!"

The cabin door swung open releasing dense smoke from within. Hawker looked round. Lynn launched herself at him from the fender. She had one thing in mind, the knife.

"Fire!" choked Nicholas at the cabin door.

Both Lynn's hands went to Hawker's wrist pulling his arm away from Olivia before she crashed into the captor and his hostage. Olivia had the wind knocked out of her as Hawker's back slammed against the cabin. Lynn twisted Hawker's knife hand with all her strength but he clasped the weapon with the inborn tenacity of a cornered animal. Olivia kicked out wildly and Lynn winced as block-heels cracked into her shins and scraped down them.

Hawker could not bring his knife down against Lynn's straight arms and holding the writhing Olivia put him at disadvantage. He threw Olivia sideways with a hard cuff on her head. His arm was free and he swung it into Lynn's side. The cabin had limited his back-swing but she began to sink and he readied to spear two fingers into her eyes. He noted a figure emerge through the smoke. He slewed to put Lynn between him and this new threat.

Lynn saw her chance. She thrust her bare feet against the deck and pushed Hawker backwards with every ounce of strength. He had been shored by the cabin wall but it was gone, his boots had scant purchase on the smooth deck and he slithered backwards. The arm of the tiller chopped against the back of his knees. Lynn kept pushing. She would go too. They splashed into the Kennet. Lynn sucked in air before she hit the surface, a lesson learned from a lifetime round London docks. She landed on Hawker, knocking air out of his lungs. He tried to breathe and drew in mouthfuls of muddy water. Panic took him, choking for air, thrashing wildly. The grievances of the wronged gave Lynn the strength to keep his head held under.

Navvies were already on the barge. She knew they would fend off anybody who tried to stop her drowning the vermin. He had destroyed her life on the river so let the river destroy his. She pushed his head deeper, made him eat mud off the bottom. Then Lynn pulled it clear and looked into the face. She saw there was absolutely nothing there to fear.

Three of the Yeomanry waded in and dragged Hawker away. Lynn was overwhelmed by exhaustion. She stepped further into the river to where she was rib deep and let the water support her.

Nicholas called from Barge Jeannie. "Are you stuck in the mud?"

"What took you so long?" asked Lynn sharply.

"I was blinded by the smoke," answered Nicholas defensively.

"You always are." A small unexpected laugh escaped from her.

Nicholas jumped from Barge Jeannie and splashed to her. He put his arms round her. He kissed Lynn. All the town watched.

Interview with Mistress Olivia Turner, Greyfriars Street

Olivia. I thought Master Middleton would show some metal and gallop into those awful navigator people to scatter them. Instead the dolt skidded to a halt. I would be mortified being at promenade with such a poor horseman. Then shame of all shames, he tried to join with the enemy, but the turncoat was knocked out by that odious Barge-bilge.

Courant. Lynn Darville floored him?

Olivia. It was delightful. He being so slow-witted failed to duck her lumbering swing and stayed down on her second. He deserved all he got. The man who showed true metal on the moment was Captain Wilson.

Courant. Second Lieutenant Wilson.

Olivia. My goodness, he is handsome in that splendid uniform. His commands carry such authority. He gave his orders and every man ceased fighting and the awful brigands gave themselves up. He is shrewd too, as shown in biding his time before effecting my rescue. I had my wits about me and he noted I was alert for his signal. All would have been satisfactory but instead I have this blight on my neck. Do you think it hideous, Mr Frith?

Courant. Some might consider it a feature, Mistress Olivia. You haven't told me how —

Olivia. Of course, a feature. When circulating London at-homes, I will be obliged to explain the saga of my ordeal and how I came by this cruel scar on my delicate neck. As I was saying, Captain Wilson had everything under control until that clumsy Middleton dolt set fire to the cabin. Out he ran like a terrified chicken, panicking the Barge-bilge to charge about like a mad heifer. I reacted instantly, using my agility to spin from my captor's grip while he was distracted. I made sure to over-balance him into the heifer who blindly grabbed him as she toppled into the river.

Even by then Captain Wilson was by my side ensuring I was unharmed.

Courant. I gather your ordeal caused you to faint?

Olivia. Indeed it did not. I was reassuring Captain Wilson he could not be held responsible for the conduct of idiots, when I heard Papa thanking the Middleton imbecile for rescuing me. Efackins! That the odious creature had anything to do with it brought a weakness. Captain Wilson, being so quick, caught me in his arms.

Courant. You haven't explained how Hawker captured you.

Olivia. Because the Aldermen's Watch are such slow-witted lamebrains. After Captain Wilson ordered the brigands to lay down their weapons, Papa was slow to thank the heroic officer for delivering the town from carnage. I took it upon myself to urge Papa to his civic courtesies. The Watchmen were but a yard from me when my wrist was taken in a fearful grip. The marks will take months to heal. Any other girl's arm would have been torn from her, and her ankle broken when dragged over the parapet onto the barge. But I am nimble and trained at dance.

Courant. And also, it appears, adept at tumbling?

Olivia. I am not! That was my natural grace.

memoirs of Sir George Crockmore

It is the wise man who plays to his advantage the unintended consequence. Far be it for me to claim this particular method, for the opening of the River Kennet Navigation along with the apprehension of the Berkshire Black outlaws, was my design. Suffice to say these memoirs reveal my efforts in laying the foundation for that which proved a doubly successful outcome.

However, there is one blot over my perspicuity. Mister Hawker was to my face captain of the Reading Militia while to my back he was leader of a gang of criminals. He was clearly an artful deceiver.

By contrast, it was through knowing the nature of Mr Hyde that I took immediate heed of his urgent request I return to Reading, that it was of greater importance than my business in London. I was correct, for everything I was negotiating in London would have been in jeopardy through a too tardy intervention in Reading.

I returned to a town in uproar and summoned to my Forbury house the Mayor along with the Second Lieutenant of the Yeomanry. I put it to both that so many violent and embittered outlaws in the gaol would overstretch the abilities of the turnkeys, for had not a girl and some witless navvies already escaped. Despite my utter exhaustion I convened an extraordinary Court that justice might be seen to be dispatched with a swiftness befitting the odium of the deeds.

First up before me was the self titled Captain Hawker, who demonstrated no respect for my authority, being full of loud invective, personal slander and defamation. I had no recourse but to have him taken down and quietened by the Yeomanry. The Mayor led the depositions, with an oratory blossomed from his newly elevated stature and fertilised by his heightened emotion over his daughter's abduction and liberation. The evidence was convincing that the accused headed a band of evil-doers, now unmasked as the Berkshire Blacks.

I ordered punishment without delay be awarded against Mister Teon Hawker, invoking the Uniformed Brigands Act, which in these circumstances did prove a most useful implement of the law. The said Mister Hawker was to remain bound and gagged during his immediate removal to Earley, there to be hanged, drawn and quartered. The other members of the criminal gang were swiftly tried and sentenced to follow their leader to the gallows.

I noted in my address that though the convict was universally detested by common man, the common man did not rise up against the evil. Such is the meekness that underpins despots and dictators and it is a point I shall heed in the future. In summing up the night's cases, I lectured briefly on the tumour of laissez faire towards criminals that had seeded and swelled large in the heart of the town. To ensure no vestige of the disease remained and by way of example, Mister Vale Clemson and his wife were found guilty of aiding the gang and a posse of the Aldermen's Watch was despatched to effect their arrest.

I omitted from my closing remarks any commendation of the newsman who unveiled the criminal nature of the so called Reading Militia. His discoveries, wandering near the lair rather than seeking it out, and coming by chance upon Mr Took, were by fortunate accident rather than by praiseworthy deduction.

A moving mooring

The Reading wharf men pulled the empty barge off the shallows and hauled her to a prime berth next to the number two crane at Orf's wharf. Lynn refused to moor there. She wanted to be through Blake's Lock with open water ahead of her to the Thames.

Emotions washed through her as Barge Jeannie dropped within the lock chamber. This was to be the last time she would work her barge through a lock, unless she could get some stay on the debts, some leeway in the contract her Dad had signed. She knew she was fooling herself.

As Mayor Turner launched into his speech from High Bridge on the benefits of the Kennet Navigation, Nicholas had forced himself from the crowd congratulating him on his bravery. Lynn was changing out of her wet clothes when he asked from outside the cabin after her Dad. Lynn opened the cabin door and walked into an embrace she would remember for the rest of her life. It was a recognition of mutual loss, a sharing of grief and fuelling of energy between the two of them. All at the same time. She felt enveloped in this other person, this man, enclosed in warm caring strength, aware she was also returning what he needed.

Nicholas knew a conscientious undertaker, a real one he laughed, and went off. He had skimmed over what had happened to his family and she felt deeply for him. Like herself with Barge Jeannie, she saw the stability of his upbringing and his hopes for the future had been scuttled. The Stores had been the yardstick of his life but far worse for Nicholas was discovering his parents as covetous fools. At least Lynn had untarnished memories of her Mam and her Dad to help her through the years to come. Nicholas must feel like a barge without a tiller. She wanted to continue the standards lived by her parents while he wanted to break with his.

Nicholas had told her Hermond was in a field behind the Angler's Tavern. Lynn walked the short distance along Kennetside with a strange feeling the horse had been waiting on the Thames side of the town to pull her through it. A chuckle bubbled from her at her silly notion.

Lynn wanted Hermond to come galloping when she called across the field. He picked up his head immediately he heard her voice and walked steadily to her. Part of her wanted to cry out "Come on, Hermond" and part knew how old he was, and part of her felt the horse always had faith she would return to him so why did he have to rush. By the time Hermond pushed his nuzzle into her Lynn was streaming tears. They were not only for the horse.

Kennetside

Sarah has a purposeful walk this morning, thinks Frith. Like himself. He has briskly stepped past the Kennet Koffee House without a glance, without a forlorn hope of a note, and is nonplussed to see Sarah step from the Watlington Wood heading for town. He catches up and falls into step beside her.

Frith hears that Master Nicholas started the smoke in the cabin and he then bundled the blinded Hawker into the river. There is no arguing with Sarah because she was there and saw it as God is her witness. She is annoyed missing the night hangings, even though it took hours to sober the hangman and he botched it so they had to tie sacks of earth to Hawker's legs. Why Sir George ordered the Aldermen's Watch to stand guard all night beggars her belief.

"Hawker had made Sir George look a fool," offers Frith. "He wanted to ensure the hanged were dead."

"Mistress Oily's doing her best to make Dragon look a fool, which don't take much. I'm the gin-bag's best friend now. Oh yes indeed. On her side against the Oily enemy. 'The floor's filthy,' says Mistress Oily. 'Is not,' slurs Dragon, and next thing they're asking me if it's properly clean or not. Whatever I say it'll be trouble from the other one. I decided I don't need that how-d'you-do. Anyway, before I could think what to say, Mr M starts mopping the floor. Dragon props herself up on my counter to watch him and telling me they were after getting rid of the Stores and Koffee House, what with Master Nicholas not being interested and Master Richard doing so well in the Army, and things couldn't have turned out better."

"Are they happy to work for the Turners?" asks Frith.

"Don't matter coz Mistress Oily's telling Dragon that Papa will knock both buildings down and build a warehouse. Dragon starts wailing how she'll be for the Poor House. So Mistress Oily offers words of comfort, 'Best start packing your bags today, so you don't leave anything behind.' Such a caring girl that one."

Sarah stops talking when they stroll across High Bridge. They walk towards High Street in their own thoughts. Sarah speaks first. "Are you going to the next hangings? Last of the Reading Militia – the Blacks or whatever they are – and those farmers."

"The Clemsons? That's harsh," says Frith, surprised. "The pair were terrified of Hawker."

"They won't be terrified of nothing after tomorrow."

They are standing outside the Saracen's Head. "What about your tomorrow?" says Frith, asking as much about himself as about Sarah.

"I ain't waiting for tomorrow. I'm telling landlord here he needs me as a barmaid, and that useless flibbertigibbet he's got is only good for scullery work." Spontaneously, Sarah gives Frith a brushing kiss on his cheek. Then she puts on her bright business face. Frith admires her adaptability and resoluteness.

Frith strides through the next door. "You have not written it?" asks Mr Hyde.

"No."

"I am pleased to see you have learnt not to misapply your time."

"A double negative Mr Hyde? In keeping with the Courant's policy."

"Superior to the newsman's exaggeration for effect, the storyteller's enhancement for the listener. I remind you there was a Royal battle in these streets but thirty years ago."

"The Irish of King James against the Dutchmen of William. Yesterday was of greater importance to the folk of this town, it was their fight not a skirmish of warring foreigners. It was personal."

"That is your problem, Mr Frith. The personal blinds you to the panorama."

The criticism catches an exposed nerve in Frith. "The personal is what people care about, their lives, their next meal. They would put up with a tyrant who kept the roadways safe until he exhorts such taxes they cannot feed their family. That's when the personal view topples the tyrant and it becomes the big picture, the panorama. History is fabricated from lots of little pictures, different coloured tiles, forming the picture in a mosaic."

"That is inference without any sound premise."

"Superior to the turnabout policy of this newspaper," says Frith sarcastically. "I see you are printing an open letter from Mayor Turner extolling the benefits of the Navigation. I quote you of but a few days ago, 'This newspaper will not print anything about the Navigation'. A week ago the Mayor was hurling stones at a barge. Two turnabouts in one article."

"Yesterday settled the issue over the Navigation."

"How? All it settled was the Reading Militia were no more than a criminal gang."

"The arrival of the Lord Lieutenant's Yeomanry was required to give the people of the town a wider perspective on themselves. Sir George had anticipated that."

Mr Hyde is suddenly silent. Frith wonders what he was about to say. Frith knows what he has to say. "I am resigning from my employment at the Courant as from today."

"Your resignation is accepted."

Dismay squeezes Frith that his resignation is so readily agreed.

"Once again you have come up against the policy of the proprietors," says Mr Hyde, more kindly. "Your dismissal, that I was about to announce, was not my choice."

"Did he give any reason for removing me?"

"Your activities and articles are not in keeping with the editorial policy of this newspaper."

Mr Hyde is uncomfortable after reciting his text. Frith is sad for the person Mr Hyde has to be to keep his job and look after his family. It occurs to Frith that Mr Hyde did not choose to become editor, that also was a policy of the proprietor.

"In view of you being dismissed your outstanding wages are forfeit."

This is definitely not Mr Hyde speaking and Frith is inflamed. "They are not forfeit. I resigned before you mentioned anything about dismissal."

The point registers with Mr Hyde, a stickler for hyphenated coughs and poxes, and for procedure. He is thinking fast, clearly under instruction from the penny-pinching proprietor. "However I must dock the hours you failed to appear in the office, and for some estimation of your time malingering during working hours."

Frith almost snorts. Another punishment, along with all his others, for loving Catherine. "I have made up more than those hours. I devoted Sunday to this newspaper. I should be paid extra for that."

"Paid for working on the Lord's Day?"

"Every day is a newsman's day."

"That was a private investigation."

"One that brought enormous recognition and increased sales for the Courant."

"The point is well received, but irrelevant to the matter of your wages."

"It is relevant. I had your word I could seek out a local story for this newspaper. I am prepared to fight my case in a court of law."

"So be it," says Mr Hyde, with a weariness.

"I shall raise my suit in the London Court," says Frith with meaning. He will not have the man who owes him wages sit in judgement on whether he is awarded his wages.

"That would be expensive." The editor can see his newsman is resolute. He walks with Frith to the bank.

A binding contract

Lynn either pottered about the empty barge or sat staring at the sky. She knew where people were, people going about their business. She was as empty as Barge Jeannie and was waiting for its fate to come to her. Her greatest concern was that Hermond might be part of the contract. She would willingly break the law again to keep him safe. Beyond that, how on earth was a girl and old horse going to survive? She could turn highway robber escaping on a plodding Shire. Her laugh was hollow air.

A dapper man in frock coat and top hat strode along the wharf carefully keeping well clear of the edge.

"Mistress Lynn Darville? Daughter of Peter Darville, deceased. My condolences," he said in one even breath. "I am Mr Joseph

Hyde acting in the capacity of agent for parties contracted in the matter of the vessel named Barge Jeannie."

Lynn invited the gentleman to board but he declined and addressed her a few feet from the wharf edge. "I am empowered to exact the terms and conditions of said agreement between your late father, Mr Peter Darville, and Messrs Hoskins of Maidenhead Wharf. Here are my authorities. Can you read?"

Lynn took the three pieces of paper, saw crests, emblems and seals, read names but was too upset by the man's tone and what it implied to dwell on the blocks of tiny scrawl.

"They appear to be in order." She had heard her dad use the phrase when accepting a manifest for a cargo.

"Bearing in mind all that you have endured, Mistress Darville, it is my disagreeable duty to inform you that the terms of the afore-said contract have not been fulfilled —"

"My barge is back in the Thames."

"The terms of the aforesaid contract have not been fulfilled to the letter. It is clear the Barge Jeannie is back in the waters of the Thames Authority but the cargo is not. Barge and down cargo are stipulated in the document."

This was it thought Lynn but she was not giving up Barge Jeannie that easily. "We carried the cargo to Reading. The Mayor and the mob at County Lock can prove that."

"County Lock is not in the jurisdiction of the Thames Author-ities."

"It's only one mile short!"

"One mile or one yard. A contract is a contract. I am truly sorry."

"My Dad gave his life to —"

"A very sad loss and you have my deepest sympathies, and those of the other parties involved, I am sure. However, such does not affect the terms of the contract. You being next of kin, assume the —"

"It must mean something!" Lynn refused to cry. She made herself angry at the impeccable man waving his inflexible papers.

Mr Hyde stood awkwardly. "As agent for the creditors of Barge Jeannie, owned at the time of signing by Peter Darville," he recited, "I am instructed by the creditors that you vacate Barge Jeannie taking with you any chattels-personal, and leaving it in good order by six of the clock this day."

"Tonight!" The suddenness was a jolt to Lynn.

"What's happening tonight?"

Mr Hyde turned to face Nicholas. "It is of no business of yours, Sir."

"He's taking Jeannie," said Lynn with defiance. "I'm to be thrown off before nightfall."

"In that case this is my business," stated Nicholas holding out his hand for the documents. Mr Hyde did not respond. "Lynn Darville and I are betrothed." He shot her a glance. "When we are wed this barge becomes my property. It is her dowry. Therefore it is my business."

Mr Hyde handed over the documents. Lynn gave Nicholas a second wide-eyed look then waited with Mr Hyde while Nicholas carefully read each page in turn. We are betrothed danced through her head until she stopped it by knowing it as a deceit of the moment.

"Everything seems to have been accounted for," said Nicholas handing back the documents. "What exactly are the grounds on which you claim the Darville party is in default."

Lynn nearly laughed. Nicholas sounded just like Mr Hyde. It had its effect as the agent assumed a more circumspect tone. Or maybe because Mr Hyde was talking to a male not a female.

"Do your homework, Sir," said Nicholas. "The cargo is behind you in Cutler's warehouse. Shall we go inspect it," he added when Mr Hyde said nothing. "The cargo has been delivered to Thames Authority waters as contracted."

"Not delivered by Barge Jeannie," argued Mr Hyde.

"Nowhere in the contract does it state the down cargo has to be conveyed the entire distance to Thames Authority water by Barge Jeannie."

"It is implicitly understood. The purpose of the agreement was to open the Kennet Navigation for commercial use. The load was unshipped one mile short of the destination."

"Implicit carries no weight in a contractual document." Nicholas grabbed back the documents. "The contract states here, see, safe and complete delivery to Thames Authority water. If you persist in your claim we will contest the issue of how it was delivered in the final mile, pointing out the contracted party at their own cognisance and expense ensured the safety of the cargo from thieves and looters when it was illegally impeded."

Mr Hyde had been out-talked by the storekeeper. Nicholas hadn't finished.

"We will ensure any hearing will be before a judge without vested interest in the agreement or associated chattels."

Lynn watched Mr Hyde contemplate all Nicholas had said.

"Your point is taken. You understand of course I, along with the creditors, had no knowledge of the cargo having been secured in a warehouse. I anticipate they will be disinclined to resort to the costs and the uncertainties of the law over this trifling issue. I am sure the necessary papers of ownership and clearance of debts will be handed to you forthwith."

"Shall we say before the end of this week at the latest," said Nicholas.

Mr Hyde gave a slight nod of his head before he turned to Lynn. "You owe a large debt of gratitude to Sir George Crockmore, Mistress Darville. It was he who bought up your father's debts and effectively funded this voyage whereby your father himself would have redeemed this barge had he lived. Sir George is a man of vision and you have the privilege of being a part of that vision."

Lynn was so flabbergasted she had no answer. Mr Hyde turned to Nicholas. "Shall we away to Cutler's to inspect the cargo. I have with me a copy of the Bill of Lading."

Nicholas left her a smile as he led Mr Hyde towards the warehouse. Lynn watched his slender back walk away and knew it was to Nicholas owed a massive debt of gratitude. It was he who had made sure Hermond was safe. She knew now it was he who had arranged for the cargo to be taken to the warehouse. Nicholas was the one who had brought the Yeomanry to legally enforce Barge Jeannie's right of passage while she was a gaol-breaker provoking a pitched battle in Brewery Gut. Now Nicholas had used his trader's skills against Mr Hyde after she had disregarded the details in the contract. When he returned she would get to the bottom of his betrothal ploy.

Lodgings room, Anglers' Tavern

The bachelors' chest is empty of Frith's meagre collection of clothes. He has ordered a slice of game pie for his final lunch, his landlady's supreme culinary achievement. She adds chopped haunch of venison, pre-stewed, to the hare and chicken meat to make it moist, and is liberal with the cinnamon and nutmeg.

The sturdy but shabby knapsack is almost full. Frith looks at the stains and scuffs on the canvas, the bright rope of the replacement drawstring. He had bought it in Carlisle and the weathered mariner had told him, "Never grow roots, me lad." The knapsack has certainly travelled and is again on the move. Frith has convinced himself he is not running from, he is travelling to. He is propelled by Catherine with her excitement over the intense, stimulating creativity in London. No Mr Hyde, no proprietors, no small town Mayor. Frith drags his longcoat from the corner and a white orb is pulled with it. Frith catches his breath.

It was in this room less than a month ago. Catherine had brought thin strips of buckram and white powder. Her laughter and their antics caused the landlord to feign a reason to knock at the door. It had him dubious but forbearing, seeing Frith's palm and fingers enclosed in fabric strips soaked in the white paste. His right hand, Catherine had insisted, for that was the one he used for writing.

When the cast was set firm, but not dry, he extricated his hand and added himself to this reversed palm. He gave her that morning's page from his journal and she tore out phrases and fragments that took her fancy, turned them face down and he picked a few to press onto the damp cast of his palm.

the great atmosphere . . . spilled out . . . to the world – was pasted along the Head line.

between them . . . there is strength through calm – traced the Life line.

there are some magnificent things in . . . a cry of passion –
followed his Heart line.

The cast of his hand is smashed by Erebus and his letters burnt
by the Darkness. This fills him with anger, not for the destruction
of those tokens but for the woman. Anger for their lost pure
connection, cerebral, emotional, physical, sexual, ethereal. He
believes that, after the long night of mind-walking in the Withy
barn. He has dismissed Mistress Olivia's spite.

Frith takes the white orb to the window and wonders about the
two turtle doves. He can accept they are about somewhere, they
just happen to be unseen by him at that moment. Frith looks over
the unfettered willow to the farms at Kennetmouth. Catherine said
he should look into the mishaps there. He did nothing. But with the
talk of prosperity not poverty from the Navigation, the farms are
extremely well positioned to benefit.

It has been niggling Frith that Vale Clemson had no idea what
was being stored in his barn, yet the forthright man had not the
curiosity to look. Frith decides to go the gaol and talk with the
Clemsons before he leaves.

Wakeman's journal – 11:00am

I needed to immerse myself in a time of happiness with Catherine.
To relive that pure joy. I opened my Journal for the day we made
the casts. Nothing. The day she came to the Courant, is followed
by 21st September, the day of our discovery by Erebus. Why did I
not write about my happiness? Why only record pages and pages
of misery? One glaring reason: I was writing letters to Catherine
and reading hers a hundred times. I was writing for the immediate
world, not chronicling in my Journal a lost past and a bleak future.

Her letters capture a glimmer of our brief history as two. They
hark to our pasts and anticipate the future. Memories and hopes
brought into my present. My journal omits incidents or something
said that later springs into mind as significant. Why can I not recall
them in the instance of writing? I do not understand memory.

So I will pull back to mind a day that doesn't exist in my journal.

I first met Catherine on Monday 8th August. To her parlour on Monday 19th September – that is too raw to think about so soon. Catherine arrived at my lodgings to make the cast on Monday 5th September. So many Mondays.

She was as excited as a field of poppies dancing in a wind. Jittery nervous in an energy of movement. Barely brushing our lips, pouted, pressing, open-mouthed, exploring. Sudden break away.

"I'm here to do work," she announced, but her chest was heaving and diamonds glinted in her eyes. She made a performance of taking from her bag the white powder and strips of linen. My palm and fingers were cast and inscribed with my words.

She asked what of her did I want to cast? The hand she uses to etch, to paint, to hug me? She'd brought an old cloth on which I stood the chair. Seated, her head resting against the wall, she slipped down the top of her dress, enjoying my awe while I saw her nipples raise from her breasts. Maybe it was the chill of the room.

I tore some strips of linen to make them narrower and put them to soak in the syrup paste of plaster. The oil poured into my hand, palms rubbed together until the liquid was warm. Kneeling before her, I placed both my hands round her left breast and held them for some seconds, until Catherine softly told me to get on with it. Her eyes were shut. I rubbed the oil around and under her breast, gently lifting and letting fall the bulk, a gentle kneading motion, the nipple and areola darkening. I sucked off the oil, replenished it. She opened one eye and fastened it on me.

The first strip of saturated linen pressed tightly round her nipple. "Make sure there are no gaps," she said, intently observing my hands working each strip against her giving breast, squishing the layers of linen firmly into each other. Pinching the wad, seeing her feel the sudden squeeze, then both of us watching the ooze of milky fluid trickle under her breast to lie in the folds of her midriff. Coaxing more strips into the deep fold under her breast.

Her left side was encased in its white hardening shield, the right breast exposed pink. I remembered how the plaster became warm as it dried round my hand and she liked the sensation on her, the warm and the cool. I bathed Catherine's naked breast with warm breath from my mouth, with oils from my tongue. As the cast hardened Catherine escaped far into her own world, holding my hand between hers between her thighs.

All of that failed to be captured in my Journal. And this cannot convey the essence of the day, the great and the tiny incidents that made it exceptional. Yet I feel her wet breast in this recall vividly enough to believe it as real as then. Far more authentic and complete than words is that which I do not understand, my memory.

from Mistress Olivia's diary

"Papa, so few people frequent the place and they sit forever over one demitasse of coffee, the last sip of which must be colder than the Kennet in January." Thus I answered Papa's enquiry about the Kennet Koffee House. As expected of someone entrusted with such responsibility I related how Mrs Middle-gone is so badly taken with gin as to have it in her veins while the husband drives away customers with his foul mouth before they can purchase anything. Papa soon resolved to turn the Koffee House into a warehouse. The errant son will work in Turner's Provision Stores serving every customer politely. The Barge-bilge will be banned for her stupidity in putting me a whisker away from death.

When I think of my terrifying ordeal I cannot help but tremble from crown to toe and issuing plaintive little sighs. Then Papa's arms embrace me and he soothes with words of comfort for me and chastisement of himself that his Princess came to such grave danger. I tell Papa of my awful dreams for it is right he should know.

There has been another benefit from my heroic action culminating in my deliverance at High Bridge. Lousy was very taken with how, though I had been roughly pushed from the parapet, I landed so gracefully on the barge. I helped her on top of our high wall along the cobbled Greyfriars but in her fervency I had no opportunity to explain how tumblers fall. She is now abed with an ankle swelled to the size and pinkness of a ham and the doctor is concerned there are broken bones from the manner she screams when touched. Lousy's wailing pains my ears but it is small price to pay for seeing her hobble through the rest of her years and never be able to dance at Balls as I.

At breakfast I bemoaned Papa's fate that I too am a burden, there being no suitor in this town worthy of his daughter. Changing the direction I said how lucky I was he had taken me the once to see the magnificence of London. I recalled our shared memories of the night in lodgings and of Mr Delpeck talking about high quality lodgings taken by the ladies and daughters of country nobles. In districts, I added, with many more constables than the whole of Reading and surroundings. All this I have let simmer in Papa's mind as he dresses for his meeting at the Yield Hall.

memoirs of Sir George Crockmore

At Leicester House, which I have made hub of my to and fro about the Metropolis, Mr Walpole is noted by his absence to his estate. I have marked him a cunning man, and expect he will return from Norfolk unsullied from the nefarious dealings in stocks. It would be, though a Whig, shrewd to first address the embarrassment of king and lords and thereby gaining a deposit for their future favour.

My standing in these exalted circles has substantially increased from my acumen as a man of business while retaining my qualities as a gentleman. I have acquired several properties and businesses in the City. At Reading, Mr Hyde has instruction to set about the transfer to my estate of the riverside farms of the freeholders who have forfeited or abandoned them. As I expounded to Maxi, West-cotte, and that archaism Burnside, the far-seeing man embraces progress with open arms, each holding an open purse. I took by example the River Kennet Navigation, bringing to my right-hand purse good and regular fees from lockage, riverage and use of the towing path. To the left-hand purse a bounteous dividend, for I am holder of much stock in the Company. My listeners were truly impressed.

The great prize of this day has been the purchase of a large house in Covent Garden, arranged through the good offices of Gertrude for a part share of the profits from our enterprise. It will cost little to partition the rooms into small bed chambers with vulgar but varied furnishings. The Duchess has approached three good women with a view to one running the house.

My undertaking greatly interested the gentlemen at Leicester House not least because my thirteen-year-old companion was dressed in a most teasing gown. Hannah is a kitchen maid at South-cote Hall and, I confided, is brought to be dazzled by and thus keen to reside in London. Maxi wondered how many pretty kitchen maids I retained. I explained this one's predecessor had run away without notice and the disgraced family had offered the younger sister in lieu.

I teased the gentlemen, declaring I intend to start a sensational fashion. I explained to my near panting listeners the Miss Charge, as I have named the device. It is an auction for the triumph of being the first man to have the girl on her fourteenth birthday. There ensued a boisterous period of ribald exchanges drawing in other nobles, that being my design to raise interest and increase the waging. The ladies came to see what so animated the men and suggested names more wonderfully lewd for the formula.

Maxi whispered to me the winner of the girl's maidenhood was a foregone conclusion. I held my tongue that Prince Lionel will not know against whom he is bidding and I shall fold when I deem the pot at its maximum. Feasting his eyes over the girl's precocious frame, Maxi lamented the Prince's excessive demands will leave the girl good for nothing. I countered he would leave her excellent for one thing.

I must put away my quill and papers for I am lodging these few nights in Pall Mall with Gertrude while we finalise arrangements for the Covent Garden venture. Breakfast today was followed by an inspection of the kitchen larder, wherein lay delicacies, including ones I have never before tasted, from all quarters of the world. Later tonight I expect some will be distinctively served to me in the bed chamber of the Duchess.

Wakeman's journal – 1:00pm

This is a landmark day, for want of naming a day. A sea-change of attitude to my life. I realise how Catherine has awakened me.

I think back to how I survived the night in Clemson's barn. What was destroying me was the doubts seeded in my mind. Was Catherine's motive truly as selfish as Mistress Olivia sowed? It is easy to destroy, far more difficult to create. A simpleton can knock down a stack of bricks but one has to use imagination and skill to build a monument. My disbelieving mind kept me locked in my prison, both mind and barn.

In the end it was not recalling the taste of Catherine's lips when we kissed, nor the stick and tissue work we made together, nor the letters, nor the exchanges that came back to help me.

She said: "It is so wonderful to know one is completely loved."

A cry of horror: "If you were to die no one would tell me. I'd never know."

None of those nor many more. It was, "Always remember, you have been loved." Not the words. We speak at the time, from a medley of motive and emotion. My faith in Catherine lies in the earnestness, the sincerity in her face, in her voice, the look. They resonate in me like a perfect bell. They united everything we had been, and had created, and had hoped in our forty-two days. Her declaration was everything Catherine could honestly offer at that moment. No wild promises. As each day goes by I believe afresh I have been loved.

I am weary. I am mourning for so much lost, which is draining. Our time was honest. That can never be taken away. I will recover and remember without heartache. After grieving.

My bags are ready, just as Mistress Olivia told Nicholas's parents, "Better start packing now." Heartless girl. Sarah said the Clemson's are to be hanged. There's something heartless about that. Do any of us really know what we are looking for? Perhaps a mother with a daughter does. Or are children an anchor rather than a mainsail?

Interview with Mr and Mrs Clemson, Castle Street Gaol
Vale Clemson. You here to gloat?
Courant. I came —

Vale Clemson. I freed you, you Bastard, and you repays me by getting me hanged.

Courant. I'm here because it was clear to me you had no idea what was in —

Vale Clemson. Why didn't you tell the Judge?

Courant. I didn't know the court was in session.

Vale Clemson. No, you was celebrating in some alehouse.

Courant. I haven't — Look, I don't live in the courtroom, I didn't know. You do live on your farm. You should have —

Vale Clemson. Not any more. I had nowt to do with any of it. I got on with my farming and minded my own business. Ain't right I'm to be strung up for a common criminal.

Courant. I'm curious why you never went near this outbuilding on your farm.

Vale Clemson. Perhaps you'd like me to check every tree in case it's stuffed with jewels.

Nancy Clemson. We were told to stay away.

Vale Clemson. Shut up, stupid woman.

Nancy Clemson. It's you who's stupid, Vale, not looking under your own nose.

Vale Clemson. I spend's all my time looking after the cows, the hens, the fields, not to mention you. What time do I have to go looking where I ain't got no business?

Nancy Clemson. That Hawker said he'd slit our throats if we went near or spoke of it.

Courant. The Reading Militia don't have the authority to make those threats.

Vale Clemson. Them guns and swords and knives is good enough authority for me.

Courant. Why didn't you tell the Aldermen's Watch?

Vale Clemson. You've seen 'em – you work that one out.

Nancy Clemson. It's our own fault, Vale.

Vale Clemson. Nothing was our fault.

Nancy Clemson. We should have checked the barn and then we would have seen what they was up to and told someone and none of this would have happened. And we wouldn't be here.

Vale Clemson. We did nothing. We ain't to blame. Not like that trash in the next cell. Telling the bastards which houses to thieve. Scum like that should be hanged, not me.

Castle Street Gaol

Dunbar slams shut the cell door and Frith jumps though he knew the crash was coming. The turnkey can do nothing quietly. In the far corner Frith can make out a heap of straw not yet laid out for a bed. There is nothing else. He thinks for a moment Dunbar with his morbid sense of humour has deliberately locked him in the wrong cell. Perhaps Frith should have slipped him some coins.

There is a rustle in the straw. Frith hates rats. His eyes adjust to the dimness and he sees a thin swathe of dark material in the straw. Looking harder he makes out the toes of a small foot.

Frith walks cautiously to the heap of straw, noticing it twitch as his boots clack on the flagstones. It is a child who, in not being able to see another, believes the other cannot see them. Frith is suddenly empathetic to the frightened youngster and speaks softly that he means no harm, only to talk. The boy continues trying to bury himself, emitting periodic whimpers.

This is no good thinks Frith. He reaches into the straw where he estimates an arm might be. He has misjudged and touches the boy's bare chest. His palm brushes the pinnacle of a young girl's breast and he pulls away in surprise, in embarrassment. Contrary to what he expected, the girl eases out of the straw, unabashed the top of her dress is around her waist. Her reddish hair is straggled across her face and as she lays back on the straw her hands start to pull up her skirt. It is mechanical, thinks Frith, his sinuses catching on the stench of strong urine off her. Frith stops her scrabbling hands and pulls down her skirt. She is disinterested in helping him.

"That is not why I am here," he says, and talks on to say who he is, that he wants to complete the story of the Berkshire Blacks. Looking at her face, his eyes adjusted to the gloom, he recalls her from the Fair. She is Hawker's girl. "Is that correct," he asks. She turns into the straw and does not answer him. She will not tell him her name.

"Why did you tell Hawker which houses to rob?" Frith sees the girl shiver, a sign of guilt. "Were you in love with Hawker? Did he bully you into telling him?"

The girl continues to cower with plaintive noises and shudders. She is truculent, thinks Frith, and this irritates him. Or she is terrified out of her wits and not taking in what he is saying. Sympathy suppresses his irritation. He is trying to fathom a way to break through to her when his mind leaps to what Nicholas told him of Lynn's breakout from the gaol. He decides to shock her into speaking to him, and fishes out his pocketbook and a pencil.

He delves into the straw and pulls her up, saddened by her absence of resistance. He holds the open pocketbook with its sketch of the gallows in front of her face, noticing how pretty she might be if her eyes were not dead. "This will be you."

The girl shakes her head.

"It will. You can't hide from the hangman."

The girl grabs the pocketbook and crosses out the gallows.

"That won't get rid of it. What have you to lose by talking to me? Nothing."

She scribbles in his pocketbook. Frith is indignant, for the girl has turned his own idea into an insult, a face with a tongue sticking out. He sticks out his tongue at her, thinking she might be retarded. He recalls hearing that some have drawing ability far beyond their vocal and mental skills.

The girl is drawing on a piece of paper she has torn from his notebook. It is a knife and she places it on top of her last effort and moves it to and fro. Frith stares perplexed and she turns her young face to him and opens wide her mouth.

Frith is nauseated. He wants to retch. He saw the crippling pain in her eyes just to open her mouth. He cannot look at her and wraps his arms round her slight body. A lifetime of anger and compassion battle through his hug. The sight in her mouth is lodged in his head, a bloody mass of lesions and sores and a stump where her tongue should be. He keeps holding her, cooing like a solitary turtle dove.

Frith groans on hearing her lamentable attempt to weep. The

droning noise pitches from the back of her throat and emits unmodified through her empty mouth. Frith realises she will never be able to cry in the way other people would recognise it and offer comfort. She begins an unnerving incessant moaning. Frith holds her tighter, wanting to smother the awful sound in her, and at the same time to draw it from her.

"I said no monkey business." Dunbar's claw hand on Frith's bruised shoulder spins him across the cell. "Trying for a free one, were you?" He is menacing Frith but holds out his palm. "Two pennies buys you one Penny. Can't say fairer than that."

"I'm not here for that."

"You'd be ploughing the same field as a lord. That's got to be worth something extra. Pretty Penny here was Sir George's whore."

"You're fabricating a story to charge more."

"Is that so?" Dunbar yanks up Penny's skirt tipping her backwards. He kicks her legs apart so she is obscenely exposed. There is a long wound of seared flesh high across her inner thigh. Dunbar runs his finger along the burn and the slender leg twitches until his boot pins her ankle. He lets his hand linger on an around the wound, as he addresses Frith.

"Possessive sod is our Sir George, and with a temper. She was his all right, branded her so she knew. Still fresh see. Don't know what he got out of her. She's got a dry snatch if ever I knew one, ain't yer?" Dunbar thrusts his groin at the girl.

"There's no need for that," says Frith, standing up and pushing aside thoughts of what the girl has been through with this savage.

"That's for me to say. She's mine now."

"She is in your charge. That doesn't mean she's yours."

"Let's see if bad Penny agrees." He pulls the girl's head forward by her hair and Frith is frozen horrified as Dunbar rams the big cell key between her lips and into her mouth. "Are you my whore?" he shouts in her face, turning and twisting the metal against the raw stump of her tongue. He forces her to nod. Penny screams an unworldly sound. Frith leaps at the bulky turnkey and his blind fury hauls Dunbar off her.

"Told you," says Dunbar, with a sickly sneer, pushing Frith off when he regains his balance.

"That proved nothing except how you enjoy torturing prisoners."

"She's worse'n shit. What she done. Deserves everything she gets."

"It must be a solace to her the gallows will relieve her from your persecution."

"She ain't for hanging. Sir George says she'll be a better warning like this. A reminder to any who might think about betraying their master. Piece of trash." Dunbar gouges the key along Fenny's scar and into her pudendum. "Better find some oil to loosen this, Whore, it's all you got,."

"Tuppence you said?" says Frith suddenly, and gets Dunbar's full attention. After Dunbar leaves the cell Frith replaces Penny's skirt over her legs.

Interview with Penny Beale, Castle Street Gaol

Courant. Let me explain who I am. I was the person who exposed the Reading Militia as criminals after I was captured by the gang near their hideaway, then stumbled across one of them in Reading with his cart filled with stolen property. Unmasking them in front of the whole town was my moment of glory.

A hollow glory. A poisoned chalice now I've seen how you've been treated. I am the cause of that, shouting on High Bridge there had to be an informer. What you did was wrong but what they've done to you is barbarous. It belongs to less enlightened times. Animals don't do this to each other.

You have no reason to tell me but, for my peace of mind, why did you tell Captain Hawker which houses to rob? Shake your head all you want. Was it a girlish infatuation? If he forced you, threatened you, you can challenge the sentence.

Note to self. The girl, Penny, makes gestures to have my pocket-book and pencil of charcoal. I doubt she can write.

Note to self. The girl has placed her hand on her sketch of a Holy
Bible. She shakes her head when I again ask if she had an infatuation with Hawker.

Courant. You swear he didn't threaten you? Or your family?

Courant. I know, your tongue. That's you with no lips. What are
you saying? Pinching your lips. You told Hawker nothing?
Nothing about the houses? I saw you kissing Hawker at Forbury
Fair.

Courant. He was after you? Always chasing you? You ran away.
The slap wasn't a lover's tease, you were telling him to stay
away. How can I believe that?

Courant. That's a gentleman with his arm round a woman. You? So Dunbar wasn't lying, you were Sir George's . . . mistress. I see. Through that you knew which wealthy gentlemen would be guests at Southcote Hall on the Fridays and told Hawker.

Shows picture of bible again. It is only your word says you did not.

Note to self: At this point, Penny lifts her skirt and points to a recent mutilation on her thigh. She holds up her sketches. It appears Sir George is violent, possessive over his mistress. The poor girl was caught between the devil wearing a black sash and the deep black jealousy of her employer.

Courant. I want to believe you but . . . Perhaps telling Hawker started in a small way, but Hawker became greedy when the navigators were being blamed.

Courant. Two churches but Reading has three. One mark, two, yes, six marks. This last is, here? The gaol? Here? Awake, asleep, awake. Today! You have drawn eleven days. Back to the gentleman drawing, Sir George, right. You've been Sir George's mistress for less than a fortnight?

Note to self: Penny uses mimes – peeling, chopping and poring – to show me she has been Sir George's kitchen maid for only a week and a half. Yet the grand house robberies started quite some time before. Why didn't you say that in court?

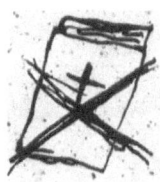

Courant. Why have you crossed out the bible? Did the court think you a witch? Over there, talking. Over here, you. No oath? Over there, here. You were not in court? Not tried! His anger must have blinded Sir George, his fury over Hawker making a fool of him. And your betrayal. If not about the robberies then consorting with Hawker.

Note to self: Something in Penny's mute fierce denial makes me want to accept her version, though believing her innocent would be my greater shame.

Courant. Help me believe you, Penny? Let us suppose you didn't tell Hawker, then who did? It's too late to force the name out of Hawker, he's already been dispatched. I agree, good riddance. Who else did Hawker speak with? Sir George of course, he was Hawker's boss. Or Sir George thought he was, the old fool.

Perhaps the coachman? They never met. You can't be sure of that. Cook would certainly know who was dining. She hated Hawker, gave him scraps food to get rid of him like a rat. It could be her ruse, pretend to everyone they hated each other.

Courant. That is Sir George? And Hawker? Shouting at each other. Me, I, floor, down. I don't understand. Drop down, me, Sir George, clasp hands, friends, together. Slowly, Penny. Hawker shouted and I drop down, no Sir George drops down. Are you saying Hawker threatened Sir George? The rogue really was getting bumptious. When was this?

Courant. A flower. After a flower? What flower? I don't know many flower names.

Courant. Trees, lots more. A wood. Not the face, the ruff. That's the flower, woodruff. And the man! Woodroffe. After Woodroffe? Ah, the burglary at his house. That was the night when one of the Aldermen's Watch was killed because they and the Militia were both lying in wait for the thieves. But the Militia were the thieves. No wonder Hawker was angry. But why rant at Sir George? It would reveal the Militia were the thieves.

Courant. A trap? Hawker shouting at Sir George. For setting a trap using the Watch. I don't see how Sir George could. He had invited guests from ten grand houses, so how could he know which one needed to be guarded? A lucky guess? Or . . . the alternative is too far-fetched.

Just supposing Sir George knew where to send the Watch because he was the one who told Hawker which house was worth robbing and would be empty. It is not credible. Anyway, if he did set up the robbery why tell the Aldermen's Watch?

Note to self: Penny parodies a greedy and threatening Hawker, pulling on his boots, larger boots.

Hawker was arrogant and greedy. He had become too big for his boots. Therefore Sir George needed to end their criminal partnership. That's why Hawker threatened Sir George. I understand, he threatened to "take Sir George down" if Hawker was caught. It all fits. Hawkers' reaction when I told him I worked for Sir George. He assumed I knew about their cosy partnership in crime. When discovered, Hawker had no opportunity to take Sir George down because he was silenced. First by trial in absentia, and then by immediate execution, all the time gagged. The judge orders a night time trial and rapid punishment to stop Hawker talking and incriminating Sir George.

But there was still one frayed end for Sir George to tie up. I had set people thinking there must be an informer. Sir George needed a scapegoat to keep the attention away from himself. That is why he silenced you. Far more cruelly than Hawker because you are innocent. He turned vindictive against the girl he took to his bed. The man is evil.

Why did I not see it? Why is it you, Penny, who has to suffer, to live with that horror wrongly inflicted on you. What is my shame, my guilt compared to that?

Townside to Plummery Ditch

Wretched.

Just a word. It cannot convey Frith's mental state. His vocabulary and his grammar are inadequate to express it. He is inadequate. He looks at the shell of a girl lying degraded and mutilated on a pile of piss-sodden straw. He put her there. He can reason he didn't do it directly, but that crumbles like a sandcastle under the waves of his emotions.

If only.

If only he hadn't shouted out on High Bridge before looking to the consequences. If only he had taken Mr Hyde's words to heart: perseverance is needed to achieve the desired. The newsman has allowed the prime culprit to escape. He has raped the life of an innocent girl, guilty only of ambition and being in the wrong bed at the wrong time. Frith only has to look at Penny to plummet the conceit of his coordinated words in his head.

He is wretched.

If only he'd gone to the evening session of the Court. If only he'd followed up his instinct and talked to the Clemsons when they untied him. He could have uncovered proof against Sir George. If only he'd thought about the pattern of burglaries. The roadway that is 'if only' is the blind alley that is stony. If only is the lament of the person who has done nothing.

Frith summons Dunbar to let him out of the cell. "How much do you want for her?" he asks.

"That piece of cold meat?"

The man is stupid, thinks Frith, disparaging his merchandise. Frith gives the oaf justification for his interest. "You said she worked in a kitchen. This one won't nag or answer back." He forces a snigger.

"She's young and strong. Pretty if you clean her up." The turnkey's bargaining faculty has woken up.

"Young, granted, but long since a virgin and dry as a desert. A girl's tongue is good for more beside talking and she doesn't have one." Frith's words are like boiling oil in his throat.

"She's experienced."

"Well used. By an ancient aristocrat. She's limp. That tells me a lack of skills."

Dunbar sees his case weakening and suggests a figure.

"How long do you reckon she'll earn for you?" asks Frith. "A few weeks at most until word gets round what a waste of tuppence she is. She'll earn you next to nothing."

Frith makes his offer. Dunbar laughs but not wholeheartedly.

"You have to feed her and keep her warm. You'll need to launder her clothes, maybe buy a new dress. Then there'll be the few days each month she won't be available except to the madhouse cases and they could slit her throat for the pleasure of it."

Frith makes a slightly higher offer. He knows something deep in him is driving him through this travesty. Dunbar is wavering. "After Sir George she'll likely have the pox."

The newsman stands Penny to watch him hand over a quarter of his wages to Dunbar. "You are mine now. Do you understand?" The girl nods.

Frith had not thought beyond the cell. He walks along Townside with Penny following several paces behind, trying to be invisible.

He stops for her to catch up and takes her arm. "You are with me."

They follow his walk of an earlier Monday towards Kennet-mouth. He takes Penny a little way along Plummery Ditch then tells her to stand in the knee-high water. He takes the soiled garments off her. She stands immobile while he washes her face, her back, her limbs. He washes her hair as best he can, pinching out prison lice. He gives a handful of sedges to her and she begins to wash her body. Frith sees her squat and bathe her bruised breasts. When she stands to wash her private parts, she has turned away from him. This pleases him.

During this rebirth Frith asks simple questions that require a nod or shake of the head for answer. He learns her family works a farm nearby but they would never take the disgraced daughter back under their roof. Moreover, her father's landowner is Sir George. She has no other relatives. To stop her shivering as well as to retain her modesty Frith gives her his longcoat.

A double confluence

"You must've had a reason for saying it," persisted Lynn.

Nicholas was filling the cabin's food locker with twice as much as it could possibly hold. "It just popped into my head."

"Often happens does it? Telling girls you're betrothed to them."

"No."

"Mistress Olivia?"

"I have never been betrothed to Mistress Olivia, nor anyone else," said Nicholas defensively.

That was good thought Lynn, one hurdle out of the way.

"Including you," he added, sticking his head out of the cabin.

"That's fine by me," she huffed.

"But I don't rule out the possibility."

She couldn't help the flutter through her stomach or her smile responding to his beaming grin. "You should. A man of your standing in the town, a hero in the eyes of everyone. I can give you a dowry of a small barge and a knackered old horse."

"When you have nothing, a knackered anything shouldn't be looked in the mouth," said Nicholas, leaving himself perplexed exactly what he had said. "Including a wife," he added.

Lynn playfully hit him and let him chase and catch and kiss her. She had been trying to keep his mind occupied on immediate matters, away from the debts and disgrace of his family. She enjoyed the results.

"Hermond is getting too old for heavy work day after day," said Lynn. "I hope you're up to it."

"Lift your skirt and we'll find out."

"Master Middleton! We're not yet walking out together."

"Quite right Mistress Darville but we have lain together." They kissed again. "Near everyone in Reading has witnessed us cuddling and kissing. That's a start. You've a locker full of gifts from me. There's a second."

"Bread like rock and cheese the colour of moss? I don't call them betrothal gifts. I want a garter with a love inscription."

It was one of those stopped moments that were occurring more and more frequently the more time she and Nicholas spent together. Sometimes it was a casual touch, sometimes a look. But this one was different.

"You will," said Nicholas quietly. "One day, when I can offer you a home, can welcome you into respectability not . . ."

Lynn set about distracting him again. "I wasn't joking about Hermond. He can't pull loads for much longer."

"You can hire horses."

"Adam was right. He said things that are bigger are cheaper to run, more competitive. It's only just struck me we were the smallest barge in London docks."

"What a pair," said Nicholas with an exaggerated sigh. "Both of us with jobs to find and a change to boot."

"River work is all I know," said Lynn flatly.

"It's a good line to be in," answered Nicholas thoughtfully. "It's going to grow. The things these people in London demand is nobody's business. There'll be plenty of bargemen's business with all these new waterways they're planning. You could be the mate on a bigger barge."

"A girl? That's the funniest thing you've ever said. As for you, how about being a navvy?" She squeezed his arm muscles, raised her eyebrows. "And that's funnier. You're a trader. You'll start your own store."

"I can't get the capital or credit thanks to my father. I do enjoy it, buying from the farms, selling to happy customers."

"Before she's thrown out of the shop?" teased Lynn.

It was another of those stopped moments.

After a while Lynn spoke. "Jeannie doesn't have to carry cargo."

Nicholas spoke immediately. "All these new folk on and by the rivers and the new navigations will need provisions." He looked carefully at Lynn.

"Jeannie could be a floating provisions store," she said holding his enquiring eyes.

"A market barge. We could have a stall on that front area."

"The foredeck," she said in mock vexation.

"Use the underneath bit as storeroom," he said to irritate her.

"The hold!"

"Staying at inns?" suggested Nicholas eagerly.

"Living on the barge."

"You're not seriously thinking ... in that poky ... That hammock will never hold two. But it will be fun trying."

"What a cart track mind you have, Master Middleton," said Lynn moving from him. "You can get a whole store of provisions in Jeannie's hold and there'd still be plenty of space."

They were about to descend into the cabin when Nicholas was hailed.

"Wakeman! Good man, how are you?"

"Couldn't be better. I've resigned from the Courant," he said, shaking Nicholas's hand and greeting Lynn.

The three went into the cabin where Lynn insisted Mr Frith drink some cider with them. She learned how Nicholas had galloped to Newbury only to wait most of the day for the Navigation Company to produce the official request for the Lord Lieutenant to enforce the Kennet Act. Next day he galloped the papers to Guildford and waited for them to be acted on.

Nicholas and Lynn heard of Wakeman's experience at the barn.

Lynn told Mr Frith how good Nicholas was arguing against Mr Hyde and won back Barge Jeannie. The newsman questioned her intently on the involvement of Sir George Crockmore in the contract. They raised their heartiest toast to Barge Jeannie.

"Neither of us gentlemen would have achieved anything but for you, Lynn," said the newsman solemnly, stemming her flow of praise for the two men. "It was you and your father standing up and doing something that made all this come about. You made it happen by taking action." Mr Frith said becoming lost in his own thoughts.

"Including breaking the law," said Nicholas lightly.

"What choice had I?" demanded Lynn. "When you're wrongly locked up, surrounded by people who hate you and not allowed to speak to anyone who might help, you have to fight."

"It just feels wrong to break the law to prove you're right," said Nicholas without reproof. "A right end never justifies a wrong method."

"I didn't know the Yeomanry were coming, did I?" She paused. "Anyway, I didn't plan the break-out."

"I know," said Nicholas softly. "That's why I love you."

"You couldn't predict the consequences of your note to Adam," stated Mr Frith. "But you took advantage of the unintended outcome. That showed mental dexterity."

"I did what I had to," said Lynn.

"The important thing is that you took action," persisted Mr Frith. "When it got unbearably tough you didn't turn back. You kept on with what you believed in." The energy in his outburst hovered in the cabin.

The newsman shook himself out of his reverie. "I must get going. I came to ask a favour of you, Mistress Lynn. Do you have an old smock I could have?"

"All my smocks are old," joked Lynn. She listened to the newsman explain the reason for his strange request, then scrabbled under the bunk. "Penny can have this." Lynn handed over the dress she had been given at Aldermaston, refusing to accept any money for it.

"I hope wherever Penny wears it she is welcomed like me when I wore it," said Lynn. "The girl would do well to go see a wise woman," she added.

"There's one up towards Sonning Common," put in Nicholas. "I'm sure she will have medications that'll soothe the girl's mouth and remedy any other consequences."

"I know the place," said Mr Frith, his thoughts hovering a short while like a settling dove. "Yedda." He stepped off the barge and turned back to Lynn. "It would be my honour to attend Mr Darville's funeral this afternoon."

"It would please me very much," she answered. "Please take these for Penny. These lockers aren't big enough for all Nicholas has brought," she added handing him a small loaf, four eggs and chunk of cheese wrapped in a piece of sacking. "Tell Penny to leave them at the wise woman's door. They never accept money."

"You'll join us for the after-wake?" asked Nicholas. Ignoring Lynn's look of surprise, he continued, "I've booked the back room of the Anglers' Tavern."

Frith looked at the two young people for a few seconds. "I would like that very much." He strode away towards Blake's Lock.

"You didn't tell me you'd arranged a wake," said Lynn.

"Wouldn't your dad have wanted one?" answered Nicholas.

"Yes. But that's not the point."

"What is the point?"

Lynn rapidly decided her point was of less importance than having Nicholas organise a wake to commemorate her Dad even if he hadn't told her beforehand. "It'll be a sorry affair with just you, me and Mr Frith."

"You'll have to wait and see who turns up," he answered, unable to conceal a smirk.

"Something else you haven't told me?" she asked punching him on the shoulder. Nicholas groaned and crumpled to the deck. Lynn bent over thinking that for all her strength she had only lightly cuffed him. He reached up and pulled her on top of him.

Herbary, Sonning Common

It is the start of a long journey for Penny. She has let Frith know, through their stylised language of his words and her signs, that he is not to accompany her. His heart is torn. He has not done enough for her, but neither could he look after her. She is making it easy for him in walking away.

They have crossed Plummery Ditch and are stepping across His Majesty's Meadows where they will cross the Thames at the hamlet called Caversham. Penny wears his longcoat, with half his remaining wages in the pocket. She has regained some of her prettiness, though there is a veil of vulnerability bearing florets of hurt. Frith wonders if she will ever again laugh.

For some reason he thinks of the Forbury Fair, the Grotesque sideshow that made him cringe and others gawp, and he has an urge to make this young girl without a tongue belong to the ordinary world. "I'm going to tell you a story," he begins. "From a time long ago about a girl who had her tongue cut out." He scrutinises her reaction and sees she did not flinch. The mutilation in her mouth must be crippling her and he draws on the mass of Zitkala, the Bird Mountain on the Mohawk lands, to give Yedda the wisdom to soothe Penny's wounds. He smiles, knowing he is about to draw on an ancient lore of a different origin.

"Far away in time and in distance, was a land called Thrace, and there ruled a King called Tereus. He was married to the beautiful Procne and by her, Tereus was father of a son, Itys. Procne was from a different land and she was lonely in the great palace of Thrace. She asked her husband to bring to her for comfort her younger sister, Philomele. This he agreed. On the return, Tereus was so smitten with Philomele he slew the escort and raped the girl. To ensure his craven deed was kept secret from his wife, Tereus cut out the tongue of Philomele, and confined her to the slaves' quarters in his palace at Thebes."

Frith watches the withdrawn girl take in the story, then gets an encouraging glance. She is stronger by the minute, he thinks. Lines from Ovid surface from his Augustinian schooling.

But Tereus did not kill her; he seized Philomele's tongue

With pincers, though it cried out against the outrage,
Babbled and made a sound that resembled "Father"
Until his sword cut it out and the mangled root quivered.

He does not say these words aloud to the girl walking beside him.

"Tereus tells his wife Procne the convoy was ambushed on their way home and all were killed. A year, two, go by and there is to be a great celebration and feast in the palace. In the slaves' quarters Philomele is busy. When the royal couple enter the banqueting hall Procne's eyes are delighted by a magnificent hanging tapestry. Through its sequence of pictures she reads about the rape and mutilation of her sister by her own husband. Procne bides her time until she can free her sister. She serves to her husband King Tereus a meal of the flesh of his own son. The sisters flee. To speed them the Ancient Gods turn Philomele into a darting, diving swallow."

Frith cannot help thinking, third time lucky at Yedda's. He heard about the Herbary first from Catherine following her urgent visit, then their blissful tryst at the place. By an overgrown pergola he puts down the basket he has been carrying.

"Let me say why I told you that story, Penny. Your —"

Penny's fingers close Frith's lips. She pulls the pocketbook from the longcoat, quickly uses a pencil. The young woman puts her lips to the cover before returning the pocketbook to Frith, her eyes raising such compassion in Frith he will never be able to express, will never write in words but will forever remember. Penny goes through the archway. Frith opens his pocketbook.

Frith wonders if he or Penny is the more akin to a swallow.

Wakeman's journal – 4:00pm

After Peter Darville's wake I cut two straight rods from my willow behind the Anglers and fashioned a travois for my things and the keepsakes of Catherine. I used ropes and sacking from the inn's cellar and a cloth from the wonderful pie-maker for a neck-harness.

A few paces down the Thames from the confluence of the Kennet, there is a cottage that goes by the name The Dreadnought Tavern. After five months in Reading this newsman had no idea it was there.

My glass is empty of its brandy. This dolour will surge periodically. It will linger a long time. There are ember memories that will glow for years. I can put all that in its due place, most of the time. My first task upon gaining the Thames was to crumble the cast of Catherine's breast into the river. A rite, destroying the inert replica so the living memory may flourish. A putting into the flowing water was a symbol of the overflowing love I had received from Catherine. My Mohawk first love would have understood.

I can allow myself to think about getting to Maidenhead with its several inns. The landlord here tells me I should follow the river to a village called Wargrave where I will find the London Road and thence in seven miles be at my destination. The towing path takes a great horseshoe bend to the north. I prefer the river route, for the running water with its changes at shallows and weir. Also for its flat towing path for my travois.

It amuses me to think I might so soon meet my beautiful past at Maidenhead. If I take the road route I may well watch white specks of plaster drift under the bridge at Maidenhead. In truth I doubt I would see them but I know they are somewhere. Catherine's letters are in my satchel and our few pieces on the travois. Everyone who has loved will understand that.

My second task was to set off along the towing path to London. That has now changed because I am advised of a more direct route. Though the new route is uncertain in my mind, I will take it.

The End

www.ingramcontent.com/pod-product-compliance
Lightning Source LLC
Chambersburg PA
CBHW032207190626
46810CB00019B/2137